D1575658

DALTON   Dalton, David.

Been here and gone.

,4

DATE			

If anyone asks you
Who sung this song,
Tell 'em Coley Williams

BEEN HERE AND GONE.

BEEN HERE
AND
GONE

A Memoir of the Blues

DAVID DALTON

William Morrow

An Imprint of HarperCollins*Publishers*

BEEN HERE
AND
GONE
A Memoir of the Blues

FIRST EDITION

Library of Congress Cataloging-in-Publication Data

Dalton, David.
      Been here and gone: a memoir of the blues / David Dalton.—1st ed.
         p. cm.
      ISBN 0-380-97676-5
      1. Afro-American musicians—Fiction. 2. Blues musicians—Fiction.
   3. Afro-Americans—Fiction. 4. Blues (Music)—Fiction.
   5. Mississippi—Fiction. 6. Aged men—Fiction. I. Title.

PS3554.A43765 B44 2000
913'.54—dc21   00-025447

Front Cover Photograph (detail) Printed by Permission:
The J. Paul Getty Museum, Los Angeles, California
Title: Savannah Negro Quarter. Date: 1936. By: Walker Evans.
Medium: Gelatin Silver. Size: 4 1/32 x 6 5/8 inches.

Printed in the United States of America on acid-free paper
00 01 02 03 04   10 9 8 7 6 5 4 3 2 1

 A Berkshire Studio Production

To all the big-hearted,

crazy-wisdom men and women

who brought us the blues—

the music God hummed

when he made the world.

CREDITS & ACKNOWLEDGMENTS

Conceived, Designed & Produced by	Martin I. Green
Written by	David Dalton
Edited by	Ross Firestone
Design & Production	Bobbi Bongard
Research Director	Leland Stein
Creative Consultant & Editorial Associate	Jared F. Green
Editorial Associate	Cia Elkin
Administrative Coordinator	Eileen Taft
Back Cover & Interior Illustrations	George Pratt
Legal Advisor	Adria S. Hillman, Esq.
Financial Advisor	Leo K. Barnes, CPA

With deep gratitude to Lou Aronica—publisher extraordinaire—for the opportunity to make this very special project happen, and for his unwavering belief and support.

Thanks to Tom Dupree for his invaluable insights and tireless efforts on our behalf; and to Kelly Notaras, Cheryl Merante and Ken Lang who, no matter how busy they were, always gave us their much-needed assistance whenever asked.

A very special thanks to Alan Douglas for recommending David Dalton for this project, and whose astute comments and suggestions on the original manuscript made the book infinitely better.

Thanks also to Edward Komara, Director of Blues Archive, J.D. Williams Library, University of Mississippi; William R. Ferris, author of *Blues From the Delta;* David Sanjek, Director, BMI Archives; and David Evans, Professor of Music, University of Memphis and author of *Big Road Blues,* for their generous assistance, time and expertise.

Much appreciation to Roger Cooper and Marc Jaffe for their usual sage advice, guidance and friendship.

Many thanks to the following for their invaluable help during the various phases of this project and beyond: Red Abare, Martha Donovan, Will Eisner, Lee Everett, Gail Firestone, Gloria Henry, Carol Kowalski, Rosie Keefe, Susan Kosko, Kim Lewis, Lillian Loving, Bob Nichols, Adele and Arthur Puhn, Nancy and Steven Rubin, Richard Rubinstein, Jessie G. Schoonmaker, Laura and Alvin Sinderbrand, Anne Sipp, Lynn Sonberg, and Lynne West.

And, of course, to my beautiful and talented partner, Mary Sipp-Green, for her wisdom, patience and love. I cherish you.

Finally, to the memory of Aaron Caesar Johnson and Dr. Norman Mendlinger—two magnificent friends and spirits who left us much too soon. I will always miss them.

Martin I. Green

Several years ago in the month of Ixtil, I received a call from the Inca (aka Marty Green). The Inca had an idea for a book. In truth, it was a great deal more than an idea. He had road maps, lists of names —names of people, rivers, towns, and cultural/historical events he wanted included. He communicated his thoughts to me and sent me pages outlining his plans. For bringing his idea to life he would pay me handsomely (but by the scroll), and interfere at will on any matter—from serial commas to the pentatonic scale—that caught his restless eyeballs. He turned out to be quite human and generous to a fault—unquestionably the nicest control freak I've ever worked for—and over the years I've grown quite fond of him. I will always be grateful to him for giving me the opportunity to write fiction (I already had some experience at this from writing brain-damaged people's autobiographies).

To Ross Firestone, a scholar and a gentleman, I owe an immense debt of gratitude. He saved me from solecisms without number—grammatically and bluesologically—and shed his benign spirit on this entire book. I am grateful to Leland Stein for lending me his blues library, finding CDs, maps and tapes, his good spirits, Hendrixology, and providing me with any arcane information I needed. And last but not least of those in the Inca's camp, my thanks to Bobbi Bongard for her elegant design and enthusiasm.

Once I had finished the first draft of the book I sent a copy of it with much trepidation to the Magus of the Okeefenokee Swamp, Stanley Booth, who kindly read it from cover to cover, patiently corrected my egregious errors, and finely tuned my Limey's-eye-view of the ruminant and mysterious South to something approaching reality.

I am forever grateful to Sharon Ruetnick for reading the MS and offering her helpful suggestions. My thanks also to Sneuques Dalton for her good heart and to Alan Fitzpatrick for the good times. And to my son, Toby Dalton, for turning down DMX long enough for me to write this book.

Finally, may flights of putti sing hosannas in the highest to my wife Coco Pekelis—first in my affections, and without whom this book would be a junkyard of howling dogs, broken pots, and rusty sentences.

David Dalton

CONTENTS

Preface / 17

Coley's Riff / 21

1   The Hoodoo Bash / 23

2   There's a House Over Yonder / 28

3   The Lady Who Seen God / 35

4   Conjure Doctors Speakin Through the Ears of Snakes / 43

5   I Seed All the Way Back to Adam and Eve / 47

6   Rise Up, Dead Man, Help Me Drive My Row / 52

7   They're Holdin a War on Mars / 64

8   The Great Blue God of Electricity / 68

9   Gonna Join the Caterpillar's Club / 74

10 The Wampus Cat / 78

11 Goin Away to a World Unknown / 86

12 I'm Goin Where the Southern Cross the Dog / 98

13 Matchbox Holdin My Clothes / 111

14 Stayed 'Round Houston Just a Day Too Long / 115

15 John Henry Doin Hard Time / 121

16 Jack a Diamonds Is a Hard Card to Play / 130

17 Blind Man Showed Me the Way / 136

18 If You Don't Like My Ocean, Don't Fish in My Sea / 147

19 Doctor Rastus Peerless Medicine Show / 155

20 The Empress of Funk / 159

21 Reckless Blues / 170

22 Phantom King of the Delta Blues / 180

23 Went to the Crossroad, Fell Down on My Knees / 192

24 Who the Hell Is Freddy Fox? / 195

25 Nobody Knows You When You Down and Out / 199

26 Pharaoh Talkin on the Radio / 202

27 Delta Giantess and a Midget in Black Stockins / 207

28 Reverend Tush Hog / 214

29 Rather Be a Catfish, Swimmin in the Deep Blue Sea / 223

30 Moon Spinnin Across the Sky, Bats Flyin in the Sun / 229

31 That Old Evil Spirit So Deep Down in the Ground / 235

32 Good Mornin Blues, Blues How Do You Do / 240

33 You May Bury My Body, Ooh,
Down by the Highway Side / 243

34 Hello Satan, Believe It's Time to Go / 249

35 Railroad for My Pillow / 260

36 Pistol in My Face / 263

37 Call It Stormy Monday / 267

38 Been Bit by the Beale Street Beagle / 274

39 Went to See the Gypsy, Have My Fortune Read / 279

40 Monkey and the Baboon Playin in the Grass / 284

41 It's Hard to Tell, It's Hard to Tell
When All Your Love's in Vain / 288

42 Sweet Home Chicago / 293

43 I Heard the Voice of a Porkchop / 303

44 When I Came to Chicago in 1951 Muddy Waters Said,
"Coley Boy, You Better Get a Gun" / 310

45 A Wolf Draggin His Tail / 316

46 If Trouble Was Money / 322

47 Got Them Eisenhower Blues / 331

48 The King and I / 340

49 Johnny B. Goode / 349

50 White Boys Lost in the Blues / 359

51 Baby, Let Me Follow You Down / 365

52 Mannish Boys / 377

53 The Jacks Are All Back in Their Boxes / 380

54 Hairy Green Buttons and the Talking God / 384

55 Gettin Ready for the Cypress Grove / 389

Sources: Bibliography & Lyrics / 397

PREFACE

I found Coley Williams in a cardboard box. That's right.

I was staying with friends in upstate New York. I'd gone with them to a yard sale in the nearby town of Treadwell. On the lawn, along with the waffle irons and gold-painted lamps and Fisher-Price tricycles, was a box of old 78s.

There was the usual stuff, "White Christmas" and "Tweedly Dee," and some big clunky albums of show tunes and light classical —*Call Me Madam, The Greatest Arias of Italian Opera,* that sort of thing. Then there was "Nine Weeks in Hell" by Freddy Fox. I had no idea what this could be. Was it a novelty record, a comedy routine? The thing that caught my eye was the faded Copacetic Records label. As an old blues hound, I knew that some great regional blues artists had recorded on that label.

I took it home. As soon as the needle hit the groove I felt a chill run down my spine. It was the blues, no question about that. The ferocious clawing at the steel strings, the .44-caliber slide guitar, the voice a cross between the howl of Tommy Johnson and the otherworldly whine of Skip James. The ancient apostolic voice of the blues that could raise up Lazarus one more time, but sung in a way I'd never heard before. The song was funny in a morbid kind of way. It wasn't all that original, actually, but I was mesmerized. Here it was: the feral, holy blues in all its glory.

Who the hell *was* this? I looked him up in Sheldon Harris's *Blues Who's Who.* There were two listings. There was a Freddy Fox from Waxahatchie who played stride piano and (later) gospel organ in the Awakeners. And there was "Freddy Fox, pseudonym of Coley Williams (see entry)." Under Coley Williams it said: "Delta blues singer, guitarist, 1889(?)—. Born in Yalobusha County, Mississippi. Recorded for: Copacetic, Victor and Vanguard labels. Played with: Tommy Johnson, Charley Patton, Blind Lemon Jefferson, Son House, Robert Johnson, Sonny Boy Williamson II, Muddy Waters...." The list was like a bible of the blues.

Like a hummingbird zeroing in on a red plastic sugar-water feeder, the thought struck me: What if he were still alive? There was no closing date on his chronology, was there? I mean it's *possible*, isn't it?

I checked the kudzu of blues websites. No Freddy Fox. No Coley Williams. No luck at all.

I went down to Arlene's Sugar Shack on Second and A to have a drink and listen to the alternate take of Albert King's "Cold Feet" —catch him hitting that B flat just right.

Arlene was behind the bar, and as luck would have it Little Willie Evans happened to be there holding down stool number three. Willie knew everybody who'd ever been anybody in the blues, and all those guys who slipped between the cracks, too. Especially those guys.

"Anybody ever come across a blues singer name of Freddy Fox?" I asked them.

"Freddy Fox, Freddy Fox...." Arlene searched her mind and lit a Camel. "Now where do I know that name from?"

"Also goes by the name of Coley Williams."

"Coley Williams?" said Little Willie. "You don't know who *Coley Williams* is?"

"He doesn't know, baby," said Arlene, rolling her eyes. "He's just messin witcha."

"I'm afraid I must take issue with you on that particular point." Willie drew himself up and testified: "Coley Augustus Williams, the esteemed South Side guitarist, played bass on Eddie Boyd's 'Third Degree.' Chess label, Chicago, 1953."

Pleased with his testimony, Willie decided to buy a round for the bar.

"Put it on my tab," he told Arlene with a wave of the arm. Since the house consisted of Willie and me, she obliged.

"Now I know where I've seen him," said Arlene, consulting her ice cubes. "On the watchamacallit channel, you know...."

"You've *seen* him?"

"One of those morning talk shows. Tall guy with the cowboy hat, chews gum? They was giving him an award or something."

Three months later, I found myself looking into the face of an ancient man. He rocked back and forth on his little stuck-on trailer porch watching me like an alligator in three feet of muddy water. Deep brown eyes, glassy as the sea. He didn't smile, he didn't talk.

"Are you Coley Williams?" I asked him. I knew he was.

"Well now," he said, "that depends...."

Within a minute of my arrival his wife, Vida Lee, poked her head out of the trailer door.

"You the book-writer what called before?"

I said I was.

"Coley, how can you let this gentleman stand out in the hot sun like that, midday? Come in, child, I'll make you some lemonade."

"Hell, Vida Lee, he ain't no lemonade drinker. Pull out that bottle you got hid under the sink."

That night he told me the story of how he'd met Robert Johnson in the graveyard outside of Lula, and then on from there. And on. And on. After awhile, I glanced up from my reverie and saw a disapproving look on Coley's face.

"Young fella," he said, "ain't you gonna take any of this down?"

David Dalton
Late Twentieth Century

Coley's Riff

Can I tell you about the blues? Baby, I was born with the blues. I seen the blues hatch outta its scaly old egg up there in Sunflower County, watch it jump and shout and let it all hang out at the jook joint, follow it down to Texas and up to Memphis, hitch a ride with it when it hit Highway 61 up to Chicago and stuck around with it ever since.

Now you be askin yourself how old is this cat anyways? Well, child, it's true I be old, ancient as Methuselah, and probably seen more wild and crazy things in my life than that old dude ever saw in his nine-hundred years.

My name's Coley Williams and I'm gonna tell you all about them sanctified and skankified legendary practitioners of the blues—the high times, the lowlifes, and all the hair-raisin, jook-joint jumpin stories you never heard. 'Cause from the saints and the junkies to the signifyin monkeys, I knowed 'em all. Hmm, hmm, hmm.

1

The Hoodoo Bash

My hundredth birthday near to did me in, if it was my hundredth that is.

They say I was found one hundred years ago yesterday. Found is what folks used to call bein borned. See, in the old days people believed that everything that ever was or ever will be was already out there in the universe. Volcanoes, baby snakes, toasters, alligator shoes, plaid pants and downhome blues. I just happen to be floatin down the Milky Way when Mama and Papa caught me, and that's the truth. You can believe it or not.

I was countin on spendin a nice peaceful day with my great-great-grandkids or whatever they is, sippin lemonade and eatin pecan pie. Vida Lee's pecan pie is one of the things that has allowed me to see this day. Right now, I'm just too tired to hunt for the recipe but if you're still around later.…

Where was I? Oh yeah, the so-called birthday. As I say, I went to bed the night before, dreamin I was in a boxcar headin down to Mobile, that's right, but I woke up to something sounded like I left the police scanner on all night. When I lifted the shade to see what all the fuss was about I wanted to pull the covers over my head and crawl right on back into my boxcar dream.

I was livin in a trailer out on Highway 61 near Robinsonville. With Vida Lee of course. Vida Lee is my wife and the lady what puts the pecans in my pie. Anyway. Out by the side of the road was a whole mess a people I had never in my life seen before. There was the local TV news from Memphis pullin up in a van, there was pick-ups and limousines and VW buses full of hairy kids. It was like the circus come to town.

There was faces at the window, there was faces at the door. Someone was knockin like a fatback drummer on a lard-pail lid.

"Who the hell is that?" I asked Vida Lee.

"Says he's Willard Scott from the *Today* show and he wants for you to come and blow out the candles on this here guitar-shaped cake."

"Tell him to blow 'em out his own damn self."

Now the phone start ringin in the hall and naturally Vida Lee got to answer, much as I am forever tellin her to let the thing ring. Damn invasion of privacy is what it is.

"Just pick it up, ya old fart," she tells me. "It's the President! He wants to wish you happy birthday."

"President of what?" I asks. She ignore me as usual.

Covers the receiver with her hand and tells me, "Now, honey, don't get mad but he seems to think you're Muddy Waters. Whatever he says just say, 'Thank you, uh, your Honor.'"

"The hell I will," I told her. "This is my hundredth. Let him say what he wants at *his* hundreth."

That, by the way, is more or less the story of how I came to *not* speak with the President of the United States. A memory I shall treasure forever.

Now how the word got out 'bout my hundredth, I still do not know for sure, but by noon people was queuing up to get in. The BBC was there, the Blues Channel, God rest my soul, French television, CNN, and *Entertainment Tonight*.

All shovin mikes in my face, askin all kinda stupid questions to which there ain't no answers anyways: "What is the blues? Where do it come from? How's it feel to be this old?"

Also: "What is your secret and can it be bottled?" And: "Is it true you knew Lincoln and Whitman and Billy the Kid?" Not to mention: "Give your opinion of kids today and what do you want your tombstone to say?"

Seems I'm the last of my kind. Like I was a passenger pigeon, or a two-headed calf. Oh man, a hundred-year-old bluesman is a sight to see.

"Woman," I says to Vida Lee, "you been down at the post office broadcastin on your own personal frequency?"

"What in hell you expect you turn a hundred years? You a celebrity, baby, a Delta dinosaur. Hell, you on the mornin news. You're historical, like Paul Revere's horse or something."

I was gettin tired. I wanted to lay down on my waterbed, smoke some grass, drink some whiskey, and watch *Hee Haw* on the television.

One thing about gettin this old, you miss the people who was close to you. You mention Charley Patton, Ma Rainey to these kids today they don't know who the hell you talkin about.

It was too many people and too many bottles. I was drunk and stoned, that's right, and pretty soon I passed out with my head in the cake.

By and by up come Marie the Prophetess, two-headed woman from New Orleans, her cowrie shells janglin as she walked. She musta been a hundred and twenty if she was a day. Had wrinkles on her like knee-socks. She didn't look all that good to tell the truth, but I was amazed to see her walkin at all.

"My my, don't *you* look good for a hundred years; still handsome I see."

'Course I know just what she's doin, so I just say, "I shoulda knowed I'd see you and your bag of tricks, today bein today and all."

"Well, I couldn't miss your hundredth, baby, now could I? You lonely, Coley? I figured you for lonely."

"With all these damn people here?"

"But you don't really *know* these people, do you? When you get to our age all your real friends is in the past."

"And a good thing too." I tells her that just to get rid of her, although I'm only partly kidding.

"But honey," she say, "wouldn't you like me to summon some of 'em up for you, just for the day?"

"Marie, you sure we should be messin with this?"

As I'm talkin she's pourin herself a big old cup of sterno. Then she spilt pig's blood on the ground and chanted some mumbo jumbo over it till the blood caught fire. A pillar of smoke went up into the heavens and down to the bowels of the earth.

Dogs was howlin, owls was a hootin, and out in the field a bull start bellowin the Lord's Prayer at the stroke of noon. My bones went cold and my flesh begin to creep.

Father Jacob let his ladder down and a pack of demons threw up Satan's bell rope. The cats and the chicks was pourin in like rats in a barn. It was a sight to behold I tell ya, all them old rounders climbin outta their coffins like it was Judgment Day. Indigo James and Automatic Slim, Big Mama Maceo and Welfare Bob. Tupelo Tom brought a fifth.

Bessie Smith was in the kitchen eatin grits and chicken wings, Charley Patton was in the bedroom rattlin the springs, T-Bone Walker was playin cards with Tampa Red. Elvis showed up in a lime green suit and hid in the baggage car.

I wept when I saw that great black moon face of Bessie's. We hugged and then I seen a cloud pass over her.

"What is it, Bessie?"

"Oh darlin, them dogs of mine worry me all the time. I been wanderin that 61 highway so long I just wanna go home and kick off my shoes and drink all the booze and sleep a *long*, long time."

"Bessie, I miss you so much. World just ain't the same."

"I love you too, baby."

Sheet lightnin flashed across the fields, the air was jumpin. Charley Patton poked his head out the trailer window. The one-time demon of the Delta looked just as squirrely as ever.

"Where the devil you been, Coley?"

I didn't have the heart to tell the old Tush Hog we wasn't livin on the same plane no more.

"Jesus, Charley," I says, "you better watchit, I just seen your old lady over by the punch bowl."

"Man, I don't give a damn what Bertha Lee thinks, I been in the dark for the past sixty years and I'm gonna have me some fun."

"How you been, anyways?" I asks him.

"Weak as water," says he. "Ain't been feelin all that well. The air where I'm livin is like a sulphur mine and pussy is as scarce as hen's teeth. So Coley, don't you come knockin if the trailer's rockin."

Over by the barbecue pit Little Walter and Sonny Boy number two was havin a dispute over a chick they knew, John Henry and Leonard Chess was arm wrestlin for who gonna pick up the tab, and the Devil hisself was sellin tickets on the Greyhound bus. Bob Dylan was there too, askin the way to Duluth.

"Daddy jive," Memphis Minnie was tellin Howlin Wolf, "stop pullin on my coat. I don't fuck no dead mens."

"I ain't dead, baby, I was just over in Arkansas."

Over on the side there was some funny lookin guy makin time with Vida Lee. I woulda punched him out 'cept when I come closer I seen that cat was me. I listened to myself makin promises I knew I could never keep. That's the kind of night it was.

It was a crazy little thing that was goin down. Old Noah was there too, dancin with three college girls from Ronconcomo. Then up pop Papa Legba smokin a cane stalk. He's rattlin a brace of bones and drinkin palm wine outta his boot. That's when I got scared. Had to get outta that dream before Ronald McDonald and the Energizer Bunny showed up.

Don't know how long I was asleep but when I woke up they was gone and someone was bangin a school bus on my head.

"Babu, wake up! Wake up, the bus is here." It was my great-great-granddaughter Nawassa.

"Where we goin on that bus, honey?"

"We gonna move to the moon and grow light bulbs."

"Sounds good to me," I say.

"Babu, you talkin in your sleep again."

"Was I?"

"Who was you talkin to, Babu?"

"Just some old friends," I tell her. "Some *real* old friends. Come on, honey, let's get outta here. Wanna go for a ride?"

There's a House Over Yonder

s we're drivin down Highway 61 outta the corner of my eye I spy a little old no-account shack fallin into decay, the kudzu and the weeds eatin it up. You might think it just a pile of junk over there, some old garage fallin in, but you know what I see? I see paradise, baby, 'cause in that old green shack is my past.

A whole lost world of the Delta in that shack. 'Cause this was once a jook joint—the hoppinest, jivinest place on the planet, where all the hepcats and ministers of shuck 'n jive congregate on a Saturday night. *A one room country shack a thousand miles from nowhere.*

You see 'em all along the highway now, boarded up and cavin in, goats wanderin through the rooms, but in their day they was palaces. Just thinkin on it, got myself so choke up I gotta pull over the car. My little great-whatchamacallit, Nawassa, sayin to me,

"Babu, why we stoppin here?"

What am I gonna tell her? That I see slick, slinky, duded-up ghosts dancin in the air, jokin, gamblin, drinkin, and singin the blues?

Blues was all 'round me when I was comin up, but didn't get me a lethal dose till I was in my twelfth year. Come by it through my daddy,

Zaiah Williams. Had a touch of the blues hisself, see, and it was passed on to me through him.

My daddy was skinny as a pole and he had one of them pencil mustaches, y'know, that he tended to like it was holy writ. He was real good-lookin 'cept that he had but one eye. One good eye and one of glass. That's right. Been kicked in the head by a mule when he was a kid. Didn't pay it no mind and his eye got poorly and he lost the sight of that eye. When he got drunk he'd pop out his glass eye and roll it 'round on his dinner plate. Us kids go wild at that but Mama just say, "Lord, Lord, I ain't got six chillen, I got *seven*."

The only other time he'd take out that eye of his was when he was gamblin—for good luck, y'know. "The un-seein eye seeth all!" he'd say, and roll the dice. It was through the un-seein eye that he won that beat-up old Sears guitar he kept under the bed. The fiddle was his instrument, mainly, 'cause he was old-time. Could play the blues right good on that fiddle, too, but the blues he was familiar with wasn't exactly same as today. They was long-meter, like hymns, and story songs, mainly. "Frankie and Albert" and "Railroad Bill," that kinda thing.

If one of us kids ask him, "Where do blues come from, Daddy?" he'd tell us, "From the hind end of a mule. Blues started right in the field over yonder, y'know, under them old hickory trees, moon shinin down. Didn't start in no city."

You wanna know how *he* come by the blues? He come by it like we all done, hanging out with bad company down by the depot. Want to know when the blues begin? I will tell you the very day, yes sir. It was a Saturday night and that I know for a natural fact. Man name of Visible Mercy was a notable guitar player in them days. He was meant to play at one of them Saturday night get-downs but the Devil caught him and push him down a well so he could take his place. On that Saturday night the Devil jumped up and played a reel and that reel ain't stopped since. Don't matter which Saturday night it were 'cause every Saturday night is the same Saturday night and it's been that way ever since dogs got tails and fish got fins. That the night the fellas get together. Gamblin, tellin lies, drinkin whiskey. And playin music.

Blues was then the new music. The sisters called blues songs out-of-order music. "Blues brings about eternity," my Aunt Mae usta say, 'cause there was always fights when blues was played.

My own initiation into the mysterious and slinky rites of the blues take place in a jook joint. This holy of holies was no bigger'n the room you sittin in. Jook joints was the very chapel of bluesology, and local chapter of the Prince of Darkness.

My daddy was a part-time preacher but like I say he play a little. Go out to a fish fry or a frolic and play reels. This pass for country folks's entertainment in them days, and I'd generally go 'long with him.

But the jook joints and barrelhouses, they was another matter entirely. That's where the blues got played. Zaiah play at them too, but I know he ain't never gonna take me there.

One night I hear Mama and Papa talkin. Papa gettin ready to go out and Mama askin where.

"Well," say Papa, "little get-together just got set up and they ask me to come by play some reels."

I follow him from a house down the road. Can you see me? There I go creepin 'long behind him, hidin up behind the water tower till he pass. But this ain't the way to the jook joint. Moon doin its crazy thing with the light, cypresses sighin, frogs scattin that African scat over by the bayou. Amblin along, keepin my distance. Man, where he goin?

Down the road a piece he look 'round behind hisself, cut across the railroad tracks and sneak over to a abandoned boxcar been made into a house. Wash hangin on the line, smoke comin outta a little old chimney, junk all over the yard and a big scroungy, yappy old hound howlin and howlin.

"Whoa, George!" I hear my daddy sayin. "Don't you recognize yo Uncle Zaiah?"

He's uncle to some strange dog? Out on the porch come a tall, skinny, red-headed high-yeller dame all dolled up. I see them embracin and huggin and carryin on and then they go on in the house for a long while. Well, I reckon that's the way the water run under the bridge. My mama was a one-way woman, my daddy was a two-way man. I'm learnin fast.

By and by they come out again and back down the road toward Dockery depot with me trailin 'em all the way. Laughin and jokin and stoppin to kiss. Disappear 'round the far side of the depot and I'm comin right up behind them and there—just like some conjure woman done pull it straight outta the ground—was the jook joint.

Big sign over the top say "Zeke's Colored Cafe," but wasn't nobody goin there to drink coffee, understand? Rusty cola and beer and tobacco signs nailed up all over the front. Place seem like it hardly fit but a half-dozen skinny people.

As I come up on it, there be so much noise and music and laughin and shoutin, place near to rockin on its foundation. I sneak 'round the back and peek in the window. It's fairly reekin with depravity in there. Like to a place where two-headed men congregate to do their hoodooin.

Coal lamps up on the mantle against the mirror castin spooky shadows 'round the room. Everyone huddled up, playin cards, rollin them bones like there was some wicked conjuration goin on. Liquor in fruit jars and tobacco smoke so thick you could hardly see the nasty lookin women slinkin up against the wall. Every vice I ever been warned against was flourishin. *Evil* goin on, baby, that's right. I was hooked, lined and sinkered.

I want in there bad, but I know I can't make my move until my daddy leave. Through the window, I see him playin his fiddle and some cat over in the corner complementin him on the guitar. Cats pattin my daddy on the back, handin him bottles of liquor and laughin, and Daddy dancin some strange steps. By and by he finally head on home.

It gets to be 'bout one in the mornin, but the party's still shakin. It's now or never. My whole bad life hangin on it, I slip inside the door and slide upside the wall makin myself thin as a shadow.

Cat in a yellow hat shakin spoons—*chukka-chukka-chak*, fella in coveralls blowin a gear-grindin harp, and two mangy cool dudes over in the corner wailin on some beat-up guitars. Whole house rockin like the bosom of Abraham.

Cat what's singin gotta be Tommy Johnson. Couldn't've been above eighteen years old at the time but he was the baddest, hippest, most dangerous blues cat of 'em all.

Tall, skinny, small brush mustache, fast hair and bad teeth, I seen him here and there, but tonight he is glowin. Someone done sprinkle goofer dust over him for sure. Sack of gris-gris slung on a snake hide 'round his neck. Also got a big old graveyard rabbit's foot killed by a cross-eyed possum. Lookin sharp and shifty as a Saturday night. Got that mojo stare, look right through you like you a pane of glass.

Toyin with that guitar like it some old magic stick. Playin that voodoo drone, sayin *I ask for a drink of water and she give me a mouthful of turpentine.* Singin in a unearthly whine that reach down into your bones and make your blood run cold. Only eerier voice I ever heard in my life was Skip James's graveyard voice. 'Course that *was* a ghost singin.

Teejay—that's what they call him—had the largest, worstest repertoire of filthy verses that you ever gonna hear:

> *I'm gonna tell you like the catfish told the whale.*
> *You can move your belly, but please don't move your tail.*

Now that did certainly give me something to think about. Yes.

He tell a long old blues 'bout how the black snake got itself outta Mississippi. Moanin *black snake, black snake, crawlin in the bush.* Now here it come again, that crazy thing he do with his voice, a octave-jumpin, mind-janglin, whoopin, field holler from Hell.

And all along, he's rappin to his guitar what he calls Mona.

"Do it to me, Mona. Cry, baby, cry! Cry, cry, cry!"

And someone shout out, "Tell it, Jelly Jaw!"

You don't never hear that kinda blues back-chat on the phonograph records, but down at the jook joints it was goin on continuous. One cat gonna jump in with his sassy-ass jive, the other cat lick it right back at him. See a friend of his come by, Teejay make up a little verse soon as the cat walks in the door.

> *Oh Willie over the hill, he done study me well.*
> *That one ole boy, goin straight to Hell.*

A blues song done in a jook joint ain't no three minute, twenty second. No, sir. Length of a song gonna depend on the kinda reception you get. Might go on for more 'n a hour just addin in them extra verses. Every blues man worth his salt know a bunch of 'em. Floatin verses was the Mississippis of the blues. Makes me thirsty just thinkin 'bout it.

Teejay was singin some old piece-together blues,

> *The reason I loves my baby so,*
> *'Cause when she get five dollars*
> *She gives me fo.*
> *What did the blackbird say to the crow?*
> *Said: "How come you don't come 'round no mo?"*
> *Crow said to the little brown hen:*
> *"I'll be back but I don't know when.*
> *Then I'll do ya like I do ya,*
> *A do do do dah dah do do do."*

Right as he finish Teejay catch me tryin to scrunch myself down upside the wall.

"Mama know you here, boy?"

They was all laughin and smirkin and goin on.

"Aw, don't you worry yo head none, son," say Teejay all smooth and sympathetic. "My mama don't know I here neither. *Hawh, hawh, hawh.*"

They all crack up at that, too, but now they laughin 'long *with* me, understand? If you okay with Teejay, they was down with you.

Fella pass me a jar of corn liquor, take me a big swig. Gettin mellow, man, I'm in with the in crowd. Someone pass me a hand-roll cigarette and I take a coupla pulls on it before the cat that hand it to me says in a low tone, "That ain't tobacky, boy. That's reefer. That the Devil's weed, baby."

Now I'm interested. I take a coupla more drags on it. He's smokin it and it don't seem to be doin *him* no harm.

Feelin just fine. Warm and woozy, lettin my mind ramble where it will go. Driftin with the song down that crazy mama-mama lord-lord road. Catchin what pass before my eye. Snakes comin outta the shakes. Daddy-longlegs crawl across my arm and damn if each one of his spindly legs ain't keepin to the beat. I 'bout to squash that bug when a big healthy girl lean over me and whisper, "Oh baby, please don't kill that thang!"

While I'm gettin my mind 'round what she talkin 'bout, I'm checkin her out. Her lips was cherry red, and up close the blue powder on her face sparkle when she speak. Her titties was bustin out of her dress like a squash in a patch of cornflowers. Black dress with bright blue flowers on it. Midnight blue in a meadow. High heels, peony flower stuck in her nappy head. She was a older woman —least thirty, I figured—heavy, homely and hungry—in other words the most beautiful thing I ever seen, and talkin to me like a angel outta a dream.

"That li'l old bug be my Aunt Flora, honey. That woman *love* to boogie down, now she come back to shake it 'round. You just gonna set there, little one?"

We start doin the slow drag dancin and I get hard in two seconds. Rubbin up against a mountain of Delta pulchritude like her, gotta be a dead man not to. In a little old coy voice she start whisperin in my ear.

"Oh baby, I thinks we got something good goin on here. My my, *mmmmm-hmmmm*! You know, I do get the feelin there some introductions need to be made here." Talk to me, baby, don't matter *what* you sayin, just don't stop.

And with that she take me by the hand into the back room. No bigger'n a closet, all pile up with boxes and crates and old cans but it had one essential article of furniture, a pallet on the floor.

She was warm and sweaty, smelled of cigarettes and cheap wine, onions and turnip greens. Her body was glistenin with a thousand tiny stars. Little river of sweat run down between her breasts like a tiny creek windin through a hollow. She was hotter'n a Delta corn row at noon. Matter of fact, she *was* the Delta. Her body stretch all the way from Vicksburg to Memphis and on it I could see all the little towns and tawny rivers and glassy lakes. Her pussy was damp as a cypress swamp. Thought I'd died and gone to heaven.

I musta fell asleep 'cause it were mornin when I waked. The jook was still jumpin, the cats was still playin, but she was gone. My head been split open by a axe and I am in deep shit. But hell, they can just go kill me now, is what I'm thinkin. I'm happy as I'm ever gonna be in this old world.

The Lady Who Seen God

I might as well begin back as far as I can remember and tell you 'bout myself. I come out of the cotton patch on March 15, the Ides of March, so you could say I been unlucky from the start. If you wanna know what year it was, lemme see…. Coulda been, oh I don't know, beginnin of the century. Or so. Depend on where you start countin. At my age a year here or there not gonna make a hell of a lot of difference. I'm about the same age as the century is all I know, though others may think they know better.

My family come out from the hill country east of the Delta, up in Yalobusha County there. That's where I come into the world, the second boy child. I had three sisters and two brothers. Zora and Septimus was the oldest, Spissy was born just afore me and James and May come after.

When I was still a child we up and left the hills and headed down into the Delta, all us together—includin Grandmaw Pie and Grandpaw Scipio.

Work was real plentiful in the Delta. In them days they usta call it a money tree. You could make real dough workin in them cotton fields. Money was mostly a unknown quantity up in the hill country. The entire belongings of most hill folks wouldn't have come to thirty bucks. Down in the Delta, people was gettin one dollar a hundred pounds of cotton in a good year and some of them guys could pick four, five hundred pounds a day. That was good money in 1902.

My daddy carry us over to the Dockery plantation, big cotton plantation down on the Sunflower River. Ten thousand acres of the sweetest, blackest earth you ever seen. Topsoil rich as cream run fifteen feet deep in places. Cotton were king, but anything you plant would grow there. You could plant a umbrella and it would sprout.

Got us a situation down there. Each family lived forty to sixty acres apart in a cabin or abandoned boxcar. Our house was long and skinny, what they call a shotgun shack, built with long poles with mortar between 'em and a roof of pine shakes that was always leakin. Walls got cracks in 'em big enough so you could put your fist through.

In the middle of the shack was the kitchen—one end was Mama and Papa's room, down the other end us kids all piled in together. Floor of packed earth and our beds made of pine poles put together with cords. Girls on one side, boys on the other.

We live scarcely but usually we ate. Mama would cook up chicken dropped in flour and herbs simmered in a big pan of ham gravy. We'd have that, 'long with ash cakes—that's meal cooked in the ashes of the hearth. Chickens and hogs and all like that runnin 'round the yard. Had a little garden up next to the house where we plant collards, taters, watermelon, greens and beans. Fish outta the Sunflower River, hunt in the woods.

The Delta was still partly wilderness. Plenty of panthers stalkin in the cane brakes. Bears lurkin in the forest, along with deer, wildcat, wolf, wild turkeys, possums. Possum pie was a regular table dish. You take a possum, skin it, take the head off, clean it, boil it in vinegar, wash it, boil it again—hell, what you need the recipe for, you ain't never gonna eat no possum.

Along the Sunflower River was heavy woods, cypress swamps, and thick cane brakes. Gators slithered through the slow yellow river all tangled with willow and reed. Blue cane grow fifteen, twenty feet high. Sweet gum, cottonwood trees shoot up fifty feet or more.

Plantation have its own doctor but you stay away from him unless you near dyin. Sixteen years old and I never seen no doctor but Mama. Didn't know what a doctor was. Mama doctored us from herbs she got outta the woods.

My mama was frequently the subject of curses and hexes, which generally bring on faintin spells necessitate her repairin to bed.

"Right away I *knew* that woman done conjure me! There was a charm in that coffee. Honey, bring me my root jar over here quick."

If the charge thrown against her been real powerful, Mama would go pay a visit to the two-headed lady—conjure woman they call Miss Evangeline. More generally she know how to fix them things her own self.

"You ever conjured," she tell us, "them medical doctors can't do you no good. You gotta fix it by your own hand. Mix it up right in your house, yes you can. First you gets yourself butter made on the first day of May, mix it with the yolk of a egg and some saltpeter and roll it into small pills."

Meanwhile all us kids goin, "You mean we gotta put that stuff in our *mouth*? Yuuuch! We'll take that spell first."

"You swallow them pills down. A conjure do you permanent damage. Might cause you to have a demon baby. But that mixture'll cure any conjurin come against you. Come by its power on account of the cow done bit off the top and bottom of every herb what grows in the woods and ain't no two-headed lady can get the better of that."

Thanks to Mama's precautions we was pretty generally safe from spirits and goblins and scaly things comin in the night. Did you know a mighty defense against witches is brooms? Yessir. 'Cause witches gotta count everything before they can cross it. So put a broom across your door at night and they gotta count every strand of them straws.

We didn't doubt that they was all 'round us. A neighbor woman had caught a tiny devil. Kept it in a glass jar. Little shrunken creature floatin in green liquid. Its beady eyes swim up to the glass when you hold it up. Hmm, hmm, hmm. The world was a dangerous place back then.

Mama believed in everything but Daddy always skeptical. He was always askin, "If this stuff so powerful, how come it don't work on the white people?" On the subject of ghosts, he'd say, "I seen too many people depart this life mistreated terrible, and I don't see them comin back to do nothin 'bout it."

My brothers and sisters could tell some whoppin terrible ghost stories. Lies to make your blood freeze in the middle of a Delta August night. Tales 'bout the Dark Thirty, Jumpin Jack-o-Lantern, Bloody Bones and Ol' Raw Head.

One night my brother Septimus was spinnin out one of his spine-chillin yarns involvin the blood-droolin, ghoul-gougin monster call Mankwake, a animal specializes in eatin the tender brains of children in the night. Septimus had just come to the part where the Mankwake was climbin upside of a house to slither through the window—when there come a very loud kat-*clank!* kat-*clank!* on the roof. Our roof.

"Comin to getcha!" shouts Septimus.

My heart near popped outta my chest and ran down the road.

"Aw, leave him alone, Sept," said my sister Zora. She was always lookin out for me when I was small. "Don't you worry, Coley, it's just some fool throwin stones up on the roof. Lookin for Pa most likely."

I had just 'bout recovered myself when a loud quaverin voice say, "Come out, damn yo niggah eyes! We're thirsty as wild dogs."

"Sweet Jesus," cry my sister Spissy, her eyes big as saucers.

We all creep out to the back porch to find what the commotion was—and there we seen it. A army of ghosts on horseback, studyin us just like a rooster study a worm.

We run for our lives and hid ourselves under the bed, stayin very quiet and small.

"Niggah boy! You hear me in there?"

"That's *you* he be callin," says my brother James. "You best go —now he know who you are." Had a sense of humor, James.

They have to push me out on that porch, I'm tellin you. The lead ghost spot me out there, just shakin like a leaf.

"Niggah boy!" says he.

"Yaaaa-ssss-uh?"

"Go fetch a pail of water. I got a powerful thirst."

I bring the water to him and I'm tremblin with fear as I hand it up. He pretend to drink the whole pail down but I seen he spilt it mostly down the other side of his horse.

"Lawdy," he say, "that sure was good. First drink of water I had since I was killed at the Battle of Shiloh." Then they all rode off into the night. Battle of Shiloh! Damn! That was some moldy old ghost, I thought.

"Hell, them ain't no ghosts, son," say my daddy later. "They think we a bunch of ignorant niggers gonna believe a pack of fat old white men in sheets is the spirits of soldiers killed in the War? There ain't no such thing as ghosts and if there was, I doubt they're gonna be that fat. That's nothin but Mr. Jenkins from the feed store and his ugly cracker friends dressed up in white sheets.

"Call them the Ku Klux Klan, son. They ever come askin for your daddy, you say he gone to visit his sick sister."

When I was seven I got baptized in the Sunflower River. First warm Sunday in May. A spirit-filled meetin linin the banks. Everybody singin glory and praises but, man, that water was cold. When the icy water hits my stomach, I cry out, "Oh Lordy!"

"You best shut your mouth and trust in Jesus," say the preacher.

Then he put his hand under my back and push me under the water. The singin seem far off, and the preacher's voice got deep. When I come up again I was walkin on clouds and everybody shoutin, "Glory hallelujah!"

Religion a livin faith back in the Delta, the church bein a mighty fortress against the armies of Lucifer. The man with the cloven hoofs was busy indeed. He was hangin in the jook joints, swimmin in that jar of white whiskey in back of the feed store, causin you to cuss. Whether it was gamblin or fornicatin, he was sure 'nuff behind it.

There was folks had seen the flame of the Holy Spirit burnin in the air plain as day. They seen the Devil and his minions hid in the night, angels battlin with devils and Jesus and Isaiah walkin like you or me down by the river in the cool of the evenin.

My mama was sanctified and she was determined that us children remain in the folds of the church and not fall into Satan's clutches. Mama tellin us that membership in the church was both eternal life and everlastin fire insurance.

When I was little she carry us kids over to visit with a old lady who'd seen God in the flesh and had information on the terrors of Hell.

There was old Ophelia Jemison settin in her garden, rockin, rockin in her chair. Her eyes roll up to see the spirit world.

"Chillen! When I was converted I went to Heaven in the spirit. Heaven be white as snow, blessed sight!

"An angel done took me by the hand and show me the stars, how they hang up there by a silver cord, and the moon was just a ball of blood—I don't know what hold it up. I seen the sun on the rim of all these, goin 'round and 'round, and Christ settin in a rockin chair over the sun.

"I seen God and the Holy Ghost—they is one and the same— set at a big table with a book of gold stretch out before 'em. God's two eyes was just like two big suns shinin, hair like lamb's wool. He got Hisself a long pen of fire and write in His book the name of the people down on the earth yet. And every name He done wrote was a spirit picture of that person, revealin each one in their own soul form. Oh, I was rejoicin, chillen, rejoicin never the like before."

This was enlightenin and sublime, but we wanted to know 'bout the other stuff.

"Please, Miss Ophelia, won't you tell us all 'bout the awful fires and tortures of Hell?"

She draw herself up tall, her eyes pop out wide and she begin whisperin in a spooky voice.

"Lord! The fire down there is sharp as a razor against the wicked flesh of sinners. A lake of burnin fire is there, a-roarin and a-roarin like to a hurricane. Burst your eardrums and the blood run outta your head *eternally*. That fiery lake, Lord, seem like it bigger than Jackson. And they got special rooms where they torture people done ungodly works in this life. Some stretched out on the rack, some with the hot needles poke through their eye—yessir!—some cover in molasses with ants bitin at 'em for all eternity."

This was awful good stuff! It bein the Hotel of Hell and all, where Jefferson Davis was registered. He was down there still, a-screamin and a-hollerin with all the murderers and cursers and dope addicts and musicianers and revenuers and sissies.

"Tell us more," we cried, but Miss Ophelia havin exhausted herself fell plumb asleep.

Blues come out from the cotton patch, anybody tell you that. Come from whoopin and hollerin in the field. You catch the fellas out in the field plowin behind the mule, you can hear 'em late in the evenin wailin out them old Bantu blues.

You in a brutal, dire condition down in them cotton fields—slave or free. Workin so bad you just had to study something for consolation. *When I gets worries it look like it give me ease*, that's right.

We chop that cotton by singin. One of the fellas hoein the rows calls a line and the others answer him and they go along like that. Just like in church the minister say something and the congregation respond to him. Every time you hear a cat sing out a word you sing it back. Keep you in motion if you got someone singin, and pass the time easier. Stop your mind from wanderin and frettin.

Looky here, I'm gonna do you a field holler and when I *lean* on that word and pause a spell, you gonna say "huhn!" okay? Like you was bringin down your hoe in the cotton patch or you swingin a hammer on a chain gang. Here we go:

> *Polk an'* Clay—**huhn!**—*went to* war—**huhn!**
> *Polk came* back—**huhn!**—*with a broken* jaw—**huhn!**

Polk and Clay, they was some old-head politicians but you put in whatever words you want what come into your head.

Say your mule won't go ahead, you holler at that mule. "Emma! Emma! Get along!"

> *Emma, Emma, don't be playin the fool.*
> *You go playin the fool, girl,*
>   *gonna find me a brand new mule.*

You know how they say a mule's bray make a sound like "hee-haw"? Well, that ain't even a close approximation of the heart-wrenchin moan and cry of a mule 'cause a mule brayin be the most soulful sound of any animal on this earth. Period. You hear a mule bray, sound like a great bucket of lost souls bein raised on a rusty chain out of a well, goes all the ways to the end of time. A wail from the bottom of the universe, same as the blues. Get rid of your aggravation good.

Down there in them cotton fields you *gotta* sing or all that worrynation gonna eat you up. Everybody out in them rows singin, hollerin, makin up verses. And that's how the blues get started. Everything mix in together. Sayins from the Bible, gossip, who puttin it to who, who be doin time in the hoosegow. They say a field holler come from a kinda Congo pygmy yodelin, but I never been there so I wouldn't know.

The Dockery plantation was a goin concern in them days. And you *know* where there's money, there's women. And where there's women *and* money there's gonna be bluesmen. Just flyin 'round like bees to a honey pot.

Crap games start 'round noon Saturday. The boys playin the blues over at the boardin house—where some old woman board half a dozen day hands who was bachelors. The men who sang the blues was generally the unmarried field hands, stray blues cats passin through for a season.

You hear the sounds comin out over the fields late on a summer night. Some old cat 'round five in the mornin wailin 'bout some woman, and he's sinkin lower and lower in his grave, oh Lord, and all that sweet sufferin jive. Nothin like singin 'bout misery for lettin the good times roll.

Eight years old, I'd hide near as I could in the field. As I lay on the ground between the cotton rows in the darkness I could feel myself floatin on the driftin sounds all 'round me. When that cat touch them guitar strings with the edge of a knife—the slider zingin over the strings—my mind went slidin with it. Eeriest damn thing I ever heard. Sound of a lost soul howlin in the night. Stung me bad as the snake what bit Adam.

If you couldn't afford a guitar you do what most of us kids done, make what they call a "one strand on the wall" or "bo-diddly." You fix a length of broom wire to a wall with a fence staple at each end and play it usin a rock as a slider—put a nail on top of the rock to give it a edge. You wanna make a high tone you slide it up, you wanna make a low tone you slide it down. You got yourself a one-string guitar, usin the whole house as your soundin board.

Conjure Doctors Speakin
Through the Ears of Snakes

Never had no education to speak of. In them days they figure educatin blacks was a waste of time and money. For what? You don't need to read no books to pick cotton, baby. If a man could write, count to a hundred and spell Constantinople he could be a teacher in a black school.

'Course, education is one thing and fireside learnin entirely another. We schooled by our mama and grandmaw.

My grandfolks was slaves. Brought over on one of the last slave ships to come across from Africa. The stories they told us of life back in Africa was the favorites of all us kids.

Grandpaw Scipio didn't talk too much. He say, "I been touched by lightnin," and that ain't all he been touched by. His eyes was hollow like he could see all the ways back through time.

But Grandmaw Pie could talk enough for both of them and then some. Tell stories, sing little crazy things. Fantastic stories 'bout *griots* and *jalis*, conjure doctors speakin through the ears of snakes, destiny stones, walkin skeletons, skulls what prophesy.

I wanna know how come Pie remember all this stuff 'bout Africa and can't remember our names?

Mama say, "That's the way old folk memory work. They can remember seein fish fly and crabs climb palm trees but they can't remember this mornin."

Grandmaw usta say, "I know too much, *too* much." Tell us 'bout how the ancient African people built the pyramids and the sphinxes and could talk to the stars and knew from the witch doctors what gonna happen day by day from the future.

"It been from de prophecy of de Talkin Skull dat we knows our fate. Say, 'Man gonna come, Olijah! Take you to far place.' See, we knew we was gonna be put in de slavery and come 'cross de sea. All dat."

"But, Granny," we ask her, "if you know it gonna happen, why you didn't run away, hide in the woods?"

"Mercy, chile, you can't run 'way from yo fate. You run in de forest, yo fate come catch you in de forest. You run in de desert, he catch you dere. Fate be fate, grandbabies, ain't nuttin you can do to get 'way from under dat."

Say she and her whole family got sold for a bunch of gunpowder and cloth. Of the crossin she didn't remember none. Pain wipe away the memory of it.

And very scarcely did Grandmaw Pie ever speak 'bout the slavery.

"You don't wanna hear such," she say. "Like lookin back into de dark—like lookin into de night.

"I was on the plantation of Marse Longthaw." That was her way of pronouncin "master."

"I heard a nigger woman done put poison in Jeff Davis's sometin-to-eat and I do same ting fo Marse Longthaw if I hadda de chance to.

"Come 'pon me as I was ridin de streetcar after freedom. I be passin 'long by de cemetery where de white father be buried. I say, 'Believe Marse Longthaw been planted here, think I get off and do him no good.' But I din't do no tramplin. Just come by to spit on dat man's grave. A dirty old rascal he been, Marse Longthaw. Now he dead and gone and I be glad, glad, glad!" And she clap her hands together.

"Tell us the story again how you come to get your freedom, Granny."

"Well, well, my grandbabies, dis de way it be. After Surrender and de War been over we was mighty afeared to stir. Just like tarrapins or turtles, stick our heads out to see how de land lay.

"'Long come man from de gubbermint tell us we's free. Long as I live I never forget de day of freedom. We was called to de big house, and dere on a hide-bottom chair be a-settin a kindly old white gentlemans. Got dem chin whiskers, his hair plumb gray, his face all fleshy and rosy lookin.

"'You darkies know what day dis is?' he asks.

"'No, suh,' says we.

"'Well,' says he, 'dis de fourt of June and dis is de year 1865, and I want you to remember dat date for always 'cause today you is free, jest like I is.'

"And on dat day I begins to live, and I gwine take a picture of dat old man in de big black hat and gray whiskers clean to my grave."

Got so as I was pretty good playin on my daddy's guitar when he ain't 'round. Wouldn't allow no one to touch it. That guitar was his heart.

"Alabama Bound" was the first piece I learned myself well enough to practice on. Got a good reason for rememberin this 'cause I got a whippin 'bout it. Come out the cotton patch to get some water and I find the house empty. So I start thinkin, Aha! Shut the door, get up on that old box of my daddy's. I tune it, more or less, and begin squallin.

And I'm really gettin into it, you know. I'm imaginin all kinda stuff, like I'm down at the honky-tonk, all the cats noddin their heads and sayin, "That boy can sure shake it," and all them pretty women crowdin 'round me, pullin up their dresses to do the buzzard lope. Yessir, if I ain't the coolest fool this side of Jackson.

Meanwhile…I have forgotten 'bout where the time have went. And I also forgotten them windows to the house been open all this time, and everything I'm playin and singin goin right out the windows and across the fields.

By and by my mother come back up the house. My mama was a Christian woman—sanctified—and she didn't want me playin no blues. Start in wailin on me with a strap.

"Where'd you learn such trash? Let's tell your daddy, see what he think 'bout it."

But my daddy, he knew, see.

"Well," he say, "you ain't never gonna stop him once he's got the bug in him so might as well let him be."

After that my daddy had me up three nights playin the blues. Like I say, he was a fiddle player mostly but he could do a few licks on that beat-up old Stella guitar—little things what had but one line to each verse.

"First thing you gotta hear is that beat, son," he told me. Learned me a bunch of them floatin verses, little old proverb lines strung together any old how.

> *the time ain't long....*
> *goin down the river....*
> *hung my head and cry....*
> *watchin that ol train rollin by....*

"Say you got a line 'bout a rooster, you sing that three time. You got a line 'bout a train, sing it thrice. Line 'bout the Prodigal Son and the swine, then 'bout your baby gettin on the train and so forth." All them lines by and by become part of the blues.

I tell you the type of blues he liked me to play—the first song I ever heard to remember was one he learned me, a real old number, fiddle tune call "Willy Poor Boy."

Strum a bit, then ask me, "You hear what I'm layin down, Coley? You hear that drum? Drum what got hid in the guitar—that drum come from Africa."

Daddy loved to paint me pictures of Africa where he never been. Make me see the flames, the palm trees, volcano smokin in the distance, birds flyin up off the beach like pink and blue clouds.

"The slave been dragged from his village, couldn't bring nothin with him. Bring with him just one thing, his body—that's all them slavers wanted. That's where the plantation dance come outta, the juba dance, see? Stampin your feet, slappin your body across with your hands—that's how they took the drummin over with them. And that drum gonna shake the world, chile, 'cause we know how to make dumb things talk. Back up in the hills the old folks was educatin chairs and bottles and tables long before they got theirselves guitars. Anything they can rap on, they'd make it talk. Teach a milk bottle to preach, a pair of shoes to sing the blues."

5

I Seed All the Way Back
To Adam and Eve

Grandpaw Scipio gettin up high in years but he still active. Diggin graves was his occupation, and in his eightieth year he still out there shovelin. Now most people think of grave diggin as unsavory, like you wouldn't sign up for it lessen it was the last damn job around. Nobody wants to do it 'cept maybe a crazy old man and his grandson. But to Scipio takin care of the dead was a sacred callin. "Freightin the souls, grandboy."

I ask him if he done this kinda work back over in Africa.

"There ain't no diggin graves in Africa. Over there they buries 'em in the trees."

I could never tell whether he crazy or puttin me on, or whether he don't remember or maybe that really the way it was. But you could never question him too much. Chew your head off at the neck if you push him too far with the questions.

Many people dyin from malaria and from influenza 'round the time he take up the grave diggin so it was somewhat profitable too. Get three dollar for every one he bury.

I ain't got no work, it bein lean times in the cotton patch, and I'm tryin to figure what can I do when Scipio take me aside and say, "Don't worry 'bout no job, grandboy. You just stick wid me."

I weren't that crazy 'bout workin in the boneyard, but I was strapped for money. A young fella always needs money, buy some nice clothes, maybe a little whiskey on the side. So I throw in my lot with him.

We settin up there by them tombs waitin for somebody to die. Playin my guitar, listenin to tall tales. Every mornin Scipio sniff the breeze like a fox and say, "Somebody gonna die today."

But since I hitch up with Scipio, nobody been dyin. First two weeks I work with him, nobody die. Three weeks roll 'round—still nobody doin any dyin. Only person dyin is me. Ain't got no coins, can't buy no corn liquor, can't buy no clothes. Don't even got the scratch to buy strings for my guitar. The cotton patch bad, but this grave diggin gonna *kill* me.

Three weeks goin on to a fourth and finally someone come by and say, "Sharpen up yo shovels, boys, old Mr. Stokes done pass."

"See, what I tell you?" says Scipio. "Didn't I say somebody gonna die today?"

"But Grandpaw, that what you say every day."

"Every day *be* de same day."

"Well okay, Grandpaw, but—"

"Everybody gotta die, chile. Everybody needin somebody to dig a hole for dem. Care tenderly for de vessel in which de soul come into de world."

One day we was diggin a grave and Scipio say, "Coley, you a songster?"

"Well, I can sing a bit."

"But can you *make* a song?"

"I dunno, Grandpaw, it's not—"

"If I tell you a story, could you write me a song?"

"I could give it a try."

"Want you to make me a song 'bout bein touched by lightnin."

"But Grandpaw, you don't never wanna talk 'bout it."

"Time have come, chile, for me to tell you 'bout de lightnin."

And 'course, Scipio bein Scipio, it ain't gonna be like, "On the 31st of June, 1878, I was standin in a field...." It gonna involve a few other things, like God and Moses and all the things what creep upon the earth.

"Dat day," he begin, "dere was a big light and I seed all de way back to Adam and Eve and de generations what come up after dem. I seed Cain and Abel and Joshua blowin his horn and de sun stop in de sky. I seed all de people dat reside inside me."

"You mean like, uh, demons?"

"Sakes no, not demons—de ancestor spirits. Didn't I never tell you of dem?"

"No, Grandpaw."

"You know who Scipio been?"

"Yeah, you're my Grandpaw Scipio who been snatched from Africa by the slavers."

"Look closer! Look *in*. Look in de eyes."

Oh man, I can tell this gonna be one of them insane conversations with Scipio.

"To know who you be, Coley, you gotta know who you been. Gotta know who your ancestors been. 'Cause you make what you made of, chile. Iffen you don't know dat, you gonna be lost, drift yo whole life like a bobbin in de river."

"How'm I gonna find that out, Grandpaw?"

"You gotta go see the two-headed woman. Conjure woman. She see into yo soul, tell you what at de bottom of yo well. Everybody got two spirits given them when they is born. Two-headed person knows how to talk with his other head. You gotta find a two-headed person as will tell you who inhabits you. Otherwise you never knows who you is."

Grandmaw Pie like me to read her from the newspaper.

Say, "Chile, come close by me and read to me what happenin in de world. Newspapers is just like dem *griots* tellin de peoples what happen."

"Well, Granny, maybe next time.... I'm not up to singin the newspaper just yet."

Then I asks her how come she never learn herself to read.

"Lawdy, chile, ain't nobody told you it were agin de law to larn a nigger to read and write? Dey chop off yo fingers dey ketches you larnin and dat's de God's truth. So read me sometin happenin in de great world. Read me more of dat big ship dat sunk wit all de rich white folk on it."

"Grandmaw, that happen *months* ago. This a *daily* newspaper."

For Granny Pie the newspaper was a endless scroll with everything in it that ever happen. All you had to do was unroll that scroll back to where you want. Pie like to hear 'bout the lifeboats and the fat cats tryin to push the women and childrens aside and such a thing as a iceberg destroyin this huge boat. She could hear it over and over.

They had a song 'round that time Blind Willie Johnson done about the Titanic, had a bunch of verses to it. Had a verse about how rich old Mr. Astor who was a millionaire could not save hisself even with all his gold.

Truth be told, not everybody all that sad 'bout the Titanic bein sunk. There was a lot of people celebratin, buildin bonfires and holdin parties on account of all the white men got sunk down with it. Anything bad happen to the white was a occasion for carousin. Hmm, hmm, hmm.

By early August I climb up the little hill to the cemetery and I come upon Scipio diggin a grave.

"Someone die, Grandpaw?"

"No, someone *gonna* die."

Not that again. He catch me rollin my eyes and gimme that juju look.

"Who you think it gonna be?"

"I *knows* who it gonna be."

"You gettin in the fortunetellin business, Grandpaw?"

"Dis grave, chile, be for Scipio."

"Jesus, Grandpaw, don't ever say that."

"It's time, Coley, my time done come. Just promise me one thing. Don't let 'em bury me in a hollow tree."

"What you talkin 'bout, Grandpaw? No one gonna bury nobody in a tree."

"Just swear it."

This time I knew not to argue. The next day he got up, ate his breakfast, kiss all us children and got back into bed. Within two minutes he was dead. We put pennies on his eyes and said prayers for his soul. Pa and me built him a coffin and took him out to the cemetery and buried him in the night. Grandmaw Pie didn't want no Christian burial. She was afraid the old gods outta Africa gonna fly over the ocean and blacken his soul, and we didn't know no African ceremonies. Grandmaw Pie was too young when she snatched from her village.

But late one Saturday night I run into Tommy Johnson. I tell Teejay 'bout my grandpaw and his wishes, and he say, "I know some stuff we could chant, man. Got it from *my* grandmaw. Let's go up upon the hill and sing the old man goodbye." So Teejay chant some verses in a unknown tongue in his high crazy whine, and we sent Grandpaw Scipio off to sleep with the ancestors.

6

Rise Up, Dead Man, Help Me Drive My Row

fter Scipio die I couldn't go on myself with the gravediggin. Brung up too many memories. So it was back to the cotton patch, and bein finishin time they need all the hands they can get.

Pickin cotton, man—you do that 'long 'bout the Fall. Stoop down, pluck them big fleshy bolls off them prickly bushes and pack it down in your sack with your feet. Hands all cut up, back achin, dust in your mouth, sun beatin down. You been out in the field nine, ten hours. Hotter'n hell, too. Make you faint and punchy in the head.

Under a heatstroke many a field hand seen the Devil turn hisself into a toad right there in the rows and nary said a thing 'bout it for fear of bein made to look foolish. You out in the blazin heat of that cotton patch long enough you gonna start seein stuff. Some weird shit known to pop outta them cotton rows. Lurkin out there, just waitin for your mind to wander.

The Delta's gonna feed them fevers 'cause it flat as a table top. Flat so you can see the earth curvin almost. Which is why I say the Delta been demonized and that's a fact. Get down below Memphis, you feel it in your bones. One of the most haunted places in the whole United States outside of Louisiana.

Flat ain't a natural condition of nature, see? Hills is natural, hollers is natural. When you got flat and empty, things naturally gonna rush in to fill it up. And what's the things fastest to fly in? Demons. Delta infested with 'em. Out in them fields you can hear the spirits of all them dead Choctaws and blacks hummin in the night air.

Why they call it the Delta, I don't know. The Delta ain't actually the Mississippi River delta, see. That's way down at New Orleans, hundreds of miles south. But never mind 'bout none of that. Delta a woman. That's right. Some kinda fierce old broad with brambledy cotton bushes growin on her, two hundred miles long and eighty-five miles wide in the middle part.

Look at the shape of the Delta on any map and what do you see? What that remind you of? A *leaf*? Aw c'mon, man, that ain't no leaf. You see it on a map, Delta look like a pussy, now don't it? Big, fat, pussy-shaped plain, what it is. That's why I says the blues come out from the Delta, and I don't care what no Texans or Africans sayin about it 'cause they don't know.

Delta the most fruitful and overripe place on this earth. So wide and flat that when you stand in middle of it you can believe that the world goes straight out forever, made by a god who gave Adam a cotton allotment and got the sons of Ham to work it for him.

But I swear it was some other kinda god with some evil sense of humor put black people down in the Delta and send along with them the fiercest magic this old world ever seen in the form of the blues. Some kinda African god who smokes tobacco, drinks palm wine, dreams about snow, dances, farts, fucks. Who delight in trickery and confusion, and change his mind frequent as he change his socks. Old Papa Legba risin outta the Delta like blue smoke off a field of burnin cane.

When I come to my senses I got outta the cotton patch right quick. I sooner fight alligators than contend with them damn weeds under the hot sun day after day.

I was 'round sixteen years old when it first come into my mind to leave Dockery's plantation. One mornin I'm out in the fields drivin them mules and wonderin was I gonna be doin the same old shit till the day I die and then have to pay for the privilege of gettin myself put in the ground.

Harsh thoughts churnin in my brain when I hear the whistle of the Pea Vine blowin. Cry just like a child. It say, "What you doin, doin, doin down there, boy? Come 'way, come 'way, come 'way!" You know how the brakeman can make them quills talk by how he let the steam go through the pipes? The words was just as plain as if they'd been writ down. Leave the plow in the row, tie the mules to a tree and walk out.

You hear that sound pullin at you, you gotta go or you gotta block your ears against it. You in its sway, baby, ain't no use resistin it. A train whistle blowin, that's just about the saddest sound you ever gonna hear. All the things what touch your heart is in that sound. All the things you lost in your life. Women, your Mama, your home. You can't wait to get off the damn cotton patch, but wherever you go you gonna spend your whole life dreamin 'bout it.

Charley Patton said it all:

> *I think I heard the Pea Vine when it blowed.*
> *I think I heard Pea Vine when it blowed.*
> *She blowed just like she wasn't gonna blow no more.*

I catch a ride on a wagon and then I walk and walk and walk and finally I get to Boyle. Y'know, where the Pea Vine cross the Black Dog? And from there ride a boxcar south, lookin for any work I can find.

One time I'm waitin down at the depot. There's a skinny cat slouched up against the wall like a cornstalk, hat pulled down over his eyes. I'm inquirin of him, does he know of any work on account of me not havin eaten in days. "There may be some work on the rails," he says, "but I ain't inclined to that type of activity." Talked real slow, like he didn't want to waste no more energy than he had to.

"Toothpick be the fattest piece of wood you gonna catch me carryin."

Just then a freight carryin pig iron come rollin through the station on its way down to Leland.

"Man, here's one we can catch," he say. "It's heavy-loaded and comin up to a rise just outside of town."

We run after it, and as it begin to climb we jump into a boxcar and roll across the floor. A minute later some old cat light a match and we see the car is full of hobos. White guys, but friendly—all liquored up.

They take one look at us and say, "Looky, looky! The Pullman porters done come on board."

"Boy, take my bags down to my stateroom, I think I'll wet my whiskers at the bar a spell."

They was a jolly crew and time pass easy till we get to Choctaw where they all jump off. We wondered why they wasn't goin further but we soon find out. Freight stop in Choctaw to take on water. Suddenly down the tracks come a bunch of rail yard bulls with lanterns and clubs bangin on all the boxcar doors. Mean laughter and grunts.

"Gonna crack me a few nigger heads before this night's out."

We're up next and there ain't no way out. They slam open the slidin door.

"My, my, what do we have here? A couple of watermelons need to get opened up."

"Gentlemen," says Slick, "we on the railroad. On our ways down to Leland to join a tampin crew." That was impressive quick thinkin but they wasn't buyin it right off.

"You *lyin*, boy, there ain't no rail construction down to Leland."

"Wait on there, Duke," says one of the other bulls. "There is a crew down there. We just sent down some ties yesterday on the flat beds. They're fixin the line runs out towards Yerger."

Man, that was close. At Leland I jump off the boxcar and look for the crew boss. Sure enough, they was workin on the spur runs out to Yerger and I sign up for it.

I work on the railroad some. Run tampers, that's tampin the ties. Done gradin track, been a section hand, carried crossties. From Yazoo City to can't-take-you city, I done it all.

Main work I done on the railroad was as a gandy dancer— that's when you linin the rails. Had them a bunch of funny old songs. One of 'em went like this:

> *Well, you got your pistol, and I got mine.*
> *Well, rap on yo cartridge, pardner, if you don't mind dyin.*

If you're on the tampin crew you need a chant so's the line crew can lay the rails. And track-linin songs generally got salty lyrics to 'em, keep the men tickled while they's workin.

> *Mama in the backyard, pickin up sticks.*
> *Sister's in the corn crib, suckin off dicks.*
> *Every time I go t'pee*
> *Think 'bout the woman that give this ta me….*

It can be fatal, see, if one cat on the line ain't pullin his weight. Got to get your rhythm down when you drivin steel, too—poundin in them spikes to hold the tracks steady—otherwise cats be bustin each other's heads. Kill you right dead, you get hit with a twenty pound hammer.

A train come in the station. Headin east, but I just wanted to get outta that stinkin railroad camp so bad. Figured I hop off in Moorhead and take the Yeller Dog north.

It was night by the time the train pull into Pentecost. Right away I was hip to something very strange goin down. At first I thought it was a fire. There was people runnin mad through the streets. Some wild outta control thing was pullin 'em along with its crazy drive. All that yelpin and shoutin made me tense up. And white folk. *Only* white folk. There was not one black person I seen on the street or by the station since I got there.

Somethin haywire happenin there and I weren't about to get in its way. I crept along the outskirts of town and had intended to get outta there altogether when I hear a woman scream. Like her heart was leapin outta her mouth. And when I heard that, I could not leave.

Make my way through the shadows, crouchin behind trees to the direction of the scream. There, the scream again. Was somebody in terrible pain. Jesus, what the hell goin on here? Towards the center of town was a big crowd down by the courthouse. People was carryin fat pine torches and shoutin, like a rally goin on, 'cept this weren't no rally.

They was shoutin at the top of their lungs. The shoutin was drownin out the screamin. I couldn't see nothin for the crowd and I sure didn't want to get any closer so I climb up a big maple.

Dear God, they was lynchin a woman. Pregnant woman. Whatever this poor soul done or they thought she done was nothin to what was bein done to her. They had her tied to a tree and three men in hoods was throwin a noose over the limb of the tree. Then they untie her and put the noose 'round her neck. The people in the square was shoutin,

"DIE! DIE! DIE!"

"Hang the nigger!"

Then they put her up on a chair and pull the chair away. They pull up on the rope with her kickin and screamin. It took a long time for her to die, and when she was only a few feet off the ground a man run out of the crowd and get up on the chair and with a penknife he rip her belly open. Out tumble the little unborn baby, which give out two tiny cries before he crush its life out with his boot.

Then they douse her with gasoline and burn her and they all cheer. Even the women was cheerin. Her face twisted up and her arms flailed and then she was still. Her name was Mary Turner and it all happen just like I'm tellin you. The lynchin of Mary Turner, man.

Just then the branch of the tree I was layin on crack and fall down. A few people at the back of the crowd turn 'round to see what it was. I was hopin they was too involved in the lynchin to take notice, and for a while they went back to shoutin and jeerin.

Then I hear a voice shoutin, "Over here! It's her nigger accomplice. Get him!"

The whole crowd turn and come after me. I ran like hell, but I was so terrified I kept trippin and stumblin over stones and they gainin on me. One of them start shootin with a pistol. I rolled down the bank on the other side of the tracks, and when I got up I heard dogs barkin and I thought this gotta be the end. Gonna butcher me just like a dumb animal.

I crawl through a sewage drain run underneath the tracks. I hear 'em shoutin on the other end, "The nigger's in the sewer! Get up on the other side of the tracks and we got him boxed in!"

Just then the train that I been waitin for come through town. I was never so glad to hear a train comin down the tracks as I was that night. On account of that train they couldn't get cross the tracks. I pull through the culvert and fall out the other side right into the river.

River well swollen, the water bein in full flood. I feared I might drown but even then I was thinkin this was a better fate than bein cut to pieces and burned alive by a crazy mob.

I come up for air and grab onto a log and just hang there as the river carry me downstream. Like some African water god had come saved me, I felt the water cradlin me in its arms.

A few miles downstream I could no longer hear the crowd yellin or even see the lights of the town and I climb up out of the water and lay among the rushes by the riverside. The moon shone above, fireflies flew 'round my head in bursts of light. I felt grateful to be alive. I felt blessed that the savage god had spared me and I entreated whatever powers that be to help that young woman's spirit rise out of this horror and be whole again, and to mend the sick souls of men.

That night I was out on the road, the wind was blowin a little bit rash, the moon shinin down like a candle at the bottom of a well. I was goin easy and slow, lookin first over one shoulder then the other, seein shadows and things creepin out of the night.

I lay down and fell into a deep, dark and dreamless sleep under a old oak tree. Wake up, it's the middle of the night and there's this little old man sittin on a rock with his back turned towards me, singin a song very soft to hisself. I couldn't hear the words, and when I gets closer to him I realize that what he's singin ain't in the English language.

> *Kusolola!*
>> *Ukaka mufu.*
>>> *Malowa mpelu.*
>>>> *Wakunyakishang'a!*
>>> *Itang'wa dineli mwitaka,*
>> *Eye eyeyeyeye!*
> *Kwimba ng'oma!*

When I'm a few feet away I see this ain't no old man at all. It's a young cat wearin almost no clothes and tossin a small white stone from one hand to the other. Stone seem to drift in the air, makin shadows as it fell. The man turned 'round and smiled. I knew him from somewheres.

"Coley," he says then he go on with some crazy string of words that when I tell 'em now don't make no sense: "Starlight bar-light neon singin night-daddy jive riffin wooly fishin wolf tone blowin the mojo sign follow that stone and moan your moan to the end of the line...." Funny thing, it all made sense then when I heard it. *Everything* made sense. Messages pourin through those words like water comin through a drainpipe in April. At that moment I knew who he be.

"Grandpaw Scipio! That you?" I says, and my heart leap for the joy of seein him again. But the moment I say his name he vanish. It was Scipio as he been when he was a young warrior in Africa. Young and strong and beautiful and proud and could read what the stars wrote on the sky. When I walk over to where he been, there on the ground was the pearly white stone 'bout the size of a nut. A piece of shiny quartz smooth from a riverbed, and as I turn it in my hand it sparkle.

"Coley," say the stone, "I lain in the woods a thousand years. I absorb the light of stars and a million suns. Whatever you desire in your heart, call to me and I come."

When I woke up it was already mornin. Birds singin, sun shinin, and the sky the bluest blue I ever seen.

I got up and head down to the nearest set of tracks. I was so turned around by what I been through I got myself on a freight goin the wrong way. I wake up and I'm in Yazoo City way down south. 'Course sometimes the wrong train can take you in the right direction. Figure I'll just ride it until the end of the line. New Orleans.

First thing, before I even took off my shoes, got into a game down on Algiers Street. Bet every last dime I had. Bet my shoes, bet my coat, woulda bet my guitar too if I hadn't already pawned it. And friend,

I lost it all. Met a weird old gent walkin on the street in his pajamas.

Told the man, "This losin streak can't last forever."

"Boy, you sure look like you need a hoodoo woman, uh-huh, hoodoo woman exactly what you need." Talked real fast like he been a tobaccy auctioneer or something, overlappin his words like he was fillin in the spaces till you made your bid. "Got a suggestion, suggestion for you," he said to me. "Marie Racine the Prophetess, woman you seek. Make a hand so you could win anybody's money, win the ring off the Pope's finger. Yessir! You got a spell put on you, she can pull it right off."

"How can I find her?"

"Hell, man, you don't find *her*. She come and fetch *you*. That's the kind of woman she be. Has that much power, yas, yas, yas. Dangerous woman, what I'm tellin you, boy. Don't go crossin her or she'll twist you like a basket. Deny her and she have you walkin like a hog. Swear! Make you bark, make you crow, make you do stuff you won't never know. Worst woman in the world!"

Seem like the Seven Snakes of Sardis ain't got nothin on Marie Racine. If all he said was true, I was disinclined to rendezvous with the woman. Unfortunately, some things in life you ain't got no choice.

Was three in the mornin. I was down in the Quarter, foolin 'round with the piano at a saloon. My head start to ache, my eyes was turnin in their sockets, I was dizzy and a thousand little hands was pullin on my coat. Walk outside to dust my brain. Standin in the doorway was a mulatto woman, smilin at me.

She wore a red bandanna 'round her head all hung with cowrie shells, her dress was covered with stars, rings on every finger and a snake stick in her hand. I tried to look away and slope off but she caught me in her eyebeam.

"You gimme a funny look, boy?" She was *hissin* at me.

"Why, no, ma'am, I—"

"You know something, you best watch yo raggedy ass, boy. Else I shrivel yo penis to a cheroot. You lookin for me?"

"Don't reckon—"

"Yes, you was. Don't lie to me, boy. Look like you seen a ghost, cousin. You 'fraid of haints, chile? *Hawh! Hawh! Hawh!*"

"Don't know I ever seen one, ma'am."

"Ghosts? Ach! Seed 'em all the time. Good company! Does I believe in witches? Say, I know more 'bout 'em than just *believe*. I been *rid* by 'em, you understand me?

"You ain't never been rid by a witch? Well, you mighty lucky, boy. Then again maybe you been and don't know it. Rid by a actual witch. Uh-huh. Right here in this house. Believe that! You ever wake up from sleepin all night long like a possum in a log and you still tuckered out next mornin like you been workin in the mine? Well, you been used.

"They comes in the night generally, just after you drop off to sleep. They put a bridle on your head and a bit in your mouth and a saddle on your back. Then they takes off their skin and hang it on the wall. And they're off! Clippity-clop, clippity-clop the whole night through. That's it. That's why some mornins you wakes up all tired out and sweaty."

"Guess I had nights like that."

"What spirit sent you?"

"I been down on my luck. Gamblin, y'know, and they said—"

"They said, they said. What trash you talkin? You seen a haint, boy, I see it in your damn eyes. What haint you seen?"

"Lissen, ma'am, I ain't seen nothin."

"*Lies!* Lies, lies, lies! You ain't see a haint why yo come to me?"

She shook a bunch of strange objects in her conjure basket. Then she pick 'em out one by one. Takes out a piece of broken green glass rubbed smooth.

"Ah! *Medilu.* Tears weepin and lamentation by de woman when they hear news of death." Pulls a tiny drum carved in wood. "*Ng'oma.* Someone been dead long time. Ancestor spirit." Next a piece of wood wound 'round with string. "*Mufu.* 'The Stiff' they call him. Mean someone passed, yes?"

"Well, uh, yeah. My grandpaw, Grandpaw Scipio. He died. Let's see, musta been, uh...."

"Shut up, I knows already."

She pulls out the shell of a water snail. "*Mpuhu.* Fame. Man who done died, great great man."

"I don't know 'bout that...."

"Fa-mous man?"

"Wouldn't say so, no."

"Great hunter. Hunter ancestor, lost his power."

"Uh-uh. Don't think so—"

"Shit! Must be my time of the month. Spirit strings a bit cloudy. Okay I got it, it comin to me now. He be a great diviner?"

"Uh, well—"

"Yes he was! Was, was, was! Don't you fuck with me!"

"He been over in Africa. Don't rightly know what he been."

"Yeah, yeah, yeah. Okey-doakey. Now we can do some things."

Hold up a piece of knotted leather. "*Matangishu*, the Twister." A black shriveled fruit. "*Mudidi*, seed of the palm wine tree. You want know what it mean? Give money! Ach! Not coins, moron! Give paper. Don't insult the spirits."

Gave her all the money I didn't have and she make me some tea outta herbs taste like shit. After we sat quiet a long while she hand me a silver mirror.

"Look in de glass. What you see?"

"I see myself."

"No, no, no! Look *through* de glass. Like de glass was a well and you is lookin down into it and de water is ripplin and takin itself a shape. *Venez vous, shabba, shabba, venez à nous.*"

She kept on this way long time, chantin softly, hissin in my ear and outta the tarnished well come fast and flashing images. Snakes, totem monkeys, gold, sweat, grass, quicksilver faces of warriors, shamans, hunters, old women rootin in the ground, men eatin ants and honey, smoke, stars, salt, familiars, masks, feathers, shells, blood and the smell of gunpowder, salt and tobacco. All the murmurous voices what lived in me was in that well that went back to the first mornin of the world.

My head was spinnin, my legs were wobbly and my hands were tremblin as I walked out Madame Racine's door.

"Darlin, you forgotten something?" she ask me.

"Uh, I don't think—"

She cup her hand over mine and let something drop into my palm.

"Open your hand when you away from here, understand?"

When I looked, there in my palm was a small white stone. It shone when it roll across my hand. I knew that stone. Hmm, hmm. Was the stone outta my dream.

On my way home from New Orleans I snuck into a barn, lay down in the hay loft. Below me a strange choir of chickens, pigs, goats and cows. I was woken by a old white farmer with chin whiskers pullin at me. I figure he gonna kill me the very least.

"You all right, son?"

"Yeah, reckon so...."

"Look like you could use something to eat. C'mon and we'll make you some eggs and grits."

Him and his wife let me rest my bones, get my strength back. I stay with them a day or two. Then Mr. Fitzpatrick take me down to the depot and give me a couple of dollars to get home. I never thought I'd be so happy to see that old cotton patch.

7

They're Holdin a War on Mars

Damn, where I go? Memory wanderin like a untethered mule. Go any way it want to. Hold on a minute while I catches up with it. Pass me over that guitar, son, get the memory juices flowin. You gotta feed the memory, y'know, talk to it and it'll talk right back to you. *Sing* to it. Here we go:

> *Vida Lee, Vida Lee,*
> *Prettiest gal I ever did see.*
> *Face as pretty as August moon,*
> *Baby, baby, gonna come home soon.*

Hold on, it's comin to me. The pictures is beginnin to fill in. Fish fry. Shimmy-she-wobble. Little girl with the red dress on.

I was goin to this Saturday night fish fry over at Ruleville. Eatin, dancin, drinkin, gossipin, eatin some more. Got a board nailed across the kitchen door, passin out plates of fried-up fish and grits and corn.

A fish fry more a family affair, which mean there not gonna be too much juicin and jivin goin down. On the other hand, you gonna see a lot of pretty young women. Your so-call respectable woman don't hang 'round no jook joint or barrelhouse.

You know how you go someplace and everything in black and white 'cept that one person? That's how it was with Vida Lee. Sparklin eyes, a mouth like honey, and a tongue like a parin knife. Wouldn't take no shit from nobody.

Her family worked on the same plantation as mine. I seen her 'round and we exchange glances. But this particular night there she look like someone just took her outta a department store window. Red calico dress, bright red shoes. Moon shinin down, stars and guitars and everything in my life leadin up to this moment.

When they start playin "Big Road Blues," I just had to ask her for a dance. Ah, play that thing, man! Tommy Johnson shakin it up on guitar.

> *Now you say you gonna do me like you*
> *Done poor Cherry Red....*

You shoulda seen me dance that night. Didn't need no gravity. Shimmyin way down low to the floor, leanin back on air.

"Stop doin that stuff, Coley. People start thinkin we got something goin on."

"A man can dream, can't he?"

Next night I bring my guitar over, serenadin her, y'know.

"You ain't gonna follow that guitar, are you?" she ask point blank.

"No, Miss Vida Lee, I ain't even thought of that."

"Well, I hope not 'cause I ain't gettin involved with no hoboin musicianer, I'm tellin you that flat out right now."

"Oh, no," says I, just lyin in my teeth. You shoulda seen her— I woulda said anything.

"I got plans," I tell her, "all mapped out in my head, y'know? Figure I'll get me my own spread over there by the river, put in three different crops...." And I went on in this manner, waxin eloquent on matters agronomic and horticultural and cotton-pickin, which is what women want to hear. The next few months is kind of a blur to me. Before I knew it I was married and out there hoein that row I swore I never would hoe. Vida Lee say she can't remember exactly whose notion it was that we get married but I got a pretty good idea.

❖   ❖   ❖

Grandmaw Pie shakin her long bony finger at me as I come up on her.

"Don't lie to me, chile, you down playin them blues again."

"Well, it ain't bad as—"

"Oh, I ain't worried, chile, I sees it all. I seen de world in flames a hundred time over. I seen everything you can picture. It don't matter none you sing bad songs or you sing holiness songs. God hear yo *singin*, dat's all dat matter. He rejoicin in His heart. All de same ting in de eye of Fate. You follows yo heart, chile, dat all what matter in dis world. Dere far worser things in dis bad old world den singin them blues.

"You knows dey got some kinda story-singers over in Africky, too. Mercy, yes! Dey got a heap of dem, awright. Call dem mens *griots*. Yo grandpaw be a griot, y'know, and de apple don't fall far, not too far at all."

My mind was filled with strange ideas. I was seein palm trees and cockatoos and I was dreamin 'bout griots and halamkatts and all Grandmaw Pie told me. Them mean old African blues was percolatin through my mind, natural and sweet, way it meant to be.

Late August, 1914. I was settin down by the tracks tryin to flag a ride when a crazy old coot come runnin up the tracks wavin a newspaper in his hand. Wearin a bunch of medals from the Mexican War or something.

"Sonny," the old fella says to me, "yo best hide yoself right quick," he say. "War been declare! Says here they gonna fight the Civil War over 'gain, gonna turn all us niggers back into slaves."

"Pops," I says, "you gotta be kiddin."

"No, I ain't. Wish I was. It's all writ in this newspaper here."

He handed it to me. War been declared all right. England and Germany was in it and Russia, France, Austria-Hungary, Turkey. Some of these places I didn't even know existed.

When I explain the situation to him, the old man was disgusted. It was as if I'd said they was holdin a war on Mars.

Then the bo weevil come through the Delta in 1915, devour the cotton crop. Same year we got floods in the summer, then malaria. And then when Booker Washington died people took it as a sign.

The only folks prosperin was the reverends, the end of the world bein the best subject there can be for a jackleg preacher in hard times. Tellin us the seven plagues of Egypt was descendin on us. They was different plagues from the ones in the Bible—war, famine, disease, bo weevils and floods—but it was close enough to build a sermon on. The Bible say man gonna wreck hisself, and by the looks of things it gonna come about real soon.

That war over in Europe come up good for blacks—mean work and money. Down in the Delta we was eatin on cheese rinds but up North there was jobs. By 1917 we was hearin 'bout higher wages than anyone could believe for packin meat, workin in the ammunition factories, drivin rivets, buildin trucks. Fellas was *swarmin* up North, clamberin on trains like ants on a tin of molasses. Next thing I heard they was signin theirselves up for the army and the army was packin 'em in transport ships and carrin 'em over to the war in Europe. Comin back them ships musta been pretty light 'cause I never did see none of them fellas again.

8

The Great Blue God of Electricity

ne day Charley McCoy come by our house on his way outta town. Charley was short and wiry, the kinda guy who never could keep still. Always hoppin from one foot to the other like he was standin barefoot on a hot pavement. Was lookin kinda shaky and shifty-eyed, rappin at the window. Fear dartin this way and that through his eyes. Have his guitar and a sack. Come to tell me Tommy Johnson got busted. So I head on down to the county jail.

Now the Sunflower County jail was like a little visit to Hell all in your own backyard. Big beefy rednecks with puffy pink cheeks and little slitty eyes with them cold blue eyeballs pokin out of them like brand-new sewin needles. *Huge* muthafuckas. Done tore the runnin boards off the police cars just from standin on 'em. You come through there, they all sittin around smirkin and crackin nigger jokes and lookin at you with one hundred proof malevolence.

Teejay look like he been through a combine machine. Had a black eye, a broke nose, and his suit was all tore up. Voice was all messed up from bein strangled, he could only speak in a hoarse whisper.

"Coley, I got something I want you to do for me. Go find my brother LeDell, see if he can get some coin up for my bail and get me the hell outta here."

His older brother LeDell was big and slow. You never seen two brothers so unalike. If Teejay was a express train, LeDell was a freight pullin pig iron up a grade. LeDell pawn a bunch of watches and rings and stuff and get the bread together to spring Teejay. Next time I seen him down at the sugar shack he shuckin and jivin like usual. When he see me his eyes brighten up.

"Coley, my friend boy!" Then addressin his brethren in his special voice he say: "Y'all know what this fella done? Brother Coley done got me out of the clink." And everybody go, "Awright! Have mercy!"

Teejay bring me aside. "Coley," he say, "you done right by me and I ain't never gonna forget it. Tell you what I'm gonna do for you, I'm gonna reveal to you—tonight!—a livin mystery. I'm gonna carry you down to the crossroad and have you visit with somebody. Meet me back here 'round eleven, we have a few libations and then head on out there."

As I'm goin out the door he say, "You got a dollar on you? For the sacraments, understand?"

"I got some at home hid."

"Bring it with you. And baby, don't be late."

When I hear that crossroad stuff, cold chills run down my spine, I begin tremblin, my hands sweatin cold sweat 'cause I know all about the gentleman he intend to introduce me to.

LeDell done tell the whole thing to me one evenin we sittin down by the river. Come to where LeDell askin me, all bug-eyed and sweaty, "What you think the reason he play so good and knowed so much?"

"Beats me."

"First off, you gotta promise you never gonna tell no one, Coley, or you a dead man."

I swore.

"Sold hisself to the Devil, that's right."

"Aw c'mon LeDell, you shuckin me."

"Swear to God. Traded his soul at midnight at the crossroad. Went down to where a road crosses this way, another one that way, met a man tune his guitar for him...."

"Tune his guitar?"

"Tune it to the *diabolical* mode. And when he hand it back, Tommy could do anything. Before that night he couldn't play for shit, and now he the king of the box in these parts. You ever heard *anybody* play like my brother?"

Even if it were pure bullshit, I was revelin in the inequity of it. Better to say it was the Devil than gettin there through *practicin*.

We sat a long time by the river unable to move, studyin on the mystery of it all. The weeds all wavin in the water, the lonesome sound of the foghorns and the ship bells in the distance already creatin a spooky atmosphere. We doin our best to scare ourselves to death. LeDell believe every damn word, which made it more creepy yet. So lost in thought we was from studyin the strangeness of it that when the first bat flew out at us we took off like we was shot from a cannon.

❖　　❖　　❖

Eleven o'clock roll around and I meet up with Teejay. Have a few drinks, smoke a coupla reefers to fortify ourselves. And Teejay could drink, man. He drink near anything. Denatured alcohol, shoe polish, canned heat. They call it canned heat when you strain sterno through a handkerchief into a fruit jar and drink it. I hand him the dollar for the sacraments and we set off down the road. Halfways from town I'm thinkin, Am I crazy? Down the highway to Hell with Tommy Johnson. But Teejay such a coolfry, goin along like nothin unusual transpirin, ramblin on about his family and stuff. Say his grandmaw been captured on the River Niger, too. Just like Charley Patton's grandmaw. So him and Charley related mostly and that the reason why they got on and why Teejay done Charley's songs so good.

Nothin 'bout the Devil, though. It's all a little too cool and collected for my taste so I bring up about them crossroads.

"Okay, here's the thing," says he. "You connect the contraries you got sparks, dig? Points of the compass—east-west-north-south, see?"

"Uh-huh," says I.

"Because that where the demons congregate. Demons naturally inclined to do their demon dance out at the mojo point where no preacher or teacher, judge or jury comin 'round to jinx them, y'unnerstan?"

Demons! Now he's talkin.

"Um, Teejay," say I, very roundabout, "LeDell tellin me…"

"That Devil shit, that what you talkin 'bout? LeDell, he simple, man. Don't want him out here in the middle of the night messin with this stuff. He likely to injure hisself, fall in a ditch, get hisself arrested or something. The Devil story is what I tell to LeDell. Ain't no Devil nohow. Well, maybe there is and maybe there ain't—but this ain't about him."

"It ain't?"

"No, man, we talkin to the Writers of Destiny, Légba and Eshu. We gonna beseech them, say, 'Papa Légba, Father Eshu, bring us the *àshe*, the power-to-make-things-happen.'"

What in the name of Jehosaphat he goin on about? After all that booze and weed and canned heat he done, he could be talkin in tongues for all I know.

"Let me ask you this," he says. "What be a agency by which demons can cross great distances in the blink of an eye, bring theirselves across from anywheres on earth?"

Travelin demons. Jesus, Teejay.

"Ee-lectricity! Yeah! Put two different kinda things together what don't belong and what you got? You got ee-lectricty, baby, you got the *power*, y'unnerstan? You run a big city like Jackson on power like that. All that power be just *streeeeeeamin* through you, wakin up your mind, every part of your body alive like a deer or a jackrabbit alive."

And here his voice modulate into the tone apocalyptic:

"I am He that liveth, and was dead; and, behold, I am *alive* for evermore, Amen: and have the keys of Hell and death!"

"For Christ's sake, Teejay, you gonna get struck blind!"

Teejay had a answer for that, too.

"Ain't blasphemous," he say. "There is only one God, one Livin God, and you think he care *what* you callin him? The Wah-diddy, Unseeable Whatever-it-is. Take the *orisha*, them Yoruba deities, Légba and Eshu, put 'em together and you got—"

He mimic two wires touchin.

"—*kreeech*! Where anything meets you got sparks, you got the sanctified language with which God speak to the angels. Can you explain lightnin? 'Course ya can't. And why not? You think they talk in English or Chinese in Heaven? Speak the language before Babel, babe. Music. That's all it is, all it *could* be. Only language that everybody understand all around the world."

"Music? What happen to the ee-lectricity?"

"Music *be* ee-lectricity. Any fool know that. Sex ee-lectricity. Ee-lectricity be sex, sex be music...."

I woulda felt ashamed at my ignorance but my mind was paralyzed. I been stung by a word-adder and I was lettin his speech wash over me.

"You followin me?"

"Yeah," I says. "I'm with you. I think.... Teejay, how we know this the right crossroads?"

"Ain't a actual spot on the earth, y'unnerstan? It be the place *between*...."

He ravin on and it too late to stop him now.

"Hey, what time it gettin to be? You gonna make us miss our assignation with all your damn questions. Got to be 'round midnight, we best start the ceremony. Okay, you chant this along with me:

> *Jigue monkey*
> *monkey-jigue*
> *nganga-jigue*
> *jigue-nganga.*"

"What it mean?"

"You never mind what it mean. It African, have big magic. This the way we call to Eshulégba the crossroads god, trickster god outta Africa—Eshulégba, the trickster god been at work provokin man to sin from forever—to bring on the anger of the gods and busybodies. Brought the human world to edge of chaos many times."

"He has?"

"Yeah! Give you a example: Tower of Babel."

"The Tower of Babel? But I thought...."

"That was his doin. Over in Africa, see, where the *first* Tower of Babel originally situated in Zar on the other side of far."

A lyin, swindlin, double-crossin god! This was far worse than meetin the Devil. The Devil at least I know about.

A cloud pass over the moon. I feel a icy hand touch the back of my neck. In a minute the wind come up, clouds rush in from the east, the sky black.

Skraaaaaachhh! Suddenly a bolt of lightnin flash down and strike within a hundred feet of us and topple the big oak we just come from sittin under. Thunder and lightnin comin out of the depths of Hell.

I'm sittin on the ground in the middle of nowhere, hunched up, tremblin and shakin, anticipatin the arrival of God-knows-what demon out of the pit, the Devil or, uh, Eshulégba or the great blue god of ee-lectricity.… I musta blacked out from fright 'cause Teejay have to carry me back to town. Next thing I know Vida Lee puttin wet towels on my face.

When I finally catch up with Teejay, he hangin by the depot, waitin for a train. Just had to ask him 'bout that night.

"Well, let's see," he say. "What *you* think happen?"

"Why you wanna give me a hard time, Teejay?"

"You given yoself a hard time. It all in your head, see? Everything be in your head, man. The stars, the Mississippi, your mama, chitlins and rice, your dick.… Everything in the world, baby."

9.

Gonna Join the Caterpillar's Club

Was back, oh, five, six years earlier the first time we heard it. Come 'bout noonday, sun blindin you in the eye. Hummin, whirrin, buzzin outta the blue, rainin terror and confusion in the fields. Cocks begin to crow, dogs begin to howl, mules boltin through the fences. Fellas choppin in the fields drop their hoes and run like hell.

Dronin—*brrrghrrrarrarr*—like a great mechanical bee through the clouds. Like something outta the Book of the Seventh Seal. We was prayin and cryin out for mercy, cursin ourselfs we hadn't repented for cheatin on our wives, for boozin and gamblin. Man, we thought it was end of the world, lyin there a-shakin on the ground, flatten under a tree, waitin for the lightnin fast sword of Judgment to slay us where we lay.

That was the first time we seen a air-o-plane, and you could not get them fellas back out in the field for *days*. They hid in their house with the shades all down. Preacher Samuels have to come out, assure 'em it weren't the Last of Judgment, but mend your ways anyhow. The overseer come by, make the rounds of the shacks, show 'em pictures and explain what it was,

"Fellas, it ain't nothin but a flyin car up there." Well now, that's mighty reassurin, boss.

By the 1920s air-o-planes was a common sight—them bein used in the Great War and all. Coupla times a week one would fly by, but

Mama never did get used to 'em. Accordin with her view and quite a number of other folks in the Delta, it was against nature.

As a boy I remember lookin up at a hawk circlin in the sky with its great outstretched wings and sayin to her, "Mama, I wish I could fly like that and see all the fields and the streams and the houses from the sky. Look down on deserts and mountains and palaces and the North Pole." And she say, "Hush, chile! Don't wish for what the Lord don't want you to have. When *I* been a chile we didn't have such so don't *you* dream on it."

But my Grandmaw Pie was different. She love to see the planes flyin.

"Heah dat air-o-plane a-goin in de air? I'm goin on a trip, grandbaby, gonna fly away, see de world wid a birdseye view."

In her mind she would fly off to all the places I read to her 'bout in the papers. She could see the big ships crossin the ocean, peek down on a famous politician takin a leak against a tree, watch football games from the air, parades marchin through big cities, men workin on the railroad lookin up and wavin to her as she pass.

"Look just like ants crawlin over a ant hill, Coley. Wished you could see it like I see it."

Of a Sunday I usta set with Pie, readin her the news of the world. One day in particular I remember. Twelfth of August, nineteen and twenty-three. Sun shinin, crickets chirpin, stalk cutter whirrin in the field, voices floatin on the wind.

"Read me out the paper, Coley."

Now you know the newspaper be full of big numbers. There's 1,126,000 marriages and 148,000 divorces happen in such-and-such a year. Thirteen million cars on the road. But Pie impatient with statistics, swat the air like a fly botherin her.

"Don' you talk dem big numbers wid me, chile. Dat ain't countin, dat *witchcraft*."

"They say if you put them end to end they stretch all the way from Memphis to Minnesota."

"Why don't dey jes say it plain like dat in the first place?"

"Oh look, here's your heartthrob Rudolph Valentino, Grandmaw, playin over at the Thalia. Movie called *The Four Horsemen of the Apocalypse*."

"Makin a movin picture of de Book of Revelation? Dat I like to see. Coley, come close by me, chile, I got something I wants to impart to you. When it come time to bury me—"

"Don't know why we talkin 'bout this stuff. You gon live long as Methuselah."

"You listenin to me? I don't want no church hymns. I don't want nobody singin no 'Hark de Tomb' and dat, hear?"

"Tell me what you want, Pie, and I see it be done."

"I want dat fella, yo pal wid de funny eye—you know, de guitar boy."

"You mean *Teejay*?"

"Dat's it. I want you and him to send me off wid a blues. Dat be my wish."

"I don't know, Grandmaw. That ain't gonna go over too well with the—"

"Tell me, pygmy, who's funeral dat be? Dat yo mama's funeral? When her time come she can have de seven deacons wid de seven psalms singin hallelujahs every mornin, noon and night. But dis ain't her time, dis be *my* time. So do what I says or I'm gonna come haunt you in de night."

She mean it, too. Figure I best change the subject.

"Ah looky here, Grandmaw, a twenty-ton meteor done hit Blankston, Virginia, made a five hundred square foot hole. Hole the size of Clarksdale, it say here."

"Dat be a message, you knows dat; a message come down from God."

"What kind of a message, Grandmaw?"

"How de devil I know? What else?"

"Well, it says here a Lt. Harold become the first member of the Caterpillar Club—parachute outta a plane and live. And President Coolidge gonna speak on the radio...."

"When I be a young-un, de fardest you could hear a person be 'bout half a mile, an dey hafta holler like a stuck hog! Now listen to de radio and hear folks talk a tousand miles away. I wish I could live 'nother ninety years 'cause I sho would like to see what's a-comin."

Pie rockin back and forth in her chair sayin, "My my, think I'm gonna join de Caterpillar's Club, take dat sky train, ride mongst de clouds and de birds." And rockin there she fall asleep. And never woke up again.

Well, it weren't easy gettin the family to agree to Pie's last request. In fact it was impossible.

"She was fuzzy in the head. She don't know what she talkin" was the general understandin. So we have *two* funerals. Preacher preach a sermon in the church and Teejay and I go up on the high ground, build a brush arbor and sung her on her way:

> *Wonder where my friend done gone?*
> *Oh, I wonder where my friend done gone?*
> *She went away in the fall, didn't come back home at all.*
> *Where you went away and you stayed so long?*

10

The Wampus Cat

Did I know Charley Patton? Hell, yeah. I'll tell you something, God made Charley so as God could see hisself. That's the truth. God wanted to see hisself cavortin on the face of the earth. Papa Légba was tired of seein God pictured as a stern old guy with a beard settin on a throne—wanted to see hisself as a wild and wooly, raggedy-ass rounder playin the blues and clownin. Any god what made the hippopotamus and the duck-billed platypus, well, you know God got to have a sense of humor.

This Charley Patton, the one they call a tush hog, or a wampus cat—he was something more than human by the way they all talk. Say his grandmother been captured by slave traders on the Niger River, but I figure he come from a long line of muddy water lizards, half human, half *something*.

Charley Patton was so uncouth, his appearance in the proximity of some quarters would likely draw a fine for vagrancy. Couldn't intermix much with the people, didn't have too much education, was what we call a "meat barrel type." Smell a little bit high, you see? Some of them bluesmen you'd come across was the stinkiest, scuzziest beasts you ever did see. You gag in the presence of them unwashed, uncelebrated blues originators. And Charley, he the foul-smellinest of 'em all.

Charley's lack of hygiene was common among the old guys what played the Saturday night suppers and chopped cotton durin the week. But blues singers of the new generation was different. They was dandies generally. They wasn't farmin, see, they was hustlin. You take cats like Robert Johnson and Son House, they dressed sharp, like sportin types almost, 'cause their business was with the public. Little string tie, pencil mustache, nice clothes—like Son House had—and the women was all over them.

But the women was all over Charley anyway. Had a cute little baby face and bold as brass. He'd catch 'em by twos and they didn't care if he smelled like a skunk—they didn't smell all that great themselves. They was sharecroppers, farm girls, y'know, and if they bathed once a week—well, never mind.

How I come to meet Charley Patton is this. I was pickin so pretty on my guitar, my Ro Anne, that everytime I got the chance I was sneakin off down to the station and playin with the boys. Shootin the breeze and tryin to collect a few tricks. Them guys was my idols. Forever comin and goin. Some come saunterin down the railroad tracks, others drop from freight cars. Pull out their harps and guitars and go into a blues while the people ate fish and dipped snuff, waitin for a train to carry them on down the line.

I was just dreamin 'bout what might be down that road when a old cat leanin 'gainst a barrel start singin. Crazy little thing, dribblin outta his head. Skinny old man who hiss like a viper when he talk. Look like he been to the sun and back. Face wrinkled like a maze of little ditches. A little mustache, grown on poor soil. He was chawin tobacco and spittin on the ground. Had some rough old songs.

> *Your mother was a zebra and your sister was a bear.*
> *Your daddy was a monkey 'cause he got bad hair.*

That kinda foolishness.

"So what's shakin, Pop?" He look like he knew. Look like he knew what kinda penknife God keep in his pocket.

"Waaal, then, there, now…" He interrupt hisself to spit out some tobacco juice. "As I hear tell, they gonna have a new guitar player hereabouts tonight—up at the next flagstop. Say he come from *way* down this road." Sayin it with awe, like this fella comin up from the end of creation.

So I say: "Where?" And he say: "Down on the *Dog* Line, hear? They're saying he look like white folks almost."

"That so?"

"Yeah, he *bright*, like a injun or a Mexican, see? Got good hair. Ain't all nappy and rough, like your'n. *Hawh! hawh! hawh!* Can beat any sonofabitch on that box, they say."

"Where he at, ya say?"

"Take the Dog one stop down the line and jus ask at the first store, Chinaman store."

So I hop my own self on the Pea Vine and as the train pull out the station the little old gnome run by shoutin what sound like crazy words: "Pattern! Pattern!"

What in hell that old fool talkin 'bout? I'm thinkin he be well-liquored up.

"Say what, old man?"

Him puffin alongside, tryin to keep up with the train: "Just remembered his name. Charley Patton what they call him." And then to all the other folks on the train who he don't know neither he hollered: "You all come out tonight, hear?"

Pea Vine pull into Boyle. Get off there and wait for the Yeller Dog goin south to Cleveland.

Just one stop down the line, what harm could that do? I'll just go down there right quick, check it out, come right back. Hell, Vida Lee'll never know I'm gone. Sure, Coley, keep talkin that talk. Tell my good self to hush. Man, you know I gotta check this out. Feel a weird kinda tinglin all through my body.

Four o'clock rolls around, the old Yeller Dog come puffin down the track. I am askin myself, Can I actually get away with this?

"Oh, c'mon," says the Devil, and I'm warmin up fast to see his point of view. He makes me buy a pint of corn liquor off a old farmer on the train. I am feelin no pain. Vida Lee, you talkin to me?

When I first come in, the Chinaman had him sittin up on the counter, to get people to come inside. When I get close I say this got to be the fella. He light-skinned, see, and his hair just laid back so. He's just settin there. A fiddle and a solo bass layin on the counter, but weren't no one playin 'em.

"This here is Charley Patton?" I say.

"*Mister* Patton," say he.

"Well, this here's Coley Williams."

Had a strange face on him. Big ears sittin out on his head like handles on a jug. Frail and short, maybe five seven, if that. Missin some back teeth. When you met him he did not exactly match up with what you heard of him. The way people would talk 'bout him, it was like he was—John Henry! Like he could chew up the railroad track and spit out steel spikes. That was his reputation, see. I'm expectin a rough fella, full of fight like a wild boar and here's this almost comical cat.

But when you hear him sing you know why they carry on. That *voice*. Already a legend in the Delta, and he was only 'round thirty year old when I meet him. But there was no real way you could tell how old he was from lookin at him. Looked like a kid even when he got old.

He sees my guitar and ask me, "You wouldn't want a little job would you, kid, by any expectation?"

And I say, "Well, maybe."

"What you play? You play a fiddle, boy?"

I say, "Well, mister, I play most anything."

Turn to the Chinaman and say, "Betcha this boy fiddle with his diddle most like. *Hawh! hawh! hawh!*"

He say, "Pick up that fiddle back there and do us a tune, son."

I could play some, so I says, "Yeah, I'll back you."

"Good," he say, "'cause I be needin a complement man. My complement man gone off. This fella, see, his name, Frankie, uh…"

And the Chinaman chime in: "Frankie No Good."

"Well, he in the jailhouse now."

"Yeah," says the Chinaman, "he play different tune now."

"Make yourself some bucks. And kid, you looks like you could use some."

"I could that."

"You looks like you need to sleep in a hollow log, live in a pyramid for a year, maybe more—pick up some of them Egypshun ju-ju vibes, visit another planet, get you some celestial gris-gris and can it."

He could do that barrelhouse banter easy, like standin on his head. Like to juggle them words any old how.

So we was settin there, me and him. Takes hisself a little snort of corn liquor. Get him *primed up* in his line, the rascal, and then he says, "Well now, Coley, I'm gonna tell ya a little story" and he goes on. Story 'bout possum could read the newspaper, mule done gone to Washington, old lady from Shady what went over the mountain and married the man in the moon. Rhyme it out and it sound fine as a nursery rhyme. Barnyard ditties was his sauce. Did me one, go like this:

> *What did the turkey say to the little red hen?*
> *"You ain't laid a egg in God knows when!"*
> *What did the hen say to the rooster?*
> *"You don come 'round often as you usta!"*

"Got any good rhymes, kid?" Rarely call you by your name. He call you "kid," "son," "fella," "nigger." He love to mess with them ditties. "Rhymin is like marriage, kid, puttin two things together what don't belong. *Hawh! hawh! hawh!*"

Charley got his trainin in the doctor shows. He knew how to grab a audience and keep 'em. He could babble from the Bayou to Babylon. Had a whole pile of junk he call out. All this right there in the middle of a dance. Didn't make no difference.

The gig we played that first night I met Charley Patton was a frolic. Did I tell you what that is? Frolic generally a outside event, held outdoors in a dirt yard. This a country affair and I am talkin country. Some of them rural folk ride their *cows* to the party. They call that ridin a stone pony.

So the croppers and plantation folk and a few people from the town are all in there, millin 'bout, talkin and crackin jokes and gossipin and pursuin the usual occupation of country folk—predictin doom and gloom. You ever come across a farmer say he had a good year? Never will, guarantee it. Always tellin you 'bout calamities gonna come to pass. Flood, drought, bo weevil—whatever terrible thing that exist, it gonna come down the pike sure as eggs is eggs. Everything gettin worse. Ain't that the truth, brother?

Some old gal sellin pies and corn and watermelon and lemonade. An old grizzled guy up behind a tree peddlin hootch but you gotta supply your own bottle. Get yourself a soda pop bottle and when he pour it in it almost *smokin*, man.

So anyways, we at the frolic walkin 'round, how'd ya do, how'd ya do, and Charley sees this cat, a mournful-lookin guy standin off to one side. Go by the name of Henry Sims. Henry was a fiddle player, thin as a piece of string and tall as a church doorway. Never took a drink but he always look like he was about to fall over. Wobbly, y'know, like a chimney pole. When he was playin the fiddle he'd roll forward on his toes and people would move back. Thought he might tip over on 'em.

"Henry," says Charley, "what you doin here, thought you was up to your mama's."

"I heard you was gonna be playin down here," say Henry Sims. "Figured I best get myself over here."

"Good thing you brung your guitar, kid," Patton say to me. "Let Henry fiddle. He been fiddlin since he found it. You can complement me on the guitar like Willie Brown done before he slunk off."

Willie Brown, he Patton's complement man. He and Charley was generally inseparable except when they was fightin, which was pretty much all the time. They couldn't get on *no* kinda way. Any old thing set 'em off. Over what key a song be in. Willie would be insistin "Jelly Roll Blues" in C.

"No," says Charley, "I *know* it in F."

"Hell, you ain't nothin but a ignorant dwarf!"

And that would do it. Wouldn't speak to each other for weeks.

Now up to this point I ain't heard Patton really play. Charley took his time. He like to get oiled up before he do his show. When the juice get high enough, he begin pickin that guitar and it don't matter what else he do, he's *gone*. He could make that guitar cry, moan, whistle, stomp, bark, chug, howl, wail, whimper, shout and fry grits.

Had a voice to him, man, one of them Mississippi River voices. Gravelly and rough. Tote-barge voice movin through Vicksburg, Rosedale, Helena. Hear all them people and places he been in that voice.

He's just a-settin there on his stool, sweat pourin off of him, goin at it like he was a one-man band. Catch the spirit right off that cat like you catch the measles. He was dangerous that night, man. A-chimin and a-chokin his guitar like a preacher down by the riverside contendin with the Devil. Tappin them bass notes, work up that hundred percent rhythm oil. Rhythm pull you through like a engine pull a freight train. Get to doin them shimmy-she-wobble bottleneck riffs and *everybody* gettin up outta their seats. Even old Grandmaw Burns shakin her booty.

Played two of his old faithfuls, "Banty Rooster" and "Pony Blues." He'd throw that big old guitar up in the air, play it behind his back, between his legs, get down on the floor and hump it, wrassle with it, and damn if he never miss a beat, never even stop pickin. I had never seen nothin like it in my life until the young James Hendrix come along.

Playin along with Charley was a tricky business. He testy as an old cook if you didn't play the way he want. Give you that face. Say, "What the hell you think you playin, boy?"

"I always heard this reel in G."

"This Mr. Patton's song, and I say to hell with your G, it's in C."

But, man, could he *cook*. Got them people fired up. Dancers just *bouncin* them floorboards or smackin their feet on the pack earth floor.

One of the things Charley would do at a frolic to make a little more money is sell old Andy Jackson's fiddle—the one Henry been playin on earlier.

"Been in my family since slavery times," says Charley, drawin himself up like a Fourth-of-July orator. "Come down to me from my father's father. It's a dear memorial of my foreparents but due to a tragic occurrence in my family I am obliged to sell it. Ten bucks. I'll take no less."

Walter Crumb come forward and claim it. You'd a thought he come into possession of a great treasure. Thing just shone like the sun in his hands (it been polished nice). I was 'bout to grab it and give it back to Charley. That fiddle belonged to the nation. It shoulda been up in Washington somewheres. But Henry seen what I was doin and he grab me kindly by the arm.

"Kid," he says, "don't fuss yourself none. That ain't none of Andy Jackson's. Now maybe his *grandpappy* be *owned* by Andrew Jackson and maybe old Andy Jackson give him a fiddle. But if he did, they been sellin that fiddle once a week ever since."

11

Goin Away to a World Unknown

First night as Charley Patton's complement man I got so nervous I kept runnin out 'round the back to get my soda pop bottle filled with corn liquor and don't remember how it end up. All I know is somehow they carry me back and let me down on the loadin dock up at the cotton mill. And I'm shoutin out to them: "Don't you leave me here. Brothers, get me on that train or Vida Lee, she gonna kill me."

"Ain't no more Yeller Dog tonight, man. That train done gone sleepytime."

"Then pour me on the next freight, I'm beggin y'all."

"Milk train don't come through till sunup, baby. You best sack out on them bales, get your bad self some rest."

"You don't understand," I'm tellin 'em, "I'm a dead man! You gotta help me some!"

They was all laughin and jivin me: "You mean this the *first* time this ever happen to you, man?"

More laughter, and as they goin away one of them ask me, I think it was maybe Charley hisself: "Kid, where you live?"

"Up to Lula."

And he say: "Boy, you a long ways from home."

When I heard them words they had a kinda sweet ring to 'em, like a line from a old blues song played on a dobro. And I was now one of that number, a ramblin rascal out in the great world somewhere.

Mornin come, I get a very rude awakinin. *Whack*! *Whack*! Somebody whampin on me with a big old stick.

"Where you from, boy?"

"Uh, Lula, I'm from Lula, mister."

"Lula, *Sir*. Ain't that what you mean, nigger?"

I look up into that porky red face with two cold beady blue eyes borin holes through me. The Man, the sheriff hisself of Bolivar County, and all he want is to beat on my hide and then put me on the next rail.

"We don't tolerate drifters and trash through Cleveland, hear?"

And that was the day I took a freight train to be my friend. Not that it was my intention, mind, just the way the day took me.

Now I did intend to go straight back to Lula, get on the next train, go on home, but while I was sittin on the platform waitin for the Yeller Dog a black tomcat cross my path. I ain't that superstitious but still you gotta be mindful, understand? Number on the front of the engine comin down the track that mornin was number 9. *Nine, nine, nine.* Now you know that train was talkin to me, man.

> *Engine, engine number nine,*
> *Say ride 'em, ride 'em, ride them blinds.*
> *Clickety, clickety, clickety-clack.*
> *Get on board, you never come back.*

All the while this going through my head I'm tellin myself, Coley, don't you give in to foolish credence of signs and portents 'cause all this mere coincidence and you know it. Still, you only gonna tempt them demons to further devilment by ignorin 'em. Might actually worsen your luck. Turn your face away from premonitions at your peril. That's what my mama say. Only sensible thing to do is to take the train down to Boyle and head over to Rosedale. And don't go sayin that crap game goin on in a tent over on Byron's Levee have anything to do with it. What? You callin me a liar?

Get myself off of the train. Figure I could increase my earnins of the night before and by this manner of resourcefulness Vida Lee countenance my return to the fold with a little more favor. Instead of the five dollars I'll be bringin home twenty-five—maybe more. Well, it's *possible*, isn't it?

I never seen such a cool bunch as the cats in that tent. All duded up in fine threads, shuckin and jivin. It was good to be among such get-along fellowship again.

Playin the Georgia Skin Game, singin along as we play. One cat sing:

> *When your card gets lucky, oh partner,*
> *You ought to be in a rollin game.*

And then everybody join in:

> *Let the deal go down, boys.*
> *Let the deal go down.*

Goin 'long pretty good there, baby. Only been there a hour and already I'm up ten dollars.

"Fellas," I say, "y'all understand if I be gettin along now, won't you?"

They weren't all that understandin.

"That ain't no sportin attitude, nigger."

"What you talkin," says I. "I won them bets fair and square."

"You deef or something? Think you can take all a man's money and not give him a chance win it back? We don't suffer no spoilers here, you followin me?"

These was serious cats with knives and guns and jail time. Had no choice but to keep on playin. My luck got worser and worser like I knew it would.

When they says, "Let the deal go down" that last time, man, I am *sunk*. Don't even have money for the fare home. I am gonna have to *walk* home now, 'less I can hitch a ride on a freight. Is there one comin through here today? All I can do is go down to the depot and wait it out.

But as luck would have it, who do I spy comin down the tracks but Charley Patton. And there I see my salvation.

"Charley! Charley! Uh, Mr. Patton, man, am I glad to see you!"

"Coley," says he, "where you been, kid?"

"God, Mr. Patton, I'm one of the Lord's poor servants!" says I, embracin him like the Prodigal Son, and I tell him the whole sad story.

"The idea of you—or anyone," says he, "winnin at them games is laughable. You think they're gonna lose money to *you*, some drifter come by for an afternoon's amusement?"

"I trust in Fate, Mr. Patton, and she let me down."

"Don't need no fortuneteller to tell me what *your* fate gonna be. You gonna end up with nothin and still be out there hustlin the nothin you ain't got."

In the twinklin of an eye before me stood Preacher Patton: "You never heard 'bout the man played skin with the Devil for his life and lost?"

"Nope, I never did."

"Well, that's you."

"I weren't playin with no Devil. Them just a bunch of pikers."

"Have you forgotten? The thirty pieces of silver Judas got by his treachery he lost by gamblin. Take heed!"

"Hell, Charley, I didn't crucify nobody. I just play a couple hands of cards."

"Slippery indeed is the descent to Hell and taken by the first step.…"

I will not trouble you with the entire speech since you can hear it any Sunday. He conclude by sayin: "Kid, I best take you under my wing or God knows what evil will befall you."

And so it was by fallin under the watchful eye of the Reverend Patton I found the rounder's religion while mislayin my original intent to return to Vida Lee and live a respectable and industrious life. As to which path I should have taken at that point, you will have to hear the rest of my story.

Charley always *say* he a preacher, but they wouldn't allow him near a pulpit nowhere. They don't allow no rounders, no midnight ramblers on that train. No boozers, womanizers or squabblers neither. To the righteous, he doin the Devil's work just by playin the blues and boozin and whorin. Some go so far as to say he *was* the Devil.

His daddy been a jackleg preacher but Charley was none of his kind. Did get the preachin bug from him though, no doubt 'bout that. Learn them hymns and fiery wheels and the Great Whore of Babylon revelations from his daddy. Charley could wax wroth in the snake-handlin apocalyptic manner. Get hisself into a fevered sermon based on the Book of the Seventh Seal and stuff straight outta his head which never was in no Bible.

> Well, friends, I want to tell you…when He come down His hair gonna be like lamb's wool and His eyes like flames of fire…. 'Round His shoulders gonna be a rainbow, and His feet like fine brass…. And He gonna have a tree before the twelve manners of food, and the leaves gonna be healin damnation, and the big rock that you can sit behind, the wind can't blow at you no more….

Son House—he keep hisself smart-looking and clean, y'know —he like to joke about Charley that he was a uncouth heathen who never could be baptized: "Couldn't dip those guys. See, they scared of water. Have to dope 'em up just to take a bath." But Charley had the Spirit. Like he say, "I don't need no church, no pastorin, kid, I be on the telephone daily to God."

Seems like one of Charley's wifes have got herself a Victrola. The subject of Mr. Patton's wifes is a tangled one, meanin it not entirely clear to him or to *them.* Let's see…there was a Udy, a Polly, a Bessie, a Katie, a Millie…. He was like a potentate with all them wifes of his, like a sultan in Turkey or something. And after havin heard several of them women referred to by him as bein wifes I ask him:

"Charley, how many have you got?"

"Shucks, Coley" he says, "never learned me to count that high. *Hawh! hawh! hawh!*"

Kinda laugh he had would roll on and on and then stop and start up again like a car with a bad battery.

"See Coley, you travel on the road you gotta have more than one wife. What good one wife gonna do? You only makin *one* woman happy. That to my mind is pure selfishness and I will not countenance it. No sir!"

They say he kingloaded fourteen wifes—not all wifes, mind, by the book. Mostly common-law. He'd just put one down and pick another one out. Like he say in "Pony Blues,"

> *I got something to tell you, when I get a chance:*
> *I don't wanna marry, just wanna be your man.*

The cat is some box player, and that'll attract women like flies to molasses. They give him anything of a hard time, he likely to tell 'em:

> *If you don't want me, you oughta been told me so,*
> *For I gotta woman, most any place I go.*

Charley and his women. You couldn't hardly get a word in edgeways. His woman yesterday, his woman day before yesterday, what he done with the woman, how long he can stay and all that. This stuff would get Willie Brown so mad one time he shout, "Goddamm it, shut up, you lappy-eared sonofabitch!"

So anyway, 'bout this Victrola.... He tellin me, "My Tunica wife, she got herself one of them phonograph players and we gonna go over there and hear some of them records they puttin out."

We go by the Tunica wife house, her name Violet or Valerie —"Mrs. Patton." She was a bird-like little woman with a huge head. Intended for someone else. When we first come in she was real genteel and polite. Kinda woman you'd only be likely to meet at a church supper or a quiltin bee. It was hard to imagine how the two of 'em ever met. She let us in her parlor, offer us some lemonade. Place all neat and trim, and right there in the middle of the room settin up on a pedestal like it the Statue of Liberty is the Victrola. Phonograph with a bulldog sittin up on top of it. Dog would sit up when the record play.

She crank it up and put on a record. Sound come out all crackly like bacon fat fryin in a skillet but you hear that voice come through loud and clear. *Nasty.*

> *Went to bed last night, and, folks, I was in my tea.*
> *Went to bed last night, and I was in my tea.*

Woke up this mornin and the po-lice was shakin me.
I went to the jailhouse, drunk and blue as I could be.

When Ma Rainey get to the part 'bout sixty days in a cell without booze seem like a year, Charley shoutin "Amen!" and "Tell it!" just like he was in church, singin along:

I can't live without my liquor.
Got to have booze to cure these blues.

In the pauses Charley mutterin to hisself like that little character he do on his songs. Say, "Girl done got a bad case of the blues and I don't blame her. They don't treat us right, them officers of the so-call law. Shame!"

Then Charley say, "My, it *hot* today, I 'clare fo God. Why don't you go down to the store, Coley, and get us some ice-cold sodies." And Charley give me a silver dollar and a big wink.

I know that bean dollar ain't just for soda. Soda cost a coupla cents. And Charley tight with a dollar. So I amble down to the store and buy us three cold sodas and a jug of corn liquor. I get back to the house and I hear shoutin and cursin. Open the door and see pots and pans just flyin through the air.

"What you lookin at?" says the Tunica wife.

"Anyone want a ice-cold soda?"

"What you got in the *other* sack?" she ask, all riled up.

"Just some vittles."

"You lyin to me, you got corn liquor in there." And she take the sack and hold up the beauteous object in triumph and then take it and pour it on the ground.

"Get outta my house, you sodden drunkard. Hell gonna freeze before I let that junk in my parlor."

We flew outta there, stuff flyin after us. He was a menace. Everywhere he go he stir it up. Just like that bo weevil what struck the Delta back in nineteen and oh-eight. Like the bug in "Mississippi Bo Weevil," a waggish, funny fellow, makin the rounds like a troublemakin blues singer:

Bo weevil left Texas, Lord, he bid me fare-thee-well.
Lordie! "Where you goin, now?"
"I'm goin down the Mississippi,
Gonna give Louisiana hell." Lordie....

You know the slide on that song? Sound like the impudent little voice of the bo weevil itself, thumbin its nose at the world, then movin on to more mischief. Always movin on down the line. Used to say, "I'm amongst strange people in a strange place and I hope it work out, but if it don't I knows which-a-way to run." Which, as it turn out, was a good thing.

Coupla days later we sittin in the back of a stake truck, Charley strummin away, fiddlin with his guitar goin,

dah dah dah *dah dah* dah *dah dah dah dah day*,
dah dah dah *dah dah* dah *dah dah dah dah day*.

"Sounds familiar," says I, "but I can't rightly place it." Then it come to me. "That from the Ma Rainey song, ain't it?" Charley go on messin with it and by the time we get up to the next town he make it into his own jail story.

Laid down last night, hopin I would have my peace.
But when I woke up, Tom Rushin was shakin me.

'Bout the high sheriff Tom Rushing and his deputy Tom Day. Come out as "Tom Rushin Blues" when it get on record.

Charley Patton, I'll give you a idea of what he compose like. Borrow riffs, words, whole verses from other songs, phrases from the Bible, anything, whatever, King Solomon, get into the song. "Oh, Susannah" come through his head, in it go. Nursery rhymes, gospel phrases, minstrel jokes like in "Banty Rooster Blues." Rhyme like a magpie, too. The way he rhyme "blow" and "on bo'd" in "Green River Blues."

Be more than just a singer. When he sing he put on a whole show. Like in "Spoonful," that's just barrelhouse theater, all them voices and everything. You got Charley's voice the way he mostly sing, you got a woman's high voice in there, you got a *low* speakin voice. And then you go to the slider. The slider like his other self, the sound of his *mind* talkin at you.

Like in "High Water," you know? You *in* that song like you in a dream:

> *Water come under his door,*
> *Rise up over his bed.*
> *I thought I would like a trip, Lord,*
> *Out on that big ice sled.*

Water comin up under *your* bed, baby. He could take you there. Like that gasp he give up in the fourth verse of "High Water"? He's drunk about now. You can hear it.

> *I hear the roar! Water up on my door!*
> *I hear the ice, Lord, went sinkin down.*

You hear that gasp at the end of that line? You know he's in there, terrified of dyin by the water. "High Water" 'bout the midnight collapse of the twenty-foot-high levee at Stop's Landing, eight miles above Greenville, what flood the Delta on April 21, 1927.

Charley make "Spoonful Blues"—what we call a rag ditty—into a little movie 'bout the cocaine crazies 'round the turn of the century. Put it in a syncopated one-two, talkin the title of the tune 'gainst a bottleneck slide. Charley talk all the time, little asides. Hear all them voices talkin to him, glidin between the speaking and the song. Got a throng of people in his head.

Charley and me got a gig comin up at Junior Austin's place, a straight-out gamblin house in Ruleville, 'bout eight mile south of Cottondale. 'Course Charley don't gamble none. He shoot no dice, play no cards, no sir. And now he concerned for *my* immortal soul.

We walk in the joint and Charley see my eyes strayin over to the card table.

"Bet you can't walk by that table without messin with it," he says.

"Yeah, I can."

"Bet you five dollars you can't."

"Make that ten," says I.

A lot of them sportin cats dress real fancy, dandified and sweet smellin, but Charley, it make no difference to him where he goin, he dress the same. Visit the Queen of Sheba ain't gonna put on a clean shirt. Ain't got one. Dress like a cowhand mostly. Greasy yellow shirt, coveralls all tuck into his raggedy-ass boots. He could afford to dress like them gamblers and pimps that Skip James and Robert Johnson dress like, but he don't care nothin 'bout his appearance.

But as raggedy and rough as he was, he didn't countenance no cussin or swearin or takin the Lord's name in vain. Or suffer no blackgurdin person when women was around. And playin the dozens, have mercy, he 'gainst that.

Now the dozens was common parlance in them joints, boastin and braggin and cussin and slaggin. And these two cats down at Junior Austin's, Frank and Ernest, was goin at it hammer and tongs. They was the two terrible twins from Jackson. One wore the plaid pants from his brother's suit and the other wore the jacket from the other's striped suit. They was just a couple of clowns foolin around but Charley wouldn't have it.

"Man, I'm the bed tucker, the cock plucker, the muthafucka, the hum-dinger, the pussy ringer, the man with the smelly middle finger."

Other cat goes:

"I'm the beast from the East, they call me Nick the dicker, the ass kicker, the cherry picker, the city slicker, the titty licker and I ain't givin up nothin but chewin tobaccy and hard times and I'm fresh outta chewin tobaccy...."

The usual shit in other words. When Charley hear that he start mumblin to hisself, but what you gone do? Common talk, but Mr. Patton don't care for it one bit. Then it step up a notch and they go to gettin *real* nasty.

"I fucked yo mama till she go blind, her breath smell bad but she sure can grind...."

Man, I thought Charley gonna choke. Sexual aspersions on one's mother, Lord! Charley loved his mama, wrote *songs* 'bout his mama.

I seen Charley get hot and bothered and I anticipatin the worst.

"Hope I don't hear you right," he say.

"Was that *yo* mama?" say the skinny cat. He's laughin, goofin 'round. Charley grab the cat by the throat and throw him down on the floor.

"Take that back or you not gonna *see* tomorrow."

Now the other cat don't want no trouble. He's a sportin dude and this shit bad for business, so he pulls out a sealed bottle of booze.

"Whoa! Cool it, man," he say to Charley, "have a swig on me. We just jivin, dig. He don't mean no disrespect, do you, Nick?"

"Not as I *knows* of," says Nick.

Charley could be a ferocious little guy when he wanted and they didn't want none of that. Didn't wanna muss their threads.

Charley say he don't drink much whiskey, but he drink it just as sure as you born to die. Drink anything if it don't say poison on it. All he want to know is, "Is *people* suppose to drink this?" Divide his boozin between a potion of moonshine and bonded brands like Doug Harper—100 proof whiskey.

Get excited just by the *look* of a liquor bottle. He say that amber liquid gonna give him the spirit of the cornfield without the fuss of his actually havin to go out into it. If he start at seven he play until four in the mornin. It would take a couple of hours of drinkin and singing before Patton really hit his stride.

Like most boozers, he have his little pet theories "Only eat the fat meat off of the ham," he told me. "That way you don't get drunk 'cause the whiskey it eat on the fat, see." If they ever ask me to write a book 'bout winin and dinin I'm gonna put that in it.

But I have more serious problems than what cut of the hambone I'm gonna eat. I am in two minds, one predicament bein worse than the other: Gettin my head beat in and havin havoc and affliction pour down on me—or life without Vida Lee.

"Don't be a fool!" says Charley, and he should know. "You go back now, she gonna whup you bad and cuss you till doomsday. What you wanna do is lay out a while. Get her to thinkin maybe he shot, maybe he drown, maybe he be languishin somewheres in the jail."

I weren't entirely convinced but I stayed on with Charley. Say it was 'cause he was king of the rounders and I wanted some of that to rub off on me. Say, "Charley Patton? Hell, I knew Charley. *Played* with him. Went down the road a ways with Charley." But I set out in the company of the Reverend Tush Hog with a troubled mind.

12

I'm Goin Where
The Southern Cross the Dog

There's no turnin back now. We headin out for West Helena. This be 'round 1923. Me and Charley and Son House. Son was runnin with us mainly to pick up some licks from Charley. Took a lot from Charley but he was a more primitive type player. A Cottondale cropper name of Athie Johnson had tagged along too. "Mrs. Cottondale." Athie was a skinny thing. Orange hair and big lips. Woman smoked so many cigarettes she looked like a crazy-faced angel comin out of a cloud.

That night we're playin a notorious barrelhouse located on Miss Street. Called the Hole in the Wall. Things goin on relatively smoothly, given the company we keepin and Charley's big mouth.

Man, he was quick to meddle. Once he get whiskey-headed there's not much you can tell him. He was one squabblin scuttlebub, a natural born squabbler. Many a time Charley look uneasily over his shoulder. Had a scar on his forehead from a bottle he been hit with.

Now, a barrelhouse a far less perilous place to be at than a plantation frolic 'cause they don't want no killin going on there. Houseman can't make no money if there was bad trouble. Always be a big old sign at the entrance say: LEAVE YOUR KNIFES, RAZORS, GUNS, BRASS KNUCKLES AT THE DOOR.

The trouble that happen that night have nothin to do with Charley. He bein sweet as pie. He brought hisself a fish sandwich and he eatin it in there when this drunken woman come up to get herself another drink and bump into him. Knock his sandwich on the floor and ruin his dinner. He didn't get mad.

"Miss, you done knock down my supper and that's all I got," he say very polite.

But what's the good of bein polite to a drunken woman lookin for a fight? Breath was pure turnip greens and turpentine, and she bark at you just like a dog.

As if she wasn't trouble enough, up come the husband all liquored up and nastyish. One of them insane husband-and-wife deals and we'd stepped right in the middle of it. The husband'd set there and watch while she sit in some stranger's lap. He liked her doin it 'cause that gave him a reason to start a fight.

"Why don'tcha pick it up, nigger, and eat it off the floor?" Start in cussin him. "You callin my woman a bitch?"

"I don't cuss nobody," say Charley.

Fella shove him back in his chair and Charley fall over backward in that chair and hit his head. Now Charley had enough. He get up and knock the fella down first lick. The guy gets 'bout half straight and Charley push him down. Man get up and run out that door. Ten o'clock and we already been through round one.

So me an Charley and Son was over there playin. We was gettin five dollars a night. Five bucks between us. Doin them barrelhouse sportin life songs like "Spoonful," "Frankie," "Hang It on the Wall," "Maggie." Stuff like that.

The big dance back then was called shimmy-she-wobble. You do it all snakey, right down to the floor. Hot and steamy contact dance, dig? Drive them women wild. You got them rubbin up 'gainst each other, guys gettin hard, comin in their pants.

Charley could chug, man, all night long. Had a long breath, drive them songs like a Midnight Special steamin down a incline:

> *Justshakeityoucanbreakityoucanhangitonthewall*
> *HollerwhenIcatchit'foreitfall*
> *Shakeityoucanbreakityoucanhangitonthewall,*
> *Justsnachityoucangrabityoucanwhipityoucanpitchit*
> *AnywaythatI*
> > *canflipitandgetit*
> > > *Till I*
> > > *Ain't in my right mind*
> > > *I*
> > > *Stayed in a little old town*

HollerwhenIcatchit'foreitfall
Sweet jelly
MY ROLL
Sweet ma'am, won't you let it fall
EVERYBODY GOT A JELLY ROLL

When he get up to it and the place heatin up he start doin a kinda hula, gyratin his hips like, y'know, he was doin it. Call it the Phantom Rider. Everybody laughin, crackin jokes just set Charley off, and in the middle of "Maggie" he start doin his love-crazed dog thing. Get down on his knees, bayin at the moon, shoutin:

"I'm a *hound* for you, baby, gonna bark up your tree."

And the guys all shoutin:

"C'mon Charley, do the Funky Butt!"

"Do the Signifyin Monkey!"

"Donkey and the Rooster!"

Charley knew a whole batch of them dirty songs. He had more of them than he did of the blues. Could sing them songs all night long—like "Jelly Roll King" and "Mama, Can't You Keep It Clean." Had so many dirty verses to it he sing it till the cows come home.

Jelly roll, jelly roll is so hard to find.
It killed the old man, and run the young one blind.

Charley had me singin that mess. Call out, "Coley, kid, now you do us a round." So I sung one of them corny old verses, make him happy:

Up the hickory, down the pine,
I bust my britches right behind.

He'd have all these kind of exclamations in his song, like Do it a long time! Good and wild! Ain't that a *shame*! Have a fit, baby, have a fit! Sink 'em down there, sink 'em! Whoop in on down! Play the board, baby! Them blues won't behave, baby....

Cats love that shit, man. Charley singin and clownin and addin in stuff and callin all them pretty women "my baby" and "my rider," which in a joint like that, man, mean only one thing: "my fuck." Call *anybody's* girl "honey" and "sugar." A real jealous man didn't have no business 'round Charley Patton. And he was some pigmeat back in them days.

All the women go: "Heh heh, chile, play it, play that thing till I get somewhere."

Meanwhile Charley's riled another cat who thinks he's been woofin up his chick—probably was, too. There is nothin worse than crossin a toadeater on a Saturday night after a few drinks. He's been hurtin all week, kissin Mister Charley's ass. I am gettin jumpy so I says to Charley: "Man, we better watch our asses, that nigger gonna lay for us and kill us on the road."

But on that I was mistaken. He was gonna kill us right there. In the middle of the floor this fool pull out a .38 and snaps it. *Craaaaack! Craaaaack!* Smoke, people screamin. People usin them hobtail knifes, snappin at everybody come out, and they all hollerin 'bout how they is shot and cut up. Then come another *Craaaaack*! *Craaaack*! This cat gets off another couple of shots. Charley been hit. Fall over on the ground. Can't tell how bad but I ain't stayin to find out.

All the people in the place got in them corn fields and hid there—me too. Stayed out there till mornin, then I crept back. Place empty, tore up. Nobody there but a coupla drunks sleepin it off—slept through the whole thing. No Charley there neither.

Ask 'round town. Nope, nobody seen him. The story was that they taken his body and thrown it in the river. "'Nother good man done gone," they said. "Hell of a shame."

Come nightfall I'm walkin down the road with Son House on the way back home. I am so rattled I begin talkin at Charley.

"Ain't you got no sense, man? What you want? *All* the women in the entire world to be yours?"

Hearin a little voice insinuatin in my mind: "Hell, man—why not?"

Son turn on me on account of my indiscretion with ghosts.

"Don't you got more sense, Coley? Addressin the dead! And in anger."

Thunder and lightnin. And just then a big wind blow up. Cornstalks just shakin like flags in a hurricane. Son cross hisself.

"By God, it's him! Talkin back to us."

"Jesus, Son, you scarin me, man. But that ain't no ghost," I says. "That some wild animal out in the rows. Could be one of them wild boars in there, rip you up good."

"Let's get the hell outta here," says Son, "before we get to be ghosts ourselves."

We 'bout a hundred yards up the road when we hear rustlin and growlin comin out of the corn. And then the thing come out. Lightnin flash. Somethin horrible and huge, standin on its hind legs, groanin and pawin the air. The thing's entirely black from head to toe, wavin a big fat stubby club. Worse than any old wild boar or scarifyin ghost. The unknown *thing*. But the Delta bein a snarlin mass of superstition and terrors, they got a name for it. At least Son did, and it weren't good.

"Sweet Jesus! It is him!"

"What *him*?"

"Fer Chrissakes, Coley, the Old Man in the Middle of the Road."

"The what?"

"Not now, fool, run!"

And we did. But no matter how fast we run it still gainin on us. By now I'm too scared to run; I'm out of breath and my head is spinnin. Then it disappear back in the corn again. Thank God! We best get to town, drench ourselves in holy water and dedicate our lives to good work—maybe return to our wifes.

We hadn't gone too far when the Thing come out of the corn like it shot from a gun, stumblin and howlin and talkin to itself.

"Yeah, them sonsofbitches," it say, "I'll kill all of 'em." Pretendin that he don't see us, arguin with his invisible tormentors and snarlin down the road.

Damned if it weren't Charley Patton covered all over in soot, his guitar blackened up from hidin up that chimney when the shootin start. One thing he *never* forget when he split was his guitar.

Son say: "How in hell you gonna kill all of anything when you comin up outta that cornfield so fast?" We joked Charley a long time 'bout that.

He was hurt bad. His leg tore open ugly from the gunshot wound.

"Let us carry you over to the doctor, Charley. Get him put some liniments on it or it gonna fester."

"Let me be," he say. "Ain't nobody taken me to no bones."

Delta folk had to be close to dead before they'd go see a doctor. Only kinda doctor you gonna get Charley to is a root doctor.

His leg heal by itself, but on account of that gunshot wound he always gonna walk a little funny. Kinda hop when he walk. From then on his walk have a splayfoot shuffle to it, like Charlie Chaplin. Knowin Charley Patton's wiles, some people thought he walk that way on purpose. Thought Charley was drawin attention to it, and he probably was.

❖ ❖ ❖

That incident in the cornfield was one of the few times he was ever in one. Charley hated work like God hates sin. He just natural born hated it. It didn't look right to him.

"I never done a honest day's work in my life," he'd say. "At least not by choice. From way back as I remember I wanted to get away as far as I could from that cotton patch. Soon as I can I am runnin down that dirt road, man, fast as my legs carry me."

"Down the Dirt Road," was his slogan. *I'm worried now but I won't be worried long.* That's the way you gotta think, see, you out on the highway, *goin away to a world unknown.*

> *Just like a doggone rabbit, I ain't*
> *Got no doggone den.*

Born wanderer over the face of the earth, Charley. A rounder, a floater with no fixed base of operations, not just some cat from a short little town. Hoboin his life, and prime subject of his songs. Come up 'round Friar's Point, but he don't tarry. *I'm goin away, baby; won't be back no more.*

A good thing for him that he keep movin on. Had a *bad* reputation. Brawler, braggart, woman-beater. Always in some kind of mess. Got hisself kicked out from Dockery's, which weren't a easy thing to do. Story went 'round that Mr. Dockery boot him off the farm on account of Charley takin a bullwhip to one of his wifes.

Charley pass 'round a different story. 'Bout the *real* reason Mr. Dockery threw him out.

"Kept them women up *all night long* playin and foolin and

jelly-rollin so they was plumb tuckered out and sleepy on the morrow. Ain't too much use in the fields after I been at 'em."

Like they say, you want to reach the spirit, somebody got to suffer. Charley Patton and Robert Johnson both have that eye, that droopy eye, like them griots back in Africa. They say that you can't be a root doctor or a exalted blues musician or a true servant of God lessen you have some kind of affliction. That a sign that the spirit be in you, they say. Blind Lemon Jefferson, Mance Lipscomb, Achilles, Jesus Christ and Hound Dog Taylor. Hound Dog have six fingers on each of his hand. You know that?

So we down on the Helena docks passin out Charley's cards, me and Charley and a bass player name of Drew. Drew was slow. You had to watch him that he didn't walk out on the street in the mornin with no pants on. But there was nothin wrong with his playin. One of the best spoon-players I ever seen. Charley was a enterprisin cat, got cards printed up with his picture on 'em. I was playin mandolin behind Charley at the time. We out on the street tellin people, "Ya'll come 'long see us over at Millie's Wall, hear?" Gig over in West Helena. A fella come by and say:

"You hear? Fancy colored band playin tonight over at the Katie Adams, a white folk dance."

"Coley," says Charley, "I ever tell you I played up 'gainst W.C. Handy?"

"*The* W.C. Handy?"

"Hell, how many is there? Played him *ragged*. Yessir, cut the old striver's head and walked right off with it."

"Aw, c'mon, Charley."

"Scared that man *soooo* bad he scuttle his way up north after that."

"Yeah, sure."

"I did. I taught Handy the blues. Yup. Without me he'd still be playin 'Turkey in the Straw' like it was a music-box minuet."

"That so?"

"Happen right here. Over on the Katie Adams." Katie Adams a wooden hull passenger boat run aground on a sand bar near Helena and after that they make it into a dance hall.

"Usta take the Katie Adams up to Dermott, Arkansas," Charley say wistfully. "Hell, them riverboat whistles all over my songs. And he begin to sing:

> *Well, the smokestack is black,*
> *And the bell it shine like gold....*

He played a little more while the mood took him:

> *I heard the big Jim Lee when it blow.*
> *She blow so lonesome, like she weren't gonna blow no more.*

"Ah, it's a shame, Coley, a continental shame. Blues singers mostly like to sing 'bout stuff that already gone," he tell me. "Money, home, women what left them or what they left, trains, and so on. In the blues that train always done left the station. If it ain't, it ain't no blues. Riverboats just 'bout gone, too, by the time I begin singin 'bout 'em. Just Mississippi flatbottom steam ghosts now."

He was gettin weepy on the subject of them paddlewheelers. This was all sad and interesting but I wanted to hear the rest of that story 'bout Mr. Handy.

"Gotta be ten, twelve years back I reckon. We was playin at this place, me and a gang of fellas, and we got told of the Handy orchestra playin at a ballroom on the river. We finish early at the jook joint 'cause I want to see what Handy puttin out.

"Over there at the Katie Adams was a bunch of planters and their wifes and girfriends and planters' children out to spend their daddys' ill-earned dollars. Lively white folk and one poetic very drunk young fella in evenin dress who latched on to us. Trailin 'round behind us all night like we was natives of the cannibal islands 'bout whom he wanted to write for the musicological society.

"'What you fellas play?' he ask.

"'Blues mostly,' says we.

"'Capital, boys! That's my kind of music.' He look at us all sly, give us a wink and say: 'Conjuration and spirits!'

"We stand in the back of the ballroom and listen to Mr. Handy's band. All them pretty white women in their satin gowns and laces all dancin so fine. He play cakewalks and ragtime, and something called 'Poet and Peasant Overture.' Jim Turner do humorous imitations of roosters and donkeys on his violin. It was well done what that little orchestra playin but there was no soul in it to my mind. Just like a windup spring toy plays 'Yankee Doodle Dandy.' Nine jumped-up niggers all in evenin dress with starch collars playin violins and cellos. Pretendin black folk be just like white.

"Handy's orchestra play whorehouses but they don't play for no coloreds. Only way colored get to see Handy is sometime he play a few reels for them after the main gig over and the white folks cleared out.

"After a hour or so, that wild young white boy been trailin us come up to the bandstand.

"'Could you play us one of your lively native tunes, Mr. Handy?'

"Now Handy's musicians are strictly sheet music boys. They couldn't play a Delta blues if it bit 'em on the ass. But he have to do something so he give the white folk 'Swanee Ribber.'

"'Good show, maestro!' say the drunk white cat, 'but would you object if some of these colored boys over here played a few dances?' And he point to us.

"Now why was they gonna object? Get to stroll outside, have a smoke and get paid for it. I was *beamin*. Gonna play on the same stage as W.C. Handy, if not actually *with* W.C. Handy. The little clockwork orchestra weren't too friendly, nobody offerin to shake hands or nothin. Some of them was so hankty stuckup they wouldn't make theirselves known to us. Like they might get a disease from us, which was possible.

"I played for white folk before, so I know what they like. We play some uptempo country tunes like 'Shake It and Break It,' hoedown numbers like 'Runnin Wild,' throw in a songster folk song like 'Frankie and Albert,' and for the slow dancin, a soppy ballad, 'Poor Me.'

"We finishes up and the white folks dancin go *wild*. Cheerin and shoutin and whistlin. And my, my, my. Down on the stage come a rain of silver dollars and quarters and fifty-cent pieces like you never seen. We end up clearin more than Handy's entire orchestra. Man, which they do not appreciate. It was after that that Mr Handy begin writin blues hisself—'Memphis Blues,' 'St. Louis Blues,' 'Beale Street Blues' and them. Half-breed blues. Half a this and half a that. Like "St. Louis Blues" is a tango in one part of it—that was the popular dance back then, and Mr. Handy he knew how to work it, baby. Sell them nigra songs to the white. Wrap 'em up in a little Cuban sugar, five cents a pop. He was a good composer of songs, Mr. Handy, but where they get off callin W.C. Handy 'Father of the Blues,' anyways? He ain't no father of nothin, least of all the blues."

Accordin to Charley, him and Handy went back further than that. *Way* back. To almost the first ten seconds when the wiggly blues universe got itself borned. Like when God leaned over from his stormy pillow and said, "Gimme an E!"

"When I seen Handy playin on the Katie Adams that night I got a strange feelin 'bout him," say Charley. "Said to myself, 'I know that cat from some place a long time ago.' And I mean *long* time ago. When *I* was a kid. I was playin a tune down at the Tutwiler station and he throws me a ten-cent piece."

I didn't think on this till many years later when I'm readin Mr. Handy's book, his autobiography, and I come to that part 'bout him hearin the blues for the first time. You familiar with the thing? Listen, I'll read it to you. Scene, man, straight out of Genesis I. "And the Spirit of God moved upon the face of the waters…." Like that. Okay, here we go. Mr. Handy talkin 'bout he's tryin to take a nap down at the Tutwiler station when he notice:

> …a lean, loose-limbed Negro had commenced plunking a guitar beside me while I slept. His clothes were rags; his feet peeped out of his shoes. His face had on it the sadness of the ages. As he played he pressed a knife on the strings of a guitar in the manner popularized by Hawaiian guitarists who use steel bars. The effect was unforgettable. His song, too, struck me instantly.
> *Goin where the Southern cross the Dog*
> The singer repeated the line three times, accompanying himself with the weirdest music I had ever heard. The tune stayed in my mind. When the singer paused, I leaned over and asked him what the words meant. He rolled his eyes, showing a trace of mild amusement. Perhaps I should have known, but he

didn't mind explaining. At Moorhead the eastbound and westbound met and crossed the north and southbound trains four times a day. This fellow was going where the Southern cross the Dog, and he didn't care who knew it. He was simply singing about Moorhead as he waited.

Now, that *had* to be Charley, man, don't you think? That Charley's song, "Green River Blues," and that the way he sing that line, three times. One of them lonesome train station songs with all them great lines in it:

> *Some people say the Green River blues ain't bad.*
> *Then it must not a been the Green River blues I had....*
> *How long, baby, that evening train been gone?*
> *Yes, I'm worried now but I won't be worried long....*
> *I'm goin away, know it may get lonesome here.*

What went down at the Tutwiler station all connected in some way to the riddle of who originate the blues. In some quarters this become the most vexatious and perplexin mystery since the pyramids. Blues come into the world like a feather on the breath of God—just some cat playin a guitar down at a Delta depot, a invisible act in the eyes of the world, and it burst out into the world and change the world into its own image. This was the music God hum when He made the world. And maybe it all went down that day at the Tutwiler station, waitin for a train.

Mustn't let myself wax too sentimental 'bout Charley Patton 'cause if you knowed him personal he could also be a sonofabitch. Didn't waste no tears on nobody.

It was right after the Handy thing, the next day, that Charley run into his old second man, Willie Brown. With Willie in tow he ain't got no use for me no more.

"Down the dusty road I go, where I end up nobody can know," Charley say all high-spirited.

"Where we goin, Charley?"

"You ain't goin nowheres. Too bad, but you plum outta road, Coley. Willie come back, whaddya know 'bout that? Best complement man I ever had. Damn if he ain't good!"

That was all the fare-thee-well I got that day from Mr. Charley Patton. His use for me bein done, it was so long, sucker! Make me madder than a swarm of hornets just thinkin 'bout it. But I can't dwell on this stuff. Ain't no pension plan in the blues, darlin. We in the heartache business, now ain't we? Shoot, guess I'll just set here by the riverside and moan. Maybe write me a song, *hawh, hawh, hawh!*

Turns out Providence was lookin out for me that day anyways. Down at the levee I run into Teejay's complement man, Charlie McCoy, lookin all shifty and sly. What's goin on here, they holdin a backup players convention here or something?

"What you doin over in these parts?" I ask him.

"Barrelhousin," he say in his fly way.

"What kinda trouble you in, anyways?"

"Hell, you don't wanna know. Say, I almost forgot. They's lookin all up and down creation for you."

He come over, shake my hand like I won the numbers.

"Gratulations, man!"

"On what?"

"Hell, you got a boy child comin, Coley! You best get on home."

"I do? Since when?"

"Since any day now."

"How you know it gonna be a boy child?"

"Madame Jane says."

"Damn that conjure lady, she usually right!"

"Say if it ain't a boy she gonna hang up her broom."

I hopped the next freight home. *Cryin Lord, I wonder will I ever get back home? Lord, Lordy, Lord.*

Got to Lula two days before her time come. Middle of the night the boy finally decide to pop out.

"Must take after his daddy, keepin hours like this," says Aunt Berenice, assistin as the midwife. Got pans of hot water, salts and whiskey. And damned if Madame Jane ain't called it right. 'Course the odds weren't all that bad.

Vida Lee, she thinks we gonna call him Willie Lee.

"Willie Lee?" I says. "You want *another* blues singer in the family?"

All the kin and all the friends come by the house, cooin and tellin her what a beautiful baby he be, but you know Vida Lee, she inclined to say just what on her mind.

"Ain't he ugly, though?"

That was Vida Lee, man. I never could tell if she was messin with me or not.

"God makes 'em that way on purpose," she tell me with that sly look on her face. "Otherwise the mother's joy be so great could not stand it."

"Well now, honey, I got to think 'bout that for a minute," I say. And I'm still thinkin 'bout it down to this day.

13

Matchbox Holdin My Clothes

You don't always know when you been bit by the walkin demon, but *it* knows. Long before you was born, it been makin its way through a thousand heads just like yours. Way back in there, insinuatin its silky line of jive, it's hip to you, baby. You gonna swallow whatever story it feedin you. Question is, will Vida Lee buy it?

When I told Vida Lee I intended to settle down, work my own piece of land, till it and bring in the crops—all that—it weren't so much that I was lyin to her as to myself. Man, I work on that farm three years. Never strayed, never wanted to, and then…one mornin I hear that double E callin me. No fuckin rhyme or reason to it.

That's how the thing come up. "Baby, we need seed money." Sound good to me, y'know? But like some idiot chile, I'm tryin to lay this shuck to Vida Lee.

"Sweetness," I say, "I'm thinkin of lookin for employment down the line. Hell, you know I ain't any happier 'bout this than you but—"

"Heh?" Just that. That one sharp-pronged word, it struck ice to my soul. Ain't no arguin beyond that. But I did anyway.

"Aw, Vida Lee, we need money just to get to next Tuesday. We ain't paid the rent collector nor the feed store, baby needs shoes and—"

"Honey…." she say in her long-sufferin, how-many-times-I-gotta-say-this voice. "We need *all* kinda money. We need seed money, feed money, tool money, mule money, leakin-roofs money, new-stove money. But that ain't why I'm lettin you go on down the road."

"It ain't?"

"Honey, if I don't let you go, I'm gonna have one drag-ass, down-at-the-mouth, moldy excuse for a man creakin 'round the place, shrinkin up like a old Ee-gyptian mummy and mumblin to hisself like some loony ol mammy. Ain't gonna do neither of us no good. So you go ahead and pack up your sack, pick up your guitar and hit the road."

Man, did I love that woman!

The mornin I set out I didn't have no care in the world. But then, you don't need no reason for hittin the road. I was quite young, mannish, in my prime, y'know? No other thought come into my mind but headin out.

Greenville, for a country boy like me, man, that is bright lights, big city. Figure I might make a few coins playin in the street, maybe chase up a few supper parties. But down in Greenville there was more guitar players frailin and pickin and slidin and lickin than I ever seen all together in one place. And I weren't exactly killin 'em with my guitar playin. Gettin more quarters for leavin than I did for playin.

The big thing comin up was piano boogie. Pianos was hot 'cause a piano cuts through the noise of a joint better than a guitar. They was lookin up and down the street for fellas could play even a fair little bit of boogie-woogie.

I had learned me a little piano while hangin out here and there. Was at least able to put on a *show* of playin. Now where I really learn to play piano was from a player piano. The actual tunes I learn off the piano rolls. Pull the catch that locks the keys, you can see which keys go down.

Barrelhouses was always lookin for piano players. Barrelhouses was noted for barrel whiskey—bootleg whiskey in a barrel, y'know—and they liked to have some music in there to draw people off the street.

At that time, anybody could walk into a barrelhouse, and just sit down and start playin the piano. Cat come in, he's lost his money at the gamblin table, or he don't have enough stakes to get in a game, he could just pull up a chair and start singin.

Nobody knows, people, the trouble I've seen.
No, you can't know, people, the trouble I've seen.
Now you know I done lost all my money
And my woman she treated me so mean.

Nothin people like better'n cryin in their whiskey. That's their story you're singin 'bout up there. Never mind that you played this tune in a thousand joints, that moment come like a revelation. Like somehow I knew this fella was gonna walk into the joint and I seen into his achin heart. Conjuration, baby!

There was an odd old cat livin down in Greenville by the levee called Daddy Stovepipe. Always wore one of them high Abe Lincoln hats like a undertaker wears—had a stringy white beard that was so long and ragged and thin it looked like it was made of cotton wool, like one of them beards on a Salvation Army Santy Claus, and a grand total of two teeth. He was a funny sight on the street, I'll tell you, and sweet as baked squash.

Stovepipe's old lady was called Mississippi Sarah. He used to go to meet the boats there, with his box. Wail on his harp, too. And his old lady—Sippy Sarah—she go 'long with him and sing to the folks comin off the boats. Used to work on all those little joints on Nelson Street. I run with him for a while and that's how I got them first gigs—by passin myself off as a piano player. Friend of Daddy Stovepipe's, y'know.

Made myself some nice money, yes I did. All right now, with that little old stash of bucks I shoulda hightailed it right back to Vida Lee. That woulda been the sensible thing to do. But see, accordin to my philosophy, common sense is a overrated quality in a man. How can common sense be the whole fuckin deal? I mean, if that was true there wouldn't be no chocolate, no smokes, no booze, no high-heel shoes. And no blues, baby, no blues at all.

While I was contemplatin this puzzle 'long come my personal demons, "52" and his sidekick Bones, and they start leanin on me heavy, man.

"Handsome, how you like to make yourself a *big* old pile? I'm not talkin this chump change you got here, I'm talkin real bucks."

And Mr. Bones is chimin in,

"Yeah, sport, how's about goin back to Vida Lee like a king? Treat that little woman like the doll she be."

Tell you the truth, didn't take all that much for the fellas to convince me. Lead me by the nose right over to the gamblin tables. Game of coon can goin down. I won a few, lost a lot more. Cards was matchin up all over the place 'ceptin in my hand. Soon my money was gone, friends was gone too. Even Bones and "52" had split. I'm sittin down by the dock watchin the barges rollin on the river.

Buy me a pint of corn liquor, soothe my agitated self. I mellow *way* down, and pretty soon I stumble into Wally's joint, fall off the piano stool 'bout five times. Can't find the damn notes. Keys was swimmin away from me, man. Damn things just wouldn't lay still. They have a few laughs on me in there and throw my ass out in the alley. Cats chewin on fish heads, dogs grindin bones, I'm lookin up at the stars and sayin, "Take me home."

14

Stayed 'Round Houston
Just a Day Too Long

In them days there was a whole nation of black men driftin like the tide, and I was driftin with 'em. Driftin here and there, hoboin, ridin the rods so long they forgotten where or why—or even *who* they was. Night come and any old lay-down was their home.

Was a kinda sickness—beyond all reason and sense. Come from back when we was slaves. Couldn't never travel nowhere—'cept in the mind. But in there—in the head of the man in chains—man, that cat gone on fantastic journeys. His home was the wind, his habits that of migratin birds.

Once 'Mancipation come, they was gonna follow down them ghost roads of their parents and foreparents like sleepwalkers. When the call come they would get up in the middle of the day and just walk out. Walk down every road they hadn't been able to walk down for four hundred years.

Never stayin anywheres more than a couple of days, then the bug would seize 'em again and they get up and leave everything behind. And Greenville was one of them places they drifted to.

Let me paint you a picture of the Greenville docks. See all them sleepin forms huddled on the levee? Crashed out under a pile of rags, wrapped up in newspaper? I was one of them cats. Truck accidentally run over one of us, nobody even notice. They just haul your bones over to the dump. It was one mournful, godforsaken sight. Like wounded all piled up after a battle. And that's what we was, baby, the walkin wounded of the South.

One of the cats I met told me 'bout Houston and the cool little scene goin on, so I headed on down to Texas. By way of Memphis. By way of Vicksburg and Jackson and a bunch of other places.

Oh, they was some tough joints, and I played 'em all from Froggy Bottom to Central Tracks. Never stayed in any place too long. Flag me a ride on the Texas & Pacific, might tarry down in Texarkana, hang around Shreveport till things settle down. Play the honky-tonks where the men from the levee go. Some of whom didn't bathe more than once in six months. Some of them was lousy. *Crawlin.*

But when I hear that whistle blowin, I'm gone. Head down the line to where the weather's fine. Some other camp is boomin, they're drillin down in Santa Fe and I'll pick myself up and head over there to the oil field at Raccoon Bend.

When I was just a little boy, a crazy man come outta the cotton rows buck naked carryin a shotgun yellin out "The Battle Hymn of the Republic," wavin his arms, jumpin in the air.

My daddy weren't afraid of nobody but when he saw this cat he just stood there in the road till that loony pass by. "Son," he said when the man gone down the road, "don't ever tangle with a crazy man. You can't reason with 'em and you can't shoot 'em—they been smitten by God."

I was way down in Texas when I had reason to remember what he said that day. I had took myself down to Houston, see some old buddies of mine. First day I get there I put out the word. By week's end I got myself a job playin in a whorehouse. Ain't gonna be too taxin a gig. Pay ain't bad neither.

I shoulda known when I seen the piano. It was shot full of holes. 'Course you can't find a road sign in the whole state of Texas that some fool hasn't nailed with his six-shooter. Still, it was a sign.

The previous cat—piano player name of Wrigley Jones—had messed up. Wrigley could play real good when he was sober. Drunk, he was a hideous sight, droolin and slobberin and pissin his pants. Fired him for throwin up on the piano once too often. If you ever got to clean up puke out from between piano keys you know why. That was my first job.

In back was a cathouse, the front was a whiskey bar—off to the side was rooms for gamblin. They got everything and anything you wanted any way you wanted it. Even had a drunk schoolteacher who'd write you a letter home.

Joints like that got a tendency to attract crazies. Blues itself'll draw your crazy individual. Anyone who ain't too tightly wired gonna drift into your jook joint.

So there I was, down at Somebody's, and things was goin on pretty fine until one night I am settin there playin the piano when in come a albino with bright red hair which I knew was trouble. They say red-haired folk you don't wanna be around when they get mad. Don't want to provoke cats with red hair and white eyes. Say they're the Devil's brood borned inside out. This freak ain't in the joint but two minutes when he starts screamin at me like I shot his dog.

"YOU PLAY ONE MORE NOTE, MUTHAFUCKA, AND I'LL GRIND YOU SO FINE THEY HAVE TO LOOK FOR YOU BETWEEN THE FLOORBOARDS!"

I knew I wasn't too good a piano player but this seem a little extreme.

"Take it easy, greasy!" I'm tellin him. "It's only a song."

"That was Mandy Jo's song. Mandy Jo and me's song. So don't you go playin that song no more."

Well okay, captain, I'll move on to something else. Songs are very personal with people—specially in the joints. Make you cry, make you mad, make you remember stuff you wish you hadn't. Songs dredge stuff up, and that's what you gotta watch out for. You don't want to stir up bad memories for a cat like this. How the hell am I to know your wife left you and this was your song?

A few minutes he comes over. "How can I make it up to you, sport?" he asks.

"Aw, forget it, man," I tell him. "Ain't nothin."

Guy'll insult you, slander your name all over town. Next minute they're cryin in their whiskey, gettin all weepy and apologetic. That's just everyday bar deportment, so I didn't pay it no mind.

One thing you couldn't miss, though, was the chick he come in with. Big tits, tight skirt, blond wig. When she wiggle across the room shakin her booty, grown men go weak at the knees. She was hot and sinful but she was this cat's girl. You didn't even want to think 'bout her. But this cat, see, he a little bit twisted.

"Know what, I got you figured all wrong. You is nice people. Brenda, warm up the piano player, doll."

That was her name, Brenda. Perfect.

"You heard me, go sit on his lap."

"I don't wanna." She had this horrible whiny voice like fingernails scrapin on a blackboard.

"Hey buddy, thanks," I tell him. "I'm doin just fine."

"Bitch, I said get your ass over there!"

"Aw, c'mon, man, leave her be."

"You ain't disrespectin her by any chance are ya, sport?"

Bouncer take him to one side. Now he's all meek and mild again. Offers me his hand. "Fair and square?" he says. "No hard feelins?"

We shake hands.

"Good deal," he says. "Hey sport, you know that Whistling Alex Moore song, the one 'bout the fella who done shot his wife?"

I said I did and he hand me a dollar to do it.

> *I shot at my woman, 'cause I was tired of so much bull corn.*
> *Policeman jumped me, I run like a rabbit from a burnin barn.*
> *She had red flannel rags, talked about hoodooin poor me.*
> *I believe I'll go to Froggy Bottom, so she will let me be.*

One minute he's gonna kill me, next minute he's my long-lost buddy. All he needs is a little push and along come just the fella to give it to him: Wrigley, the piano-key throw-up artist. Lanky, knock-kneed, trippin over hisself when he walked.

Even though he don't work in the bar no more, he is still hangin out at the joint, and he been lookin for a way to get back at me.

Now he found it. The sonofabitch starts tellin this guy Sam that I'm the back-door man been diddlin his chick. That's the kinda snivelin little snake in the grass he is.

"Shut up, Wrigley. Come here, Coley."

Out of the blue he smacks me upside the head. My head was all broke open, there was blood in my eyes and from somewheres I hears someone shoutin, "Watchit! He got a gun."

I'm lookin up into the barrel of a .44. He's shovin it up against my nose.

"Eat it!"

"Sam, baby, you know this is bullshit."

A man with a gun'll rattle you, a *crazy* man with a gun gonna spin your brain. Just then Brenda trot over to calm Sam down.

"Jesus, Sam," she's whimperin to him, "don't *shoot* him for crissakes, he ain't done nothin."

She's standin behind me now and I feel something hard and sharp rubbin up against my shoulder. My first thought was, Christ, now she's gonna stab me in the back, too. But what she was doin was slippin me a knife. I reached back and grabbed it. I had just caught hold of it when Sam fired. Bullet caught me in the leg. Hurt like hell but I was still alive. Sam cocks the gun and puts it up against my forehead.

"Say your prayers, muthafucka!"

He was gonna make sure he didn't miss this time. Without knowin what I was doin I went at him with the knife. He stood there for a few seconds, rockin on his heels with a creepy smile, gun pointed right at my eye. Then he fell over backwards onto the floor.

"Christ, you got him in the gut," I heard someone say and then I blacked out.

When I came to I was in some house with a woman puttin cold compresses on my head. It was Brenda.

"How long I been here?"

"Three days. You lost blood and passed out."

I might have got away that time, but Wrigley squealed on me. He musta wanted his job back *real* bad. Cops come and lock me up. Brenda figured the judge would let me walk. I did too when I first seen him. He come in the courtroom very jovial. "Good mornin, sinners," he says. Sweet-lookin old guy—but he weren't no Santy Claus. Which came very clear when Brenda began to make her explanation.

"Your honor," she said, "this man been wronged. What he done, he done it in self-defense. Sam had it comin." But the judge weren't impressed one bit.

"Lady," he say wearily, "we all got it comin. Five years hard time on the Central State Prison farm.... Next."

15

John Henry Doin Hard Time

*B*ason and Brock will arrest you,
Payson and Boon will take you down,
You can bet your bottom dollar,
That you're Sugarland bound.

From the moment they came to get me outta that jail and send me to the state pen it was nothin but bad news. Bud Russell was the transfer man, the fella who took prisoners from one prison to another. He was the size of a canteen icebox and just as cold. Nothin but pure malice put on two legs. Evil kinda spirit that kidnap black men into bondage. He put a chain 'round my neck and dragged me to "Shorty George," that's the train runs outta Houston to Sugarland, the Central State Prison farm. Gets its name from the nearby Imperial Sugar Refinery.

Chained me onto a dozen other convicts bein taken to the joint. It was just like Blind Lemon Jefferson said in his song:

I hung around Groesbeck,
I worked in hard showers of rain.
I say I hung around Groesbeck,
worked in hard showers of rain.
I never felt the least bit uneasy
till I caught that penitentiary train.

Sugarland is in the Brazos river bottom twenty miles west of Houston. *That Fort Benn country bottom is a burning Hell.* Soon learn the livin truth of them words. Slavin in the fields from sunup to sundown, and muggy as a steam room down there. Guards was mean as snakes and their whips was crusted with blood. A climate designed to break a man's spirit and his mind. *When I die I'm goin to Heaven 'cause I spent my time in Hell.* Hmm, hmm, hmm.

The leader of my work gang was a man they called Leadbelly. Texas songster doin hard time for murder in the first degree. He usta say, "Sing while you sweat, boys, keep your ugly mind employed." He'd sing,

> *Number one leader, I was rollin some,*
> *I was rollin, honey, from sun to sun.*

His born name was Huddie Ledbetter. It was in Sugarland that Huddie got his nickname of Leadbelly. Without a nickname you was lower than a bug on the floor without no pallet. They called me "Muddy," which they called any cat from Mississippi.

Huddie was one scary-lookin fella. Had a ear-to-ear scar. Doin thirty years hard labor. Not-so-hard labor by the time I got there. He was head nigger in charge. Dude what knows all the scams.

The guards liked his guitar playin so he don't spend too much time on the work gangs. We come back from the cane brakes, there was Huddie just settin up in the shade playin his guitar. They'd bring him sandwiches and whiskey, treat him just like a king. I figured if I play my cards right I could cut myself into this deal.

But Leadbelly weren't the kinda fella you get close to. He didn't like nobody. Didn't require no company. Didn't give a good goddamn. But there always was the mystical fraternity of blues pickers, and I was countin on that.

I send him a message by way of his "wife," a pretty yeller boy named Ponce, that I would like to talk to him, that I was from Mississippi and maybe he like to hear a few Delta licks.

He was just like they said. Sullen, silent, hostile as shit. Settin stiff as a statue of Robert E. Lee. He had a big long face like a Indian.

His mama been a Indian. Had one of them faces where he always looked mad.

"Wanna hear something, man?"

"No," is all he said.

We sat across from each other for a coupla minutes, silent. The weather didn't look like liftin, so I got up to go.

"Let me take a look on your box there, boy," he say very slow and deliberate. I hand it over. He's examinin it, sniffin it, lookin down the neck like the sight line of a rifle.

"Nice lookin piece of wood you got there, son," says he and for a minute I thought it was gonna go pretty good between him and me. But right then he took my guitar in one hand and smashed it— *whaaack!*—on the cement ground and it broke into a hundred little pieces. Then he got up and stomped on it. Then he bent down and picked up a little splinter off the sound box and put it in his mouth like it was a toothpick and chomped down on it. He had style.

"There ain't but one musicianer in Sugarland, and that be me."

Well, good mornin, sunshine! A opportune beginnin it weren't, and I figured that was that. Then one day on the detail he speak to me.

"You gonna second for me, boy."

"With what? You turned my box into firewood."

"Leave that to me."

He had pull and got me put in the cell next to his. Leadbelly was a cat had trouble sleepin. He hated electric lights, and in Sugarland they had 'em on day and night, even when you sleepin. They wanna see that you dreamin regulation dreams. Man, did he bitch about that. Bitch and sing. *Lord, I been down yonder where the lights burn all night long.*

Huddie had a long memory—specially for grievances. Anything what happen to him bad—and that would include most things—he could reel it out just like he was watchin a silent movie in his head. But of Fannin Street, down in Shreveport, he had only happy memories. Fannin Street was the most notorious street in the world. Twelve blocks of wood-framed buildings, brick houses and warehouses. With dance halls, brothels, boarding houses, bars, and 'round-the-clock mischief and mayhem. You could find guys lyin in the street cut from ear to ear. Sometime stark naked, even the clothes been stole off of 'em. Throw 'em right out the window! Sporting class of women runnin up and down the street all night long. Not too long 'fore Huddie hook up with one of 'em.

"When I be a boy, I put on long pants," he says by way of tellin his story, "and my daddy give me forty dollars. I was a big shot, sure, when I had that forty dollars. Go down to Shreveport. My daddy say, 'Go down sell the produce, buy seed, get a new plowshare and come right on home. And Son, whatever you do, don't you go down wastin yo time on Fannin Street, ya hear?'

"'No sir, Pappa!' I'd say, but that's just where I headed. Fannin Street. Just the word was conjurin things in my head. Fanny and pianos and.… Finish up the errand I been sent on and I scamper down to Fannin Street fast as my shoes could carry me."

One night, he run into this demon—his truly beloved. A whore by the name of Jarlene that seem to be as close to the Devil with a blue dress on as you are ever likely to meet in this world. But Huddie, he don't see her that way. To him she the most gorgeous thing he ever known.

Huddie had a song 'bout it. A born showman if ever there was one—do all the bits, all the voices, and throw in a song just to make the story go along. He stopped and sang me a verse:

> *My mama told me—my little sister too,*
> *Woman on Fannin Street, son,*
> > *they gonna be the death of you.*
> *Oooh, oooh, oooh.*

Middle of the night in Sugarland they don't consider this lullaby material. He was workin out a song with a fella called Dicklicker —a more unfortunate name for a man in jail I never heard. They callin their composition "Dicklicker's Holler," which they shout to each other 'cross the block. You got cons—and they ain't all that particular musicwise—shoutin down the cell block,

"Shut up!" "Stuff it!" "Can it!"

Huddie kept a pencil and paper under his pillow so he could wake up and write down his songs. "Midnight Special" was a song he worked over in Sugarland. It was a old-time song that Huddie put some new words to—"yonder come Miss Rosie," "get up in the mornin," "jumpin Judy," and such. He'd yell 'em over to me in the middle of the night, "Coley, what you think of that?" And someone would yell out, "Can it!"

Midnight Special left Houston every night 'round eleven o'clock on its way to San Antone. It come by Sugarland 'bout midnight, headlights flashin in the cell windows. Shine your ever-lovin light on me. Stand in your cell and let that light touch your hand like it contain the whole of life on the outside. You could taste a glass of whiskey, smell a woman's body, feel the sun shinin on you like you was a free man in Dallas.

Only ray of sunshine come into my time at Sugarland was when I got a letter from Vida Lee tellin me we got a second boy child—she was callin him Lonnie. I liked the name. I always felt she done it for me, namin him after one of my favorite blues singers, Lonnie Johnson.

"Shorty George" come out on Sundays bringin families, wifes and lovers. If you stocked up some good behavior or you'd done favors for the guards—like Huddie, he'd play birthdays and stuff for the guards' kids—you could have a woman come in for a "all night long." This were the first time I seen the "beauteous Jarlene."

She couldn't've been more'n twenty-eight but she looked sixty. A junkie, skin pitted, eyes sunk, hair thin and fallin out. Her head was like a skull pokin through her skin. A ghost before her time. But Huddie didn't see none of that. Six months later she got knifed by a pimp. Or croaked on the Chinaman's dope, we never did get a straight story outta it. And that was the last person Huddie ever cared 'bout.

Huddie had told his stories for so long he'd just drift in and outta them like he was in a dream and you was just catchin up little scraps here and there.

"Let me, see...musta been at that supper back in nineteen and fifteen—yup, that be the first one."

I'm lost.

"Huddie," I say, "the first one what?"

"First fella I ever shot dead. Happened at a breakdown, fella botherin my Eula Lee. Shot him through the eye. That be 'round the time I got my first guitar, when I met up with Blind Lemon Jefferson."

Now this interest me 'cause I heard of Blind Lemon's reputation, even knew a few of his songs. Blind Lemon had one of the biggest fames around. People speak his name like he the seventh son. And he was—the youngest of seven. Huddie claim he ran together with Blind Lemon quite a while.

"Lemon weren't older than teenage but he already lookin like a old man. Sometimes he play the guitar with a knife or a bottleneck, and that's where I pick my style. He play real pretty, sing them *plinkety-plinkety* melodic type blues nice and easy. The womens sees him and they come runnin. Lord, have mercy! They'd hug and kiss us so we could hardly play."

But Huddie had a bitterness to him. He could never say nothin good 'bout no one without he'd counterdict it by his next breath.

"He play okay, but hell he ain't nothin but a fat, drunken lecher who ate his food with his fingers. Make hisself a fool in them cathouses. They foist the real wrinkle-up, old whores on him and he don't know the difference. Shi-it, they laugh at that dumb sucker till their side splitted."

Well, you sees what you sees in a man. Generally you sees who *you* is.

Leadbelly been locked up so long he was kinda a livin museum of black music. Time had stopped for him. He hadn't been outta the clink long enough in his life to know too much 'bout how the music was changin.

Folks think of Leadbelly as a folksinger, but he could do near anything. "The Grey Goose," spirituals, prison songs, country reels, work songs, blues, ballads—he could even do cowboy songs—as well as the ones he's known by: "Take This Hammer," "Easy Rider Blues," "Rock Island Line," "Midnight Special," "Alberta."

Only old-timers was doin this stuff anymore and even fewer cared to hear it. For many blacks these songs had a bad taste to 'em, remind 'em of times they just as soon forget. You know, house niggers sayin, "Yassir, boss" down on the slave plantation. Songs that the old mammy in the bandanna usta sing.

"Goodnight Irene" probably his most famous song. Most people assume it's a old black folk song. But accordin to Huddie it was a old music hall song, wrote down by some Irish cat up in Tin Pan Alley.

❖　　❖　　❖

Eventually he sung his way outta the joint—or so the story goes.

It was January of nineteen and twenty-four, Governor Neff and his wife and a bunch of women was payin us a visit, seein how the other half lives. Eight of us got called to provide the evenin's entertainment. Captain Flannigan come onto the cell block.

"Listen, you sorry sumbitches. Guvnuh Neff comin by today. You'all do the right thing by me out theah and you boys can count on fair rations. You fuck this up and it's gonna be fatback and black-eyed peas for dinner. You got that?"

Leadbelly been plannin this day for a long time. Got his glad rags set. Had hisself a clean white prison suit, paid a boy to wash it and put creases in it. Got a song settin there in back of his mind in case he need something spontaneous to lay on the Big Man.

Governor Neff was settin on the front porch of the warden's house slunk back in his chair with his arms folded and his legs crossed over, a ten-gallon hat that just about covered his whole face. But he didn't look relaxed. His face was tense, and in his stiff white collar and bow tie he look just like a preacher.

Each of us parade by the governor as the warden call our names. Governor Neff just nod and say, "Glad you could be here, son." Little smile come on his face. When it come to Leadbelly he perk up directly.

Huddie was one sly old dog, know how to put on a good show. Stoopin and shufflin like a old Uncle Tom prisoner who repented his ways and had a good heart and had learned his lesson and was ready to become a useful member of society, yassuh boss.

"How you bearin up, Ledbetter?" ask Governor Neff.

"Just dandy, your honor, suh."

"Good, good. Gonna give us a dance are you?" Turn to his wife and says, "You gotta see this nigrah dance."

"Sho can dance, suh. Dance all night, yassuh."

"Boy, you sure are some nigrah. What you gonna show us, tonight?"

"I calls it the Sugarland Shuffle."

Whirlin round, pluckin a boll of cotton over here, pluckin a boll of cotton over there. Fast-pickin that cotton like a machine gone berserk. They was fallin off their chairs laughin.

Huddie followed this with "What a Friend We Have in Jesus." Religious number is always a good thing to throw in, coupla cowboy songs—soften the heart of King Saul. Then the governor ask, "Can you do 'Ole Dan Tucker'?" So Huddie did him a coupla hillbilly tunes like "Down in the Valley."

"Give the boy a drink of whiskey," he say, "and a slice a watermelon."

Killin folks was only a sideline with Huddie—his real talent was as a actor. Governor wanna see a man who have put his bad deeds behind him and play a pretty tune on his guitar. And that's what he was givin him, humble Huddie. Tell 'em what they want to believe, that was Huddie's philosophy.

The governor's wife was a nervous little blond woman in a print dress and a straw hat with a swallow on it. Huddie had that woman clear in his sights. He was workin her just like a shill in the doctor shows.

"Ma'am, I never gonna trespass 'gainst another agin."

"If a man provoked you, what would you do?"

"I'd surely rebuke him for his action and tell him, 'Brother, you have offended me but I forgive you.'"

They was well satisfied with this malarkey. Now he got to his ace in the hole. Gonna do his *special* song. Man, if he didn't put everything he got into that song but St. Peter's bicycle. He got Mary the mother of Jesus into it, a verse from the Bible, something he learned off Reverend "Sin Killer" Griffin. Stuff 'bout if you forgive the trespasses of a poor man made one bad mistake, then the Heavenly Father gonna forgive *your* trespasses if you have any. Hankies was comin out all over the place. The women was suckers for this stuff.

Then he come in for the kill.

> *Nineteen hundred and twenty-three,*
> *When the judge took my liberty away from me,*
> *In nineteen hundred and twenty-three,*
> *When the judge took my liberty away from me.*

I left my wife wringin her hands and cryin,
Lord have mercy on the man of mine.

This picture near had *me* cryin. Poor old Huddie bein drug off from his weepin wife. She's clingin on him and a-beggin the judge to not take Huddie from her. No mention of him havin murdered anyone or nothin like that. Or that he and his wife, Lethe, done split awhile back. Into the song he slip in the Governor's name—ol Pat Neff. Try rhymin something with Neff. Ain't easy. Like tryin to rhyme "orange." He always had that touch, puttin in people's names and places in a song to particularize it. And of course he had to fudge the date too. It was 1920 he been sent up river but that wouldn'ta rhymed too good with "took my liberty away from me."

They was as moved as when we used to do the dyin-granny-callin-out-for-a-drink-of-water-and-her-blessed-Bible scene in the medicine shows.

"You make this up extemporary, boy?" Neff ask him.

"Yassuh, just come right in my head when I saw your worship." Then Huddie got hisself weepy as a crocodile.

"There there, boy!" says the governor. "I'm gonna turn you loose after a spell. Not directly, understand. Gonna keep you here so you can pick and dance for me when I come down." They all clap at that.

Next time Governor Neff bring a whole passel of folk with him when he come. Musta been upwards of thirty carloads. Had a big party and Governor Neff was well pleased with his prancin boy. Last official act when he left office was to free Huddie.

January of nineteen and twenty-five, Captain Flannigan come in to his cell and tell him, "You a free man, boy, papers come through just this mornin. Goddamn if you ain't one sly nigrah. Get yo uglified black ass outta here!"

'Course, Huddie been sent down for seven to thirty years and when his pardon come through, he already done more than six, so I figure Mr. Neff done cover his ass by waitin till Huddie's term almost up. But singin his way outta prison, man, it was such a good story no one could resist it. Leastwise Huddie hisself.

16

Jack a Diamonds
Is a Hard Card to Play

It was snowin the day they let me out of the joint and cold as a banker's howjado. Merry fuckin Christmas, baby.

Train rollin by them little Texas towns: Buffalo, Crockett, Palestine. To listen to all them names, you'd think they was great big places, but they was just flag-stop towns when you come up to 'em. Places have three or four stores and a stable. Town called Crockett was named after the old frontiersman, but it weren't no more of a town than Lula was. Small and straggly. No work, no jooks, no Negroes. Skipped outta there and hitched on a wagon to Buffalo, got on a T-model truck from Buffalo to Palestine.

Dark by the time I hit Palestine. Now when you first get to a town, you don't go roamin 'round at night. Bein a black drifter you are a prime candidate for jail or worse. Police lookin for who been breakin into stores or what have you, they take the most easy-to-catch fella, which usually be the hobo.

Me and this fellow rounder had found ourselves a wooden crate to take shelter in. His name was Bosworth and he was a amusin individual. Had moist bright eyes—so jet black you could see your reflection in 'em. The old sinner did card tricks, and claimed he had book-learnin. Claimed he knew who come first, the Greeks or the Romans.

Me and Bosworth was makin ourselfs scarce, drinkin a little canned heat down there by the depot. Some whores come waltzin by. White whores. All we says was "Evenin, ladies!" right friendly—a habit of mine, greetin workin girls—and they says it back to us and that was where it lay. But soon as them two white girls have gone, they call a police.

"You all 'round here been meddlin with white girls? Say you stole their purses."

And we says, "No officer, there ain't been no girls by here."

They knowed we was lyin 'cause they'd fucked them chicks earlier in a baggage car and seen them walk down 'long the tracks where we was.

Throw us in the clink overnight just because. Next mornin they carry us to the railroad track and tell us to get out fast. Which we did, and never went back *there* no more.

One time I was hoboin with Speckled Red. Got his name 'cause his skin had patches all over like a certain kinda spotted fish which I can't remember the name of. Red was a guy who never felt at home except on a train. But ridin the rails can be a hazardous way of travelin. Hoboin on trains, you get shot at, clubbed and beaten by the railroad dicks. To kill a nigger ridin freight was a kinda sport with them. One time Speckled Red and me came near to gettin killed in Christmas—Christmas, Texas. We was comin into town and soon as they seen us they start shootin. We're runnin down the bank, fallin over ourselfs gettin down the hill. I was sure we was goners.

Next town we come to there's a bunch of crackers standin by the silo down at the depot.

Big burly old boy in overalls and a straw hat come over to me. Had a flat nose and piggy eyes and a jack o' lantern face with enough teeth missin to be real scary. Thought he was gonna do me some kinda harm, but all he says is, "Do us a tune on that machine of yours, son."

I start in with a good fast one. "Ella Speed" I think it was. But he say, "Fuck that coon shit, boy, do us a *tune*."

They wanted merry-go-round stuff. Y'know, hillbilly crap. So that's what I gave 'em. Had to play for quite a few ignorant folk in my day.

❖　　　❖　　　❖

So I'm standin by the railroad tracks, gettin them old Texas & Pacific blues. Little Son Jackson's song driftin through my mind.

> *You know I'm through with gamblin,*
> *Some jack stropper can have my room.*
> *Pretty women may kill me, but gamblin will be my doom.*

I was runnin my own games there for a while. Thought myself one pretty slick dude while it last. Coley Williams the cat to see if you wanna get into a game. 'Cept Coley could not keep his *own* self outta that game. Did not know when to stop. See, money is something I was never trained to handle. Oh, I could get it, but I could not keep it. Always this little voice tellin me, "You can't stop now!"

Followin this philosophy I eventually went bust, ended up owin a bunch of bread to people you don't want to owe money to. Broke, desperate, and mean-hearted, I lit out on the lam. Guess you could say that was my idea of fun in them days.

Cut a fella for his money, put a pistol on folks, stealin anything ain't nailed down. Stick up fillin stations and stores. Banks I steered clear of. Robbin banks was for cats that got cars and plans and gangs. Kept mostly to the small-fry stuff. I stick up one particular bar, scored six hundred dollars, but it didn't last long. Found a game down on Fillmore and Elm in a basement. Lost every penny of it right there. Next day I was out on the street askin for a handout.

> *Say, meet me in the bottom, bring my boots and shoes.*
> *Meet me in the bottom, bring me my boots and shoes.*
> *I'm gonna leave this town, 'cause I got no time to lose.*

A crueler, more relentless mistress than a pack of cards and a brace of bones you ain't never gonna meet. Jack a diamonds was there whisperin in my ear late at night and gettin me up outta bed in the mornin. Let the bones decide! I'd throw dice, tell me should I stay or should I go. Should I hop a freight or meet my fate?

> *I fell down on my knees,*
> *Tryin to play a jack a spades.*
> *Jack a diamonds is a hard card to play.*

Well, I played him against the ace.
He was a starvation in my face.
Jack a diamonds is a hard card to play.

I would bet over how far you could spit, that's right. If it gonna rain. Will the three-leg dog cross to the other side of the road. I've missed weddins, funerals, recordin sessions, barbers, gigs and trains waitin for that jack of spades to show.

As long as you in it you can't see it, follow me? I was always gonna make that big score. Sometimes—a very infrequent occasion —I did strike it rich. You think I'd take the money and run? Hell no, I'm on a winnin streak. 'Course you can't stop if you losin neither.

Hundred years old and I'm still a gambler, that's right. I quit the cards and the bones but the gambler's gospel stuck right with me. Whether you takin your chances or hedgin your bets, it's all a crapshoot. You can go to church and say your prayers till the cows come home, but none of that gonna change a thing.

Take farmin. Ain't nothin in this world more a gamble than farmin. The sun, the wind, the rain, God, Mother Nature. Some odds. Y'know, like James Cotton sing, *raisin good cotton crops just like a lucky man shootin dice.*

Among the despised of the hoboin nation, musicians was the privileged ones. The conductor or the guy in the mail car is doin that same stretch day in and day out. He's lookin for some distraction, wouldn't mind passin the time listenin to you playin him a few tunes. So frequently the musician rides in style.

Only time you jeopardize your ride is when you get too stinky and I was fast approachin that limit. Hadn't changed my clothes in months. I was afraid to take 'em off to tell the truth. Afraid to see if they'd growed right onto my skin. They say that happens.

Beginnin to feel I got the mark of Jonah on me. People start shunnin me. Hobos, drifters, rounders and ragpickers givin me the evil eye. When them sort start to turn from you, you know it's bad.

Learned how to peddle dope in all forms, and used it to a certain degree. One time had me a hemorrhage in the nose from the cocaine. Got scared then, thought I was gonna die, but it didn't stop me dealin.

My home was a freight train boxcar—that's all I had left. My luck was runnin out all over the place. Even my dice wasn't playin.

Got a few coins in my pocket and I'm feelin lucky. I'll play pitty pat, shoot the bones anytime anywhere. I'm good in the wrists, know how to even-roll, pad-roll and so on. Trick is you don't shake 'em, you just click 'em together. Uh oh, here I go.

'Course, after a few swigs the Georgia Skin Game start eludin me. With the Georgia Skin, the cup is the problem. Too complicated a thing to go into right here—I don't know if people still playin it even. I will have to look into that.

Suckin on a bottle of Forbidden Fruit one time I won, oh, maybe three hundred dollars from this Mexican cat with a cast in his left eye. He worked that angle, the juju thing. Got his mojo workin but it sure weren't doin him no good. His friend was a freaky little *mestizo* whore with a high-pitch voice. She was eggin him on, tellin lies, screamin in his ear sayin I cheated him. And right outta the blue the Mexican pulls a long-barrel .44 on me. Thought nothin of it. Figured he was just clownin. I was loaded myself, unclear as to what was what.

"Sonny," I says, "you best stow that water pistol before you wet your pants."

Cats crackin up at that, which he didn't much care for, as you can imagine. A lot of them characters got a thin skin. Ain't got much of a sense of humor neither.

When I seen that little tear comin outta the corner of his eye, I knowed this cat ain't kiddin around. He's hurtin and somebody gonna have to pay. Bare bulb swingin over the table, castin spooky shadows in the hall. Everyone's face frozen. It get so quiet you can hear the tickin of the clock on the wall.

Crazy pictures flippin through my mind like someone shufflin cards. Vida Lee, Willie Lee (that's my boy), that stretch of track outside of Palestine, divin into the Sunflower river, runnin up a hill with my brother, Septimus....

He was shakin bad, the gun wobblin in his mitt. Little hands was wavin 'cross his eyes like a clock gone crazy. Slowly he take the gun, point it at his head and pull the trigger. Blood flew out the back of his head. Splattered on the wall, splattered on the light bulb. Splattered on me too. The whole room turn red and begin to spin.

Seem to me the Devil be a busy, busy man.

❖   ❖   ❖

Woke up in a field. It was night. Sky in Texas is high and wide. The stars cold as little chunks of ice. I was alone, afraid and drunk most of the time—nothin seem real to me no more. Just tumblin over and over through endless space—down, down into that bottomless pit. There weren't a livin soul to take pity on me 'cept myself, and I was fresh out.

> *Now place your deuces, Lord, and your fours and fives.*
> *Say I saw cold water from the poor boy's eyes.*

17

Blind Man Showed Me the Way

Headin westbound towards Dallas on the Texas & Pacific. Train come into a little town name of Waxahachie. People dancin in a field, food bein set on tables and such. Out the slats of the cattle car I see they holdin some kinda supper. Little old country gatherin goin on, and right in the middle a fat guitar player has 'em jumpin. Well, I'm hot and tired and dusty and I ain't in any hurry so I hop right off that train to see what is what. A Buffalo Association picnic. That's okay, I don't know what that is neither, but that's what they call it.

Chunky little fella in overalls settin on a chair playin guitar, big smile on his face.

> *Baby, I can't drink whiskey,*
> *But I'm a fool about homemade wine.*
> *Ain't no sense in leavin Dallas.*
> *They makes it there all the time.*

Had a high, lonesome voice, accompanyin hisself on the guitar. Do a soft strum, follow it up by lopin, single string runs. Sometime he paint his words, make his guitar whine just like a mosquito.

Right then a woman with a jug of cat whiskey offer me a swig. "Mr. Al Capone couldn't make better shit than this," she says. When she laughed she put her head back like a wolf and kinda howled.

She had not one tooth in her mouth. She goes, "Ain't that Lemon the cat's pajamas? I do love that man so."

"That Blind Lemon Jefferson playin here?" says I.

"Now who else ya know can pick like that, boy?"

So this was the mighty Blind Lemon. He and Lonnie Johnson were the champions, 'long with Charley Patton, as everyone heard 'em said.

Guitar was rusty as a old terrapin. Beaten and banged with holes in it. He done a weird, lacy version of "See See Rider." Gently stingin them notes with guitar slides.

There was a little kid with a guitar hangin 'round Lemon who had a little guitar hisself. He was strummin along to "See See Rider." Lemon look up and say, "Who that playin guitar?"

"Oh," they says, "that just a little boy knockin on his daddy's guitar."

"No, he ain't," Lemon say, "that boy can play. Come here, boy." He start feelin down low till the boy come to him.

"This here what was pickin the guitar?"

"Yes sir, Mr. Jefferson Blind," say the boy. And Lemon commenced to playin and the boy was playin right with him, copyin him note for note.

"Say, that my note, chile," Lemon say. "Keep that up you gonna be a *real* decent guitar player." And you know who that little boy was? That was young Sam Hopkins. That's right, the young Lightnin Hopkins. Hmm, hmm, hmm.

Little Lightnin a showman even back then. When he finish playin he take a bow and make a little speech, talkin real slow, Texas style.

"'Bliged to y'all for hearin me play," he says like he was announcin the second comin of sliced bread. "And now Sam Hopkins ain't got nothin more to say."

Took off his cap and people was just pullin their pockets inside out to give the little tyke coins. But here's Lemon Jefferson gettin upstaged by a little kid and he don't care for that one bit.

"You done well, young Sam," he says. "Come over here, boy." And he took that cap from little Lightnin and poured all the money into his sack. Told the boy, "That's for the lesson, hear?"

❖   ❖   ❖

I had to track this Lemon Jefferson down so I am askin, "Where can I catch him?" and "Does he play suppers 'round in here often?"

"Nah, he up in Dallas, man, playin on the street."

So here I go takin the interurban up into the city of Dallas. Had them electric cars still runnin up and down.

That was a lot of people's alibi, way they passed their time. Settin by the tracks, catchin whatever fly by. Lemon was suppose to hang 'round on the track down by Elm Street and Central Avenue. What they call Deep Ellum. Deep Ellum run five or six blocks on Central Avenue and a coupla blocks on Elm. Call it Central Track because a railroad run right down the middle of the street.

First person I ask 'bout Lemon's whereabouts is a jittery young dude with a orange tabby cat. Kid seem to know his schedule like a train timetable.

"Mornins he start out 'bout 'leven o'clock from where he live down by South Dallas. 'Round one or two he get up to that corner over there where Central Tracks cross Elm Street. This time of the day you gonna find him over at Jezebel's—y'know, the cathouse over on Central."

As I'm walkin away he says, "Hey, you wanna watchit."

"Somethin wrong?"

"Yeah, you got chalk on your pants, fella, best brush it off quick. Yellow Britches put the mark on you. Stooly who work for the cops. Whenever he find a stranger in town, he mark you with a piece of chalk. They gonna throw you in jail for a drifter."

Jezebel's weren't no tent down by the levee or upstairs room in a barrelhouse. More like a fancy hotel. Big plush place with tiny palm trees and red flock wallpaper and pictures of naked ladies on the walls. In the main parlor downstairs was Madame Jezebel. Tiny mulatto woman sittin cross-legged on a big mahogany table, wearin a fancy gown and fannin herself with a fan as big as she was. When a customer come in she'd start up chantin, "High-yellah, brown, uptown, Mexican or Creole—take your pick, lowlife, high-tone, short, tall, fat and lean, finest girls this side of New Orleans!" Small groups of hussies in shifts was lyin 'round on sofas gigglin.

There I see Lemon with a bunch of girls. The girls was playin the original blind man's buff with him—he was blind and they was in the buff. If he could catch one of them whores he could have her.

It didn't seem all that attractive a game, but Lemon was enjoyin hisself and so was the girls.

Lemon stumble, fall down, get up again, bang into a chair, but eventually he gonna catch that pussy. He couldn't see where it was but he sure gonna smell it—had a nose like a dog. And just like a dog he didn't have no shame 'bout followin his nature neither. When he catch up with the girl, he just unbutton his fly and take her right there doggy style, in the middle of the room. Button hisself up and say, "Oh, mama! Let me down easy! Daddy feelin mighty fine!" And he'd go straight to playin and singin,

> *Well, the sun's gonna shine in my back door some day.*
> *Ahhhh it's one more drink gonna drive these blues away.*

And the girls all say, "We know whose back door *you* shine on, Mistah Jefferson."

Next mornin I went down to see him under what they call the Lemon tree. Standin 'round down there on Central under a big old shade tree. Call it a standpoint. Had a tin cup wired to the neck of his guitar. And when you'd give him something he'd thank you, but don't give him no pennies. He don't abide no pennies.

Man step up, drop a penny in Lemon's tin cup, he rattle that cup to determine the coin and his face come over all sour. "*One* cent?! One lousy cent? Don't play me cheap. Put some silver in my cup or come back here and take it out 'cause you must need it more'n me."

There was quite a few fellas hangin 'round catchin onto Lemon's guitar pickin and takin it up their own selves. I was doin it too.

Lemon twirlin 'round in his spot singin,

> *Ghosts, ghosts, all 'round my place.*
> *All you shadow mens, why don't yo show yo face?*

"You knows I can hear you pick-tone boys out there spiderin up and down yo boxes," say Lemon. "But you can't catch me, fellas, I am *waaay* down the track. Train left the station and y'all don't even got a ticket to ride. Got eyes on my bones, ears in my toes and where I'm headed nobody knows. You gotta be blind and fat to play like me. Blind, black, fat and horny."

They all laugh over theirselves.

"You gotta bump into every lamppost, trip over every dog, roll in the mud for a pillow and—"

He pause and sniff the air,

"Who all be out there today?"

A bunch of guys jokin around, soundin off: "Tops!" "Jimmy!" "Shine!" like they was on roll call.

"Travelin boy over yonder. Man, I can smell that Texas & Pacific soot a mile away."

My clothes was all smoky from the train.

"That me, boss. Coley—"

"What you doin down here, Smoky Coal? Guitar player?"

"Uh-huh."

"Figures. Sometimes all's I get out here be a mess of damn pickers. Where you from, mister? Don't tell me. Play a bit and I tell *you*."

I play a few licks and right away he say, kinda sneerin like, "'Nother damn cropper! You Delta boys is all alike. Groanin and slidin. Can't pick a clean note to save your lifes. Muddy on, Brother Coley. Mississippi where you from, chile. I can smell them bo weevils crawlin through yo nappy head."

Well, he did sniff me out. That's why they say Lemon got juju eyes. Got more a owlish look to him than a raggedy-ass bluesman. In his high-button jacket he resemble a old-time country schoolteacher. Confuse people 'cause he don't look like your common blues singer, all shabby and threadbare.

'Course on a bender he could get hisself ragged as a pet pig. Generally, though, he stand straight as a pole. His speech was lovely and direct to the word. Didn't have no glasses when I first saw him.

"Uh, Mr. Jefferson, Huddie say to tell you hello and—"

"Huddie, huh? Been wonderin where all he went to."

"Been in Sugarland all these years. Just last year got hisself pardoned."

"That where you knowed him from?"

"Yeah."

"That's one hellhole I don't *ever* want to be acquainted with. Place too ugly for a blind man, *hawh, hawh.*"

Lemon was suppose to be completely blind, but I do believe he could see a little. More'n one people suspect he weren't plum blind. Just don't attempt to take no money from him! Could feel his way 'round them women real good too, and that's the truth. And his hearin was uncanny.

He was kind of heart and generally cordial but sometimes he'd grow crabbish. Fella's blind, he relies on his habits—'spectin things to be done his way. Like if a fella didn't lead him exactly right, why he'd raise sand.

Presently the little kid who been leadin him had enough of Lemon's snarlin. That's how I come to lead him 'round. Not that he really need anyone. He could just walk along and ask, "Which is the direction that I'm goin in?" and anybody 'long the way was happy to take him wherever he was headed. I got used to his salty moods soon enough.

'Round five o'clock I'd go down to the station and take him wherever he playin next. Frequently he'd play at the Big Four, popular club down near the terminal. Start singin 'bout eight and go on till four in the mornin. Sometimes he got me or another fella with him, playin a mandolin or a guitar and singin along, but mostly it was just Lemon sittin there and playin all night long.

First night I'm there Lemon say, "Gonna skip the joints. Ain't feelin too good. Figure to head on home. Gimme your arm, kid."

Didn't need me to lead him, just follow the tracks back home like every day. This was his way of sayin, "I know you ain't got no place to go. You best come stay with me."

Had a nice setup over there. Big fat mama of a wife, bunch of kids runnin 'round. He was a enterprisin cat. At his house he had a still, a whole bootlegger operation goin on. When he gone durin the day his wife sell the whiskey outta the parlor. 'Course his wife like to sip on the product and Lemon he don't care for that. She'd sneak a snort or two thinkin the old fool never gonna notice a itty bit sip like that.

"How you doin, baby?" hc ask her when we get there.

"Mighty fine, mighty fine, Mr. Jefferson."

"How'd we do today—sell any 'shine?"

"Nope, nobody bought no whiskey this day."

He take that bottle and shake it. Lemon tilt his head like he weren't convinced. Had ears on him like a bat.

Dallas was the most excitin of all the places I been, 'specially its red light area down in Deep Ellum. Barrelhouses, gin mills, dance halls and night clubs. Let me tell you, the pickin was good. On either side of Central Track was Fat Jack's Theater and the Tip Top Club—'long with shoeshine parlors and beer joints and the Pythian Temple.

An old preacher with the holy shakes was preachin flesh-creepin stuff there. Prognosticatin that Jesus gonna come—to Dallas and he named the day—June 14, 1927. I watched a pickpocket liftin a wallet from a man standin there with his mouth open listenin to the end of the world news.

Business, religion, hoodooism, gamblin, stealin, pimpin, pawnin, moonshinin, druggin and dancin—all mixed up together agreeably in that thieves market like they was made for each other. Kinda place where stuff gets brewed up.

Lotta blues players come through Deep Ellum. Lonnie Johnson, Little Hat Jones, Texas Alexander, Funny Paper Smith, Bobby Cadillac, Mance Lipscomb, Lightnin Hopkins. Bunch of jazz cats, too. Charlie Christian, Herschel Evans, Hot Lips Page and them. All came outta Dallas.

You could get anything you wanted, includin dead. There was a alley call Death Row, and if some cat didn't get hisself killed there it weren't a regular Saturday night.

Lemon took me 'round the beer joints and clubs. The Tip Top—it was on the second floor of the Hart Furniture warehouse, Ella B. Moore's Park Theater, Hattie Burleson's dance hall, the Green Parrot.

In the barrelhouse they wanted them songs low. Mostly settled down to the slow lowdown blues, and they'd slow drag to 'em. Dance to that, you see. Just bear down on the slow blues. Lemon could swim with them moods just like a fish, go whichever way they led. Could be mean as a adder, too.

I done swallowed some fire,
Taken a drink of gasoline.
Put it up all over that woman,
And let her go up in steam.

Or he could mellow down easy, slip it in like a eel.

Long distance well, and it's blowin oil, that's all.
Ain't nothin to hurt you, sugar,
Ain't nothin that's bad.
Ain't nothin to hurt you, honey.
Ain't nothin bad, it's the first oil well
That your little boy ever had.

He got that freight train beat, that easy-roller rhythm. Can you tell me what's the difference between one blues wizard's playin and another? Their rhythms, that's right. Every blues player got a ghost drum in his guitar and he lays his melody over it. Tried to estimate how he was doin it—that broken time thing. Sometimes I thought he was puttin too many bars in a song.

Lemon was a tough teacher. Wouldn't let you go till you got it down. "Hammer them strings, make that slide *sing*. We can stay here all night and then some."

Guitar was his answerin self, Lemon Two. He could do just about anything with that thing. Made a churchbell ring in "See That My Grave Is Kept Clean." His guitar was scaly as a terrapin, but it was the only thing he ever did get tight with. Hmm, hmm, hmm.

Like I say, Central Track run right through Ellum. Crossin point where the Texas & Pacific meet the H&TC. They'd come there and take you to pick cotton over in Collin County, so there was always a crowd of men waitin 'round. Sharecroppers been wiped out by the bo weevil come to town lookin for work.

One afternoon we was standin under Lemon's tree when a white fella approach. Somber-lookin gent in a dark suit. Tryin to look more confident than he likely was, in the middle of a mob of black men didn't necessarily wish him well. But the crowd parted for him like the Red Sea. Is it a police or some trouble comin? Man introduce hisself as R.T. Ashford, owned a local record store. Boogie-woogie piano player name of Sam Price worked for him, said Lemon was the best man out there on the guitar.

"Ain't done no recordins," says Lemon.

"Well I know that, and that's what I come to remedy. Fella up at Paramount wants you to come up to Chicago and make some phonograph records. Get you a ticket so's you can ride in style. Just tell me when you wanna go."

When I heard Lemon was takin off for Chicago to make his recordins I went down to the station to say goodbye. Shine, one of them cats hang 'round Lemon, see me there.

"Yo! Coley!" he say. "You lookin for Lemon? He over on the other side catchin forty winks on a baggage wagon."

As I'm makin my way 'round the back a tall, serious cat cut me off.

"Your name Coley?"

"Might be...."

"Coley Williams?"

"I know you from somewheres?"

"You don't. I just come down from Mississippi, man. Got a message from your wife. She need you to come home right quick. There's been some trouble."

"Is it 'bout Willie Lee, can you say?"

He shook his head—then I knew the worst.

"Oh, Jesus, not Lonnie. Hell, I never even got to see him—been gone so long."

"I'm sorry, man, real sorry to be the bearer of bad news."

"How long it—"

"Pneumonia. Three weeks ago."

A whole new life had come into the world and gone out before I even got to see his face. I sat on the packin crates and cried. I was cast in utter darkness. I felt I been the cause of it, just by not bein there.

Next thing I knew, Lemon was lookin down at me, his big round baby face like a little chubby sun.

"Why you cryin, baby? What's wrong?"

I told him and he swung his head way back like he was swoonin and muttered "Dear God!" over and over. And then he couldn't say no more and neither could I. We sat there in the late afternoon sun and then very quietly he begun to sing:

> *Hey, long distance, I can't help but moan.*
> *Mmmmmmmmmmmmmmm, I can't help but moan.*
> *My baby's voice sound so sweet,*
> *Oh, I'm gonna break this telephone.*
>
> *I think I'll use deadly poison to get this worry off my mind.*
> *I think I'll use deadly poison to get this worry off my mind.*
> *This long distance moan*
>   *about to worry me to death this time.*

As it happen Lemon's train come in long time 'fore mine. That train pullin out into the night was the last I seen of Lemon for awhile.

> *The train's at the depot with the red and blue lights behind.*
> *Say, train's at the depot with the red and blue lights behind.*
> *Well, the blue light's the blues,*
>   *the red light's a worried mind.*

I was eaten up with sorrow, torn apart by guilt. Bible knowed all 'bout them things, that's right. Knows when the bad times come you gonna blame yourself—curse yourself—and wish you was dead. All laid out there in the *Book of Job*, baby. Like God could peek into your life through a pane of glass, and foresee all the afflictions life gonna lay on you.

As if things weren't bad enough, people was throwin the Scriptures right in my face. Tellin me the Lord is testin my faith. A little too much of that kinda consolation and I was startin to curse the day I was born.

Dread seized upon me and my bones begin to shake. You know the end is near when you start hearin the Devil whisperin like a dozen spiders in your ear, "Skin for skin! Skin for skin!" That's when I knew I had put myself in his scaly clutches and I begin to shout out into the night, "Get behind me, Satan!"

When I get home I was too beaten down to speak. Vida Lee, she just have to look at me to know what I been through and she didn't say a thing to me. Laid not one accusin or reprimandin finger on me. The sorrow cut too deep for that.

"How long is it been, honey, since I saw your face?" was all I could say.

Vida Lee say, "It's gonna be okay, baby. We been through the worst thing you can go through. We gotta hold our head up, honey, and count the blessins we got. 'Cause no amount of tears gonna bring my baby back, and I already cried all the tears there is in the sea."

I told her how everybody along the way have told me God punishin me for my sins. But to that Vida Lee just say, "I am surprised at you, Coley. If you listen to what fools and hypocrites is sayin, you just as much a fool as they. Bible don't say *none* of that. You think you can change the world by gamblin and boozin and whorin and fightin?" She read to me 'bout where God speaks to Job.

> Where were you when I laid the foundation of the earth? Tell me, if you have understanding…. Who shut in the sea with doors? Have you commanded the morning since your days began? Has the rain a father? Can you guide the Bear with its children? Can you send forth lightning, that they may go and say to you, "Here we are?"
>
> And Job answered the Lord, "I have uttered what I did not understand, things too wonderful for me that I did not understand."

And when I heard Vida Lee speak those words it was like cool water splashin on my brain. I really was one ignorant fool. Hmm, hmm, hmm.

If You Don't Like My Ocean,
Don't Fish in My Sea

Stayed 'round Lula a few months. Vida Lee was happy and I was happy to be there with her. Not that you ever get over the death of a child. There ain't one day you wake up you don't think 'bout it. But it's hard bein 'round others when you is troubled in mind. And sometimes it's hard bein 'round someone who is feelin the same pain as you.

Time go on, I begin to feel if I don't get away, this thing gonna end up tearin us apart. I'd find myself all the time tryin to explain why I drifted away, why I stayed away so long.

One mornin we drinkin coffee, not speakin a word between us.

"So let me ask you," says Vida Lee. "When you plannin on leavin again?"

"Who says I'm leavin?"

"Honey, it written all over your face."

"But this time I'm gonna do right by you," say I. "Buy you some fine clothes, a big old diamond ring."

"Lord have mercy."

"See, I been thinkin…."

"Here we go."

"It bein summertime and all I might get myself on one of them tent shows. See, I figure I can do a season, get us straight and then —I swear on Noah's naked ass!—I come back and sit at your feet the rest of my natural life."

"You know, baby, I'm beginin to feel like I married a damn sailor —and I only get to see you on shore leave, baby."

"Honey, I know...."

"It gets goddamn lonely takin care of everything myself. Mr. Green down at the feed store flirtin with me. How'd you think I feel when some redneck tell me, 'Darlin, we can always take it out in trade'?"

"Jesus, what am I thinkin?"

"You *ain't* thinkin. But hell, there ain't no work here nohow. Cotton ain't king no more, there's borers in the corn. Even when it's good they ain't payin nothin for it. But this time you best come back with a bathtub of silver dollars or you gonna find me gone. *Gone* gone, y'understand? Won't be nothin waitin for you but your mule."

One day I'm playin down on the corner, waitin for a tent show to blow through Clarksdale. Just doin my thing when I see a big lady standin in the crowd. She just laughin and laughin, a wide old gold-tooth grin. 'Course I knew this was Ma Rainey, 'bout as famous as you gonna get in the chitlin circuit.

She give me a sign to come over to her, puts her arm 'round me and says, "I'm a sucker for them lowdown blues cooked up with gut-bucket humor. What's yo name? Never mind, we'll get to that later. You gonna do just fine. Mama gonna take you away with her, put you in her show."

Pinchin my cheeks like I was her little boy child. When Ma decide something there weren't no arguin with it. You don't argue nohow with a force of nature like Ma.

"Honey," she tell me, "you just hang 'round and catch the show 'cause tonight I'm gonna be singin just for you." And she laugh and laugh, 'cause every person in that audience believed Ma singin to them.

And that night was the first time I heard Ma Rainey, in the old Rabbit Foot and Silas Green from New Orleans minstrel show. There was a big, *big* crowd. Packed in there like rice in a bowl.

Ma's shows was like bein in some crazy dream where the furniture gets big and the people all shrink down, crawlin in and out of pots and pans. On one side of the stage is built a huge Victrola—a giant's phonograph, eight feet high. A girl come out, puts on a record big as herself. The band picks up the "Moonshine Blues." Ma's hidden back in this big boxlike affair. Big Victrola bathed in bluish light.

Ma sing a few bars inside the Victrola, and then the big old doors of the cabinet swing open and Ma jump out into the spotlight throwin kisses and smilin wide as the sun with them big old gold teeth of hers. Gold-toothed, gold-neck woman of the blues waftin a ostrich plume fan, face lightened with grease paint powder and rouge. Looked like *she* was made of gold.

Diamond-studded tiaras, rings and bracelets. Long triple necklace of shiny twenty-dollar gold coins coverin her chest like armor on some ancient queen. Diamonds flashin like sparks of fire fallin from her fingers. All them jewels reflectin the blue spotlight dancin on her sequined black dress.

When this fat, friendly phantom of the blues leap out from the hokey little pasteboard temple the audience go wild. Nobody would ever accuse her of bein goodlookin, but once she begin to sing audience forget all that. She was their big, black goddess in a sequin dress. And she had one of them voices you never could forget. Like your mother singin a lullaby to you before you was born.

You got a lot for your money at one of Ma's shows. Generally lasted two hours or more. There was a guy did eccentric dancing, then Willie Jackson come on and sing *Il Trovatore*. And there was John Pamplin did that devil act—rattled a big iron ball and did a lot of jugglin. Plus some acrobats from down in New Orleans called the Watt Brothers. And Delmon Miles the contortionist—turn hisself 'round completely. And Ma even had her adopted son, Danny, doin a routine of female impersonations.

Ma would finish the first half with "Ma Rainey's Black Bottom." The curtain'd come down, and there'd be a olio, hodgepodge of between-acts stuff. A fella'd come out to the center of the stage and tell a tale while the rest of the people behind the curtain be dressin.

Second half. Lights flash, curtains rise, and out come a bunch of young men and women—dancers. Long Boy ripples minors on the black and yellow keys, then Ma Rainey herself come back out dressed in a real long maroon dress, like the Gay Nineties, tellin jokes 'bout her cravin for young men. Her name for the young men was pigmeats. If they was very young, 'round eighteen or nineteen, she call 'em bird liver.

"Yeah, I likes my pigmeat. I ain't got nothin for a old man to do. I like mine young and tender."

Then she say, "Boys and girls, I'm gonna tell you 'bout my man," and she sing "A Good Man Is Hard to Find." She'd do "Walkin the Dog," which she also danced to a peppery Charleston with her partner, Broadway Frank Walker. She weren't no spring chicken neither. Musta been 'round thirty-nine at the time.

Ma could move through the emotions like they was strings on a guitar. Show how things can oppress you, make you mad enough to kill the jerk. Like in "Leavin This Mornin," where she gonna go after a no-good man with a Gattlin gun. Sing 'bout how things never gonna get better nohow. Tell 'em the down-and-dirty truth straight out.

> *Black cat on my doorstep, black cat on my windowsill.*
> *If one black cat don't cross me, another black cat will.*

> *It's bad luck if I'm jolly, bad luck if I cry.*
> *It's bad luck if I stay here, it's more bad luck if I die.*

She end with her famous "See See Rider Blues."

> *I'm goin away, baby, won't be back till fall.*
> *Lord, Lord, Lord.*
> *Goin away, baby, won't be back till fall.*
> *If I find a good man, then I won't be back at all.*

> *I'm gonna buy me a pistol, just as long as I am tall.*
> *Lord, Lord, Lord.*
> *Gonna kill my man and catch the Cannonball.*
> *If he don't have me, he won't have no gal at all.*

This got loud calls for a encore. Then the whole cast come onstage and sing and dance the finale. Took seven curtain calls.

Yeah, she was a bona fidy tent show queen. *The* tent show queen. Bessie Smith may have beat her as far as audiences in the theaters and up north, but nobody could contend with Ma in her own territory, and that was the tent shows.

My gig was to introduce Ma—call her the Black Nightingale—then we go straight into the sketches. Ma seen her life as a ongoin drama, and that's the way she sang it.

Sometimes the skit run right through the song. There'd be singin and talkin all through the thing, like in "Blues the World Forgot."

The skit begin with Ma boozin heavily. I'm strummin a twelve-bar blues while I describe the alarmin activities goin on outside the window. Went something like this:

Ma: Lord, Lord, Lord, I got the blues this mornin and don't care who knows it. I want all you boys to lock your doors, and don't let nobody in but the police.
Me: Lookit here, Ma, what's the matter with you?
Ma: I got the blues.
Me: What kinda blues? Money blues, boy blues, achin blues or nothin shakin blues?
Ma: The blues what the world forgot.
Me: Woman, I believe you is drunk.
Ma: Drunk? Lord have mercy! The way I feel this mornin I don't mind goin to jail!
Me: Ma, don't talk so loud—don't you see the sergeant standin out there on the corner?
Ma: Tell the sergeant I said come on in, and bring all the corn mash he have with him!

Here there'd be a loud caterwaul—George Hooks Tilford would make the sound on his sax.

Ma: What was that?
Me: They done turn all them black cats loose in the alley.
Ma: What do I care, let 'em bring all them drunken cats. Where's the bootlegger? Tell him I'm gonna drink all the whiskey made this week. I feel like goin to jail!

The spirit of the thing so mixed-in together you can't exactly tell where the jokes stop and the seriousness began. The farce come in where a reasonable individual—part I play—tryin in vain to restrain a rowdy and outrageous Ma. Naturally she ain't gonna shut up. Gets deeper and deeper in trouble and drags me down with her. Audiences love that.

Back in her dressin tent Ma look like a big black Christmas tree—just a-glitterin and a-sparklin. Her gowns was always very elaborate. Rhinestones, bit of jewelry. Was a fanatic on jewelry. All kinds of diamonds and gold pieces. Any number of necklaces. But for all that fancy stuff, Ma never forget where she come from. Born dirt poor, second of seven children, workin the shows since she was a little girl. That's why she could sing them down-home blues so good.

She'd look at herself in the mirror and shake her head, "I don't know, I don't know." And laugh so the whole tent would shake. "God sure didn't bless me none with good looks, Coley."

"Ma," I'd say, "there are two things I never seen."

"And that be?"

"A ugly woman and a pretty monkey."

"Bless you, darlin, for a kind heart and a lyin tongue."

Ma'd make fun of herself, and didn't have no respect for nobody else's dignity either. She'd make the strait-laced squirm.

> *If you don't like my ocean,*
> *Don't fish in my sea.*
> *Stay out of my valley,*
> *And let my mountains be.*

On stage Ma wanted the folks to enjoy theirselves even at her own expense. And if a little pandemonium break out now and then, so much the better. Like the time the rattlesnake in the new snake act got loose and headed for the footlights. Or the night the stage starts fallin in and she begins singin, "If you don't b'lieve me I'm sinking, look what a hole I'm in."

She didn't have no airs. No secrets neither. She talk to you 'bout anything. I heard a bunch of stories about Ma and Bessie so I asks her, "Is it true, Ma? You know what they say—"

"Probably."

"Y'know, 'bout you and Bessie."

"My, my my! Me and Bessie have some wild old times together."

"I mean 'bout how you suppose to kidnap her and all when she was just a little girl."

"Oh, honey! I don't hafta kidnap nobody. People *follow* me around, you know that."

"Figured it was—"

"You know peoples say anything what fly through their heads. Just the kinda foolish nonsense old men hangin on the liars' benches tell. And lotsa times these stories is better than the truth, anyways. Almost *become* the truth, been told so many times. Who knows? Maybe our whole life some kinda dream, and reality just be who can tell the best story. So come on over here, baby, put on my gold pieces and hush your mouth, 'cause I got a story to tell you tonight."

In the long hours between shows Ma like to ruminate. She'd known everybody somewhere down the line. All the fine dudes, jive-asses, tail-shakers and jail-breakers what ever snaked through the southland.

Ma been singin the blues since the blues begin. Been in vaudeville since her teens and in the minstrel shows. Minstrel shows go way back. Grandmaw Pie seen 'em. Jungle scenes, blues scenes, novelty acts, comedians, jugglers, vaudeville teams. Scenes of plantation life, spirituals, marching units, refined singers, dancers, and specialty acts. Generally followed the harvest, in the south, ending up in New Orleans. That's where Ma met Joe Oliver, Louis Armstrong, Sidney Bechet, Pops Foster. She sang in Kid Ory's jazz band.

Ma was from back when, before things got differentiated. When blues just one tributary in the big River Vaudeville.

"Darlin, I goes so far back downriver I remember the first blues *anybody* heard."

Guess I didn't look all that persuaded, 'cause she says, "Now just look at yo face, Coley! You don't believe Mama, do you? Well, Mama know, 'cause Ma been singin the blues since nineteen-and-two, baby.

Weren't no blues afore that nowhere. Blues is invented by a li'l girl no more'n twelve. You best believe what I'm tellin you, y'hear?"

"I believe you, Ma."

"One day come 'long raggedy li'l girl from town. Come up to the tent one mornin. Just standin there. I say, 'What you want, li'l girl? You wants a apple or a crust of bread?'

"Didn't say nothin back to me. Just stand there with her big wide eyes. After a big old minute she begin to sing in a high weird tone 'bout how her man done left her. I practically fell over laughin. Little pickaninny singin 'bout her woes of love. But she kept on with that pie-pan face till she end her song and then thrust out a rusty little tin cup. Strangest and most saddest melody I ever heard and I ask her to teach it to me. Learned that song from the little girl, and sung it for many years."

One night Ma summon me to her room. Lookin weary and troubled, sittin there in a big armchair she tell me with a heavy heart:

"Coley, Coley, Coley. What am I gonna do with you? Things gettin close to the rind 'round here. We ain't got the audiences we used to. I am sorry, honey, but I ain't gonna be able to carry you no more; gotta trim my troupe or we *all* gonna starve."

Ma get up, she hand me a twenty-dollar gold piece and say:

"Come here, honey, give Mama a hug. I'm gonna miss you when you're gone. Mama want to keep all her kids close by but the world gettin bigger, Coley, I swear."

19.

Doctor Rastus
Peerless Medicine Show

I'd got lucky and then I'd got unlucky. That's the way it can go. One day you're in show business singin the blues and the next you are lookin 'round for your shoes. I was out on the street again, hustlin for nickels and dimes, doin whatever that took, y'know, and drinkin it up pretty much soon as I made it.

One day a medicine show come through town and I told the man was runnin it that I had recently come from a tour of the South with the great Ma Rainey but I was willin to hire myself out to his organization at a slight reduction in my usual fee.

"No shit!" he said. "You ever clean a elephant's cage?"

"No, sir."

"Good! 'Cause I don't got no elephants. Get you ass on that truck."

I start out doin "low pitches," workin with a Doctor do his spiel from a box on the ground, and gradually I worked my way up to the big-time shows, kind that travel by railroad car, bring along a big troupe of actors and singers, snake handlers, wrestlers, jugglers and magic acts.

In Greenville, I hooked up with Doctor Rastus Peerless Medicine Show, as scurrilous a bunch of rapscallions who ever went forth to dupe the public. 'Course people *want* to believe in foolishness: tonics that cure toothache, heart disease, heartache, sleeplessness, rheumatism, piles, pox, pimples, sour breath, blisters, and the sins of the flesh. And why not? Water into wine, walk on water. Make my lover come back to me. Folks is always countin on miracles. You probably waitin for one right now.

Medicine show be just what it sound like, a travelin routine where a self-proclaimed "Doctor" hustle his nostrums—tonics, pills and so forth. The show is just his way of drawin people in. That's where I come in, entertainin the folks before the "Doctor" come out and sell his patent medicines. Ain't got nothin in 'em but a shot of booze and some herbs. Don't do no harm though, s'far as I know.

I sing a few songs, do a little dance. When the Doctor come on he give his speech. Dr. Rastus dressed in a top hat, a fancy walkin stick with a gold-plated top. His clothes was fancy but past their prime. Collar of his coat so greasy it looked like it was made of satin. Hat frequently tipped off his head like he was havin a battle with it. Drunk too much of his own medicine I guess. He'd hand me the bottle to demonstrate the potency of his potion, a magic elixir suppose to cure all your ills. I take a swig and suddenly I'm a changed man, make a lunge at the nearest women. Folks believe what they wanna believe.

You worked on one of those shows, you had to be ready to do just 'bout anything in the entertainment line. Play trumpet, sell medicines, liniments. Whenever the people start to wander off, Doctor say, "Tide's going out, boys, you'd better reel 'em in quick."

We had singers, shake dancers, magic acts, comic routines, dramatic recitations, a play what's based on Shakespeare, *Faust* or the Bible. We'd do any kinda singin the situation require: country stomps, ragtime numbers, prison songs, and square dance calls and a few no-doubt-'bout-it blues. "John Henry" always popular. "In the Jailhouse Now" was a medicine show favorite, too. We'd act it out. There was upside-down dancers, all kinda crazy stuff.

Novelty acts was much sought after with the doctors. There was a trumpet player who could fan the bell of his horn and make it say "yes" or "no." And a guy called DeFord Bailey could do a cacklin hen, a contented lover, a speedin locomotive, just with his breath and his fingers.

While I was travelin out on the circuit I met everybody in the business. That's where almost everybody got their start back then.

White fella by the name of Jimmie Rodgers who go on to become a big-time hillbilly record star. Roy Acuff, Fiddlin John Carson, Uncle Dave Macon, Hank Williams. And Buster Keaton the movie actor, that's right.

I got vexed with all this nonsense after a while, especially after they had me doin that hobo-in-the-henhouse routine. I played a bum who breaks into a hen coop. There was real chickens in there and while I'm crouchin down a few of 'em was sure to let some droppins loose on my head. Then another fella from the show come out in white face and chin whiskers playin the mean old farmer. He's lookin 'round to see what all the commotion is about.

"Who's in thar?" he shouts. "If I find you I'm a gonna fill your britches full of buckshot."

That's when I say, "Ain't nobody in here but us chickens, boss!" That got a big laugh. Then the farmer shoots off his shotgun and the chickens all fly up in the air and across the stage. And I would run like hell. It was the highlight of the show—none of us on either side of the footlights was that far from the farm, understand? It was the stupidest thing I ever done. Well, *one* of the stupidest. Them chickens was trained so that they wouldn't fly out into the audience but it was my job to catch 'em and put 'em back in the cage. Scratchin and peckin and chicken-shittin on me four times a night. Have to get drunk just to get through it.

We was playin Durham, North Carolina. One night I got more drunk than usual and passed out on the grass. They just left me there. Cat who was playin the farmer was jealous that I got all the laughs— probably been schemin to take my place all along. Damn, he was welcome to it. I wasn't doin too good in the show business and I was too ashamed to go home and tell Vida Lee.

I was layin down by the station with all the trash that gathered there when a train stop to take on water. On the side of the front carriage was a big banner sayin: THE INCOMPARABLE RABBIT FOOT MINSTRELS. Damn, if that ain't Ma Rainey's troupe, I said to myself, and as the train was pullin out of the station I jumped on board.

Ma was sittin in her compartment with a sweet young boy on one side and a plate of chicken wings on the other. She was glad to see me all right but she didn't have good news for me.

"Oh chile, we's no better off than when you left us. Things is gettin so lowdown I'm thinkin of quittin the whole business, open a motion picture palace. Yup, just might do that. You know, Coley, I'd take you back on in a minute but, hell, it's these times, darlin. There might be somethin, though."

"What that be, Ma?"

"*Might be*, hear?"

"Might-be's is soundin mighty promisin to me these days."

"Well, Bessie's doin real good right now and that guitar player she got—Denzel? Well, he take off with one of them cute little chorines Jack have his eye on—and Bessie too, most probably. They so damned pissed at him they won't take him back. They lookin for someone to replace him, hon. So you go along, see Bessie, she's playin at Raleigh this weekend. Tell her Ma sent you."

20

The Empress of Funk

"Ooooh hooo! Which one of you boys gonna fuck me first? I am as horny as an old goat tonight and Mr. Jack ain't nowheres in sight!"

First time I met Bessie Smith, man, I was terrified. Like a frog in a fryin pan. Year was nineteen and twenty-five. May. Raleigh, North Carolina. One of the roustabouts carry me over to Miss Bessie's tent. Bessie sittin there smokin on a big fat cigar, lookin like some kinda funky Empress of China.

As we come in, Bessie be tellin a pretty young girl: "Ruby chile, fix my feathers!" When she catch sight of us without missin a beat she say: "My, my! Two *fine* lookin specimens, *uh-huhmmm*!"

Talkin that dirty talk just like Ma. Hell, I'm thinkin to myself, these blues mamas all alike.

"Ma'am," I start to say. I got my little speech prepared, but suddenly all that stuff about "bein honored to work with a legend such as yourself" is beginnin to seem pretty foolish. Anyways, Bessie interrupt me before I can get it out.

"Who you callin ma'am? Am I your mama or something?"

"Ma'am—Miss Smith…"

"Bessie! You boys best call me Bessie or don't call me nothin, y'hear?"

"Bessie, Miss Smith, I ain't no boy. I got more'n twenty-five years on me…."

"Shit, I can see that, but you got the right equipment in workin order, don't you?"

"Last time I checked."

"Then you is a boy. Don't argue with me, you never gonna win. Nobody ever does."

She see the look on my face.

"Aw, cut out that hang-dog face. Don't you know I eat boys like you for breakfast? What's shakin?"

"Uh, this here Coley Williams, Miss Smith," the roustabout say, introducin me. "Ma sendin him over on her recommendation. Thought you might have a use for him."

"Yeah, I have use for him, all right. Hah, hah, hah!"

Bessie's dressin room was in a little tent off to the side, and the Empress was sittin holdin court in there, smokin and drinkin and cacklin. That was Bessie. Onstage she look larger than life; offstage she just look big. Big-boned, big-mouthed. In that little tent she seem like a bawdy giantess with not enough room to move around. Every time she turn around she seem to be knockin something over. But when she was performin, everything she did—includin fallin off the stage—look graceful.

That was my first acquaintance with Miss Bessie. Next day I joined the show, playin guitar in the pit band, doin a bit of dancin, announcin the acts—whatever was needed.

With Ma's recommendation and all, gettin the gig was gonna be the *easy* part. The hard shot was goin to be explainin it to Vida Lee. It was now over a year since I left, sayin I be back in the spring. 'Course I didn't say *which* spring. My first thought was to tell Vida Lee I couldn't return just yet because, see, I am a necessary part of Bessie Smith's new tourin show. Vida Lee idolize Bessie, so I know if I can somehow figure a way to link my destiny with Miss Bessie's, I be all right....

So I tell Vida Lee that Bessie *insist* I come on the tour. Couldn't do the tour without me. Man, am I a cryin fool thinkin she gonna fall for that shit. Anyway, I run my line of jive and, like a flash, Vida Lee come right back at me.

"Coley," she say, "you talk about as good a line of bullshit as Herbert Hoover. The day Miss Bessie Smith can't go on without you, she better hang up her dancin shoes. Try another one, baby, and at least show me enough respect to make it a *good* one."

Long pause, and then Vida Lee—you coulda blown me over—she say: "Okay, you go along. Do what you gotta do, make us some money, and for God sakes get Miss Bessie's autograph and one of her feathers for me. And you best be back before *next* spring or I will personally hunt you down and I will show you no mercy."

Goddamn, I love to hear that woman talk. Kinda reminds me of Bessie, come to think of it. Probably best to keep those two women apart.

It was somewhere 'round the beginnin of May, time for the summer tent shows, and Bessie had a big followin in the South all 'long the eastern seaboard. She was the biggest high-salary black star in the world, or something like that. Headlinin eight acts and the pit band. Have a cast of sixty performers in a comedy extravaganza, tunes and topics called *Harlem Frolics*.

Everybody know when Bessie come to town. The band members come out in their short red coats and march through the town to drum up business playin "St. Louis Blues." Parade of other troupers wavin signs advertisin "A hot show tonight—Bessie Smith and her gang are here!" Wherever she go she stir up a lot of dust. There was posters and handbills and ladies' fans with the name of the show on it everywhere. You live in Burlington, Chapel Hill, Durham, Raleigh, Louisburg, Oxford, Henderson or Franklin—any of them towns Bessie comin to—you have to be deaf, dumb and blind not to know the Empress of the Blues was makin a royal appearance.

At the fairgrounds a huge round tent set up. Outside, they're hustlin tickets. Fifty cent gets you a wooden seat in the back, seventy-five cent for the padded ones up front. Hawkin programs, sellin Crackerjacks, hot dogs, soda pop and any old cheap novelty item.

I sneak up front just as Bessie comin out onstage. Man, it was like a Fourth of July parade. She coulda been Cleopatra comin down the Nile on her barge. Big beautiful black Cleopatra is what she be, all decked out in her exotic costumery. A white and blue satin dress with hoop skirt covered all over with strands of pearls and rubies and that crazy headgear only she coulda carried off. Looked like a cross between a football helmet and a tasseled lampshade.

Bessie goin into her last number. She seem a little wobbly to me —her drinkin sprees was legendary—and when she get to the last verse she step off the small makeshift stage, slip, grab onto a pole supportin the canvas roof and take the entire stage coverin down with her. After a minute or so Bessie come out all raggedy, her hat tilted off her head, laughin, take her bow and the whole place cheer. They stampin their feet and hollerin. As she come offstage she shout to the stagehands: "Well, I fuckin brought the house down tonight, boys, didn't I?"

You never seen Bessie perform? Man, you missed something that ain't never gonna be repeated. I'm gonna take you along so as you can catch yourself one of Bessie's shows. Might be your last chance. I'm gettin too old to tell this story, that's right, get tired just thinkin 'bout them days. Hmm, hmm, hmm.

Curtain go up and there is, for instance, the act of Rastas and Jones, a duo workin under cork—doin their act in blackface, see? You burn the cork and then you smudge it on your face. Even black folks in vaudeville use cork. Followed by Margaret Scott, a prima donna singin a ear-splittin operatic aria in Eye-talian by way of Alabama. Then comes the rightly named Three Baby Vamps, whose dancin abilities and scanty costumes generally stop the show. Then come Whistlin Rufus who finish his act with some fancy knee drops accompanied by a lady pianist. After him Little Marie come on and do a ballet dance number, a little more Ponchatrain than Swan Lake, but no matter—the audience like a little high-tone hokum. Next, Robinson and Mack come on with their bootlegger nonsense 'bout moonshine, revenuers and pissin in the still for their expensive brand. Stuff probably make no sense at all today. Didn't make much sense back then. Skit go on with some songs featurin howlin hounds and sirens and such and a bit of tipsy dancin. And then—we probably gettin to the end here but you never know—maybe there'd be a yodeler from Arkansas, followed by the Baby Ali Company and the all-singin, all-dancin trio, and then Tim and Jerry Moore with patter, songs, and hokey down-home dialogue. Tim Moore, y'know, he later be Kingfish on the *Amos 'n' Andy* TV show.

And then, *Tah-dah!* the big noise, Bessie herself! Grand entrance, bowin and throwin kisses and shakin her hips. Just this side of sultry, buxom and massive, but stately, too, shapely as a hourglass, with a high-voltage magnet for a personality. Drippin with beaded fringes, a Spanish shawl loosely draped around her shoulders, a string of pearls, a skullcap with beads and pearls sewn on to it, and a wig with shiny black hair runnin down to below her neck. Backdrop is a silhouette of magnolia trees in front of a orange sky with a big fat moon hangin there. But all that flummery and costumery she wearin in wicked contrast to the funky, down-and-dirty songs she singin.

> *You better go to the blacksmith shop*
> *   and get yourself overhauled.*
> *There's nothin about you to make a good woman fall.*
> *Nobody wants a baby when a real man can be found.*
> *You been a good old wagon, Daddy,*
> *   but you done broke down.*

She pick out a guy in the audience and "walk" him, fix him with her eyes and make him think she singin this song just for him, and this cat get so mesmerized he get up outta his seat and start walkin towards the stage like a man in a trance.

When she start singin *It's true I loves you but I won't take mistreatment any mo*, a young girl standin underneath the box begin testifyin: "That's right! Say it, sister!" Eyes wild, hair flyin like at a Pentecostal meetin.

Come the fall we head on up North. New York, Philadelphia, Chicago. In Chicago they love her, man. She in all the newspapers. Big buzz goin 'round. Out on the streets, Bessie's "Sorrowful Blues" blarin out of record stores along with Ida Cox's "Chicago Monkey Man Blues."

Bootlegger Richard Morgan wanna throw her a party. Morgan one cool-fry dude, decked out like Mr. Sportin Life hisself. Green raw silk suit, handmade shoes and a purple satin shirt with a yellow tie so bright you go blind look at it too long. Rich, flashy, let-them-good-times-roll hipster.

Richard furnish whiskey, bathtub gin to all the dives and speakeasies on the South Side. Anybody—any*black*body—servin liquor in Chicago, that was Richard Morgan's stuff. He hear Bessie gonna be in town to do a show, he'd throw a big old pigs' feet and moonshine party in her honor. Plain loved music. Crazy 'bout piano players. Anybody plays a tin whistle or a saxophone gonna be to Richard's bash.

To get them musicians in there all you gotta do is lay on a big supply of booze, broads and all the chitlins they can eat. Any given night you gonna find the musicocracy blowin their brains out and havin a ball. Jelly Roll Morton and Louis Armstrong cuttin through the smoke-filled air. You got people leavin their own funerals to attend one of his parties.

Naturally Bessie not gonna miss this one. She poke her head in the door, smell the fried food, liquor, smoke and sweat and she say: "Oooh, mama, the funk is flyin!"

Out there in the main rooms you got hustlers, gangsters, fat cats and hepcats. All the slickest, coolest jivers and smoothy strivers you ever seen in one place all duded-up in their silk and satin threads. It was the color-blindest fashion parade of dandified dudes you ever did spy in one place at one time, all jivin and high-fivin. And Richard Morgan's little nephew Lionel Hampton sittin over there in the corner.

Ain't nothin like a bootlegger's party, and you gotta take my word for it but this the best party I *ever* attended. You got Louis Armstrong on cornet, Miss Lil Hardin on piano, and now the great Bessie Smith herself gonna sing. She get up there and Richard—he in awe of Bessie—hush everybody up. Morgan didn't do that for *nobody* else, not even for Louis Armstrong. Bessie known to have a wicked temper and he didn't want no Tennessee hurricane tearin his house apart. All the folks laughin and talkin and carryin on, but he make everybody be quiet. *Shhhhhhhh!*

She sing the "Empty Bed Blues" with all them double meanins and Louis Armstrong's humorous cornet like a goofy cat clownin at a party. And let's see, oh yeah, she done the "Sobbin Hearted Blues" from the session she cut with Louis back in New York. This was so great to hear live, man, with Satchmo answerin Bessie phrase for phrase. Like when Bessie sing "daddy" Louis plays "daddy" on his cornet. But he learn to cool it on the improvisin shit when Bessie around—Bessie don't want no cat on a horn upstagin her.

> *You brag to women that I was your fool.*
> *Now I got them sobbin hearted blues.*
>
> *The sun may shine in my back door someday.*
> *Oh baby, the sun may shine in my back door someday.*
> *But I won't take mistreatment any more.*

Man, that was something. Louis blowin curlicues of blue smoke around them words.

Bessie was by nature a generous soul, more into raisin people up than mashin 'em down. She hand out money to strangers on the street. Her generosity extend even to "them bitches" (her sisters in the profession). But not always! The so-called refined type of singer like your Mamie Smiths or your Ethel Waterses, now them girls really got under her skin. "Them Miss Mamies and Miss Ethels can kiss my royal ass!" *Ladies* of the blues, you know. "Fuck, ladies ain't got no goddamn business in the blues in the *first* place. Let them missies stick to that Tin Pan Alley shit and leave the funky stuff to them what cooks."

Them skinny, good-lookin, high-yeller broads with "good" hair that appeal to the fancy folk up North really got up her nose. "Go ahead, let 'em sing to the ofays. See how long they gonna keep eatin by singin the blues to *them* folks. Hah!" What really got her goat was them chicks was sellin records like you would not believe. One time down at the "91" Theatre in Atlanta I see Ethel Waters comin in backstage, gonna stop by and pay her respects. Ethel was skinny, good-lookin, light-skin and high-tone. You wouldn't need much more than that for Miss Bessie to find a grievance with you. Soon as I seen her there I thought, "*Oo-oo*, here it come!" But Ethel, she one cool lady and have a sense of humor to go along with it. You come around Bessie you *better* have a sense of humor.

"Come here, long goody." say Bessie. "You ain't so bad. It's only that I never dreamed anyone would be able to do this to me in my own territory and with my own people. And you damn well know you can't sing worth a fuck!" Ethel just laughed.

Did I ever tell you about Bessie and them high society types? Well, 'round this time, you got some elevated white people goin through one of their periodic bouts of idolizin the primitive, untutored soul of black folks. The present crop of seekers after the savage soul come swarmin uptown to Small's Paradise or Connie's Inn or the Cotton Club. They have foresworn Beethoven and Tchaikovsky, and they are mad for jazz and blues and the aboriginal souls who produce this tribal jive.

The leader of this pack was Carl Van Vechten. "Carlo" to his friends and us fellow savages. He was so misguided and foolish that it was almost impossible to take offense at him. He'd written a book 'bout the nice niggers he have met up on 125th Street. Have the fuckin nerve to call it *Nigger Heaven*. After much consideration of the problem, the man have come to the conclusion there be good niggers, too.

Carlo loved the blues and big black men. He had this fancy decorated-up apartment on West 55th Street. Black ceilin, silver stars, moody red lights. Done up like a high-tone whorehouse. His wife, Fania Marinoff—she once been a Russian ballerina—was a tiny woman with a high squeaky voice. Fania and Carlo hold court in that apartment.

Bessie was in town 'round then doin a show called *Mississippi Days,* so every night Carlo and the tiny Fania would come by the theater and stop in Bessie's dressin room and gush. Carlo worshipped Bessie. He call her "my big beautiful Black Aphrodite."

Porter Grainger, who composed music for the show, got very tight with Carlo and Fania. He was a dandy—pressed suits, spats, walkin cane, tilted derby—and a homosexual, so he right at home in this scene, baby. He so afraid of Bessie that he even went to bed with her on her command.

Porter the one I figure set it up, this big party they wanna throw Bessie. They want Bessie to *sing* at it, too, so all their fancy friends can hear the Tennessee Nightingale. When Porter tell Bessie about it, she not all that overjoyed. "Some fuckin party," she say, but she go anyway. Gets me to carry her over there. Spendin so much time at the Empress's elbow I have become something of a confidant to Miss Bessie. Not that discretion was ever one of her failins.

"They think I am some kinda freak, y'know, but fuck 'em. They are the freaks, baby, they just don't know it."

Bessie breezes past all them highfalutin people payin her compliments: "Oh, Miss Smith, you were *soooooo* fabulous…. Oh, Miss Bessie, you are the diva of syncopation" and all that high society jive.

"They say you can sing two diatonic notes at the same time, Miss Smith, is that true?"

To which Bessie come back: "What kinda pickup line is that, Jack?"

"So refreshingly direct, isn't she, Carlo?"

Bessie feel the way things goin she need to get a little *more* direct:

"Fuck this shuckin, get me some goddamn booze!"

"Well, of course, darling, how remiss of me. How would you like to slip into a nice dry martini?"

"*Whaaaaaat?*" Bessie's voice like a foghorn honkin across the room. "Slip into a dry *what*? What kinda girl you takes me for anyway? Ain't you got some whiskey, man? I don't know about no dry martinos, nor *wet* ones neither. The only thing around here I want wet is my—"

Porter Grainger musta felt it might be a little early in the evenin to get *this* down, so he grab her real fast and pull her over to the piano.

Carlo confer with the butler: "Mario, I am sure we can scare up something in the line of what our ebony diva requires, can't we?"

Bessie not about to wait for this whiskey search. She pick up a vase, throw out the flowers, fill it up with damn near a pint of gin and downs it. You might as well be pourin gasoline in the fireplace. It was gonna be a night none of 'em was ever gonna forget, and Bessie's singin probably the least memorable part of it.

Every time some society cat come over to pay her a compliment she reach down and grab his crotch along with some salty critique of the man's equipment: "Where's the fuckin hambone, Jack?" or "Hell, this ain't gonna be *no* use to me."

And as for the women, Bessie have no use for any of 'em.

"*Oweee*! I tell you there some *ugly* old pussy runnin 'round here tonight!"

It was gettin to be a mite more primitive than they bargain for. Best thing was to get her to sing.

Grainger start playin a few chords and everybody clap and that the only cue Bessie need.

She go into a funky version of "Workhouse Blues," her boobs bobbin up and down like two black puppies. Every time she hand Carlo a empty glass he refill it. Oh mama!

"This gonna be it," she say as she go into her last song. Some of the guests just about faint when she move into that raunchy Lucille Bogan number, "Shave 'em Dry":

> *I got nipples on my titties big as the end of my thumb,*
> *I got sumpin between my legs will make a dead man come.*
> *Aw, baby, won't you shave 'em dry?*
> *Won't you grind me, baby, grind me till I cry?*
>
> *Now your nuts hang down like a damn bell clapper,*
> *And your dick stands up like a steeple.*
> *Your goddamned asshole looks like a church door,*
> *And the crabs walks in like people,*
> *Oh, shave 'em dry....*

Soon as it's done Grainger grab me and say: "Let's get Mama outta here quick before she pull down her panties."

As she leavin, Fania Van Vechten grabs her by the arm.

"Miss Smith, *daaarling*, you are surely not departing without giving me a goodbye kiss?"

Little Fania close her eyes and plant a big wet smack right on Bessie's lips.

And damn if she don't belt Fania with a right hook, flatten her and sweeps out of the joint draggin her ermine coat behind her. But listen, this how smitten Carlo is with Bessie. He leave Fania groanin on the ground and follow Bessie out into the hall like she's the fuckin Queen of England.

"It's all right, Miss Smith, I hope you weren't too put out. And may I say how *magnificent* you were tonight!"

We manage to drag Bessie into the elevator, still bitchin and complainin.

"Watcha doin, you bunch of pansies? You boys meant to be *protectin* Bessie."

The idea of Porter Grainger and me protectin Bessie, it would be like some crazy zookeeper sayin to you, "Stand over here inside this cage and see no one come along and bother this rhinoceros while I'm gone."

She milk that story dry, tellin and retellin it for months, and it get wilder and woolier each time she repeat it. Whenever she high and in a good mood out it come.

"Shee-it, you shoulda seen them ofays lookin at me like I be some kinda singin monkey. So I asks them motherfuckas, 'You want to see the genuine article?'" And who cares if it never have happen the way she tell it. It *could've*. It almost did. And, you know, we hadn't of been there, she would have, too. Pulled down her drawers and show them folks her pussy. They woulda probably applauded her for that, too.

21

Reckless Blues

We out on the road again, Bessie gettin restless and ornery. In a low mood on account of things not goin well in her affair with Lillian, a sweet-faced, sulky-tempered chorine that Bessie was sweet on. Type that could seem cute if you thought she was cute, if not, not. She was the little dancer Bessie initiate at the eggnog and corn liquor Christmas party back in Tennessee. Didn't I tell you about that one? Hell, if I was to tell you about every damn party we had, we be here till doomsday. Anyway, things not goin too well in Bessie's love life.

"She's pouty and I wanna get rowdy," says Bessie. "C'mon Ruby, let's go have ourselves some fun." Ruby was cute and perky. She was light-skinned and sophisticated but real fun and game for anything, which you had to be to run with Bessie. And off they slink to the buffet flats. So-called "good time flats." A buffet flat is a place you get anything you want. Bootleg booze, gamblin, a different sex show goin on in every room. Caterin mainly to thrill seekers. And for a little more bread you could also join in the action if that was your thing.

Bessie was well-known in them places. You have to know somebody to get into this sort of joint because them buffet setups always was in someone's home. Stuff goin down in them establishments make your eyeballs pop outta your head, singe your whiskers. Men dressed as women, women actin like men, lesbians, threesomes, tongue baths—you name it.

Bessie mainly like to peek in at the shows. Time I go with her there was this fat broad billed as "the educated pussy," does tricks with a cigar and a Coca Cola bottle. Bessie love that nonsense, man, talk 'bout it for days.

Bessie weren't all that political but the buffet flats was Bessie's idea of one of the basic freedoms. "It's in the Constitution, baby. Life, liberty, and the pursuit of whatever you damn well please." Between the climb and the fall, Bessie have six of the most glorious, debauched, blessed years that anyone ever lived.

The spookiest presence on them tours was Jack Gee, Bessie's husband. Tall, handsome, illiterate and violent scoundrel. Been a night watchman, and one time the cat save Bessie's life durin a holdup, which was the last entirely unselfish thing he ever done for her. Things start to get really messed up when Jack decide he gonna manage Bessie—Jack couldn't even manage hisself. He could count the money, though. Loved handlin that bread, man. Bessie usta do imitations of Jack hunched over his piles of greenbacks, countin on his fingers and toes, stackin 'em up, and tyin 'em up with rubber bands.

Jack usta play the troupers for their wages, generally win, too. Deck always stacked in his favor. The chorines and the stagehands constantly complainin to Bessie but Bessie say, "You dumb enough to play him for your money, he *should* take it back." As long as the money rollin in and he gamblin and connivin, Jack happy.

Bessie a party girl. That swingin, reckless broad on a bender in "Gimme a Pigfoot," that's Bessie right there, man. 'Course Mr. Jack always put a pall over everything if he suspect other people havin fun. Bessie have a trick when she want to ditch him.

"See that man back there?" she tell the taxi driver. "The mean-lookin sonofabitch wavin his fist at us? He just held up somebody with a gun. So step on it, cabbie, 'cause he after our asses."

But she catch Jack foolin 'round, man, Bessie ready to haul off and pull hair. She was hell on wheels once you got her riled. Might say of Bessie what she say about Black Mountain people in that song —they use gunpowder just to sweeten their tea.

Jealousy her main defect, the main cause bein the notorious Mr. Gee who always messin with them chorines. Jealousy—and cheatin —their main folly. They get theirselves overheated 'bout just nothin, which I surmise mean they was in love. They was meant for each other, those two.

"That did it! That done did it but good!" Never mind what or who or when, 'cause when you hear that operatic chittlin voice rattlin the china you don't need to know the details.

What occasioned this particular ruckus is Jack gettin involved with a brownskin chippie from another show. This Gertie was a ambitious little hussy who was ready to do anything it took to get out of the chorus line, and she seen Jack as her ticket. Jack, he love them yellow women with red hair. Now this one was sendin Bessie right upside the wall.

Still, no little chippie gonna stop her show from goin on. Now, one of the routines Bessie do was a Southern kerchief-headed mammy number. Bandanna, red dress with white polka dots, and her behind all padded out with a big pillow stuck in the back. Look like a enormous overstuffed rag doll. Part of the skit involve her sweepin the floor. The most dramatic sweepin you ever gonna see. She could sweep the Pharoah's army into the Red Sea with that broom, I tell you. This was pure Bessie. Sweepin "all the mess" outta her sight —which was just what she intended to do. At some point them chorines come prancin onstage all in their peasant costumes with the ribbons and wreaths on their head. Doin a Russian-type dance, you know. What Russian dancers doin in a mammy skit don't ask me 'cause I do not know. This vaudeville, baby.

Bessie come in wieldin a broom, sweepin the stage and givin the girls a look of aggravation. They gettin in her face and she sweepin them off the stage just like one of them old mammies would. "I don't care what kinda dancin fools comin in here, they ain't gettin in the way of my housekeepin!" Like that.

Now Gertie was a aspiring singer herself, so on top of her havin a affair with Bessie's husband, she *studyin* Bessie. Good luck, baby. You can study a tornado all you like but can you *be* one?

One night, smack in the middle of her act, Bessie spy this Gertie lurkin in the shadows, tryin to watch the show from behind a pillar. Forget the sweepin, forget the Russian dancin girls, Bessie stop the show dead in its tracks.

With her boomin voice, she holler: "Gonna buy you a damn ticket, let you sit up front, bitch, 'cause you my best customer."

The audience all laugh. Gertie start runnin up the aisle.

"Stop that woman! She done stole my man!" Bessie shoutin at the top of her lungs and as she climb down the stairs into the orchestra pit, all the while swingin her broom like it was a two-headed axe. This old Southern mammy with her broomstick chasin a chippie up the aisle. The spectators still thinkin this part of the performance, they laughin and laughin until they fallin outta their seats.

"You motherless bitch, you can't keep up with me, you better get outta my way."

The women down with this 'cause they have heard *themselves* sayin it more than once. So up the aisle come Bessie, barrelin like the Midnight Special. She bustlin so hard that the pillow stuck in the back of her dress fall out. The audience go crazy. Bessie start laughin, too. Nobody laughin harder than Bessie herself. But then she remembers what she after. Out through the doors and into the street after the terrified Gertie go Bessie still dressed in her costume. Audience follow her out onto the sidewalk; they have never seen a performance like this in their entire lives. Tremblin, Gertie is tryin to find sanctuary by sneakin into the hotel across from the theater. But she have another thing comin if she think that a hotel lobby gonna intimidate Bessie, who bustles into the hotel in all her wide outfit—like a sofa tryin to squeeze through the revolvin doors—and then get stuck there.

Half the town come out to see what goin on. Big fat red mattress with red polka dots on it, *jammed* in the door and hollerin like hell had broken out into the world. It take two porters to pull Bessie outta the door where she stuck. Now she in the lobby of the hotel and her voice sound like a boomin soprano in a opera.

Grabs Gertie by her long hair, drags her outside and through the mud. The two of them women goin at it rollin in the mud, Bessie beatin on her with the broom. The both of them look like mud pies—you can hardly tell one from the other. Jack by this time have heard about the ruckus downtown and come to see what goin on. Confronted with Bessie and Gertie lookin like two clay-covered statues, Jack glued to the ground hisself.

This frozen moment give Gertie time to get up, still screamin.

"One of these days I'm gonna climb up there and...."

"You ever get up on my stage they better start sellin tickets—'cause, bitch, I'm gonna make you jump through a hoop and bark."

'Round about the end of my time with Bessie come the Great Flood of 1927. The heavens darken, the sun blot out from the sky and it rain and it rain both night and day. A visitation from God, they say, for the wickedness of men. The real cause most likely bein them engineers messin with the Mississippi, buildin levees and jetties and such. Want to tidy up the big old river. Straightnin the Mississippi, are they outta their minds?

How many people drowned, no one really know, and black folks hit the worst. Herded into detention camps, pressed into forced labor. Like in Biblical prophecy, the whole world comin to an end.

The first we see of it is at the end of January 1927 outside of Vicksburg, when Bessie's train pull into the station. The tracks run along the levee, up on the high ground, see? Water, water everywhere. Flood gettin worse and worse, gatherin force. Levees overflowin, houses washed away. You see families huddled together on the rooftops, old ladies stranded up trees. Beds, iceboxes, bloated carcasses of dead cattle, cars and coffins floatin down the street.

Along come a lady clingin onto a torn-apart outhouse hollerin. We all laughin, you know, not at the woman's plight, mind—more like you can't keep them Delta women down. As she come floatin down by the station I notice something familiar about this woman. Somethin mighty familiar. "BESSIE!" she shoutin. "MISS BESSIE SMITH!" Bessie goin on and wavin to her, "God bless you, chile! You know the Lord gonna take care of you. Lord take care of *all* his chillen." But the woman not lookin for a blessin from the Empress of the Blues, thank you very much. She on a *mission*. She lookin for her man and, *uh oh*, as soon as she draw near to where we standin I know who she is. The unstoppable Vida Lee. I duck down behind Bessie and crawl away behind the baggage cart. Lord, I am a miserable coward. But you the bravest man on earth you never gonna win with a woman under normal circumstances; now, how you gonna make your point with a woman floatin down the middle of the street on a outhouse?

Vida Lee carryin on at full throttle:

"You see that no-good Coley Williams been travelin with you, you tell him get his sorry ass back home right quick or there ain't gonna *be* no home. He expect me to wait around for him, he badly mistaken." And she goin on and on in this fashion all the while floatin by down the street. As she disappear from sight, you can still hear her callin: "I'm gonna move over to Memphis, get me a job...."

"Why, you old sly boots!" says Bessie. "You got yourself a good woman at home and you roamin the land winkin your big brown eyes at every pretty girl come around? Shame on you, Coley Williams! I think I been a bad influence on you. You best put on your wadin boots and find that woman. That is *love*, baby, and you abuse it you gonna get what comin to ya, hear?"

Water was already so high they come to meet us at the station in rowboats. Hotel was all flooded up, too, so they carry us over to the funeral parlor next door to the theater. Not the kinda accommodation Bessie used to. She ain't pleased one bit.

"You best think again, you get a notion I'm gonna stay *here* tonight. I ain't sleepin with no dead men." Bessie so agitated she can't sleep. But there was nowheres else to go. There was a lot of other people takin shelter there and soon as they see Bessie was among them they all start to hollerin:

"Please, Miss Bessie, sing us the blues 'bout the flood." "Yeah, do us them 'Back Water Blues!'"

Well, Bessie didn't know nothin 'bout no "Back Water Blues." She hadn't never even *thought* 'bout it, but that not gonna stop her, however, no sir.

"Get your guitar out, Coley, we gonna entertain these good folks."

I begin strummin and Bessie just improvise a few verses on the spot of her "famous old song," the "Back Water Blues."

Mmm Mmm, I can't move no mo.
Mmm Mmm, I can't move no mo.
There ain't no place for a poor ol gal to go.

Back Water Blues done caused me to pack my things and go.
Back Water Blues done caused me to pack my things and go.
'Cause mah house fell down, and I can't live there no mo.

Hearin that I began thinkin about *my* house and set out to find Vida Lee. Now you would think a woman on a outhouse would be something to be remarked upon but nobody remember seein her and I began to fear the worst.

On the other hand…I *know* Vida Lee. Ain't no li'l old Mississippi flood gonna hinder that woman. She made of hard wood, sound hinges and a powerful dose of what-you-mean-I-can't-do-that? So I'm not all that worried, see? More concerned what gonna happen to *me* when she catch up with Coley Williams. More afraid of that than of the damn Mississippi jumpin its levees. So I proceeded on my cowardly way till I could figure out what I was gonna do—or say. Show must go on, right? You see Vida Lee, be sure and tell her that.

When it rains five days, and the sky turns dark as night,
When it rains five days, and the sky turns dark as night,
Then trouble's takin place in the lowlands at night.

But neither flood nor hail nor dark of night keep Bessie from her appointed rounds. Bessie a force of nature. When we play Concord, North Carolina you see not even the Devil hisself gonna mess with Bessie. It was a hot night in July, hot as Hades itself. The generator we use for the electricity and the lights was heatin up the tents something fierce. It was *broilin* in there, man. I close to passin out. I don't play on the last couple of numbers before Ruby come on so I figure who's gonna miss me? Well, you *know* who. But I was too hot to care right then.

I step outside and walk around the tent. Smokin a cigarette, you know, takin in the night air, when I see outta the corner of my eye a bunch of hooded figures gruntin and mumblin in the dark—must've been ten, fifteen of them. They gettin ready to collapse the tent. A dozen or so Ku Klux Klanners in their robes intent on shuttin down Bessie's "nigger show."

The Klan didn't mess with Ma Rainey's shows on account of Ma playin mainly to black people. You didn't see too many white folk comin to Ma's shows, but Bessie was different. Sometimes maybe a third of the audience white. They sittin in a different area, separated off from the rest of us.

I wasn't scared, I was paralyzed. My hair was standin up on my head, my brains had froze and I hadn't a damn clue what to do.

From outside the tent I could hear Bessie just comin off the stage—she take a short break about then and Ruby do some dancin while Bessie go backstage to change costumes. I know it's her break 'cause I can hear the audience hollerin for her to return. I sneak back inside the tent. When Bessie catch sight of me I see her open her mouth—it was all happenin in slow motion, understand? The fear is causin everything to slow down. She about to shout at me for not bein in the pit with the band when I blurt out what I seen.

"*Some* shee-it!" says Bessie—her standard response to any aggravatin situation. "Tell the prop boys follow me out, I gonna see what this mess be."

Everybody else but Bessie draw back as they approach. The fear was so strong you could taste it. Bessie just standin there, hands on hips, ten feet from them Klansmen. She take one look at them white hoods and say:

"What the fuck you boys think you doin? I go get the whole damn tent out here to kick your sorry asses if I have to. You just pick up them silly bedsheets and go back where the hell you came from!"

At first, the Klansmen don't do nothin; they was too stunned even to move. They just stood there lookin back at Bessie cursin them. Then they slink off into the night like they fadin away.

"And as for you fools," she tell us, "you ain't nothin but a bunch of sissies."

Bessie finish up her performance as if nothin happen. Nobody—
nobody!—dare mess with that woman.

Bessie could read the signs like any of them doctors in the Delta.
And she was right about them omens. Somethin bad was comin down
the pike. 1927 was the worst year there had ever been for black theaters.
Radio and the talkies slowly encroachin on what was once the territory
of vaudeville. People begin thinkin the travelin shows too crude and
countrified for them. But it was the new talkin pictures that really
did 'em in.

Ma Rainey have to shut down her latest show, the Arkansas
Swiftfoot, and hitch up with Boize DeLegge's Bandanna Babies,
and even they wasn't doin too well. Several of the big Harlem clubs
close down. Things was goin to hell all over.

There was rumors goin 'round that Bessie had been reduced to
sellin chewin gum and candy in the theatre aisle, but that ain't true.
It weren't like the old days, but she was still makin a livin. When
the TOBA, the Theater Owners and Bookers Association—the agency
that booked Bessie and Ma's shows and all the other black travelin
shows, Tough On Black Asses, we called it—went outta business,
you didn't have to be no gypsy to read the writin on the wall. You
know the world fallin to pieces when Ma Rainey and Bessie Smith
havin trouble gettin work and two white crackers doin blackface voices
on the *Amos 'n' Andy Show* got the most popular program on radio.

With the way things goin, the show gotta tighten its belt. Bessie
couldn't carry me no more and time come for me to split. I knew it,
but nobody sayin nothin, hopin it gonna just go away.

Then one mornin the Empress call me. She have a dream and
she tellin me what she saw, because this the celestial news and am I
gonna take heed? You best believe I will, 'cause Bessie, man, she
was the funky prophetess. She don't have to go out in no wilderness,
she just tap right into it anytime she want day or night. And like any
respectable Southerner, she believe in the power of dreams. A snake
talk to you in your dreams, you sit up and listen.

"Coley," she say, "I seen stuff last night that trouble me."

"That so?"

"Yes, it *is* so, and it happen to be about *you*, so may I continue?"

"Do I have any choice?"

"Chile, what I seen in this dream be a great big terrible flood. A worse flood than the Mississippi flood, understand? This thing comin, gonna be *vast*. Like Noah, baby. The whole damn world under water. You only see the top of the Rocky Mountains peekin out. All the big cities flooded, all the people in the world lamentin.... And you know what that all say to me?"

"No."

"It tellin me you best go to your burrow, baby, take care of your nest. Go back to your woman and pray like hell she take you back. Get down on your knees and beg. 'Cause any woman got *you* on her mind while barely keepin from drownin in that big mutha flood, she gotta love you bad, baby. You go through your whole life with a lantern lookin for a woman like that."

And so I went on home. The Delta look like the bottom of the sea where everything lost in the world ended up. The fields strewn with sheds and cars and suitcases and rusty iceboxes. Like a shipwreck on dry land. The flood have devastated everything.

I tried to point out to Vida Lee that it was actually a good thing I went on the tent show circuit with Bessie.

"Look honey, had I been home and planted the corn and cotton it woulda been washed away anyways. Now we got a little money left over from bein on the road with Bessie. We can buy that piece of bottom land we talked about, some seed, and a mule. Maybe even fix the house a bit from what I saved up."

"That's as may be," says Vida Lee. "But from now on, you even *think* about driftin off, you a dead man."

To which I could only reply: "I love you too, honey. I love you too."

Phantom King of the Delta Blues

The Delta flat, flat, flat. Flat like a drum. Out in the countryside, sound travel like a telephone wire. You hear things a long way off. Conversation goin on miles away you hear it clear as a bell. You the least bit troubled in mind it can mess your head. Start hearin wiggy things out there. Spirits talkin at ya outta the darkness. Any place flat as Coahoma County gonna have ghosts in it.

That particular night my mind was in open tunin, my nerves was singin. Beginnin to feel those old blues in E comin on. Talkin to myself, talkin in my sleep, wearin out the rug, drinkin the whiskey river dry. Whatever I do, I hear that crazy sound goin 'round and 'round my brain.

Have a mind to call the operator, say, "Hello, Central, gimme 209, I just wanna talk to my baby one more time."

'Round this time Vida Lee and me was havin our usual disagreement. In the form of either you settle yourself down and take care a business *or else*. So I'm doin a little or else for the time bein. Small type experiment in livin on my own. Meanwhile, meet a lady at a jook joint.

Now the lady in question, Miss Ella, did not tell me she married. I ain't lyin to you, I am too damn old to mess with marrieds. Say she *estranged*. Not estranged enough, though, 'cause her daddy come back and he a *big* muthafucka. Six-foot-four, two-hundred-and-fifty pounds of pig-eyed spite.

She say, "Gimme a coupla weeks, Coley, and I straighten it right out, I swear." Meantime her man was workin over in Tunica and he hear we been seen together and he didn't care too much for that so he's aimin on comin by and *kill* me. Sonofabitch mean and ugly enough to do it, too. Shit! I ain't no brawlin fool. Still and all I is in *love*, nothin messy, just wanna *see* her, know what I mean?

All them thoughts runnin 'round my head as I pass along the outskirts of Lula that night. I was already shook up, when across the night air I hear a sound so high and strange I stopped where I was. A eerie *Ooooooooh-hooo-hoooo* echoed by glass scrapin on a bone. What that sound like to wake the dead?

> *Ununnimmin lilimminnim.*
> *Blues fallin down like hail.*
> *Blues fallin down like hail.*

Black rain, black rain seepin all through my brain. A steady *ka-chunk-a-ka-chunk ka-chunk-a-ka-chunk ka-chunk-a-ka-chunk* like a old freight train short of breath and pullin outta Clarksdale depot in the freezin rain. Blink of your brain, that freight turn into a rollin boogie piano. Steam-engine piano pantin up that grade. Sound of big shoes walkin across the hot Mississippi night.

Grave spider fingers runnin through them strings. *It keep me with ramblin mind, rider, every old place I go.* A voice moanin, like the wind itself worryin your mind.

> *I can tell the wind is risin,*
> *Leaves tremblin on the tree.*
> *Minnumn-lunninumn-limminnim-lunninumn.*

Somebody playin guitar out there in the night. Whoever he was, weren't no sharecropper strummin "Careless Love" on his porch. Cat holdin a seance with that guitar. Agitatin the spirits. The *notes* themselves was spooked. Conjurin up dark pictures. Take your mind with 'em step-by-step, stumblin down, down, down some doomy staircase. Silence and terror, baby. It weren't long before I heard the sound again. Had it been a hundred years, I woulda known it.

Couldn't go straight through town on account of a little matter of not wantin to run into that gentleman thought I was sweet on his wife. I was more scared of gettin shot by Jimmy Culpepper than any old ghost. Fact is I'd like to meet some ghosts and ask them a few questions. Straighten a few things out. Blues bein the ghost music.

Got to the big iron gates wrought all with angels and saints. Weren't gonna walk *through* no cemetery. I ain't that crazy. Creepin along the stone wall I got under the old cypress tree and I hear a sound so chillin my blood froze. A high whine like a power line hummin. A demon! I ain't all that superstitious, understand, but it's a whole lot easier to disbelieve in demons if you ain't never *seen* one.

Moon slip behind a cloud, creepy sound of a whippoorwill—who ever said the cry of the whippoorwill a pretty sound? It the cry of a departed soul if you ever heard it.

Heard my sainted long gone granny singin: *Coley, Coley, Coley, where you goin, chile?*

Just 'bout died of fright. I hid in the bushes.

"Fool! Come forth!" say a loud mockin voice.

Thought it be Cousin Guede, graveyard spirit. Look up and see a man—or were it a demon?—sittin on a tombstone lookin as slick and shiny as if someone just took him outta a bandbox. Pinstripe suit, big old starch cuffs shootin out of his sleeves, fedora hat on his head, shoes got a high polish on them. Holdin a Kalamazoo guitar, the one Gibson used to make with the big hole in the middle. And he commence singin that crazy ditty again:

> *Coley, Coley, Coley, where you goin, chile?*
> *Been waitin on you a long, long while.*

Man talkin to hisself in a graveyard is generally something to be avoided. Man *singin* in a graveyard, you best run like hell. He smiled me a big grin.

"How you know my name?" I ask him.

"Oh man, I knows a whole *mess* a things. Seen 'em through my moon eye, dig? Seen stuff you ain't never dreamed of. Seen the table set at Judgment Day, seen angel wings of satin. Hear *you*, uh huh, talkin in your sleep. Hear what the *dead* say...." Here he paused.

"And your case bad, Mr. Williams, real bad. I see two trains runnin and, baby, they ain't runnin your way. *Hawh, hawh, hawh.*" He commence laughin and laughin till he fall down on the ground.

Up close he not all that scary. Short, baby-faced dude. Small bones. Frail. And drunk. Had a pint of Doug Harper hundred proof, which he had near killed. Offer me a swig. Wavy hair, sportin fine clothes. Seem no more than a kid. A kid that can't stop hisself from laughin at his own stupid joke.

"What so damn funny?"

"You. You got that look, Coley. Who the bitch?"

"Now looky here!"

"Ooooh we got it bad, baby. Got them mean old kiss-the-pillow-take-a-mouthful-of-sugar-drink-a-gallon-of-turpentine-blues."

He was toyin with me all right. But he done it in a light, humorous way. Play a little funky riff on the guitar.

> *I got this notion, got it lodged inside my head.*
> *I got this notion, got it lodged inside my head.*
> *Hole where I used to fish, Coley fishin there instead.*
>
> *Monkey stuck his finger in that old "Good Gulf Gas."*
> *Monkey stuck his finger in that old "Good Gulf Gas."*

Go on and on in this manner for a time. Seem like he could have gone on into next week. All the while I'm wonderin is this the same cat as was playin them melancholy blues back there? Hell, no way that could be. See, this fella here weren't nothin more than a common joker.

"I know how it go," he tellin me. "One day you fine, the next day you in love. You need to get yourself a hand, boy. Some kinda conjure woman what you need. Go see the gypsy, pay the doctor a visit, knock upon the Mysterious Ethiopian's door. Folks nowadays don't believe in that conjuration shit and I feel sorry for 'em. Back where I come from, you have a problem you go see the two-headed lady. That witch could make a jug of lemonade into a pint of Wild Turkey. You was in trouble, she was definitely the bitch to see. 'Course you need a charm bag. 'Bring me shavins from a elephant tusk,' she gonna tell you. 'Plus a toad's eye, one gator scale, and a feather of a kingfisher.'"

Jesus, now he offerin up advice 'bout root doctors and such. There was no way to determine did he believe in this hoodoo stuff or was he shuckin me. I got up to take a leak. *Outside* the cemetery—even I am too damn superstitious to pee on the dead. When I come back he was sittin with his back to a headstone playin his guitar.

The mood had changed. Paid me no mind whatsoever. It was just him and his guitar in that graveyard. Long delicate spidery fingers that creep out and grab the strings.

There was that sound again. The notes was paintin a dark, starless road with a lone stooped figure makin his way through the chilled rain. For him everything is lost. *Uhhh-uhh-uhh-ummmmm.* Creepin along my spine like the moan of a lost soul. West African bird of the brain howlin down your mind. High, eerie, lonesome hellhound sound of that old spirit so deep down in the ground. Mean old moanin animal wake you up outta your bed, bother you all day till you let it out.

Which is how I came to meet Robert Johnson. In a graveyard, that's right. Fittin place to meet up with the Phantom King of the Delta Blues.

Coupla weeks later I'm out on the street. Hush, somebody callin my name.

"Coley, Coley, my man, you just the cat I want to see."

I am his buddy, his hangin-out-with simpatico dude. Don't ask why.

"They tell me you a mean muthafucka with a guitar."

"RL," I says. That's what they call him on account of his first and second names—Robert and Leroy. "RL, I heard you playin up there in the cemetery and I ain't never gonna be close to touchin you, man."

"Friday night, cat, I got a gig out at Harper's Ford, country supper type thing. Figure I could use a extra pair of hands."

What would I say to playin with this cat? You gotta be kiddin. But duetin ain't exactly what he got in mind. When I come to meet RL outside the feed store I see him sittin there for his ride. But wait a minute.

"Ain't none of my business but seems to me you done forgot something, RL."

"What's that?"

"You ain't carryin no guitar."

"Pawned it. Figure we do the gig, make ourselves twelve, fifteen bucks and then I can break my guitar outta the shop."

Robert got a restless spirit. You want to hang with RL you best put on your travelin shoes 'cause that dude always ready to move on. You *gotta* move, like the song say. Stay in a town three weeks, you wear out that town. They got you down, heard everything you got. Get outta town before they draw a bead on you. That was RL's philosophy.

"A drifter be a natural target, man," RL say. "Everybody beat on you. Cops, women, preachers. You wanna hit the road before they clock you. Slide back into town three, four months later. Everybody be sayin, 'Where you been, man? Ain't nobody been through here play like you since.' They *love* your ass, but if you had of stayed there, they have run you out on a rail. Human nature, Coley, can't ponder it. You gotta watch your tail feathers."

RL played all over the Mississippi Delta and Arkansas. Clarksdale, Rosedale, Friar's Point, Lula, Coahoma, Midnight, Sunflower, Jackson, Itta Bena, Tchula, Drew, Yazoo City, Beulah, Lamont, as well as Tunica, Robinsonville and up in the northern Delta area—Marianna, Hughes, Brickeys, Marvell. Sometimes he ditch me, go on alone. I catch up and he slip off again. Sometimes he glad to see me, sometimes he groan when he see me comin. And if he left me along the way I doubt he hardly notice the fact that I be gone. I *know* he ditch me on purpose many the time, but I pay it no mind.

Catch a train, hitch a ride on a pickup truck, back of a corn wagon. Sometimes we had money, sometimes we didn't. Sometimes we had food, sometimes we eat as the swine did eat. Sometimes we had some place to stay, sometimes we bed down in the alley, up in a hayloft. It was a fine way a life, that's right.

Up and down the county, all through the Delta, RL got people talkin. Everybody say RL the new thing. New King of the Delta Blues. Folks lookin for the new Charley Patton.

He was increasin, Charley was decreasin. Robert Johnson's boogie spread over the Delta like wildfire. Started out late twenties, playin standards like "Pallet on the Floor." Friday nights he hobo down to Jackson. Most musicianers, talkin about back in 1931 or '32, if you was gettin four or five dollars for playin, you was gettin good pay.

RL study Charley 'cause he the one to put it all together. He was the Book of Genesis for the blues. But Charley was a clown, see, a rowdy type a guy. Tall stories accumulate about Charley, but no such yarns formed 'round RL. He was too slippery for that. Stories 'bout RL begin to happen only after he gone—dead and gone. *Spooky* stories. People always ready to believe almost anything of RL on account of him bein so secretive and sly. You could not read that cat.

Robert in his early twenties and I'm like pushin forty but that make little difference in this kinda life. We both bums as far as the world concerned. A young bum and a old bum ramblin down the road. Happy to tag along with him even when I weren't that welcome. You don't meet too many cats like him, man, and, well, when you hang with the wizard, you just gotta learn to swallow your pride.

'Course trouble follow you everywhere if you a drifter, and you add the blues to that, you gotta keep your eyes open. Playin the blues attract strange people, crazy people—'cause see, the blues is the other path. One time we playin down by the depot, it hot as Hades and this skinny little girl come on by all sweet and "My, you do play good, what's your name, sugar?" and stuff, and she be siddlin up next to me with a handkerchief—I could smell the perfume and all—like she was gonna mop my brow. Hey, this the kind of treatment we deserve, baby, is what I'm thinkin. Then suddenly Robert reach up and grab that girl's hand. "Watch it, old man, she got a razor in there." He save my life that day. Street smarts keep you alive out on the road and RL got them in spades.

A master trickifyer, too, RL knew all the scams. But just as frequently he outsmart hisself. Like the time we go down to Clarksdale to play this club he heard of. And when we get down there it's not exactly a *music* gig, y'understand. It's a poker game and he knowed for a fact, RL that is, that there was two easy marks from Kansas City gonna be there. Hear from a reliable source. Fella workin as a porter on the Illinois Central have told him. All we gotta do is bide our time and we clean out the joint like *that*. Make ourselves a little bundle and then maybe we head up to Chicago. Sound good to me, Robert.

We get to the club and sure enough there are two overdressed guys who seem like they barely been introduced to the game of poker. Sayin shit like, "Do I take another card now, mister?" We laughin up our sleeves. But after a few hands it was clear who the easy marks was. Wiped us out of all our bread, and when RL put up his guitar as a stake I had to split. I figured at least we'd have *one* guitar left.

I go out, sit by the tracks and await the so-called inevitable. I'm watchin the Yeller Dog come rumblin through town and I'm thinkin we could be *on* that train when RL come runnin out of the club shoutin. "Get on the fucker, Coley! That our train!" Pursued as he was by a posse of irate card sharps.

The last boxcar *clickety-clack* shuntin *clickety-clack* across the crossing rise *clickety-clack*. She wheezin up the incline and I'm runnin alongside keepin one eye on Robert who is just a couple of steps ahead of his playin partners.

Now the way your guitar get lost is when you try and get it on that train, 'cause if you don't get on *with* it, you kiss your box goodbye. Ya gotta do it just right. When the train slow down for a bridge or a station, you get up to speed alongside it. First you slide the guitar across the floor of the car, see, like this, and then scramble yourself aboard.

So I slide my Gibson in, climb up myself and put my hand down to pull RL up. He's about halfway up when his grip slips and I fall back and land on top of old Ro Anne and crush that guitar to smithereens.

You ever ridden a boxcar? Well, it's as unusual a manner of seein the country as you'll ever experience. Like the movies, 'cept *you* the one movin. Big old screen unfurlin right smack in front of you. Fields of grain from a movin train. Just lay back, watch the whole world pass by: chain gangs, old farmer with his overalls down, women in the fields, their brightly colored bandannas, baptism goin on by the riverside, mules plowin, lovers in the corn, towns, churches, shacks, prisons and children waitin at the crossin jumpin and shoutin.

Sittin there in the darkness the lights of the passin towns seem more mysterious than the stars in the sky. Nighttime sounds comin to life: dogs barkin, owls hootin, donkeys brayin. Then the orchestra of the train start up, all them mysterious mechanical sounds: mournful sigh of the brakes comin down a hill, clank of the hammer on the steel wheels, fireman's bell, shrill cry of the engineer's whistle, steam puffin on a grade like an old farmer in a whorehouse. It's all in there in the blues. Hauntin your memory just like that young girl's face under a pool of light, standin on a platform with her beat-up suitcase. You catch her eye and she look back with a face so sad that it could melt the Arctic Sea and in that one instant you fall in love, baby, and you live a whole lifetime in just the time a daydream take. That lost moment is the blues, baby.

Long, flat rows of cotton flickin by like to hypnotize your eyes, rhythm of the track lull you to sleep at night. That de-de-dum de-de-dum beat behind many of RL's songs. Like on "Walkin Blues" or "Stones in My Pathway." That ain't walkin, that's the train comin up to speed. And naturally "Love in Vain." Hear it go clickety-clack?

Robert didn't talk too much, didn't like others to talk too much neither. When he think I'm talkin too much he say, "You buzzin like a fly in my ear." He was close only to his own guitar.

RL got peculiar ideas about the guitar which I only once or twice heard him talk about and which afterwards he deny he ever say. These concern the "Jonah sound" and the Hawaiian god.

He'd bend a note, string twang so fiercely it about to snap. "Hear that? That's the sound of the cat what can't get back in. The Jonah sound, hah!"

It was RL's opinion that the slide was the voice of the Hawaiian god.

"The catgut god have deserted us and moved to Hawaii. He may be extinct over here in the U.S. of A. but he was once *alive*, man, over in them cannibal islands. And that's the way he talk, like a snake talk if a snake *could* talk." Here RL do a imitation of a slitherin viper with his bottleneck.

"A prayer to the catgut god what it is," say RL. "You playin the slide you prayin to him, dig? Voice of the Hawaiian god tellin of volcanoes and typhoons, parrots, palm trees, naked women and coconut wine."

When you travel together two, three hundred mile in a boxcar even the close-lipped Robert must sometime talk.

Didn't talk 'bout nothin personal, though. Like me to believe his life begun the day Son House arrive in Robinsonville. When Son House and Willie Brown come to town, *man*, it was like John the Baptist and his cousin have come to spread the gospel. They brought the gospel of the blues with them that they got from Charley Patton, and which Charley Patton got from the Mysterious Element that worked on Dockery's farm.

"There was four jook joints in the vicinity of Robinsonville in those days," RL tell me, "and Son and Willie played 'em all. Every night I'd sneak outta the house and head over to the jook joint where they was playin and, *man*, they could tear the joint up, I tell ya.

"When Son and Willie take a break—say, 'Let's go out in the cool' —I pick up one of the guitars and play. Make people mad, you know? Come out and say, 'Get the guitar away from that boy, he's runnin people crazy with it.' Son would come back and scold me.

"'Don't do that, chile, you drivin people nuts. You can't play nothin, why don't you go on play the harmonica for them?' But I don't want to play harmonica, and I don't care how Son get after me about it, I play guitar anyways.

"Kidded me to about make me crazy. *Terrible* stuff. Make me wanna crawl in a hole and die. 'Cause I worshipped the man, you know. 'Forget about pickin guitar, boy, you best get out in those fields and start pickin *cotton*.' At which point everybody start laughin.

"'You ever catch me pickin cotton you better lock me up, man, because you know I have lost my mind.' That's what I told them.

"'Boy, you sure got the attitude down, now all you got to do is get the *aptitude*.' He made it much worse than I actually was," RL tell me.

These cats livin saints, dig? Son House, Charley Patton, Willie Brown. They was a different breed. Like they came up out of the ground. Son House was burnin up that guitar. Tormented. That's why he tear at his guitar the way he do, grabbin at it like it was a demon and he gonna pull out its heart. Too intense for some folk. Outside of the Delta he scary to people, that's right. Just one crazy cat.

❖   ❖   ❖

Freight pull into Jackson, we jump off. Freezin our balls off out there. But once inside Sippy's jook joint we okay. Sippy was short and dapper and smooth as silk. He was real glad to see us. Made us feel just like a pair of kings. Put his arms 'round our shoulders, offer us a unsealed bottle. They got a potbelly stove goin, bunch of people in there and it get real toasty. We do every song in our book, in Charley Patton's book, off the radio, and from the movies. And we throw in a coupla Christmas carols for the hell of it. What's the hurry? To get out into the weather? Finally the last cats slink their sorry asses outta there and the houseman wanna close up.

Sippy say he don't wanna show money 'round the joint. Encourage the raggedy element to rip him off. "You can understand that, can't you, fellas?" Say he meet us at a bar downtown, but guess what, he never show up. No money, no crib to flop in. We was on the street and it begin to hail. Ain't no *blues* fallin down like hail, it hail fallin down like hail.

Many songsters die from this. Comin out of a overheated shack into freezin weather, especially up north. You catch pneumonia and you're a dead man. But Robert got a plan.

He walk into the swankiest black hotel in Jackson and me just creepin behind him, hopin nobody notice me. Manager of the hotel, she notice *everything*. Cool, waxy, blown-out woman with a haughty manner. Woman who'd seen every scam in the book. She knew right off there was something fishy goin on with us but she couldn't figure it. She stood there in her porkpie hat with her hands on her hips tryin to assess what exactly was goin down. Robert looked real fine. Pinstripe suit and tie, shootin out his cuffs, layin on as smooth a line of patter you ever heard.

"I am not at ease." I tell RL, "Let's get outta here before they kick our asses out."

"Coley, you *so* country," says he and launch into his slinky, sophisticated rap with the lady at the desk. She wary of him but gonna give us a room nevertheless.

Mornin come. 'Round about sunup RL leap outta bed like something bit him, run downstairs screamin, "Thief! Thief! Come back here!" RL's out in the street pursuin some varmit who has stolen his guitar. Whoever it was, man, he sure could run.

RL, he come back in the lobby, pull hisself up to his full height and address the lady at the desk in the grand old Fourth of July manner.

"Madam, what kind establishment this you got here? Thiefs comin right in peoples' rooms, steal their merchandise right under their noses while they is sleepin."

The lady was suitably unimpressed by the foregoin speech and she tell him to fuck off. "You *got* to be kiddin. Whoever stole from you musta been in a bad way."

"I'll have you know that was a thirty dollar guitar, ma'am, that got stolen outta my room. Man come in expectin to get a decent night's sleep and security for his possessions. Why this ain't no better'n a Shreveport ho-house."

By this time a group of guests at the establishment hearin all the carryin-on start comin outta their rooms see what the commotion be. Lady who run the hotel may not believe one word of this bullshit tale of RL's but she was gettin a might concerned that the guests not be familiar with wildlife of RL's stripe. She tell him she'll forget about payin for the room if he'll just hush his mouth up.

I'm tuggin at his sleeve, sayin, "Come on, Robert, let's split. She may be dumb but even she got a limit." You think he split? Why would he do a thing like that? He run back and got the guitar he'd hidden behind the bathtub and jump from the window. *Then* he split.

Went to the Crossroad, Fell Down on My Knees

RL wake me up one mornin say, "Coley, we going on a expedition."

"Count me out, baby."

"We ain't goin to the North Pole, man, we just goin down the road a piece."

"What kinda piece?"

"Just by River Road and Highway 61."

This soundin worse by the minute. "Why we goin all the ways out there when we can hop a freight right here in Clarksdale?"

"Ain't *about* trains."

"Now this intersection," I say, "it wouldn't have anything to do with that crossroads shit of Tommy Johnson?"

"Might, might not."

"Man, what the matter with you? You *want* to die young?"

"What you 'fraid of, eh? Devil gonna get your soul? *Hawh-hawh-hawh.* You been brought up on them old wife tales, little boogeyman with horns, funny lookin stingy brim hat and a pitchfork and a leathery old tail."

"I already *been* through this scene once before with Tommy Johnson, dig?"

"Heard you passed out you so scared. *Hawh-hawh-hawh!*"

"Maybe so. Glad I did. Who knows what kinda ugly shit I'd a seen?"

"What you talkin, Coley? You know the Devil just a boogeyman to frighten the little chillens and ignorant folk. Ain't no such thing as the Devil—that's for old ladies. Devil be taxes, stayin in one place, bein married to the same woman your whole life, teetotalin. Devil be the *man*. Sheriff Jenkins, Big Boss Thompson down at the mill, revenuers. Or when your sweetheart's the luscious young wife of some other joker. Devil's got modern. You think he dress up in tights like he in a old Shakespeare play? *Hawh-hawh-hawh*! You simpler than I thought. I have to consider whether I would want someone so foolish as you along, honestly I do."

He could be very persuasive, RL. So we walk a ways. It gettin darker and darker when we come to a swamp. Particularly creepy type swamp. Vines and reeds and trees with moss creepers look like they reachin out for us. Near about landed on a snake. Lanterns flyin 'round, lights blinkin on and off, hollerin frogs croakin. I am so scared, I'm hearin frogs talkin to me. Some critter come by *barkin*, two eyes like bullets floatin on the water.

"Just a gator," say RL.

Things out there barkin, croakin, moanin. *Kersplash*!

"Holy God, what's *that*?"

"No doubt some li'l old animal splashin 'bout in the swamp make a sound like that. A possum, yeah, that what it be."

"When you ever hear a possum sound like that?"

"That's a Arkansas grisly possum."

"Jesus, RL, look over there, birds ain't got no heads!"

"Jus the swamp wakin up, Coley. Swamp wake up at night, now you know that. Birds got their heads tuck under their wings on account of the mosquitoes. How long you live in Coahoma County and you don know 'bout swamps?"

"Well, if there's no Devil to sell your soul to, why we going down to the crossroads?"

"I reckon Tommy Johnson *made up* that Devil story so as no one else be fool enough to try it. Whatever it be he wanna keep it for hisself. You get out there and there's owls hootin and varmits scratchin. Pretty soon you scared outta your cotton-pickin wits and you hightail it on home. Just 'cause there ain't no Devil don't mean there ain't no *secrets*."

So we get down to the place where 61 cross River Road. Lonesomest place as there is on this earth.

"Here, you better take a swig of this," RL say, "calm your nerves." Took a swig and then another and another and another till I was finally calmed down enough to tolerate myself. For a long while nothin happened, and feelin sleepy I lay down on the mossy ground and soon fell into a dark, deep and dreamless sleep. That sleep where all the lost things in your life collect in your head and hold a crazy party. I woke up and the ground was shakin. Clouds of black smoke and a scream that came from the jaws of Hell itself. RL musta took a coupla swigs hisself and fallen asleep too, because when I woke up he was layin on top of me just howlin. RL pleadin and cryin in a pitiful voice:

"Have mercy, now save poor Bob! Yeee-oooo! Oooo-oooeeee! Poor Bob sinkin down!"

Seemed like there was lightnin and thunder and graves bein upturned and a scaly figure outlined against the sky. Now I say *scaly* but the truth is I don't honestly know *what* I seen. Somethin. Coulda bin a pricker bush blown by a gust of wind but I have told this story many times, and after a few tellins it grow horns and breathe smoke from its nostrils. Even I begin to believe I seen Beelzebub. But it coulda been the Illinois Central makin its midnight run, see what I mean?

Anyway...not too long afterwards, RL and I was walkin down the road when RL stop and grab my lapels and his one cloudy eye lookin mean as sin and he say, "If you ever say so much as one word about this I will personally skin you alive and feed you piece by piece to the gators." But some stories you cannot contain, and I figured Robert, bein the contrary fool he was, actually wanted me to tell it.

That was the last I saw of RL for some time and the last I *wanted* to see of him for a long, long while. Whenever I see Robert after that he always say, "See ya in Hell, *hawh, hawh, hawh!*" Like it was a big joke.

Who the Hell Is Freddy Fox?

Everybody hustlin to get theirselves recorded. Black Boy Shine and them cats. Whole world gonna get itself phonographed. Blues was *hot*. Record companies found theirselves a big new market—call it "race records." At one time in the mid-twenties you coulda got a recordin contract for a bumblebee backed with a grasshopper playin fiddle.

Hell, I was sayin to myself, if Willie James can sing on a phonograph record I can too. Just then a scout come down here from Chicago. Fat little man with a bow tie and beady eyes who sold Bibles and dinner plates on the side. Didn't know anything more about the blues than he did about the pyramids in Egypt. Went about his job like everybody else in his line. Man in the bow tie says he's lookin for this cat that's been recommended to him from a bunch of guys hangin out on the liar's bench outside the barber shop.

"Your name wouldn't be Freddy Fox by any chance?"

"What's it to you?"

"Some fella says you can play blues."

"Well, I can play some," I tell him.

Vida Lee, settin up on the porch rollin her eyes so loud you can hear 'em click.

"We're recordin at the Nelson Hotel down in Jacksonville. Think you can be down there next Sunday?"

Vida Lee gonna put in her two cents' worth.

"Damn if I don't know what you got on your mind, Mister," says she. "You gonna tell my Coley a big long story and take him away from me. 'Cause Coley like to believe just 'bout anything. But you just suit yourself 'cause anything I say ain't gonna make a damn bit of difference to Mr. Freddy Fox here."

Man from the Copacetic Recordin Company got his equipment set up on the top floor of the hotel. Portable machine, one of them old wax deals. Windows all draped 'round to make it soundproof. It was dark and hot and no air to breathe. Like you was layin down in your tomb.

My first recordin session, so I was scared silly. Couldn't hardly play none, my hands was tremblin so. Man, some drinkin went on alright. Part of the deal, I suppose. They'd all but pour it down your throat. Didn't steady me none, though. Booze or no booze, it ain't easy to tell the story right, sittin in a tiny little old room no bigger than a closet with a sour white guy who don't know blues from bottled milk.

Plus you gotta make your song fit into a three minute bag. Ain't ever *been* a blues song that was three minutes long before phonograph records. If a audience was diggin it, you make it long as you can. People throwin in verses of their own, gettin you to repeat stuff.

Made six numbers for Copacetic Records without paper. Didn't give me no contract whatsofuckinever. I didn't play good on none of 'em songs nohow, but they was too dumb to know how bad I was. Which I considered a definite possibility since it didn't seem to make no difference to the so-call engineer whether I sang "This Old Man" or "Me and the Devil Blues." He was just a-cuttin wax like we used to chop in the rows.

After awhile the recordin company guy come back, want me to do another session. What did I do *right*, baby, know what I mean? This time I play something good. Wrote me one good song went something like this:

Come one, come all, chillen,
    don't you hear that lonesome bell,
I said, come right in, little chillen,
    don't you hear that lonesome bell.
All ya gotta do is sign right here, chillen,
    get your twelve weeks in hell.

Called it "Twelve Weeks in Hell Blues." You heard a that? Really. Well, well. Yeah, that was one of mine. Never a big seller accordin to them, though I know for a fact that it sold twenty copies—I own 'em.

Took a long time in them days to figure exactly what had been sold and what was gonna get melted down, go back in the wax factory. And while this process goin on, by some fluke I got me a reputation. Everybody sayin I was one hot bluesboy. All the scouts and the salesmen had heard the name of the song I done and they liked the sound of it, liked sayin it. And, y'know, every time a new guy come through with something they think is good, they wanna know, "You got any more like that?"

You have yourself a handy tune like that, you change your name 'round and make disks for different record companies, dig? Give it a new title while retainin the hook. Like I done "Crawlin Twelve Weeks in Hell" and "Down and Dirty Twelve Days in Hell." Then I got a bit creative: "One-Hundred-Seventy Days in Hell." I recorded that particular song quite a few times under a lotta different names: Shorty James, Freddy "Fox" Foster, Furry Blue, Big Eleven (my shoe size), and finally, Woolly Fish (that was the nasty version—for the party records, y'know).

Man come to see me from Okeh records. He was wearin a seersucker suit and smokin a big cigar—looked prosperous, anyway, and he seemed to actually know something about the blues. Could rattle off some names. Bessie Smith, Blind Lemon Jefferson, Leroy Carr. Say he heard my record—which one?—and want me to do a recordin session for his company. Say can I make it down to this big hotel in San Antone. Man's gonna give me money, make a bunch of copies, advertise it in the papers. Now I figure my time comin for sure. Took Teejay with me for company. We was makin our way to San Antone, but slowly. *Very* slowly. Had a few days before we was due so we drank a little wine, figured we'd have ourselves a fine old time. Get in the groove, baby, get *way* down in that groove. Got plenty of time to get to the place. Begin to write us a song we took off of some old number that was lyin there under a tree:

> *She got a Waterbury watch, same like to mine.*
> *Said she got a Waterbury watch just like to mine.*
> *Both keep runnin, Lord, but mine don't run on time.*

We so pleased with ourselfs we decided we would ramble a bit. Well, we walk 'round the corner a few times, and damn if we didn't get on the wrong train out of wherever. Got into a boxcar to take a little nap, end up on the bad side of a redneck town, got pinched for fuck all and blew that stinkin recordin session. They called it vagrancy. I spent five days jail time and end up missin my big chance. I coulda been up there with Muddy Waters and Freddy Fox—whoever the hell *he* is. But that's me all over again, ain't it? If the odds was too good, I had to play with them a bit. Make the game more interesting, see what I'm sayin? By the way, do me a favor, will ya? You run up on her, don't even mention none of this to Vida Lee. She is as ignorant of this as a llama in Yokahama, which suits me just fine.

25

Nobody Knows You
When You Down and Out

The seven lean years come upon the land all right. We was makin bricks without straw and don't even know it. You wouldn't think it'd make a wick of difference to us what the hell them fools up North dickerin with on Wall Street, but things couldn't've been worse in the Delta. And worst off of the worst off was the blues singer. When the sharecroppers and farm hands and sack shakers got no money, they sure don't have no money to give any raggedy-ass, shiftless bluesman.

Record company guys stop comin 'round long time. 'Round 'bout nineteen and twenty-nine they stopped right quick. Think a field hand gettin next to nothing a hundredweight gonna pay seventy-five cents for a phonograph record? Things was bad, baby. Gettin worser. What you gonna say? What so different 'bout *then*? They always have been bad times ever since the time of the Pharoah and probably a good deal before that. But 1930s was one of them times when things got downright ugly. Things so bad even Charley Patton ain't makin it. They seen that suit hangin in the store window and pass on. Stuff considered played out, y'know?

Great Depression all but killed off the vaudeville blues singers like Bessie Smith and Ma Rainey. Them weren't jook joint gals or goodtimes ladies. Not in the usual sense of the word. These was tent show queens. But devastation like a train—whatever happenin gonna happen to them down the line. Man, you hear that train a-comin. And that was on the main track. Their fame tied to the show business, dig? When they shut down the big travelin shows they lost their gig. They sayin Bessie takin Mammy parts in cabarets. All this aggravation goin on her drinkin got worse, which made it naturally more difficult to find any kind of employ.

'Round that time I recalled Bessie's dream, one she told me when I quit from her. Often I pondered did she think of that vision when she come to record that song, "Nobody Knows You When You're Down and Out."

> *When I began to fall so low,*
> *I didn't have a friend, and no place to go;*
> *So, if I ever get my hands on a dollar again,*
> *I'm goin to hold on to it till them eagles grin.*

Come out on September 13, 1929. A *Friday*. Now dig this, one month—hear what I'm sayin?—after it got released Wall Street lay a giant egg. What you all think of that?

Mr. Gee and Bessie broken up by this time but whenever he run into Bessie he always say, "Baby, now look what you done. You brought on the Depression down on all the people's heads with that song." Bessie mildly flattered by this Tower of Babel type compliment, as who wouldn't be?

"You saying *I* cause the stock market to crash?" she say. "Well then, you best stay outta my path! I am a *dangerous* woman."

Bessie knew it gonna happen just like Moses foretellin the plagues of Egypt. Like Isaiah seen them fiery wheels. What the hell *was* that? Never could figure out what it was but, man, what a riff. And Bessie bein a prophetess in her own right, she naturally gonna sense stuff. Beans in her rice just don't look right to her, see what I'm sayin? Hair ain't layin right on her head. World bein a incomprehensible muddle and a mystery, why should it make any difference if the cause is a song or an eclipse of the moon?

Can you explain why the ungodly flourish and the righteous be downtrodden? And why do something like golf exist? Or golf *attire*? Them dopey plaid pants and white shoes and tammy shanters with the little bobbins on the top? If that ain't a imponderable, nothin is.

26

Pharaoh Talkin on the Radio

Only blues singer come close to sellin as many records as Bessie was Blind Lemon Jefferson. Matter a fact, it was on account of him that the recordin craze in the Delta got started. That's right. Field trips by record companies begun around 1927 as a result of Lemon's huge record sales. He was the most imitated bluesman of his time. People *studied* Lemon's songs, especially once his records was out, 'cause he come up with one of the best styles of blues ever to be heard.

I was gonna say I never seed Blind Lemon again after I left Dallas but I am forgettin 'bout the time he come through Mississippi. He was settin down by the Clarksdale station, all button up in his suit, specs on like a professor and a crowd 'round him. Always a crowd buzzin 'round when Lemon singin.

'Cept on this particular occasion he weren't singin. He was preachin, preachin his crazy-ass head off.

When I come up close on the crowd I hear him declaimin in a loud voice, "Woe to Assyria! Woe unto them that toil in the vineyards of iniquity and turn from the word of the Lord! Brothers and sisters, I have come among you to cast out demons."

A type of speech I am familiar with—the high apocalyptic manner. 'Lijah pronouncin the comin of the Age of the Holy Spirit to the righteous. And to all you other suckers, sackcloth and ashes.

Jackleg preachin was an affliction come over blues singers on a regular basis. Bluesmen know in their heart of hearts that in the eyes of the Lord what they doin is evil. When they get old and sickly, distressed in mind, or feel the wing of death pass over 'em, they start lookin at theirselves with the eyes of others and what they see there ain't pretty. Gonna run right over into the embrace of the sanctimonious before you can say "dust my broom."

"Lo, I seen a old raggedy man eatin grass! Black bird a death settin in a tree. Bell ringin in the church without human hands. Plagues gonna come upon the land, yessir, just like in Pharoah's time. You gonna see the Nile—great Mississippi river—turnin to blood. And the voice of the Pharoah—the President's voice what you hearin over your radio—be magnified so all the people in Egypt land can hear him. In the days to come the livin will copulate with the dead, God almighty, crucifixes gonna bleed with the blood of the Lamb and weevils will descend and consume the fields like fire."

It was impressive stuff and we all stood silent a long while ponderin the aftermath of the Lord's terrible swift sword. I was mostly impressed that the Bible had foretold the invention of the radio and foreseen the President usin it to deliver his address.

"Lemon," I says, "gotta ask you something. The part 'bout the radio bein spoke of in the Bible, the Pharoah's voice bein magnified and all? Where exactly that come in the Bible?"

"It's all in there, Coley. Everything is in the Holy Book. Everything, baby. Been written there by the Mysterious Hand."

"That part you talkin 'bout, would that be in the Book a Exodus? Don't see nothin 'bout no Pharoah's voice bein broadcasted over the land of Egypt. You sure you—"

"Brother Coley, you gotta look at the scriptures with the second eye. Eye of faith. Read between the lines. Pick out them blue notes, follow me?"

There's no talkin to a man who delve into such matters as the Mysterious Hand and the second eye. Best to leave it lie. Lemon been holy-rollered but he ain't too sanctified to help hisself from frailin a little skanktified blues. Writ hisself a real nasty blues, too —'bout the slipperiest I ever heard.

Um-um, black snake crawlin in my room.
Um-um, oh yeah, there's a black snake crawlin in my room.
Yes, some pretty mama better get this black snake soon.

That black snake crawled right outta Victoria Spivey's song and slipped into that little girl's room and, baby, got but one thing on its one-eyed mind.

"How you and your woman gettin along, Coley?"

Tell him things been better. Vida Lee layin down the law like Solomon and I'm sittin there in misery.

"Struggle and worryination, brother Coley," Blind Lemon tell me. "Cain set against Abel, Jacob against Esau, and Satan against all. 'I will put enmity between thee and the woman,' saith the Lord, 'and between thy seed and her seed.' Genesis chapter three, verse thirteen."

Goin on and on 'bout a infirm king or some crazy thing.

"King done lost his power. That how come we got famine in the land."

And that was the last time I seen Lemon. Durin that night I had troubled sleep. I dreamed I walked along in terror with Ezekiel. We was among the slaves by the river of Chebar and the heavens opened and I seen Babylon turn to dust and locusts coverin the earth. I awoke suffocatin and the sweat pourin offa my face.

There's all kinda stories 'bout what happened that December night Blind Lemon died up there in Chicago. Some say Lemon left the party drunk, got lost, and couldn't find his way through the bitter cold streets. Never would have cried out for help, not him. Who gonna hear him, anyway, with all that snow dampenin down everything?

Lemon, what you doin out there in the snow all by your lonesome? Don't you got better sense than that? Hell, if I'd been leadin him 'round that never would have happened. And where was all the cats from the club? Lemon always have a big crowd 'round him. He was famous, man, famous as you can get in this blues line.

Say, remember Walter Taylor and John Byrd's "Wasn't It Sad About Lemon?"

> *The weather was below zero*
> *On the day he passed away,*
> *But this is a truth we all know well,*
> *That's a debt we all have to pay....*

No use speculatin 'bout it, Blind Lemon dead and gone a long time. But what a cryin shame, die all alone and a long way from home, nothin but the howlin wind to hear your cries. 'Course they say it don't matter where you be or who you be with—when the Lord gets ready, you gotta go.

❖   ❖   ❖

He was a original, Blind Lemon, that's for sure. Master carpenter of the blues, hmm, hmm. Knew how to make blues real good. What was it that John Lennon said 'bout the blues? I always loved that thing.

"Blues is a chair." he said. It's a chair for sittin on, not for lookin at or bein appreciated." But you know who built that chair, don't you? Blind Lemon. That's right. Before him, all the cats what plays on the street corners could make in the music line was a magpie blues. That's when you pick stuff up from here and there, make a song from loose lines you heard around. We all done like that. That was the way Blind Lemon done it, too, in the beginning.

I'll show you now how it's done. You take a line like "Blues come to Texas, lopin like a mule." Now that's some great line, ain't it? What you gonna follow that with, though? With anything, just so it rhyme. That's the only thing you gotta worry about. So, this is how that Blind Lemon thing go:

> *Well, the blues come to Texas, lopin like a mule.*
> *You take a brown-skin woman; man, she's hard to fool.*

Now these two things, they ain't got nothin to do with each other, understand, but did you notice it? No, man, 'cause it just slide along. Come to think of it, I like it better that way. The verses themselves, they didn't have nothin to do with each other either. You could put 'em in any order you liked.

Now, Blind Lemon knew more of them magpie lines than anybody. King Solomon may have known a few more—he wrote the book of Proverbs, y'know—but that was long ago and he was a king and Blind Lemon weren't nothin but a blind hobo wailin on the corner. Blind Lemon been on the street fifteen years before he come to make a record. He been pickin up them old-time rhymes since he was a little kid. But after he'd made some thirty-odd records he looked in his box of old lines and find it empty. Just stuff like "where in the world my baby gone?" and "down the road I go." Hardly enough to make one more verse. So 'round nineteen and twenty-eight he begin makin 'em up his own self and at that he was real good. He fiddled with it until he come up with something you could sit on.

> *Peach Orchard Mama,*
> > *you swore nobody picked your fruit but me.*
> *I found three kid men shakin down your orchard tree.*
> *One man bought your groceries,*
> > *another man paid your rent,*
> *While I work in your orchard and givin you every cent.*

No more loose lines 'bout roosters and mules and bowlegged women all cobbled together. And it all was put together real nice. Run good as a Model-T. Sold a whole mess of records when his bluesmobile hit that dirt road. Once we seen how he done it, we could make our own. If you wanted to make a blues, you went and took a look at what Blind Lemon done.

His music was just like him, sunny and laid-back. There was nothin dark or creepy 'bout Lemon. It was blues but it was honey blues, blues to make you feel good. Still, he knew all 'bout the dark side—like you overhearin some ugly daybreak scene: *I say, fair brown, where you stay last night. Your hair's all down, and you know you ain't talking right.*

To hisself Lemon was the sun. The whole flukey, violent, unstable world whirlin 'round him like a twister—but Lemon just a-settin there like a possum in a tree, regalin us with his crazy wisdom stories, dishin out his little old folk proverbs. *Tough luck has struck me and the rats is sleepin in my hat. I'm gonna drink muddy water, sleep in a hollow log.*

Sure hope they buried him with that Stetson hat a his.

Delta Giantess
And a Midget in Black Stockins

Was 'round the beginnin of July, nineteen and thirty something. I was layin at the Hunt Hotel in West Memphis, one down by the bus depot, y'know? Woke up one mornin look 'round for my shoes. Yeah, I did. 'Cause upstairs they got some terrible bottle-party racket. Carryin on, singin and thumpin. Feet poundin, someone playin guitar loud as a bell and a bass player *ka-thump ka-thumpin* and what all. Quite a little combo they got swingin. Wonderin just what it were. People laughin and talkin. Hell, can't sleep no more—*thwump a thwump athwumpiddy thwump*—might as well go up and join 'em.

Get out to the landin, proprietress come bellowin up the stairs. "What in the blue hell is all that tumult? Don't you know there's a baby sleepin upstairs?" Tell her I go up and see about it. Through the door I hear some cat announcin the next number.

"Fine ladies and kind gentlemens, uh-huhn! Don't care if you high or low, bring you music gonna transport your soul. I'd like to play you a little song, goes like this." Like he's in a club or something. And he start in to playin "Take a Little Walk With Me."

I knock louder. Door fly open. I am expectin to see a small gatherin of hip cats and chicks; instead of which there is one little guy, smokin a cigarette, so skinny he barely cast a shadow. Who but him! Robert.

"What's shakin?" I says.

"You, brother."

"Uh, see, I just come up here to—Mrs. Prendergast she gettin riled on account of you wake the baby."

"Did I ?" he says and pulls a humorous frown down across his face. "I'll go in there and sing it a lullaby I got. Chile gonna go right out under it."

I look 'round the room. No other cats. Just Robert and this chick. That left foot of his keepin time on the floorboards get him thrown outta more places than you ever imagine.

He took up with some weird broads. In Friar's Point there was a runty girl named Betty. There was the Witch of Lula—the woman who was the plague and the terminal ugliness put together. In Clarksdale there was the Delta Giantess. Six-four and two-hundred-fifty pounds of black passion.

But this chick here was the strangest I seen him with. Female midget, dressed in a lacy slip and black stockings. She run errands and did other stuff for Robert. In every town in which we stop, there was someone to take care of him. Women, to Robert, was like motel rooms. He might use 'em repeatedly, but he left 'em where he found 'em. Heaven help him, he was not discriminatin—he loved 'em all. A little like Jesus, in his own way.

Man, he could croon like Bing Crosby, signify sex like a bedroom snake. They go wild for his stutterin when he sing, *When I mash down on your s-s-s-starter then your sparkplug will give me fire.* And that mournful slide of his cause many a woman to weep. Many a man, too.

Robert was different from your parish blues player who only can play in their own one particular style. RL could play just about anything. Popular songs of the day, hillbilly tunes, polkas, square dances, ballads, "Yes Sir, That's My Baby," "My Blue Heaven." Robert could play all that shit. Play in the style of Lonnie Johnson, Blind Blake, Blind Boy Fuller, Blind Willie McTell, and the hillbilly singer, Jimmie Rodgers—he could do that too. Ragtime, pop tunes, waltz numbers, polka! Even his *guitar* do impersonations. Trains, rain, wind. Dogs too.

One time Robert and I come in to H.C. Speir's general store. Mr. Speir was round as a apple. Had his pants pulled up with suspenders right over his belly. He looked just like Humpty Dumpty—with a real twinkle to his eye. He loved to joke. You'd always know when he was gonna tell one, he'd move his lips around like he was chewin tobaccy.

The store was a long narrow place with a shelf and stools down the one side, the other a counter with bolts of cloth and dry goods. In the center there was a potbellied stove. Mr. Speir had just install a radio and people come in to hear FDR deliverin one of his fireside chats over the wireless. After the President finish there was a big discussion all 'round the store and in the background the announcer come on and say: "Now here's Bing Crosby's newest record, folks, you're hearin it here for the first time on WVOX." The whole time RL talkin with people in the store there. What it mean for Mississippi croppers and talk like that. Robert naturally not too occupied with questions relatin to farmin, but still he have an opinion on it.

Everyone slowly move out to the courthouse steps. RL take out his guitar. A man there goes, "Why don't you play us that Bing Crosby song came across the radio?" And everybody says, "Go on, Robert, pick it!" And I'm thinkin he shoulda listened back there, but without blinkin an eye he plays that Bing Crosby song note for note. Play it just like you heard it. Picked songs outta the air. I swear there was two RLs. How else explain it?

Sometimes you could actually see the two Roberts fightin behind his eyes. You seen them two photos of Robert? In the one there's this dandy with his creases as sharp as a knife, and then in the other there's the smolderin don't-fuck-with-me dude. You can even see the two Roberts in the same picture. Cover over the left eye and you have a nice lookin well-behaved black kid. Cover over the right side and you got a African mask. Haunted face 'bout which you can believe anything you like.

His manner especially at jook joints where there was other musicians 'round was mighty wary. He was very jealous of revealin his playin techniques, turnin away from other musicians if he felt their eyes on him. Ever catch some young fella watchin while he's playin, eyein him too closely, he get up and leave the room. Fella ask him how he play some riff he say, "Just like you."

His mind compose the words, his fingers bend the strings, open his mouth, move his lips, something worryin his fingertips. Hear him speakin them invisible words before he say them. Like he was in a room where he can see everything and all he have to do is describe what's in there. Yeah, now I'm home.

All blues bein more or less come-on songs from a loner. Robert was a "outside child," illegitimate, and he put across how that felt—like lookin in the windows of people's houses at night, see families settin together at dinner.

For the next year or so we travel throughout the Delta usin Hazlehurst as a base. From now on his home was street corners and jook joints, flophouses and bus depots. But however much he travel down that dusty road he always stay neat as a pin. He usta roll his clothes up and keep 'em in a paper bag, They'd come out slick and starched and unsoiled as if he just step outta his house. Shoot out them cuffs of his and they white as snow. How, I don't know.

Some of them places we go was so small they didn't even have names. But even before he made phonograph records, his name went 'round. It was in the air. Guitar was freedom back then. Play guitar like them guys, you can go anywhere. No more toilin in the field, bailin cotton. You set down on any street corner, down by the depot, on the courthouse steps. People come by and throw money at you. Women throw *themselves* at you.

We set down and play in front of the local barber shop, stood up in front of restaurants, in town squares. Play jook joints, house rent parties, country frolics, wide-open river front saloons, and plain old down on the corner. In them days you didn't need nowhere to play. People would just pick you up on the streets. They'd see you with your instruments and they'd say, "Man, you play? Play me a piece." They know right away you not gonna be playing for *free*. Play two or three pieces and, hell, you got twenty or thirty people 'round you. Play all night in the jook joint for a dollar and a half.

When RL return to Robinsonville, Son House and Willie Brown get a surprise, 'cause, see, they don't know what he can do.

Willie and Son, they was playin again, out at a little place east of Robinsonville, called Banks, Mississippi. They playin there one Saturday night and we come into the place where they was at.

These two was some pair. As unalike as Mutt and Jeff. Son was skinny as a pencil and goodlookin—but snappish. Cussed as a damn possum. He'd get nasty right in your face, that's right. When he was young he'd killed a man in a fight over a girl at a Saturday night supper and been sent to Parchman Farm penitentiary.

His mom and dad was honest folk and they pleaded with the judge, "Let the boy go! He got in with bad company but he seen the error of his way or I'll woop his butt." Got him out after two years. When he come up before the judge in Clarksdale, judge say, "Boy, I ain't gonna see you 'round this town no more, am I?" And Son tell him, "Your honor, boss, you let me go and I will cover as much ground as a fox can in two days with a pack of hounds on his tail." He walked to Jonestown, caught a ride to Lula.

Over there at the train station he run up on this woman named Sara Knights, ran a restaurant type of deal a little ways from the Lula depot. She ask him would he play his guitar at her place, draw the people in. She was makin good money sellin bootleg whiskey and when Son seen that he was all over her like gravy on mashed potatoes. He could talk that trash real smooth, y'know.

"I can run my mouth just as fast as that damn Charley Patton." He sweet-talked that Sara Knights until she ask him if he would care to lodge with her. Would he! He's the one had put the idea in *her* head. Later she caught him in back of the place with another woman and kicked him out. That's when he come to Robinsonville.

Son could be as contrary as hell. Wouldn't agree with nothin you said. If you said the sky was blue he'd give you a argument. Whatever side of the fence you was on he was on the other side. Ornery as a damn mule and disputatious as a deacon.

Now Willie Brown was entirely a hog from a different litter. He was smallish and squirrcly—they called him "Little Bill." A chubby thing and old lookin before his time. His face, even when he was in his late twenties, was wrinkled all over like a Georgia prune. Had a scraggly mustache and his lips was discolored with bright spots. Peculiar lookin and his eyes was none too good. They watered like he was cryin most of the time, especially when he drank, and drinkin was a full-time occupation with him. Dressed like a farmer and washed hardly at all.

Willie was one of God's poor creatures. Didn't say much. Would allow anythin you said and agree with it. That's what made him such a good second man. But his bein so agreeable and quiet is what provoked the devil in people. When he played behind Charley Patton, old Charley would bug him until he blew up. He'd point to him and say, "Look what just crawled out from under the house. Man is so ugly that water runs away when he comes by." Willie put up with it for a while, but by the time he left he hated Charley somethin fierce. Claimed he could play better than Charley, pick more notes than him, and called him a fool.

Son and Willie had a similar type thing goin but it was more of a joke with them and after a while it become somethin of an act— you know people love that, two cats squabblin. They had this riff down, sort of like the dozens. Son would tell Willie, "You a damn fool, Willie, you goin to the Diddy Wah Diddy place for sure."

Willie say, "Where's that at, man?"

"On the outskirts of perdition, built when Hell was no bigger than Baltimore."

And then Willie say, "Oh, *that* place. Ain't no town, ain't no city that I ever heard. You mean the place where the sun don't shine and it hardly ever rain?"

And Son would lick his lips and say, "Hmm, might head over yonder myself."

They got their little scene goin, Son and Willie. They was like little kings 'round there. Now in come Robert and me. Robert got his guitar swingin on his back. Son say, "Bill," he say, "who's comin through the door? Praise goodness if it ain't little Robert. And he got a guitar!"

Son and Willie they laughin about it. RL had a reputation in the Delta, but evidently they ain't heard of it. Robert wriggled up to them through the crowd. Son say, "Well, now you got a guitar, huh? What can you do with that thing?"

"Well, I tell you what," he say. "Lemme have your seat a minute." "All right," Son say, "but you better do something with it too." He wink his eye at Willie.

So RL sat down there and finally got started and, man, he was so good. When he finished, all their mouths standing open. Son say, "Well, ain't that fast? He's gone now!" This was the best, havin the benediction of Son House. But RL weren't about to linger long in Robinsonville. Robinsonville a farmin town. The shadow of King Cotton gettin too long on Robert. Have to move on down the line. I head back to Lula.

Reverend Tush Hog

Long 'bout fall who should come by Lula but Charley Patton. Figure he had hisself a sweetheart out there somewheres, 'cause Charley had no end of women. Always had plans. Was goin to a frolic in Itta Bena and would I tag along? Just a one day deal. On the way he wanna buy hisself a gun on account of the panthers and bears lurkin in them woods between Sunflower and Itta Bena.

"When the last panther you seen in the Itta Bena woods?" I ask him.

"When the last time you *been* in the Itta Bena woods?"

Oh, hell, weren't no point in arguin with Charley. Just get yourself all riled up. Gimme ten bucks and I buy him a scrappy old .44 at the pawn shop.

After the frolic I tell him I gotta get myself home but he won't hear of it. Gotta help his old buddy Son House out. Like that was what the cat needed, help from us.

"Son pastorin over at Belzoni," says Charley, "church up 'gainst the creek over there."

"That so? Blind Lemon got religion, too. Thing might just be contagious."

"Problem with Son is he got hisself a unruly congregation. Can't get a hold of them people nohow."

"Why ain't I surprised at that?"

"Thought you and me, Colcy, we go by his parish and raise him up."

"Now why would I want to do that?"

"'Cause you got a good heart and are a child of God yourself."

Hell, he could talk you into anything. Anyways, we get over to the church and Son is preachin away. He was goin on pretty good but every now and again he'd get in the middle of his sermon and then his eyes would wander out like he was watchin a bird flyin high up in the sky. He was as torn a man I ever seen in the blues-sanctified line. That's why he tear at his guitar the way he do.

This was a tough gig he got hisself 'cause it was one of them split-off church deals. Members break off from the big church, see, 'cause they was all nastyish and couldn't get 'long with nobody nohow. They all turn out to church and just set there. Son was shoutin his lungs out and they wouldn't even give him a "Amen."

Now when Son seen us settin there in a pew, his eyes wander all the more. Lose his place in the good book. Was it the loaves and the fishes or the fishes in the deep blue sea? People gettin restless, lookin over to us. We wasn't in our go-to-meetin duds exactly.

Charley figure he could use some help so he go up to join Son in the pulpit. Son cursin him but he don't pay it no mind. Charley say, "You peoples out there, I'm a-talkin to you all. This man here preached to you for two week and nary a one of you has given him so much as a 'Amen' or a 'Hallelujah!'" But see, they still ain't budgin. They settin there, arms all folded like a pack of laundry.

Charley wouldn't abide this. No audience, sanctified or skantified, gonna ignore old Charley Patton. Do so at their peril, see? Right then Charley pull out the .44 and say, "Hark to me, you gabardine swine. BOW DOWN! SING OUT YOUR PRAISES!" And he fire off a coupla shots over their heads.

Which is more or less how we landed in the Belzoni jail. Charley wrote "High Sheriff Blues" 'bout that time we spent there. Charley loved to clown, even in jail.

> It takes boozey blues, Lord, to cure these blues.
> But each day seems like years in a jailhouse,
>   where there is no booze.

Deputy Webb was a big old boy and dense as a mule. Too many words at once could confuse him, and Charley could talk a ring around the moon. Charley got Deputy Webb's ear while I was sleepin. Told him the ruckus in the church weren't none of his. Told him I done it all. "It been his pistol, Deputy, he bought it from a pawn over in Rising Sun." Which was true, far as it went. But Charley didn't stop there.

"I am myself a man of the cloth, Mr. Webb. I would no more discharge a firearm in a place of worship than piss on my mother's grave."

Convinced the deputy that he been wrongfully locked up and I a dangerous rascal who should be kept chained to the wall. That the only reason he himself been in that church in the first place was he been afraid to part company with me I was so vicious a individual. Webb let him go, no doubt figurin this was the only way to shut him up.

Got outta the slammer, snuck back home, told Vida Lee what all happened to me, omittin a few details here and there. Things goin 'long okay for awhile, like they always do. And like they always don't. My walkin shoes weren't talkin to me no more but when you start dreamin of a yellow dog chasin the jack a diamonds you know somethin's up.

'Long 'bout March, that's plantin time for the cotton, I'm out in the field puttin in seeds with a plantin stick when I see a preacher come by, ridin up on a mule, give me a tip of the hat. Big brimmed hat, dog collar, Bible stickin out his long black coat. Vida Lee have a soft spot for them preachers, and they all got a nose for a soft woman and hard liquor. Used to call 'em "lady greens" on account of them bein so genteel.

Don't see no preacher comin out of the house in such and such a time so I head back. Open the door and, man, do I get a big surprise. "What the hell is he doin here?"

"Oh," says she, very pleased with herself, "This here's the preacher I been tellin you about, Elder J.J. Hadley."

"Woman, that ain't no reverend nothin, that—"

"Brother Coley, how you doin," says he, oily as a undertaker. "Many years since we last crossed paths. Too many, too many."

"Don't you brother me! What you up to anyhow, sneakin in my house?"

"Coley, you do me a disservice. I ain't up to nothin, just passin through. I remember you live by Lula and thought I stop by pay my respects." Vida Lee smilin.

"Don't let him deceive you," I tell her. "This is the biggest liar, braggart, woofer, drunkard and coward that the world have ever seen."

"Oh," says Vida Lee brightly, "so you two know each other."

"Brother and sisters, mercy! I am a sinner, I confess it, but I have seen the light."

"Bull*shit*."

"Now, Coley," he say, "one thing you know I do not abide is swearin. Life is but a fleetin affair, brother. The flower cometh up and flourisheth a spell. Miss Vida Lee, would you be so kind as to read to me out my Bible. I have forgot my glasses. Ecclesiastes or Proverbs is my special texts."

This was too much for me. I take Vida Lee by the arm, "Woman, come out on the porch. I want to have a word with you."

When we are alone I ask her, "Don't you find it a little strange a preacher drinkin whiskey, and can't read his own Bible?"

"He forgot his glasses, didn't you hear him?"

"He ain't got no glasses. What the hell would he need glasses for? He can't *read*. Don't you know who that is? Remember that crazy muthafucka Charley Patton I told you 'bout, got me slung in the hoosegow?"

"Charley Patton, the guitar player?" And without missin a beat she turns and goes back inside. To hell with the Reverend Hadley, she's got the Reverend Tush Hog in her parlor!

"Mr. Patton, now why didn't you say who you was? I heard of you, everybody 'round here heard of you. You is famous. Sally Mason got a bunch of your phonograph records. 'Pony Blues' and 'Banty Rooster.' They's just about my all-time favorites."

"Thought 'Bird Nest Bound' been your all-time favorite," I says.

"Oh, hush your mouth, Coley. Won't you do us a tune, Mr. Patton?"

"I hate to disappoint you but I am done with that mess. Only sing in praise of the Lord now."

"Wouldn't you oblige us with just one number, Mr. Patton?"

"Well, maybe just one."

"Oh, Mr. Patton, I liked them blues you played 'bout goin down this old Jackson road. Uh, the flood thing, 'High Water Everywhere.'" He sing a couple of lines and Vida Lee go all to jelly.

> *Lord, the whole round country,*
> *Lord! River is overflowed.*
> *You know I can't be stayin here;*
> *I'm—gotta go where it's high, boy!*

But he's got other fish to fry.

> *You my all the time dream.*
> *And I wonder, Lord, I wonder*
> *What this woman done done to me.*

Clownin is one thing but now you know I had to put a stop to this pattycakes. "To hell with that shit!" I shout and walk off down the road. Slowly. Hopin Vida Lee will catch me up. But it ain't Vida Lee come runnin after me. It's *him*. Got some crazy plan and he ain't gonna rest till he get me tangled up in it.

"If it was just me, it'd mean nothin," says he, in the contritest voice you ever heard. "Absolutely nuthin. You still sore 'bout that jail thing and I don't blame you. I can understand that. But see, it's not 'bout me, it's 'bout Son."

"Whatever it is count me out."

"Coley, he needs our help. Last time 'round we done him a disservice."

"No kiddin."

"Coley, I appeal to your good heart. You know he don't respect me none. Figure me for a fool. But you he respects, that's why I'm askin your help. I have a idea to make it up to him. Have a idea for a holiness record. You, me, Son, and Willie. It would astonish the angels, make the little hills skip like young sheep."

And such. Foolish talk, but he was gettin to me. As usual. Could be mighty persuasive, wind you anyways he want.

"Your problem, Coley," says he, "is you too smart and lazy to be a farm hand. You gonna be miserable and make Vida Lee miserable long as you pretend you a farmer."

"Well, I'm farmin, ain't I? See that field out there?"

"Kid, you a *sometime* farmer. Like me. A don't-work-unless-you-absolutely-have-to farmer."

"I ain't even finished settin the cotton seed in the ground."

"Ah, plantin is woman's work. Vida Lee can go 'long with a stick just as good as you."

Saturday night Charley decided I needed to get that mean old blues right outta my system and the only way to do that properly was to spend a night playin and boozin at a barrelhouse. Which we did. So it was unfortunately Sunday mornin when we got over to the Reverend House's church in Commerce.

The congregation was singin "Jesu, Lover of My Soul" when we arrived and the high spirits from the night before havin spilt over we joined in. But as the hymn progressed Charley began to digress in a loud voice:

> *Thou of Life the Fountain art;*
> *Freely let me drink of Thee.*
> *You take one bottle, baby, I'll take three.*

The service come to an abrupt end with the congregation chasin the Reverend House down the hill and into the river, shoutin "Judas!" "Satan!" and "Herbert Hoover!"

Son did not take the congregation puttin him out so bad as I woulda thought. Seemed kinda relieved, if you ask me. What had went a long ways to soothin his afflicted soul was that Charley come up with a idea of formin a gospel quartet. Charley was a celebrity back then; every music store in town, you wouldn't hear nothing whoopin but Charley Patton.

The four "saints"—Son, Willie Brown, hisself and me—met in Skene to rehearse. Call ourselves the Locust Ridge Saints, Locust Ridge bein a bluff over behind Boyle, next town over. Take the train from Boyle down to Jackson to get a audition with Mr. H.C. Speir.

Charley done up in his Sunday preacher outfit. Dog collar, big brimmed hat pulled down over his face so Mr. Speir wouldn't recognize him. 'Course he did, right when Charley walk in. Near bust a gut. After we sung a coupla hymns Mr. Speir ask Charley if he knew any blues by any chance? Charley laughed so hard he choked.

Son House was disappointed H.C. not recordin the gospel quartet right on the spot! But Speir's recordin machine was strictly a vanity operation. All kinda people includin the actress Tallulah Bankhead come in to record. He'd make a vanity record for any artist he didn't want to recommend on up to a commercial company.

But Mr. Speir had good news. Paramount Records wanted Charley to cut some more records. Since Blind Lemon died, Charley was their main guy. The Depression all but wiped out the recordin business but lately we had two race records that been hits: Memphis Minnie's sexy, slinky "Bumble Bee," and Walter Vinson and Lonnie Chatmon's "Sittin on Top of the World." This was good news for Delta players.

Only problem was that Paramount made terrible records. The reason they got into the recordin business in the first place was to sell furniture. Paramount Records come into the recordin business backwards. They was desk and school furniture manufacturers, the Wisconsin Chair Company, and in order to sell cabinets they got themselves in the record makin business. Sold 'em in furniture and drugstores. Their talent scout was a lumber salesman! Mr. Laibly. Laibly claimed he didn't know a twelve bar blues from a two-by-four. Like he usta say, "Bidness is bidness. Wax or wood—it don't make no difference." But he couldn't have been as ignorant as he professed. He the one discovered Blind Lemon.

We set off for Grafton in two cars. Mr. Speir and some others in one and the rest of us in Wheeler Ford's Buick. Put our Stella guitars in Ford's car and down the dusty road we go. Tickled Charley, his name, I mean. Several times over he'd say, "Look what we got here, a Ford drivin a Buick."

Wheeler Ford was just about the tallest fella I ever seen. Practically had to fold hisself in two to get in the car. He was a long-sufferin individual—which would be a necessary requirement to be the chauffeur for the present company—and had a dignified air to him. Practically the only one of the bunch of us 'bout who you could say that.

Wheeler knowed the way to Grafton, but Son didn't like the route he takin. Why was we makin a detour 'round Robinsonville? "Why we goin over here? This ain't the way." Charley was pretty much hooked up with Bertha Lee right at the time but he had hisself a side-track out there called Louise Johnson and that's why we was goin there.

She was a nice lookin woman with tight hair cut short in a mannish fashion. Couldn't have been above twenty-two, twenty-three year of age. Mouth on her make a sailor blush. She and Charley set up front and didn't do nothin but drink and sing the whole time.

Louise was one lippy broad. Didn't mind nobody. Just studyin on low jokes all the time. After a while she was gettin on Charley's nerves.

"Hell," Charley sayin, "I only brought you 'long in the first place to keep the fellas happy."

"That so, meat barrel? Well, let me tell you something. I only come 'long with you to get myself a record made."

Charley slap her hard across the face. Her answer to that is to climb into the back seat and sit on Son's lap.

When we get to the Eagle Hotel the man was handin out our keys to the rooms but when it come to Son House he didn't give him none.

"I got our key," Louise says.

Son say, "*Our*? What you mean, 'our'?"

Then the light goes on. "Oh!" says Son, "'Scuse *me*, honey! All *right*! Okie-*doak*! Well honey, I'm ready, willin and able, but don't know *how* that comin out, you bein my old pal's used-to-be woman."

We was all expectin a ruckus to come of this, but turns out Charley didn't care. That was Charley. Weren't possessive of nothin or nobody. Just in it for the good time.

Next day we down at the studio. Now when I says studio you gotta understand one thing. Ain't nothin but a tar paper shack no bigger'n a chicken coop. Set right there by the tracks. Fact is they had to time their recordins so as not to coincide with the trains.

Wasn't no auditions or nothin. You just set down and play while the other fellas sat and listened—or, like in Charley's case, made comments—like he'd do at a frolic.

Mr. Laibly tried to get us to do a version of Blind Lemon's "See That My Grave Is Kept Clean" 'cause the company made a lotta bread offa that piece and they wanted to repeat it. But none of us wanted to do it. Couldn't match the *beat* Lemon had. After a day or so Son come up with his version, which he called "Mississippi County Farm." Didn't sell too well.

They got Charley and Willie Brown to cover the big hit of the moment, "Sittin on Top of the World." Charley called it "Some Summer Day." Do his usual number on it. Nine-and-a-half bar bottleneck with some of his weird lyrics onto it: *Now Henry's gone; Johnnie don't you worry, he stealin some summer day.*

With all them characters together, boozin heavily for three days, something gotta blow. When it come time to record Louise Johnson's numbers, Charley was gettin very merry. Encouragin her, doin the usual wild shouts he did at frolics. Put on a good show. "Do it long time, baby!" he was hollerin as he jump about. "Lord, what a *shame*! Good and wild! Good and wild! Come over here, woman!" His antics was aidin and abettin the others who started in makin jokes, flippin comments.

Son got mad—she was his girl now—and he begin tellin Charley to shut up. Didn't do nothin to quiet him, though. Next, Son take to abusin Charley and shovin him. Then Willie join in, grabbin Son 'round the neck and they tussle there in the middle of the floor until Charley lose his balance and they all crash into the wall of the studio—which weren't nothin but old, rotted board and batten—and the whole wall collapse to the outside. Then the roof pull away and the other three sides fall down just like a house of cards. There we was a-settin in the middle of a field, Louise still at the piano. And here comes the 11:15 rollin through. A bunch of hoboes settin in a open boxcar. Louise plays 'em a few bars of "Bumble Bee" and they all applaud like they was attendin a concert at Carnegie Hall.

Next day I slept late at the boardin house. When I come down for breakfast they'd took off, no one knew where. Never did see Charley again neither.

29.

Rather Be a Catfish, Swimmin in the Deep Blue Sea

Summer of nineteen and thirty-three. Model A Ford, loaded down with gear. Cots, pots and pans, beddin, tents, foldin chairs, oil lamps, kerosene stoves and some five hundred pounds of equipment on a platform in the back. Like they was goin on safari. But what they huntin ain't all that clear. Two white men, suits and ties comin to my door make me mighty nervous. Gotta be some kinda trouble. Government, police, taxman or some fool tryin to sell encyclopedias to folks who can't read.

"Let me introduce myself," says the elder one. "Lomax is my name, son, John Lomax."

He was a jowly old gent, pompous looking, like a politician or a bookie. Smokin a stogie, snappin his suspenders while he talk to you. The other fella was a fresh-faced college kid, very friendly and enthusiastic.

"How are you doin on this fine mornin?" Mr. Lomax ask me.

"I don't know 'bout the mornin but I ain't doin so good myself."

"And this here is my son, Alan Lomax."

"How'd ya do," says Junior and I says it back to him.

"Now son," says Senior, "we are here to collect folk songs for the Library of Congress and we have reason to believe you might be able to help us in our search for authentic Negro ballads."

Before we can even invite him into the house he reads off a long list of songs out of a ledger, and does I know any of 'em? Well, I offered as I might. Hell, just 'bout anybody would.

"Excellent," says he. "We'll begin at once. We need to get the batteries and equipment out of the car. Alan, show him the equipment."

The back of their car looked like a miniature telephone switchboard in there. Whole bunch of wires and knobs and microphones and a disc-cutter on which they made their recordins. And with that I became not only a contributor to the mighty Library of Congress, but Mr. Lomax's valet.

His career in this line started when Thomas A. Edison's widow give Mr. Lomax a old-fashion Edison cylinder recordin machine. His contribution to civilization up to this point bein "Get Along Little Doggies" and "Home on the Range," both of which he collected off of a black trail cook sometime back. Now he got hisself some brand-new equipment, gonna search the world for unlettered expressions of sufferin humanity and set 'em down for posterity.

I sung him what I could but I tell him, "Boss, this ain't exactly my line." These was plantation songs he was collectin, children's songs, old work songs. Everybody knew 'em, but they was out of fashion. But ain't that collectors for you? They ain't interested in what's shakin down on the corner. Them folklorists is in quest of the fallin-in, vine-covered cabin down on the Swanee river. You give 'em what they want.

After Mr. Lomax got done puttin down all the songs that I knew, he ask could I accompany him on his expedition. Times was hard so I said I would, despite the protests of Vida Lee.

"Let me get this straight," she says. "You goin off with them guys and they ain't given you nothin—"

"Tell you the truth, baby, I'm in it for the ride. I'll go with them down to Greenville, then find passage back upriver. Score myself some gigs—won't spend but my board and food—and I fly back to you just like a kingfisher."

"You don't have to explain why you goin. Think I got that part down by now. Just don't be so sure I'm gonna be waitin on you when you get back. Lord, when I think of the men I coulda married. Men with jobs, and steady, oh I don't know...."

"Yes indeed, baby, yes indeed. I am one lucky man and I know it."

"Well, that's as may be," she say. "Just don't expect me to hold my breath."

Vida Lee's way of givin me her blessin, or so I thought.

❖   ❖   ❖

So we set off for Greenville. City life weren't what Mr. Lomax lookin for, but I didn't much care. I intended to take me a little trip down the Mississippi.

When we get to Greenville I lead Mr. Lomax into the first, funkiest and lowdownest barrelhouse I could find. In his eye this was utter depravity, what with prostitution, bootleggin, gamblin and exchange of stolen goods all taken place in the same establishment, along with boogie-woogie piano playin. Considered it "corruption of the folk spirit."

Weren't no sense in tryin to persuade him so I point him down the road, sayin, "Well, Mr. Lomax, sir, what you lookin for is old-time. For that you gotta go where time gets locked up."

"Good man!" says he. "And where might that be?"

"Why, in the prisons, boss. You take a guy that's doin life, he ain't heard too much new stuff. That cat's gonna know a whole heap of old-timey songs."

I told Mr. Lomax I knew just the guy for his puposes. Leadbelly. He'd shot a fellow rounder and they slung him into the Louisiana State Pen in Angola. Man, what a stroke of genius on my part. Only problem is Mr. Lomax wants me to go with him. One minute I'm sayin, "I ain't visitin no penitentiary," next minute I'm ridin back there with the equipment on my way to the pen.

I knew Huddie be glad to see us. He weren't gonna get outta that place none too soon, neither by pardon nor by breakout. Angola was pretty much escape proof, havin the Mississippi river on one side and tangled woods on the other. Place was locked down tight night and day. Enterprisin cats who'd tried burrowin out underground had frequently got buried alive when their tunnels collapsed in the muddy soil.

But Huddie weren't tryin nothin. Been on his best behavior. They made Huddie a trusty. Set him in Camp "A" headquarters as a laundryman so's he could entertain visitors.

Mr. Lomax addressed the warden, Mr. Jones, in his usual high-falutin manner of speakin.

"We are making recordings for the Archives of Folk Song in the Library of Congress and Mr. Coley Williams has directed us here in the hope that we might capture authentic Negro songs."

"That right?" said the warden, playin for time while he figured what just been said to him. Sly-lookin, bull-necked dude in his forties. So relaxed that when he tilt back in his chair with his hands clasped behind his head he seem almost asleep. A mannerism much cultivated among Texans. "Well, I'll be a toasted armadillo. I got just the boy for ya. Huddie, come down here, son, got a perfesser here to see ya."

Huddie greeted me enthusiastically with a big bear hug come near to crushin my ribs. With Huddie it were a short step from affection to harm. In my ear he hissed, "You my ticket outta heah, boy. Knew you'd come get me free." He was way ahead of me. He'd figured it out settin there in his cell. In the glass house you got a lotta time to ponder.

I introduced Huddie to Big Boss and Little Boss. Huddie saw a opportunity just settin there—but Mr. Lomax, he was somewhat wary of Huddie. Huddie was big and mean lookin. Looked like the kinda ornery nigger might whack you with a hammer while you was sleepin.

Big Boss and Little Boss set up their equipment in the run-around. It was Sunday afternoon—prisoners didn't have to work for Mr. Charley that day—so the inmates was hangin in their cells. Soon as Huddie begin singin they dropped their cooncan card games. Mr. Lomax beamed when he heard Huddie's twelve string and "fine baritone voice," as he called it.

First Huddie done "The Western Cowboy," then the one 'bout cocaine, "Honey Take a Whiff on Me," then "Angola Blues" and a long version of "Frankie and Albert"—what Huddie was callin "Frankie and Johnny." Also a badman ballad 'bout a murder in a Dallas saloon, called "Ella Speed." When he come to the part where Bill Martin shoots Ella with his colt .41, he advised a startled Mr. Lomax, "Don't none of you boys kill no women. When you kill a woman, you is gone." Advice that no doubt give Big Boss pause 'bout shootin Mrs. Lomax on his return to Connecticut.

Huddie wind up with his special song, a waltz called "Irene." "Good Night, Irene" become a hit song twenty or so years on for the Weavers. Then for a encore he done the song he'd writ the year previous for Governor O.K. Allen:

> *In nineteen hundred and thirty-two,*
> *Honorable Governor O.K. Allen, I'm 'pealin to you.*
> *Had you, Governor O.K. Allen, like you got me,*
> *I'd wake up in de mornin, let you out on reprieve.*

Pretty much the same song he'd writ for Huey Long when he was governor. Bein canny and a born hustler, Huddie knew the Lomaxes might be his way outta the joint, so he not only sung for them but told 'em his unhappy life story as well, layin on all the pitiful incidents and omittin—naturally—certain grisly details. It was a tale of misunderstandins, done-wrongs and coincidences which fitted certain folk songs Mr. Lomax familiar with.

He was doin fine. Big Boss was gettin weepy hearin all 'bout them terrible injustices. But Huddie went too far. Get down on his knees and grab a startled Mr. Lomax 'round the legs. Goin for grand opera, now.

"Bless you, bless your kindly heart," he pleaded. "You won't ever have to tie your shoes again, Big Boss." Begged him to take a recordin of his plea song to Governor Allen.

Warden Jones was horrified at this breech of etiquette. Pulled Huddie off like he were a rabid dog, apologizin to Mr. Lomax for the presumption of his prisoner. Mr. Lomax went on about how he forgive him, then quickly got the hell outta there.

Huddie kept thinkin Big Boss gonna spring him. Which was his only hope 'cause he weren't eligible for parole till nineteen and thirty-six at the earliest. We had took the recordin over to Governor O.K. Allen's office when we split from Angola and left it with his secretary. And there things set for a while. Eventually Governor Allen did sign a order commutin his sentence and Huddie got let out the followin year. Had nothin to do with Mr. Lomax or the song he writ for the governor though. His discharge bein a routine matter—the double good time provision. Gave Huddie a pair of overalls and a pair of ugly shoes and let him loose with a sugar sack packed with all his earthly belongins. The rest is history, that's right.

Mr. Lomax so taken with Huddie when they got back together that he make him his chauffeur. Huddie was a master at sizin up his audience an givin 'em what they want. Anyone willin to listen and pay for the privilege was okay with him. Leadbelly saw his meal ticket comin down the road first time Big Boss and Little Boss walk into Angola. In the twinklin of a eye he turned into a old Negro songster.

End of that year, nineteen and thirty-four, Mr. Lomax take him up to New York, where he marry Martha and get his own radio show on WNYC. Play at colleges, hootenannies, Communist Party get-togethers. He created a whole new audience. Woody Guthrie come outta that, Pete Seeger, Harry Belafonte, Joan Baez and the young Bobby Dylan.

So Mr. Lomax and Huddie was set up to bring folk music to the white masses and I was where I wanted to be—done with the whole monkey business.

30

Moon Spinnin Across the Sky,
Bats Flyin in the Sun

I was passin through a little old town south of Rosedale when I run across RL again. RL had hisself a small band and he was workin with a piano player, drummer, horn player. Big bass drum with his name on it just like Duke Ellington. This the way things goin. Muddy Waters playin regular with a string band and Son House duetin with Little Buddy Sankfield on trombone. But RL soon tired of playin with a bunch of cats. He didn't like one other person hangin with him too long, never mind two or three.

Me and Robert travel to St. Louis and on into Illinois. While there we was passin through a little town outside of Elgin when a man in a straw hat and checkered jacket come runnin outta a furniture store. He's all over us, friendly as a puppy. "Boys, you look like you could use a sandwich and a drink, come inside and I'll fix you something." We hadn't seen a kind face in days and it was real comfortin to run into someone who was concerned with our welfare. He's inquirin of us, "You boys musicians by any chance?" And we say, "Yes, sir." "Can you do us a few numbers?" he ask. "I'd be much obliged." We figures the guy usin us to sell furniture—nothin wrong with that. "We'd be glad to play. What kinda music you want to hear?" And he say, "Oh, don't matter, you play anything you used to playin." Now this is peculiar. If there's one thing people have definite opinions about it's music. They want to hear *their* music.

Another thing, all the people comin in are white. Peckerwoods comin to hear us play the blues? Wake me when it's over, man. RL start with a boogie, "If I Had Possession Over Judgment Day." Everyone like to hear a little boogie. I'm right there with him. People pay twenty-five cents a head and we get to play whatever we want? We musta died and went to heaven, man. Durin the break I walk outside and I hear this guy out front yellin, "Special attraction! Three nights only! Come see two niggers from Mississippi black as coal playin genuine coon music. In the flesh! Two bits cheap! Stay as long as you want." They wasn't there for the music at all. They come to see our black asses. Hicks gawkin at us, people which never seen black people before. They try to get us to stay. The manager thought we wanted more money but we just wanted to get the hell outta there. They were the freaks, not us. Scared us to death.

We was ramblin up and down the levee camps, road gangs, jook joints, clubs as far away as Chicago. But every now and again RL needed a place to stop. He settled in Helena on the Arkansas riverside for a while. There was a whole bunch of clubs in West Helena, about seven mile from Helena. At night it was jumpin over there, man. West Helena hot spots was famous. Night clubs, bars, jook joints. Everybody come through Helena one time or another. Robert Nighthawk, Elmore James, Honeyboy Edwards, Howlin Wolf, Hacksaw Harney, Peter "Memphis Slim" Chatman, Johnny Shines. You stop there long enough the whole damn world come by.

RL was livin over there with Estelle Coleman and her son Robert Lockwood, later become a great guitar player in his own right. He hold RL in such high esteem he take to callin hisself Robert Junior in honor of his common-law daddy. RL basically adopt Estelle's family as his own.

Robert took to the ramblin life like a fly to jelly and his fame spread up and down the land as far as eastern Tennessee and southern Mississippi. Main problem for a ramblin singer was how to project a acoustic guitar up against all that racket at a country dance. The way RL done it was by his stompin feet and usin his boogie-woogie walkin bass to provide the beat.

He had that beat down, man. Those feet pursue him through every song. Some shadow thing in pursuit, things gainin on you. Time to go. If it ever catch up with you, watch it.

The other technique he use was his high-pitch falsetto to throw the sound. The high sound you hear better. That piercin field-holler sound.

Sound carry a *long* way in the country. What's the song he sang in that high-pitched voice? "Kindhearted Woman." His voice was carryin it way out in the fields. Didn't have too much trouble makin ourselves heard in those days. People that was dancin, they'd just pick up the beat, and if they got out of earshot, the rhythm stayed with them and kept right on dancing. Robert know that two-day sound and he intend to stay one step ahead of it. Hang 'round a week, ten days, then come mornin he'd be gone. Made him the subject of endless speculation, that's right.

RL would go anywhere, tolerate any kinda nonsense to hear a new record of Charley Patton, Leroy Carr, any of them. And now he was ready to have the recordin angel inscribe his own tunes on a metal disc.

Was 'round the middle of November of thirty-six we set out with Mr. Oertle of the Vocalion record company for San Antone. We played together on the street and in the joints along the way. Took us a while to get to San Antonio because Mr. Oertle was stoppin off along the way to sell records, and while he doin his business we pass the time playin for people, give RL a chance to try out the tunes he was goin to record.

On Monday the 23rd we arrive in San Antone and Mr. Oertle take us to the Gunter Hotel where ARC recordin director Art Satherley set up his equipment. They been there for several weeks already recordin. They got a suite in the hotel set aside. One room hold the equipment. The other one was the band room. All the furniture stacked up against the wall.

Bunch of musicians there already. Gents in sombreros and ornate Mexican fiesta outfits, dudes in cowboy gear. Did a lot of their recordin in Texas on account of all the western swing and cowboy-type bands that was there.

Don Law was the big daddy. He was lean and athletic—but short. He was a English cat and compared with most other record company guys he dressed pretty sharp. V-neck sweater, white pants, white shoes. Like he was gonna go play a game of golf when the thing was over, which he probably was.

"Heard a lot about you, son," Mr. Law say to Robert. "You gonna show us something?"

"That depends," say Robert, "on what you ready to see."

The Mexican hombres was Hermanas Barraza and his band, a Mexican guitar group bein recorded. They was sittin 'round pickin. To break the ice, Mr. Law say, "Why don't you show these Mexican fellas how you boys from Mississippi pick it?" Now this the very thing Robert *don't* wanna show them, so when he played he turn his back to the Mexicans and face the wall.

This amused Mr. Law. "First time this young fella been to a recording session, folks," he say to the cowboys. "Bashful, don'tcha know?" And everybody laugh. Eventually Robert calmed down enough to play but he never faced them, always got his guitar turned away. Didn't want people pickin at his soul. Just set there playin like a old-time root doctor conjurin over his jars and sacks.

RL play his trump card, "Terraplane Blues." He stomp out the beat with his feet, play a chordin shuffle rhythm and a high treble-string lead with his slider all at the same time. Mexican cats was speechless, lookin 'round for the *other* guitar player. *Mysterioso amigo.*

That night Mr. Law take us over to a colored boardinghouse and before leavin he say: "Now I want you boys to remain here in the house and get some rest. We start recordin tomorrow morning at ten o'clock sharp. And by the way, cops down here are a vicious bunch."

He wasn't gone ten, fifteen minutes before Robert walk in all slicked up and ready to go on the town. "C'mon man, I hear there's some mighty fine lookin women in Texas." I thought I had talked him out of it but when I woke up the next mornin RL gone. Bed not even slept in.

'Round ten o'clock Mr. Oertle show up lookin for Robert. Nobody seen him. There was only two places he could be: some woman's house or jail. And that's where he was. A miserable sight, too. Clothes all ripped, face bruised and his lip cut. Cops had picked him up on a vagrancy charge. Worked him over, smashed his guitar.

With some difficulty Mr. Law get him released. Give us forty-five cents to go have breakfast, but Robert don't wanna spend the money. "This coin could come in useful sometime down the line. Why waste it on eatin?" But savin it for a rainy day was not exactly what he had in mind. As he went out the door he said, "Gonna find that bitch

I lost last night. *Betty Mae, Betty Mae gonna find that girl someday.*" Now Betty Mae was a workin girl and she naturally want to get paid, so five minutes later RL's on the phone to Mr. Law tellin him he's lonesome.

"You're lonesome?" Mr. Law was amazed. "What can I do for lonesome?"

"Well, there's a lady here wants fifty cent and I lacks a nickel."

Mr. Law have a good old laugh over that one. The session on the last day sandwiched in between the Chuck Wagon Gang, a popular western swing group, and another bunch of Mexican fellas. RL laid down seven songs and the next day we left.

Mr. Law gave Robert a train ticket which he immediately cashed in down at the station. I went down to the station with my ticket in my hand. Rode the rods right back to the Promised Land.

A few months later "Terraplane Blues" come out on a record with "Kindhearted Woman" on the flip side. Sold some four to five thousand copies. Most the King of the Delta Blues ever sold.

We was standin there on Johnson Street in Greenwood one time and this lady come walkin by and say, "You know that number, 'Terraplane Blues'?" And Robert brighten right up like a little kid, say, "Miss, that my number, that my song I just recorded." Like that. And she say, "Yeah, and I be Eleanor Roosevelt." RL, he say, "Gimme fifteen cents and I'll play it for you, ma'am. And if it ain't just like the one on the phonograph record you can have your money back again." Lady just stood there with her mouth open. "I never did meet someone made a phonograph record."

Then he sung that lady a song will haunt me all my days. You probably know it.

> *I went down to the crossroad,*
> *fell down on my knees.*
> *Asked the Lord above, "Have mercy now.*
> *Save poor Bob if you please."*

On down to the end, still gets me every time.

You can run, you can run,
tell my friend-boy Willie Brown,
Lord, that I'm standin at the crossroad, babe,
I believe I'm sinkin down.

When I heard that, I begin to wonder did Robert really believe something happened that night, 'cause he was now tellin the crossroads story hisself. *Singin* 'bout it. Even tellin it to me.

A minute or two go by, RL say, "Did I get you goin? Well boy, you got *me* believin that you ain't got no more sense than a mule." He laugh and laugh. *Hawh-hawh-hawh*! Had to sit down beside the road on account of he was laughin so hard.

Now I was really confused. The only thing make me wonder if there weren't something in it is what I heard from my Uncle Ezekiel. He a kinda root doctor hisself, and shortly after the thing went down at the crossroads he tell me he know something strange have transpired that day.

"Singularities and freaks of nature was aboundin," he say. "Weird shit start happenin for no reason. Blight on the crops, women leavin their men in the middle of the evenin meal, well water turnin blood-red, moon spinnin across the sky. When you see bats flyin in the sun and bees swarm at midnight, you know something been messin with the divine clockwork."

Back then, people studied about magic and such things all the time. Talk to Jesus, the saints, and their long-dead friends. Didn't have to meet with the Devil at no crossroads. You let the Devil in your mind, that's the same thing. RL communed with the dark spirits, no doubt about it, seen the movin unseen shapes in the night.

Early this mornin, ooh
When you knocked upon my door
And I said, "Hello, Satan,
I believe it's time to go."

The wind was howlin in his brain, blowin up from Hell itself. Some things you summon up, you never gonna get rid of them.

31

That Old Evil Spirit
So Deep Down in the Ground

Woke up one mornin—we was in Greenville—looked 'round for Robert but he'd split. Gone into the blue. I hung 'round Greenville just to see what I could see. Played piano for my keep. One day I come up on Daddy Stovepipe again.

"Why don'tcha head up to St. Louis?" he says. "I hear they got a scene goin will melt the shoes right off your feet."

"How am I gonna get there with no money?"

"Son, just get yourself on the Excelsior."

"Meanin?"

"Meanin that's a floatin cathouse, man. You never heard of the Excelsior? Call it a women's boat. Floatin whorehouse of the Mississippi. I'll introduce you to Captain Hogg—piano players is always welcome on the Excelsior."

So that was my ticket to St. Louis. All the women would follow that boat, pay fifty cents for cabin fare and ride it from Memphis down to Rosedale and back all the way up to St. Louis. That's how they made their bread, up and down the river. Boat was carryin Uncle Sam's mail so the women was well protected.

They usta keep their gold twixt their legs, hung on a sack. They had so much money that when they got back to Memphis they'd be walkin in all funny from the weight of it. I woulda stayed on her for the return trip but bein it's St. Louis they got their pick of piano players to come on board.

First job I got was down on Main Street, a furniture store. A piano was settin in the window. Big old grand piano. I ask the guy, "Can I play it?"

"Go right ahead, maybe it'll bring folks in the store. Give you a nickel for every person comes in."

That went along fine till Willie Somethinorother come along —there was a whole lot of Willies around at that time: Willie Jones and Willie Smith, Pinetop Willie and Willie Ezel. This particular Willie claim he can play *any* tune. You name it, he could play it. Couldn't compete none with that. I told the man, "Give Willie my stool. I think you just found yourself a new piano-playin fool."

Next job I got was playin piano at the Hole in the Wall. Lost it the second night.

"Two white men snoopin 'round here earlier askin after you," says the houseman. "Look like vice, or revenuers maybe. They can shut me down and send me up river, man. Them cats is from outta town. You can't even bribe them muthafuckas."

Ah, shit! What is this? Just some mix-up. Maybe the guy was makin the story up. Just didn't care for my playin. Maybe I wasn't drawin like he figured.

So I nailed me a gig at Addy's, the very joint where the boogie-woogie come from. Addy's Place on Mulberry Street. That is where "Vicksburg Blues" and "44 Blues" come outta. People dance to them numbers, and that's what you was hired to promote—dancin.

Addy was a old-time hipster and he'd seen no reason to change. Dressed in a style that was the height of fashion twenty years ago— bowler hat and bottle-green waistcoat—he talked in old-time slang, too. He loved musicians and, man, I was flyin high in my little old sky. Makin fifty cents and a chance to hang out with Roosevelt Sykes and all them cats. Play *all* night long. From seven in the evenin 'round to four in the mornin without stoppin, and the chicks in the life sashayin through. In them places it was strictly blues all the way.

Never got more than a dollar and a half to play but you couldn't of paid me ten dollars to *leave*. I was glued to that piano. Got to check out all the big-time sports comin in and spendin all their money. Pimps and prostitutes and such—I was glad to be around that kinda folk. People in the sportin life the best audience you can find, that's right. But my employ as a piano player was goin downhill fast.

"Two guys was here lookin for you," says Addy. "White. Suits."

Damn! The two suits was still on my tail and they was messin me up bad. Nobody wants the heat.

"Just keep 'em far 'way from my joint, man." Addy's tellin me.

"How can I do that when I don't even know who they is?"

"Just take care of it, Coley."

Next day I run up on Peetie Wheatstraw. You heard his name run all 'round the town. Call hisself "The Devil's Son-in-Law" and the "High Sheriff From Hell." Man, that cat was so fly he was *spittin* in the Devil's face. Looked a little like the Devil, too. *Long* head with pointy ears. Piano player, rounder, whiskey drinker and pavement pounder. Lived over in a rough section of East St. Louis called the Valley. Kinda shantytown full a crime, vice, bedbugs and lice.

Peetie sung in a gangster's swagger, draaaawlin out the words so slow and slurred and cool.

> *He makes some happy, some he make cry.*
> *Well, now, he made one old lady go hang herself and die.*

Talked in a high-speed slangy patter. Jive type of don't-give-a-damn individual.

"All it take to get along in this mean old world is a little shit, grit and mother wit. And man, I was born with all three."

In the days I come up in, I was well acquainted with Tom Turpin, Ell-Zee Young, Speckled Red, any number of blues players. Boogie-woogie was hot. Spreadin like a brush fire down through the camps and the joints.

St. Louis Jimmy, you heard of him? He was famous in his day. Jimmy Oden was his real name. He was a real skinny cat with a long head. Bony featured. Stuttered real bad. The words would come outta him all mixed up. Except when he was singing and then it went away entirely, even though he spoke part of his songs.

St. Louis Jimmy had a tune called "Going Down Slow." You mighta heard of that. Another one he done was "Monkey Faced Woman." Many good blues he had. The one that really took off was "Night Time Is the Right Time." By the next mornin it was all across town. Next night it had syncopated its way up to New York, and by the next day you got lumberjacks up in Alaska requestin it.

Still goin 'round, far as I know. A good riff like that will run like perpetual motion. *Night time is the right time, to be with the one you love.* Hmm, hmm, hmm.

When it got 'round one, two o'clock in the mornin, that's the time to soften way down on the pedal, that's when the police come through with their gang. S-l-o-w down, get real smoky and funky.

There was so many places to play in St. Louis. There was a bunch of joints down there on Johnson Street. That's where "Frankie and Albert" originated. It was always full of people over there 'cause all the riverboats would come in there and dock. All the fancy people would come down there for their slummin and sinnin.

Robert Nighthawk played at the 9-0-5. He was always goin off someplace. Down to old Mexico, up in Chicago. Teddy Roosevelt Darby was around then. They used to call him Future Darby. And then there was Pappa Slickhead and Pappa Eggshell too. 'Cause his head was bald as a eightball. It was Pappa Eggshell sittin on my stool when I come in to do my gig.

"Why's Pappa Bear settin in my chair?" I ask Addy.

"Coley baby, you don't work here no mo."

"Whaddidido? Ain't done nothin."

"Them cats as what was lookin for you was back again last night. Crabtree pulled all his chicks outta here and now nobody's comin in. The action's movin down the street to Zack's. I'm dyin in here, man."

Shit, now I'm gettin worried. What I done to draw government heat? Hell, musta be some kinda government mix-up. They done put the wrong papers in the wrong box or something.

Run up on Peetie Wheatstraw, he tells me there's a openin over at the 9-0-5 Club. Ended up losin that gig to Chee Dee. Coal black he was, a shiny little black dwarf and one of the old-line players. He would carry hisself from one gin mill to the next like a little old gnome pushin a cart with his wares. Whosoever he come upon playin in the barrelhouse he'd kick 'em off their stool.

Had this little trick he fooled with where he'd cover the piano with a sheet, then play with the sheet coverin up the keys. They would blindfold his eyes and he'd play trumpet with one hand and piano with his other. It was a novelty act, but people ate it up. People love all kinda stupid shit.

When you see stuff like that goin down—and you is still pumpin and grindin—you know it is time to move on. Seem like every day some new gunslinger come 'long gonna cut my head and knock me off my chair.

Got myself one last gig. Score some bread for the road. Was at a lowdown, scruggly joint named Slugger Nelly's. Nelly was made of solid brass. You cross Nelly and she'd plow you right under. But she gimme a job and that's all I cared. First night I show, everybody from the club is all out on the street.

"What the hell's goin on here?" I ask.

"Feds, baby. Givin some poor sucker the third degree."

"Who all is in there?"

"It's St. Louis Jimmy."

"What they got him on, F minor sevenths?"

Sure was some strange shit goin down. But now was my chance to get the jump on them two. Sneak 'round the back, climb up on a garbage can and chin myself to the window. When I finally get myself situated so I can tell what is goin on, you know what I see? The Lomaxes, that's right. I been runnin 'round St. Louis all week, dodgin a coupla professors of folkology.

I slip away quietly. Next night I'm playin down at Slugger Nelly's whiskey house and damned if they don't walk in the joint.

"Oh Mr. Williams, we're so glad to find you at long last" and all that stuff. I'm not all that delighted to see them and neither is Nelly, what with Big Boss interruptin me after each number with where did I first hear that song and from who?

One thing them sportin life cats hate is people askin questions. And Nelly, man, she coulda killed me, 'cause ain't nobody in the joint gonna believe these two ain't feds.

Finally Mr. Lomax come to the point. He want me to take him on to another penitentiary. Did I have a place of incarceration I could recommend to them? I told him I didn't have all that much experience in the prison line and didn't especially want to broaden my knowledge of it. But I knew unless I got them cats outta town soon they was liable to get me killed. I weren't that crazy 'bout doin a tour of southern prisons so I told him I'd take him to the gates of Parchman Farm and then I'm gone.

"Here you are, boss," I say when we get to that godforsaken place. "Far as I go. One penitentiary enough for me."

Good Mornin Blues,
Blues How Do You Do

Nineteen thirty-two been the leanest year for Bessie since she come up, but she never was as low as the stories they told 'bout her. No little old worldwide depression gonna set the Empress of the Blues back none. Bessie dump the goofy headgear and the fancy costumes and squeeze her ample self into a white shimmerin silk evenin gown. The sophisticated Miss Bessie comin to your town.

She was leadin the highlife—by this time she and Richard Morgan, y'know the bootlegger from Chicago, had moved in together. Richard's former common-law wife was naturally not too delighted with this arrangement. She was short and stubby and a holy terror if she didn't get her way. 'Course there was no way in hell she was gonna get her way with Bessie and Richard. So one day she stop by where they was stayin wieldin a tire iron, demandin him back.

Bessie goes, "Honey, you outta your mind? What do you think, I'm holdin him here against his will? Tell you what I'll do. I'm gonna leave now, go down to the store. If he go with you while I'm gone, he's yours."

She always did know which way the wind blow. Things change, Bessie get right with 'em fast. She taste the new scene and say: "Times is hard. Nobody want to hear blues no more. Folks wanna hear novelty songs. I'm gonna go get myself modernized, baby!"

She got two flat feet planted firmly on the floor and practically overnight she transformed herself from old style up-from-the-blues beltin to doin popular songs of the day like "Smoke Gets in Your Eyes" and "Tea for Two." Like she said, "Times is hard, baby. Times is hard."

❖   ❖   ❖

In the fall of 1937 I'd heard Miss Bessie was comin through Memphis —figured this would be a good time to go home and mend my bridges. If I could bring Vida Lee up there so's she could meet her idol I'd be sure to get some time off for good behavior.

Bessie was doin real good by this point. Gettin gigs up North, singin in nightclubs in Harlem, got herself invited to the blues and jazz concert at the Famous Door on 52nd Street. She even nail down a six-week gig at Connie's Inn. Future was brightnin, there was talk of another movie, maybe a new recordin session. Got her own show and a new Packard.

"La Smith"—that's what they was callin her—was a *huge* success in Memphis. Singin all the new stuff, "Pennies from Heaven" mixed in with the old risqué songs, "Kitchen Man" and "I'm Wild About That Thing." The plump proclaimer of the blues could still knock 'em dizzy.

One day I am in Memphis, carryin Vida Lee down there to catch Bessie's show. When we get backstage Bessie was mighty high on herself.

"Coley," she say, "I figure I keep on keepin on pretty much indefinitely. Retire myself oh, say, 'round nineteen and sixty. Be sittin mighty pretty by then. Have myself a butler, cook, ladies maid, swimmin pool, big old tub with gold handles and as much pig's trotters as I can eat."

"Sounds good, " say I, but it was not to be. Bessie got x-ray specs, but some things even she could not foresee.

Her next appearance scheduled to open in Darling, Mississippi on Sunday afternoon. But Bessie, ever restless, want to get outta town *now*. Wants her and Richard to get a head start on the troupe and drive down to Clarksdale. They leave Memphis 'round one in the mornin, September 26, 1937, draggin Richard kickin and screamin away from his poker game.

Bessie and Richard about seventy miles outta Memphis. drivin through Coahoma, just a few miles from Lula, when the car struck a Uneeda Biscuit truck stalled in the middle of the road. Bessie badly injured, arm near cut off, she lyin there moanin and groanin. A Memphis surgeon, name of Dr. Hugh Smith, come down the road with his fishin partner. They summon a ambulance but after a long while, no ambulance show up. Dr. Smith and his friend try to lift Bessie's two-hundred-pound body from the wreckage into the back seat of his car. They doin that when the doctor's own vehicle get struck from behind by a car driven by a partyin couple. So now you got *three* badly injured people, and Bessie dyin by the side of the road. Still no ambulance.

Eventually a ambulance come and take Bessie into Clarksdale. Take her to the G.T. Thomas Hospital, a *black* hospital. You've heard all them foolish stories about how she first brought to the white hospital in Clarksdale and they wouldn't treat her? Well, in 1937, no ambulance driver black or white even think of puttin off a black person in a hospital for white folks. Anyway, by the time they get Bessie to the hospital and amputate her arm it was too late. She died the next mornin.

In my memory she still dressed in one of them flapper gowns, all silver and black with her wig hat on and more feathers than you find on a cockatoo. But that may just be my memory harmonizin with the songs—"Careless Love," "Empty Bed Blues"—and the music sweepin everything along, changin everything into its own sultry rhythm, the world itself just part of that song and the song itself a history of the world. World's pain just a love story gone wrong— all you can do is sit down by the river, put your head in your hands and laugh.

33

You May Bury My Body, Ooh, Down by the Highway Side

Alittle before then RL show up again, on his way to Dallas. I asked him, "Can I hang with you a while?" He didn't say no.

It was June of nineteen and thirty-seven. As if it weren't hot enough already where we was, we was goin to Texas, gonna fry like catfish on a Saturday night. And weren't I right 'bout that? It hotter than a poker down there. So hot you could fry a egg on the sidewalk, but Robert didn't care. He was there to cut a record and to hell with everything else.

They was recordin in a empty warehouse above a Buick showroom. The sessions was on the weekend but still there was traffic noises from the street. To keep them out they have to shut the windows and cover them with heavy drapes. Inside it musta been 120 degrees, and no air. All us have to take our shirts off because we drippin. Big fan blowin air over a block of ice hardly cool it down one degree.

Outside the sun was shinin like a lamp in Hell but inside the mood was dark and bleak. It was all doorknobs a-turnin by theirselves, liens on his soul, mojo hands, and spooks swarmin 'round his bed. And that was just the lighthearted and dirty-minded songs: "Milkcow's Calf Blues," "Honeymoon Blues," "Little Queen of Spades," "Malted Milk," and "Drunken Hearted Man."

Suspicion, betrayal, and doom was all in his mind then. Such that some people said they was omens, that you coulda read it like a sign.

Then there was the truly eerie songs: "Stones in My Passway," "Hellhound on My Trail" and "Me and the Devil Blues." He was settin on a rock in the wilderness of Moab, starin into the end of time. Dark moods rolled over him like a thunderhead on the Brazos River—he conjurin that atmosphere. Pullin little demons outta the pit by their scaly tails.

You listen to "Hellhound on My Trail" lately? I played it just the other day for my great-grandboy, Nace. Man, that song set your mind awry. You ain't listenin to a song no more—you in a world of shadows.

Aside from the hellhounds and the Devil, RL doin fine. His fame spreadin throughout the South, records comin out one every month or so. By Spring of '38 he was 'bout as famous as you get in the Delta, but he was more ambitious than that. Said he was goin back up to Chicago soon. That woulda been somethin, huh?

Saw him in Memphis when he come through. Then just as soon as he arrived Robert left again. When I caught up with him in St. Louis he ditch me again. He was a hard guy to stick to. He'd say, "I'm goin to take a leak," and disappear for two weeks. Caught up with him again in Memphis, spend a few days together and then he's off back over to Helena, back with Robert Lockwood's mother.

Strange things start happenin to Robert 'round this time. His hat catch on fire while he playin over in a club in West Helena. He got into a accident where he fell off the fender of a truck and had to lay up three, four days. People started to say his luck was runnin out. Pact with the Devil come due and such. I was gettin a funny feelin myself. Robert went over into Mississippi and I didn't like the thought of Mississippi right then, don't ask me why. I start to cross the bridge from Helena into Mississippi but something stop me. You could feel it comin across the bridge. Robert always make fun of this stuff but that don't mean he didn't believe. Probably feel same thing I did, just don't care. *Believe my time ain't long.* Someone tell me he was headin up to Robinsonville, another say he heard Robert on his way to Greenwood. Next thing I hear Robert dead.

News travel slow through the Delta. It was 'bout six month before friends of RL learn of his death. Story changin as it went from hand to hand. Even his cousins was sayin maybe it was his pact with the Devil at them crossroads. "Believe the Devil come for his due." And on like that. Some say he stabbed to death, some that a lady poison him, others say it was pneumonia. To tell the truth, most folks surprised Robert live as long as he did. I never did get the straight of it until some thirteen years later. People kept tellin me, "Coley, you best talk to Sonny Boy Williamson." They say, "You find Sonny Boy and he tell ya, man. He *know* what went down 'cause he playin with Robert the night he got killed."

So when I come up to Chicago in the early fifties I arrange to meet him at the Cadillac Baby's, funky little lounge on the South Side. Inside it's dingy, smoky, Christmas decorations still hangin, a little stage over to the right, neon signs blinkin and cracklin, jukebox playin Lightnin Hopkins' "Santa Claus Boogie." They sure like Christmas in this place.

Sonny Boy sittin in a booth by hisself and he look scary. Kinda his regular fiendish look, what with the little goatee and his eyes hard and cold. We talk a while and then I bring up RL's death. Does he know anything about it?

"Man, I was there," he tell me. "Summer of nineteen and thirty-eight. I was goin by the name Little Boy Blue at that time. Livin in Greenwood, goin out to play Three Forks on the weekend. Robert and me been playin out there several weeks runnin. The houseman who own the jook name of Ralph I think. Live way out in the country but he come in the little city, that be Greenwood, pick up the boys gonna play and carry 'em back out into the country, unnerstan? A good steady gig but RL complicate the situation by messin with the houseman's wife. I say, 'Robert, you like to get yourself killed and me along with you.' But RL don't care. Like he need the danger or somethin. Need a woman to sing to. Preferably unavailable."

"Santy Claus" come on the jukebox.

"That's mine," Sonny Boy say. It was that crazy Christmas song he done.

"The night Robert get poisoned we play 'If I Had Possession

Over Judgment Day.' What Elmore James do as 'Rollin and Tumblin' now. It always get everybody out on the floor. Most everybody drunk, clappin along, whoopin and hollerin. Rollin and *stumblin* mainly. It was *hot*, brother. August, y'understand.

"This guy out in Three Forks who own the house, he a little god in his town runnin everthin for the black folks. Which mean shit to us. They real bumpkins out there, man. Bein Robert's elder, I was keepin a eye on what was goin down, dig? I observe Robert's attraction for a skinny girl but I can tell by the faces of certain of the people in the house somethin ain't right. They keep lookin at this Ralph like ain't you gone do something? I'm watchin and watchin. Durin a break in the music they play records on the new Wurlitzer. Robert dancin with this chick, bendin backwards, slidin on the floor. Bad, bad scene, man.

"Robert and I standin together and I see the houseman give this other guy some pint of whiskey and point to Robert. Why don't he just offer the bottle to Robert hisself, dig? Give it to Robert to drink. Why? Because he have it in for Robert, see, and his wife or whoever she was. But aside from wantin to kill him, he still keep Robert to play for him.

"So here come this weasely little guy bring Robert a half pint with a broken seal. Robert about to drink from it when I knocks it from his hand and the bottle smash on the ground. 'RL, don you *ever* take a drink from a open bottle,' I tell him. 'You don't know what could be in it.' Like that. Robert come right back at me. 'Man,' he say, 'you ever knock a bottle of whiskey outta my hand again I tear your fuckin head off.'

"So when the fella hand him a second bottle of whiskey I could only stand by and watch and hope. Robert's still playin but soon he don't have the breath to sing."

Sonny Boy was into his third round of whiskey sours with Bud chasers. He looked beat-up and tired and old and his watery eyes was hard and beady. Had him a rough and violent life and it showed. Sonny Boy grab the waitress.

"Sugar, bring us another round."

She examine him with some cold contempt. "You best slow down or your old lady be haulin you outta here on your ass again tonight."

"I love you, too, babe," he say. "Anyways, where was I?"

"The poisoned whiskey...."

"Well, 'round one o'clock in the mornin Robert slow *way* down. Folks sayin, 'Wassa matter, Robert? You okay?' He say, 'Can't talk, can't play none neither.' Then he say, 'Sonny Boy, you go ahead take this one.' Robert was the leadin man, see, and this was very unlike him to hand over his spot. He say, 'Take me home, I'm not able to play no more.' Two o'clock, he's so sick they have to bring him back to town.

"He was out of his damn mind. Shiverin, prayin to God, cursin God, cryin for his mama come cover him, and this in middle of August in Mississippi. Lookin *real* bad, man. Have a putrid kinda glow 'round him like this here Budweiser sign.

"Robert be pale as a ghost, shaky, green at the gills. The poison do terrible things to poor Robert. His blood boil up till his tongue be hangin out like a hound with rabies. His—whatcha callit?—his liver shrivel up to like a piece of crispy bacon...."

"Whoa, Sonny Boy! I get the picture."

"No you don't. 'Cause I ain't told you the strange part yet. The closest you ever come to seein a man turn into a animal. He wasn't human at the end. And who ever heard of a man crawlin on his hands and knees and bark like a dog without hoodoo bein involved?"

"So, you sayin…"

"Lay down for several days and toward the end wrote something on a piece of paper, what it was I never knew. He give it to.... Hell, I can't remember. Died in my arms, yessir. Right before he go out—I'm weepin, right then, tears pourin outta my eyes—I say, 'Robert I'm prayin for you, man!' And he say, 'Whatever you do, don't you pray for me, Little Boy Blue.'

"Damn shame, man. Lissen, I gotta go blow my harp, man. See ya."

Only his mama and brother-in-law at RL's funeral. Buried in a unmarked grave in a pine coffin furnished by the county in the old Zion church graveyard near Morgan City outside of Greenwood. Just a stones throw off Mississippi Highway 7.

You may bury my body
Down by the highway side,
So my old evil spirit
Can catch a Greyhound bus and ride.

There never was a investigation into Robert's death. At that time the death of a black man didn't mean no more than the death of a mule. To most folk he just a no-account jook joint guitar player that got what comin to him.

But Robert a giant—like Gulliver among the little folk. He ate up everything that came before him. Brought the Delta blues to its glory. There weren't any further you could take it short of electricity and even that he could mimic.

He foreshadow all what to come. Chicago blues of Muddy Waters, Elmore James, Sonny Boy Williamson II, Howlin Wolf, they all made his songs into hits. To them he remain the master. But he was also the last. No more saints after Robert. Mystery gone out of it, see? Robert come from a world where facts and magic was livin side by side. Where you could imagine the Devil come knockin on your door. A world as far away as the Middle Ages. World of mysteries and conjuration, where a root doctor write a name on a slip of paper and that curse fly across the Delta and strike you down. And all the doctors in Hot Springs can't help you none.

Hello Satan,
Believe It's Time to Go

Do I remember Memphis? Hell, as if I ever could forget it. Funky, funky Memphis, big, bad slinky harlot of the Nile. Did I say Nile? I'm gettin old, I don't need to tell you. Old where all the rivers flow into the sea, all the pharaohs turn to glass, all the women run together in your mind.

Memphis, Memphis…Tennessee. Come back to me, baby, won't you please come back to me. Now for myself, *that* was home, man. Place you know you was meant for—like the first time you with a woman. Know where you belong.

When was I there? Let's see…musta been 'round '41, '42 first time I come through Memphis. Probably in '48, '49 when I pass through again. But I'm gettin ahead of my story, 'cause I haven't yet told you 'bout Helena and Detroit and Los Angeles and all that. What got me ramblin down the road again was a electric guitar. That's right. Led me right by the nose. This story is in E minor, dig, with a whole lotta changes in it. Goes something like this.…

❖   ❖   ❖

One day I'm scufflin my way home, when down the road apiece I spy a funny scene goin down. Back window of a house shoots up, out poke a big head. Big head lookin south, big head lookin north. Presently a smooth dude clambers out that back window.

"Well well," says I to myself, "looky there, some slick cat makin his midnight creep." Laughin up my sleeve, y'know. As I get closer suddenly it ain't that funny no more 'cause, brother, that was *my* house the creep was creepin outta.

"Hey, muthafucka!" I shout. He turn just long enough to flash me a grin. By the time I get up to the house he's long gone through the corn.

Man, this looks *baaaad*. Evil goin on in my happy home. Never figured on no claim-jumper come knockin on my door. Oh, I sung all a them songs 'bout cheatin hearts and two trains runnin and backdoor men. Down at the jook we all usta laugh at some fat old man gettin cuckolded by a slick young cat—who was you. You, baby, remember? You was always that cat, the one slippin and a slidin outta that window soft and low.

But when it happen in your own home, brother, that's a other whole mess. Still, I was cool.

I spy Vida Lee sittin up on the porch, smokin a big fat reefer. Lookin mighty pleased with herself. Now I'm thinkin evil stuff. Like, that's just what *we* usta do when we make love. Smoke a big old reefer and fuck. I'm steamin, man.

"Woman, you best tell me who I seen sneakin out back or I'm gone—"

"Ain't nobody climbin outta no window, honey. Sure you feelin all right, baby?" You know it real bad when the women start to sweet-talk you.

"You think I'm blind?"

"So, what 'bout it, baby?"

"That cat climbin out the back of my house is what 'bout it."

"C'mon sugar pie, your 'magination workin overtime." What she done next is what I least expected. My worst nightmare.

"Anyway," she said, "you got your women, why can't I have my men?" Bold as brass.

I tell her, "You ain't thinkin right."

And in her tiny little girl voice she comes back, "Told you you shouldn't have left me all on my lonesome for so long."

"Jesus, Vida Lee! You talkin trash."

"I'm tellin you the truth. You can't take the truth?"

"Depend what it is."

"Oh honey, calm yourself. It's just Jimmy."

"That self-righteous little brother of yours you always tellin me about? That Jimmy?"

"Uh-huh. Listen, honey, he lost his job where he was workin and Mr. Perkins over at the mill offer him a job. He's a good steady worker, churchgoer. Responsible and reliable individual."

"If he so all-fired respectable, why's he jumpin outta windows?"

She didn't answer and I just let it go.

Jimmy took a little gettin used to. Could be a sanctimonious sonofabitch. Polite, no cussin, always rushin to do the dishes. I made a note to myself. Got to educate this fool some. He dressed just like the big old dumb farm boy that he was. Overalls, straw hat, hobnail boots. He was not familiar with my nasty past. Vida Lee had misled him into thinkin I was a travelin salesman—that's why I been gone so long.

So when he heard I done time and was still committin crimes I thought his hair gonna fall out.

"Oh, y'know, Coley done got hisself into a little bitty scrape with the law," say Vida Lee. "Ain't nothin, really."

"Ain't that like harborin a fugitive?"

"Aw Jimmy, come off it. You carryin on like some peckerwood."

The cat really got under my skin. Who he think he is with all them questions? Askin, "What he done?"

"Just a few robberies," says Vida Lee.

"Stickups?"

"What other kind *is* there?"

Once he get over his fussiness 'bout the law, time pass pleasantly enough with Jimmy around. Even had a few things in common, me and Jimmy. Played a mean harp, too.

'Round this time, Devil got to me. Man, he knew my name. Whisperin and hissin in my ear. "Been lookin for you, Coley, up and down the cotton patch long time. Now, you know you can't hide from me, baby."

One night I says to Jimmy, "Man, it's gettin fuckin close in here. I'm runnin outta oxygen and that ain't all. Why don't we step out a while?"

My idea of steppin out was some *big* steps. Trip down to Clarksdale what I had in mind. For a cropper that's a serious undertakin—two stops on the Pea Vine, five stations south on the Yeller Dog. Pack biscuits and a chicken wing for a trip like that. For me it was just a run down to the corner. I'm thinkin, buy me a Alabama special, hold up a few joints, get crazy, tear a hole in my soul.

Jimmy'd heard they got electric guitars someplace. Read it in the paper and I told him I heard of a cat as had one and would he like to hear what it sound like? He's figurin maybe we was goin over to this barrelhouse on the edge of Clarksdale, but I had other plans. Me and the Devil walkin hand in hand. "No," I says, "that ain't the place."

Take him down to the main drag. Clarksdale. Nothin but a dusty, flat treeless place with a bunch of stores. The beautiful thing itself settin there in a window of Gavin's Music Store. A hollow-body electric ES150 Gibson. Gleamin all brand-new in its stand. Had a card on to it that say,

THE LATEST ELECTRIC GUITAR MODEL
AS FEATURED BY CHARLIE CHRISTIAN

"You mean we come all the way to Clarksdale just to *look* at the damn thing?" Jimmy was disappointed.

"No baby, we gonna very shortly be the proud *owners* of a electrified guitar. Hand me your boot."

"C'mon Coley, stop messin with me." Jimmy was turnin pale as a sheet.

"You know of Charley Patton, right? Now what would the old Tush Hog have done if he'd been here?"

"Aw Coley, quit it! Charley Patton, man, this ain't none of his."

I look up in the sky and start shoutin, "We doin this for you, Charley baby, and, uh, you too, Robert. We doin it in your skanktified names."

And—*whack*—I smash the glass, climb in the window, grab the guitar and wave it in the air, dancin 'round like a cat who has won a trophy at the county fair.

"Hey, forgot the little black box," I say. "Ain't gonna work none without that little black box."

They had them *tiny*, little old amps back in them days, kinda like a Pignose. I jump in the window and grab it. What the hell, I'm already in trouble.

We catch a milk train back to Lula, but I ain't 'bout to take this contraption home with me. Somehow I don't think Vida Lee gonna appreciate my new toy. We move over to Charlie McCoy's. *Y'all remember that rubber-legged boy.* Passin a evenin with that man could be a interestin experience. Had a twitch that increased with the amount of alcohol he was drinkin. At the end of a night he was like a windup toy gone crazy.

Showin Charlie what this new doohickey can do. Get it set up and it was a bust. Damn thing buzzed and whined and hummed like it was gonna blow up. You just *touch* one of them strings and it *scream* back at you. We didn't know what feedback was, see, and that's what it was doin, feedin back into the amp. It made such a evil whine I was sure the damn thing gonna fry me.

"This ain't no electric guitar," I told 'em, "this a electrocution guitar."

I didn't care for it one bit. Stupid thing was just a damn gimmick.

I was gettin restless. Man inside my head makin plans for me, big plans. Plan on me takin a big trip for one thing. But much as I liked the idea, I was hangin back some. Gettin used to bein home watchin the crops come up, sittin on my porch and sleepin in my own bed instead of some cold loadin dock.

My kids was growin up. Willie Lee *was* grown. Still lived with us in the house. Frequently I wished he didn't. He grown up all contrary—just like his mom.

I coulda smacked him when he come over that way 'bout Joe Louis. Joe Louis was my idol, man. I *loved* that cat. He didn't take shit from nobody. When he KO'd that Nazi sonofabitch Max Schmeling back in '38, he said, "Smellin never tetched me more than a fly on my jaw." I loved that!

But Willie Lee had a bug up his ass. Always. You know like

when Joe Louis fought Buddie Baer? He gave his purse to Navy Relief, which far as I was concerned was a patriotic thing to do. But Willie Lee, he was slanderin his name all over the place, callin him a Uncle Tom. Joe Louis a Uncle Tom!

"Yeah, he is," says Willie Lee. "What else you gonna call a man who gives his money to the Navy. Are there any Negroes in the Navy? Answer me that!"

I tell him, "Don't ever let me hear you talkin 'bout the Brown Bomber that way. He's world champion—best guy we got and you be lucky if you could even come near to touchin what he done."

Willie Lee just snorted at that. "He ain't nothin but a ignorant cropper like the rest of y'all."

And he stormed out, slammin the door behind him. Peace at last.

Made a good team, me and Jimmy. Started hittin the jook joints up and down the line. We was doin just fine. Coupla weeks gone by and I managed to get some sounds outta that electric guitar, and that was our key to the highway. See, most of them jook joints by this time had juke boxes. Now who wants to hear a coupla old guys strummin on guitars when you can hear anybody you want to? Duke Ellington, Robert Johnson, Blind Lemon, Ella Fitzgerald, Bing Crosby.

The whole world was on that box, and there was half a million of them boxes out there, they said. The day of the ramblin bluesman was numbered. But the electric guitar was a novelty. People wanted to hear it played even if you could only do "Three Blind Mice." Well, I could do "Poor Boy, Long Way From Home," stuff like that, and we got invited to gig just from havin that guitar.

One thing you couldn't mostly get on a juke box was what they call "party records." The nitty-gritty down and dirty dozens. I mean they did make records but you couldn't always find 'em so if you could play the dozens you was welcome in any of them places. We could do that Champion Jack Dupree thing,

> *I want to pull up on your blouse, let down on your skirt,*
> *Get down so low you think you're in the dirt.*
> *Now when I say "boogie"—I want you to boogie....*

A boogie mean fuckin, see. Code for fuckin. 'Cause boogie-woogie was dancin music and the kinda dancin people did to it was raunchy.

Yonder go your mama going out across the field
Runnin and a shakin like a automobile.

That's one I learned from Speckled Red when we was hoboin together. The words on the record, that is. The actual words to this was much worse. Or better.

Dirty dozens. You know that come originally from Sunday school? That's right. From children learnin rhymes, learn about the Bible: *First God created the earth, second He rested*, and so forth. That's what Speckled Red was riffin on:

God made him an elephant, he made him stout.
He wasn't finished, until he made him a snout.

Dirty Dozens where the word muthafucka come from. Uh-huh. Don't tell me blues ain't contributed nothin to civilization.

❖   ❖   ❖

Vida Lee like havin her brother 'round, and I'm enjoyin hangin with him too. But all along I knowed it wasn't gonna last. Jimmy just pourin salt into the wound, sayin shit like, "With a cat like you, Coley, trouble stick like flypaper. Hell, it's only a matter of time." It's true, of course, but that ain't the point.

One night we was playin at this barrelhouse outside of Drew when the cops raid the joint. They was shakin the place down but the houseman wasn't payin up or wasn't payin enough so they gotta send a little rent-due reminder. Beat up some customers and drag a few off to jail. They take one look at me, they had me figured. Nigger with a attitude. They could just *smell* it on me. *Plus* we got this electric guitar with us. We fly outta that place like a cat outta a barrel of rainwater. Can't catch me, baby, *I'm long gone John from Bowlin Green.*

We crouchin down under a bridge, and just then Jimmy decides to come over all righteous. Says he's gonna explain he had nothin to do with it and it weren't even his idea, stealin the guitar.

"Jimmy," I says, "you think they give a flyin fuck *which* nigger stole that Gibson? You turn yourself in, they gonna have you breakin rocks and choppin logs out on the county farm for a long while. So you go ahead, tell 'em what you want. I'm outta here."

"Okay, okay," says Jimmy. "Take me with you. Let's hit the road."

"How the fuck we gonna hit the road? We need wheels, man!"

Meanwhile I spy something down the road a ways. A beat-up old Ford pickup pulled up on an embankment.

"Tell ya what…we gonna just take my vee-hicle an hightail outta here."

"You got a car?" says Jimmy. Boy wasn't thinkin straight.

"I do now!" says I.

Tearin along them country roads, Jimmy near died of fright. But soon he gets into it and we start tradin lies 'bout all the terrible crimes we've committed and the hearts we have broken and all. "Ah'm soooo bad that.…" All that shit. We was havin such a ball it took him a while to realize we wasn't exactly headed home. We was on Highway 61, *old* 61—a route I knew well.

"You is headed north, Coley. That was Robinsonville you just flew through."

"You positive?"

"Yeah, I'm positive. That's where Robert Johnson from. Lula the other direction. Turn 'round, man."

"I don't think so, boss," I say. "Not with a stolen guitar in a stolen car."

We drove through the night into the mornin sun. Flat, dusty country roads. Fields of cotton and corn. Country stores with rusty soda pop signs and gas pumps out front. White clapboard churches. Old sharecrop farmers settin on the porches of their shacks, kids playin in the dirt, sellin fruit at wayside stands.

I'm gettin punchy, little high. Right then up pops the Devil. "Gonna ride you like a witch ride a broom, Coley. Yes, indeed. You and me gonna get along just fine."

I'm laughin to myself.

"What's so damn funny this time?" Jimmy ask.

"Just tell me one thing...."

"What?"

"Where'd you get them clothes, man—off a scarecrow? We gotta get you some threads, baby. We can't go to Memphis with you lookin like some old cottonpickin daddy."

"We're goin to Memphis?" He's losin his nerve again.

"You got a better idea? Come on, man, we're goin on empty. Got some coin for gas and a bottle of wine?"

He empties his pockets, give me what he got. I tell him, "Scoot over to the driver's seat. I'm gettin a little too jangly to drive much more." But I had another reason. I come runnin out of the store like I'm on fire.

"Step on it, Jimmy, or they gonna pop my ass!"

We get down the road a little ways and he asks me,

"Man, what was that 'bout? Didn't I give you money?"

"Got a little surprise for you. Bought us a gun."

"You spent our last dime on a gun?"

"Yeah. As a investment."

"Oh, really?"

"Damn right. It's a stake in our future."

"A stake in gettin our asses jailed."

"Man, I can't believe how *dumb* some of them country crackers are. The jerk sold me the gun—and a box a shells. 'I'll throw in the bullets,' he says. I ask him can I try it, see if it works and he says go ahead. So I did. 'Open the cash register,' I say. 'Now put your hands in the air.' And he does. So I says, 'You're right, it does work. So long, sucker!'"

"Jesus, Coley, we'll be lucky if we make it to Memphis."

"Aw, you worry too much, Jimmy. See, this the beauty of the cross-country trip. Them crackers ain't gonna cross over no state line on account of some gas station been held up. Besides, you stay too long in one place you gonna get dust on your soul."

Did you know you can cure a spell bein put upon you by travelin? Truth. Conjurin don't work on cats what move around. It a disease of settin still, that's right. Witches can't cross no state lines, neither.

Movin on, that was my entire philosophy of life. Hard to hit a movin target.

In Walls just outside of Memphis we sold the car to a guy who worked in a mill, swung onto the Southern and headed into the big, bad city. We made some pennies playin up and down Beale Street, got ourselves a "hot" room in a bordello. You could rent 'em cheap durin the day. Come five o'clock they'd chuck you out—which was fine with us. Sleep all day, spend all night in the bars and clubs. Yes indeed, this was the life.

You know all that whiskey they got piled up in the back of them clubs? Well, one night Jimmy come back to the room and I got it all piled up with boxes.

"What the hell is this?" he asks.

Man, I was just *beamin*.

"Ta-dah!" say I.

I open one of the boxes, you know, proudly displayin my bottles of booze.

"Where'd you get this stuff?" he asks. I'm startin to feel downright unappreciated.

"Boosted it," I tell him. "Right under their noses."

"Which club?"

"The Monarch."

"*The Monarch*?"

"Yeah, what's the difference?"

"Jesus! Coley, you outta your fuckin mind?"

"Hell man, the stuff just settin there."

"Did it occur to you that there might be a reason no one touches them boxes in back of the Monarch?"

"Nice name, huh?"

"You know who owns the Monarch? Jim Kinnane, that's who. He'll kill a man for breakin the mirror behind the bar. You can imagine what he gonna do to us."

My mind start singin, *Train, train....* But you know I just could not abandon all that booze. Got myself another bright idea: "Let's just take a coupla of them boxes down to the station." 'Course sellin old man Kinnane's booze at the Memphis train station was close to committin suicide. But I wouldn't hear of walkin out on all that booze. We gave a bunch of boxes to the madam and took a few ourselves.

It was Thanksgiving and the station was packed. People goin to their families, servicemen home on leave. We was down to our last three bottles when a young kid in a hooded jacket come over, clamp his hand on mine.

"Fifty cents cheap. Get 'em while they last." I'm runnin down my spiel when the kid looks in my face and says, "Shut up, Dad, it's me." I nearly jump outta my skin.

"Willie Lee!" I shout. "This, uh, ain't what you think."

"Keep it down, Dad, there's MPs right behind that pillar."

"What's the matter, son? How'd you get outta the army? Don't tell me—you on the lam?"

"No, they insisted I take a vacation. 'Course I'm on the lam, Dad."

"Lord have mercy."

"Gonna go join the Army Air Corps. Ain't gonna be lookin for no army deserters at two thousand feet."

"They let—"

"Yeah, Dad, they let niggers fly. Gotta go before them donkey dick cops spy me. If you see Mom tell her I'm okay, and if I see her I'll tell her you still up to the same old shit."

With this, my ramblin boy slipped back into the crowd.

"Apple don't fall far from the tree, I guess," says Jimmy.

"Yeah," I says. "Ain't it a beautiful thing? C'mon, Jimmy, we best split, too."

"Gee, we hardly got to know the fuckin place, y'know?" says Jimmy.

"Yeah, I know. Gotta come back sometime when there ain't guys out there with meat hooks lookin to punch holes in my hide. Best take ourselves a ride somewheres *far* away from here."

I wanted to go north. I'd told him all 'bout St. Louis, but he had a better idea.

"No, man, that's where they'll figure we gone. Let's head south."

35

Railroad for My Pillow

They appreciated our company so much the railroad even gave us a free ride. Imagine that! Jumped off at the marshalling yards and hoofed it into Helena. Sonny Boy was livin there, got hisself on the radio. Had become such a hit they broadcast it over the Delta network. Carried his program on the Clarksdale station. This was a big deal —blues on the radio.

We was hangin out in the park where the blues guys hang and there is Sonny Boy, just a-settin there like he was a statue in the park. On his belt was a string of Hohner harps in different keys. Reminded me of little tiny six-shooters.

Sonny Boy was wearin a yellow shirt with his name stitched on it. Call hisself Sonny Boy Williamson. Rice Miller is who he was. Mostly people call him Sonny Boy the Second, to distinguish him from the original Sonny Boy, John Lee Williamson. But don't go callin him Sonny Boy the Second to his face.

Jimmy run over to him, say, "Hey, man, heard you on the radio. Heard it way back in Clarksdale."

"Thank you, thank you, thank you," says Sonny Boy and bowin his head like a old Chinese every time he say it.

"How long you cats been doin this shit?"

"Hell," says Sonny Boy, "we been doin it close to a year now, ain't we, Junior?"

His partner Robert Junior Lockwood settin there up next to him. Robert Junior was real quiet. Look down at his shoes when you talked to him. Sonny Boy been playin with Junior in the streets of Helena awhile before they got theirselves on the radio. Junior mumbled something and Sonny Boy repeat it like he was interpretin him, "Said it was last year, 'round Thanksgiving. Nineteen and forty-one, uh huh."

Now, some people say that what really clinched the deal was that Sonny Boy, who previously been known as Rice Miller or Little Boy Blue, told Mr. Max Moore over at the Interstate Grocery Company that he was Sonny Boy Williamson, the singer up in Chicago what already had a bunch of successful records out. Mr. Max thought he got hisself a genuine star, goin 'round town crowin, "I got Sonny Boy Williamson, the big Negro star, on my program."

Sonny Boy and Lockwood got so successful doin their radio show they started puttin out a Sonny Boy Flour, brand of flour named for Sonny Boy. Had a picture of a grinnin Sonny Boy on it ridin a ear of corn. Got so famous they'd go out and play dances and suppers, sellin Sonny Boy white cornmeal. Had a little band of Pine Top Perkins, Stackhouse—Houston Stackhouse, et cetera. I'd string along, sit in for cats who didn't show. Had a flatbed truck and Pine Top'd sit up in the back and play the piano—'cause it was too heavy to be taken down and set on the ground.

Sonny Boy's band had so many requests he asked if we'd play some of his gigs for him. *As* him, it turned out.

"No one gonna know no difference. Can't *see* us on the radio, what do they know?"

So me and Jimmy, we'd go out and play for suppers and stuff.

One time we played a fish fry as Sonny Boy and Junior in this section called Helena Crossing. Later that night I spied a gas station ripe for the pluckin. The attendant was a old codger, so I stop by pay him a visit, relieve him of about eighteen bucks and go on my merry way.

Man at the gas station calls the cops. Cops ask can he describe who done it.

"I can do better than that," the guys says. "I can tell you his name. It was Sonny Boy Williamson. Had his name right on his shirt."

So the cops say, "Any idea where this creep hangs out?"

And the attendant tells 'em, "Yeah, you can find him any day of the week from noon to twelve-fifteen up at KFFA."

So the next day they show up at KFFA, maybe fifteen cops, and they put Sonny Boy away. Sonny Boy had a alibi down cold but still they put him in jail, rough him up a bit. When he come out we was far more scared of Sonny Boy than of any law. Most a judge gonna lay on me was a stretch on the county farm—and that was just a second home to me—but Sonny Boy, there was no tellin what he'd do if he'd a caught up with us. Six-foot-two of bile, and *huge* hands. Weird lookin, y'know, with them puffy eyelids? And that goatee—whoooeee! Cut slits in his boots just to cool his heels.

We got ourselves a gig on the Excelsior. *Jimmy* got us a gig. Strolled in the bookin office and two minutes later he come out sayin we got the job. She wasn't a floatin whorehouse no more, much to my disappointment. Just a gamblin den cruisin up and down the river.

We was on board and headin upriver before I learned why we'd been booked so quick. Voice come over the P.A. that "radio stars Sonny Boy Williamson and Robert Junior Lockwood will be entertainin you tonight in the Beaulieu Lounge." Now wouldn't Sonny Boy just have loved to hear that?

We got off in St. Louis. Got kicked off as a matter of fact, once they figured us out.

We walked quite awhile until some hog farmer gave us a ride in the back of his truck. Took us into St. Louis. We was fast runnin out of cities in the South. No choice but to head north. Jimmy started singin that old Robert Johnson number "Sweet Home Chicago."

But I had a better plan,

"Let's make that Detroit. They got cars in Detroit."

We tossed for it with a silver dollar. Tails it's Chicago, heads Detroit. Detroit it was, thanks to my lucky old two-headed never fail ya silver determinator.

Pistol in My Face

Here it was, city of my dreams. Tall buildings, factories, clubs, big stores, and pretty women. Jimmy and me got us a situation in a factory. Bars and clubs and dives and blues everywhere. Hastings Street was the main black drag in Detroit. There was all kinda clubs down there. You could hear just about anything you wanted. Hell, on a Friday night you could catch John Lee Hooker doin his back-country hoodoo down at Henry's Swing Club.

Electric blues was just wakin up and me and Jimmy was promotin its pussy, havin in our possession the noise bringer, bell ringer of the blues, a electric guitar.

And, man, these joints was just filled with pretty young things lookin to boogie down and we intended to give it to 'em. There weren't all that many men around so we pretty much had the field to ourselves. It was like openin the pasture gate and lettin the bulls in.

I met a cute little girl from Selma called Berenice, a parachute maker. Way they make 'em is just like a sewin bee. Women sit 'round a big table and gossip. I was spendin more and more time over at Berenice's. She didn't care all that much for the blues. She liked the smooth stuff. Big bands. Swing. Count Basie, Jimmie Lunceford, Erskine Hawkins.

Jimmy was a straight-arrow cat but he loved pussy. In between the women Jimmy was pursuin his other hobby—cars. Fast Freddy worked over at the Ford plant on the assembly line and he had his own little dealership goin. He smuggled parts outta the plant and put 'em together in his garage. Car he built for Jimmy was like nothin you ever seen or will see again. Assembled on a chassis from a '36 Chevy outta the junkyard. That's how Jimmy got hisself a baby-blue convertible—well anyways it didn't have no top. Jimmy was now definitely lethal to women, long as it didn't rain.

Things was goin along pretty smooth for awhile there when along come the *big* trouble. You ever heard of the Hastings Street riots? Some of the best riots this country's ever seen, that's right.

It was late January, nineteen and forty-three. Things was tense between blacks and whites. Every night there'd be some brawl. Blacks comin up from the South movin into poor white neighborhoods. Like throwin a stick of dynamite in a trash-can fire.

Most of the whites we workin with was guys who couldn't make it in the army. Older guys, guys with some infirmity. Mean-hearted sonsofbitches with chips on their shoulders. Almost any damn thing could set them off. Stupid argument over a wrench. Who left what where.

Tired and wired from boozin and fuckin the nights away. Then some dumb peckerwood start tellin me I'm activatin the foot pedal too slow, *nigger* slow. That did it. Fuse got lit and it was hissin down the wire.

"Go stick your nigger dick in a watermelon!" he tells me.

"Hell," I says, "your bitch was so hot, had to cool my tool off somehow."

"What you say?"

"Said I fucked your bitch everyway but—"

"Why you sonofabitch!"

In two seconds flat there was one big ball of hate lungin at me with a claw hammer. I grab this cracker 'round the neck, stick his head on a band saw plate and hah! turn it on. Blood was spurtin on the walls, on the machines. Everyfuckinwhere. Oh man, I really wanted to slice that redneck's head clean off at the neck. Jimmy pull me off the guy just before I beheaded him.

Place just blew. People was swingin and throwin shit and pushin over benches and smashin equipment. Cops came and cleared everybody out, so we just took the riot on out to the street. Hundreds of whites and blacks goin at it. Lootin and house burnins went on right into the next day. President sent in the troops. Took six thousand soldiers to cool things down. It was some fuckin scene.

By the end of it, twenty-five black and nine white been killed. Hell, I just intended to separate some redneck from his neck—didn't mean to start no riot. Didn't mean to kill him, even. Just them dark clouds rollin up over my head and followin me down the road.

First night of the riot I haul my ass indoors—figure I'll get myself outta the line of fire. 'Round midnight we hear a big commotion down on the street. Jimmy leans his head out the window and shouts down,

"What the hell you think you're doin down there?"

"Torchin your car, nigger."

"The hell you are!"

Jimmy and me ran down the fire escape. By the time we swing down to the sidewalk they was gone.

"Fuckin spineless peckerwoods."

We put the fire out but it wasn't a brand-new shiny automobile no more. It was the convertible from Hell. As we're headin outta town the troops got a roadblock set up. Stop us at the city line. Jimmy tells 'em,

"Man, they beat me up *and* burned up my car. Hell, we're gettin outta this town *fast*."

They took one look at the car and waved us on. They was only too happy to see our backs.

Car died in a coffee shop parkin lot in one of them little prairie towns north of Peoria. Frank Sinatra come on the jukebox croonin some pretty little ballad, kinda thing you usually hear outta the corner of your ear.

Before I know it I'm comin over all weepy. Frank Sinatra, he could get to you like that. You could see how all them bobbysoxers was goin wild for his dream tunes. Strange thing, soon as I walked outside, that cotton-candy song flew right outta my head 'long with any thoughts of home and Vida Lee.

Wind was risin, stirrin up leaves and scraps of paper across the road, the corn shucks was rustlin, and way in the distance I hear that sound, lonesomest sound ever devised by man or beast, a train whistle blowin. Jimmy come outta the coffee shop and I grab his arm.

"C'mon man, let's grab that rattler."

"Hold on, Coley, that's the Santa Fe."

"So?"

"It's headed *west*, Coley, to Oklahoma."

"They got black folk in Oklahoma. Man, they got black folk in Alaska. We *all* over this damn country."

Come mornin we was in Topeka. Now I'm really into my California kick.

"California, baby, they ain't never gonna look for us out there. Ask me no questions and I'll tell you no lies."

I was tellin Jimmy all about all the job opportunities in the shipyards. Jimmy's lookin puzzled.

"Somethin the matter?" I ask.

"Just that this don't exactly sound like you, Coley. Let me get this straight. You goin out to California for the *work*?"

"Dig, Jimmy, where there's work there's money and where there's money—"

"There's gigs!"

Call It Stormy Monday

Pulled into Los Angeles Central Pacific Station summer of '43. Los Angeles was hummin. Southeast side in Watts, along the side streets off Central Avenue and Broadway. And more black folk arrivin every day to work in the defense plants and munitions factories. Yeah, there was plenty of work in the war projects of Oakland and Los Angeles and over in San Joaquin and Imperial valleys.

Whole bunch of money out there lookin for a home. For the folks from back home, man, music was the pipeline. Wanna hear the blues and there wasn't that many blues cats out on the coast at that time. So there was a whole heap of work for bluesmen out in L.A.

One night I was down on Central Avenue, me and Jimmy checkin out the clubs. This was the height of the zoot-suit scene. Long one-button jacket, padded shoulders and a knee-length key chain swinging as you walked. Broadbrimmed hat to top it off. Jimmy had to get hisself outfitted with one of them right off.

So we was walkin past this tumble-down nightclub called Little Harlem and we hear a strange sound snakin outta that lounge. Damn thing stop us right in our tracks. Jimmy ask me,

"What *is* that, a guitar?"

It was *wailin*, man, just like a horn. We duck into the club and up there on stage is this slick, skinny dude playin a hollow-body electric. Long, white lamé jacket, outrageous bow tie. Doin splits, swingin the guitar 'round his back, playin it behind his head. He'd kneel down, holdin that guitar straight up by the neck, wavin at the audience with one hand while he's still squeezin out jazzy, jump blues with the other. Concluded his set with a finely executed split and the crowd go wild. Never seen nobody—well, since Charley Patton—bein that acrobatic with a guitar. Charley liked to clown, but nobody ever gonna call this T-Bone Walker a clown.

After the show I caught up with T-Bone backstage. Dapper cat. Little mustache, hair so shiny and slick looked like it was made of wax. We begin talkin, y'know. Turns out we almost coulda met a bunch of times our paths crossed so often. He'd been lead man for Blind Lemon for a while down in Dallas same as me. Lemon was a good friend of Walker's family, coming over every Sunday to have dinner and drink home-brewed corn whiskey. T-Bone have worked the medicine shows and I knowed he played guitar for Ma Rainey 'cause I seen him with her that time at the Fat Stock Show in Fort Worth.

He was charmin as hell, but for me meetin T-Bone was a disaster. Ever run into some cat who got the same vices you got and 'bout as much sense? Two fools slippin and a slidin on a slippery slope, and I ain't even told you the spookiest part of it.

It's 'bout three in the mornin, that three-in-the-mornin blue smoke when the world is spinnin and you're wonderin how come you don't fall off and drift into space. Then you see that look come through his eyes—like *uh-oh*!

"Shit! I done forgot all 'bout Vida Lee," he says.

Holy snakes! What kinda deal goin down here? How does he know 'bout Vida Lee?

"I know what I'm gonna tell her when I gets home," he says. "Gonna tell her I been led astray by this cat—that's you, my man. You don't mind bein my I-can-explain-honey, do you? Say, 'Now, honey, you can understand that, can't you, two cats haven't seen each other in ten years—we was both with Ma Rainey and that was some trip, baby. Just me and my buddy Coley talkin trash and that's all, I swear, Vida Lee.'"

I knew I was stoned but strange thoughts was passin through my brain. Vida Lee moved out to the coast and moved in with T-Bone? Turned out his wife's name was Vida Lee, too, but there was a message there somewhere. Message I'd been trying to avoid for quite awhile.

❖   ❖   ❖

The thing with the two Vida Lees kinda rattled me, y'know? Like a lotta cats that moved away, I planned to bring Vida Lee and the kids out when I got settled. Trouble was, as time went by I was gettin more and more *un*-settled. I was gonna get the little bungalow thing together—hell, even a coupla rooms over a furniture store woulda been good enough—but somehow I never could make it happen. Be on my way over to check out a place and I'd stop by a bar on the way and I'd forget why I come over to that part of town in the first place.

Closest I'd come to gettin a place is lookin at some rooms somewhere someone told me of but when I seen 'em I'd go, "I dunno…. Is this what Vida Lee woulda chose?" Nothin seemed just right. If it was downtown she'd a found it too noisy—comin in from the country, see? If it was outside the city she's gonna say, "Why you stickin me way out here?" See my problem? Then one mornin a lightbulb go off in my head.

"Fool! Just get her out here. Let her choose her own nest. Ain't you got more sense than to second-guess a woman?"

When they drop the bomb on Hiroshima, figured I'd better get her out here before the whole damn world blow up.

Went downtown for the parade, though. VJ Day. People throwin all kinda shit outta the windows: torn-up telephone books, shoes, hats, newspapers, panties, wastebaskets, socks. For one day there wasn't no black nor white, just people glad to see the whole mess done with.

Took a coupla months before all the arrangements got arranged but finally the day did come. Oh, happy day, indeed! There was Vida Lee and the kids gettin off the train with suitcases and bags and sacks and boxes tied with string and teddy bears stickin out. And there was Vida Lee with that "Okay, now what?" look on her face.

We found a little place out in Watts. Tiny lawn out front, size of a doormat but a big yard out back, big enough to have swings for the kids, little flower and kitchen garden. Got ourselves a radio to listen to *Fibber McGee and Molly, The Green Hornet.* All them shows. We was livin just like white folks.

December of '45, that's when Willie Lee got out of the Army Air Corps and came to stay with us. We was mighty proud of him

—our own Willie Lee a war hero. Ace flyer in the 332nd Fighter Group air combat unit. Won hisself the Distinguished Flying Cross.

We was expectin to see him get off the train wearin his uniform and all his medals. Forgot it was Willie Lee we was talkin about. Tells us he's *burned* his uniform. Called his medal the Distinguished Flyin Fuck.

Aw, his mom was so upset.

"Don't talk like that!" she told him. "You should be proud to wear that uniform. Didn't you help win the war?"

Willie Lee, bein Willie Lee, weren't about to give an inch.

"I fought for nothin, Mama. And now that I'm back it feels like *less* than nothin."

"My poor baby," say Vida Lee, "bein negative ain't gonna get you nowhere in this life or the next."

"Do believe there's such a thing as colored blood?" says Willie. "'Cause the Red Cross do. They segregate the fuckin blood."

"I don't know nothin about that," she say, "but I do know you won that the medal for bravery and I'm proud of you."

"Well I say, fuck the Distinguished Flyin Fuck!"

Ain't kids grand? It was like World War III from mornin to night with him. Plus he *hated* the blues. To him that stuff was embarrassin. Droopy overall, bo-weeviled mule droppins. His thing was bebop. Dizzy Gillespie, Charlie Parker. Now you gotta excuse me, but that stuff was strictly from Mars. Played mostly by wigged-out cats who was gettin high on some weird outer-space weed. I didn't get it, didn't *want* to get it.

Jimmy and me was still boogieing. Had ourselves a little local hit. Lucked out with a number we pulled together called "The Dead Cat Bounce." A jitterbuggy blues thing that went over big. Made a recordin of it for Victor. Sold a few copies, that's right. Scored a whole bunch of gigs off of that. Race records come back after the Depression and with Cecil Gant's "I Wonder" toppin the Harlem Hit Parade in *Billboard* we was back in business.

Vida Lee was startin to act funny 'round Jimmy. Now why was that? With brothers and sisters who can figure? It end with her askin me to tell Jimmy he shouldn't stop by no more.

Jimmy and me hung for awhile—the little combo we put together was really smokin—but now that Jimmy had a regular job and all, he was movin away from me.

"Coley, I do not want to be playin on the street for quarters the rest of my natural life. Hell, I'm pushin forty and don't care to end up bummin a dime for a bottle of wine like you gonna be."

"Suit yourself," I told him. "Just don't come crying to me when I strike it rich."

Life was sweet. Had me a fine job at the plant. I was makin good money. Just about paradise those few years in L.A. Jackie Robinson playin for the Brooklyn Dodgers, man. That was enough for me. Meanwhile Vida Lee gettin into a serious funk. All them letters from Willie Lee layin shit on her head. Then you got the Reverend Deakins over at the church preachin doom and gloom and how things gotta change.

When some asshole burnt a cross on the Reverend Deakins' lawn and beat up his son on the way home from school, Vida Lee had enough. She wanted out. Wanted to go back to Mississippi. Yeah baby, you go on back to Dixie where folks is *real* liberal and understandin. But there was no persuadin Vida Lee.

At first I thought this just crazy talk, but when "Stormy Monday" come out—that was T-Bone's big hit, y'know—them lyrics was talkin to me.

> They call it stormy Monday, but Tuesday's just as bad.
> Wednesday's worse and Thursday's also sad.

How the hell did I ever think workin in a factory was for me? After four years of punchin the time clock, hoein the rows down in the bottom was beginnin to look mighty good. Tyin the mule to the post, comin home for lunch. Must be goin crazy, thinkin thoughts like that. Musta been away from the Delta too long.

Vida Lee went on ahead. They was gonna give me a bonus if I stayed out the year. If we was gonna get back into farmin we could sure use that money. See, they wasn't plowin with mules no more.

Everybody was usin tractors and stuff now. So I had to wait till the eagle flies. That's what I told myself, anyway.

I was feelin outta time, all goin too fast for me—bebop, jump blues, jitterbuggin. But T-Bone, he was hip to all that, he was movin on. They say blues gotta progress—like everything else. But I don't see it. Blues is blues. What it is. I'm as you find me, down-home, always will be. Muddy-river boy at heart. Still, I suppose if the blues gonna last it gotta get its funky butt customized some. Got to, if it don't wanna become a folklorical old relic in some Washington warehouse.

T-Bone breathe a new spirit into the blues—what you might call the *gumbo* blues. Little jazz, little Texas funk and a whole lotta swing. Smooth, sophisticated blues that's gone to town and hung around. Zoot-suited blues. It was catchin on fast with the white folks, too. T-Bone playin almost as many gigs in the white clubs 'round Hollywood as he was on Central Avenue.

He'd learned a lotta tricks playin with the Les Hite Orchestra, but durin the war big bands was too expensive to carry on the road. Now with electrified instruments you didn't need a big orchestra to put out a big sound. That's where the combos came in. Five, six cats. What they call "small big bands." He had hisself a hot jump blues band and he was goin places.

One night I'm down at the Trocadero Club and I run into T-Bone. He is flyin high. Y'know after "Stormy Monday" hit he was a big star. They was bookin him from the Rhumboogie Club to Ronconcomo. I offer to buy him a drink.

Tells me he can't drink the hard stuff no more on account of his doctor says. He got the ulcers like a lot of blues cats got. "Just beer, from now on, baby. I'm gettin off my stool to piss every five damn minutes now."

We drank a few beers and listen to some smoky jazzy blues on the juke box. "I'm Gonna Move to the Outskirts of Town" by Louis Jordan and his Tympany Five. He loved that stuff.

"That's the kind of blues I like to play. A more smoother and more softer type a thing, dig? I like that up-to-date sound, not the way down-home blues. No brother, no more of that for me."

Tells me he's openin the W.C. Handy Theater in Memphis, and him and his band and a bunch of guys, see, they gonna christen the place.

"Coley, why don'tcha come along? Get on the bus, take the trip with us."

That was all the encouragement I needed. Memphis had slowed down durin the war but it was wakin up again and I wanted to be there when it did. I figure fuck the bonus, this is real life. And hey, it's on my way home, ain't it?

Been Bit by
The Beale Street Beagle

Beale Street was quite a depraved work of art in them days. Been the main drag since the Civil War. Memphis was a city of sin and slick livin, and Beale was the center of it all. Anything your messed-with mind conceive of, you could find it on Beale Street.

There's a place where you could go where you pay your fifty cents and see anything you want. Crimes against nature, what have you. A guy there would sell his sister, but it ain't like that no more. All cleaned up, spruced up, spit and polished and please dispose of your trash responsibly. Sanitized, homogenized, and Disneyized it. Tourists, y'know. Like their fun good and clean even if it's the down and dirty they come to see. Sort of a blues theme park these days. "Come to Deltaland—take Exit 94A and follow the signs."

You got your T-shirt vendors down there, your souvenir shops, high-price bars, and blues preservation societies. Only thing you wanted to preserve in my day was your hide. In the sixties and seventies *nobody* come down there. Everything all boarded up and burnt out. Nothin but pawn shops and plywood far as you could see.

But back 'round '48, Beale Street was cookin. May have looked like just a jumble of cheap hotels, whorehouses and pawn shops durin the day, but at night, man, the joint was jumpin. Preachers, pimps, lawyers, gamblers, doctors (root and medical varieties), *and* the blues. Like I say, anything and everything. And it wasn't real clear which was which.

The depravity wasn't as open as it been back in the twenties when you had bodies flyin outta windows and johns runnin naked down the street—still it was a tame Saturday night if only four bodies were found in the morgue Sunday morning.

Beale Street pretty much hit its peak 'round three o'clock in the mornin—so thick with people you could hardly get through it. All seekin that spoonful—hootch, pussy, cocaine. Zoot-suited pimps like Fashion Plate Frankie and Pretty Boy Bennett paradin down Beale like they was little oriental kings.

There were barrelhouse piano players, country pickers, bottleneck sliders, and any variety or shade of jug band musician you can mention —Memphis was the jug band capital of the world. There was lots of musicians but there was plenty of gigs to go 'round. Whatever was goin down in that town there was blues attached to it. Gamblin, poolroom, serenadin up and down the street, playin for classy white dances, businessmen's stag parties. Musicians was only gettin two dollars and sixty cents for their work but that was enough to live on easy. A dime of that went for carfare. Rest of it was for the musicians.

On that street was more people than lived in Babylon. Rail workers, pullman porters, cotton farmers, drifters, gamblers, musicians, hustlers and hookers of every price and persuasion to service them. Down by the river was the cotton market and exchange. A more rowdy, lawless, violent bunch of roustabouts, boatmen, and levee workers you never seen. They were the cats that kept the levees built up to protect the city from the river. They was rough cats and the kinda entertainment they was lookin for weren't too refined.

The Monarch, situated at 350 Beale, was one wide-open joint, most notorious dive on the strip. That was the place I boosted all them boxes of liquor from last time we was through. It was a gamblin house at that particular time. You mainly played poker there. Fella played piano—blues goin all the time. All night long. Joint was so tough they searched you when you come in just like they would if you was goin to jail! I shot some craps, rolled some dice, but I never did make even one lousy dime in that joint.

There wasn't anything to control gamblin back then. If you got out of order the house would handle it, and these cats weren't kiddin 'round. This guy named Bad Sam took care of anybody gettin rowdy. There was regular killing in the Monarch, and Bad Sam'd just dump the bodies outside like he was puttin out the garbage.

There was a crap house called the Panama operated by a boy named Howard Evans. Over at the Panama was a conjure woman who'd read your palm, do the tarot cards. Mary the Wonder, a voodoo lady. Used to be a woman there, call her Razor Cuttin Fanny. Didn't give her a piece of change, she cut your throat! It was just great in them days.

Second day I got to Memphis I walked into a joint, sat down at the piano, and began to play. Great big woman called Jenny come waltzin in, smellin of wine and cheap perfume. She had the blues, baby, had 'em bad. Got them old it-feel-so-good-to-feel-so-bad blues. That night I played Sunnyland Slim's "Four O'Clock Blues" for her and she started hollerin loud. Playin the blues and drinkin that White Mule moonshine and this big black mama was moanin and groanin the blues all night long. I was home.

Big turnover of piano players in that place. Sunday that first week some coked-up cat shot my piano full of holes on account of I sung a song with a girl named Delilah in it. His girl had that name. Shook the piano so much a statue of Venus toppled off it and cracked me in the head. I just kept on playin. In them joints if you stopped playin they'd stop shootin the piano and shoot *you*.

Eventually the blood was runnin in my eyes so bad I couldn't see the keys no more and I staggered outside to see if one of them ambulances would take me to the hospital. They was just settin there all in a line. They'd come and take you away if you was injured or bleedin.

I hadn't got but to the curb when Jenny grab me by the arm.

"Anytime you feel like committin suicide," she says, "just jump in one of them hearses 'cause that what they is—death wagons. They'll stick you with a hypo, you be dead before you get to the morgue. Come on with me, honey, I'll put a plaster on that cut for you, give you a little tender lovin care and you be a new man by tomorrow mornin."

She lived over a Chinese laundry on Hernando Street, a tiny place. She wasn't much of a housekeeper. Clothes and bottles and junk all thrown around. She pulled out a bottle of shine, splashed some on my head and poured the rest into a couple of glasses.

Next mornin I am walkin down Front Street, by the river, and strangest damn thing happen to me. I spy someone walkin down the end of the street lookin just like Vida Lee. Turnin the corner in a red straw bonnet with a bow. Sassy walk, floral print dress just like the one she got. Hell, that *is* Vida Lee. I run 'round the corner to catch up with her but when I get over to the next street there's no one on it but a vendor sellin apples off a cart.

"Did you see a woman come by here, red straw hat?"

"Nope. No one been by here in a while. I'm considerin pushin on over to Main."

"It was just a minute ago. You musta seen her."

"Nope, can't say as I have. Care for an apple? I got McIntoshes, I got Pippins—did you know apples is the only fruit people buy by name? Truth! They'll say, 'Gimme a pound of—'"

Everybody in Memphis was a damn philosopher. They could hold forth on any friggin subject, but I didn't have time to tarry. Took off down the street in pursuit of my wife. Could not find that woman high or low. Maybe I seen what I seen or maybe I didn't. Could she be one of them Beale Street haints, the shadow men and women that drift up and down the street at the end of your mind?

One day I'm feelin low, draggin myself along the street and a little owly-lookin guy corner me as I'm goin by. Says, "Shame! Shame! It's a cryin shame, mister."

"Say what?"

"Said, dog done bit you."

"Ain't got no dog."

"Yup. He's there all right. Howlin in the wind all night and day. And you know what he say? 'Been a mighty long time since my baby went away.' Fact."

"Man," I tells him, "you crazier than me."

"Beale Street beagle. You ain't been bit by the Beale Street beagle?"

"Uh no, I don't believe I did."

"Good. 'Cause that dog nip you, that might mean the end of you."

"Rabid dog is it?"

"Well now, it is and it ain't. You know there's many folks that come to Memphis and moseyed down to Beale Street and never could get out. They just bodily cannot leave. And that mean only one thing —you're gone, baby, into the skantified church of bluesology. Got bit by the dog."

"Well, I'll watch out for him," I says, and believe me I did.

Went to See the Gypsy, Have My Fortune Read

One day you're doin fine, next day you bummin pennies for a glass of wine, that's right.

It was a rough-and-tumble kinda life and I started to act rough myself. Guess I never quite did get over seein that mirage of Vida Lee. Got thrown outta Jenny's house, got into a fight with the owner of the joint I was playin at and lost my gig. End up I'm livin on a roof.

I'm workin along Beale Street trawlin for pennies when along come the owly-eyed character. Hobblin along, grinnin ear to ear. Like a idiot, as I thought. Words to that song come in my mind, *Kid man done got so buggy, 'clare that the fool just could not keep it hid.*

I wasn't in the mood for no Beale Street beagle rap that mornin so I turned my head away. Wasn't in a state where I'd find that humorous. But he pulled out his leg and sat down anyway and began to play,

> *This ain't my home,*
> *I got no right to stay.*
> *This ain't my home,*
> *Must be my stoppin place.*

That little thing he was singin put me in mind of the Prodigal Son. Like he's written a letter back to me from yonder's town. When

I heard them words, I began to cry and I cried till I could cry no more. Why did I leave Vida Lee and Lula and my kids? Hell, I was crazier than this crazy man settin next to me.

"Here son, wipe your eyes." This was the limit—this owly-eyed cat was comfortin *me*. "Sun gonna shine, grass still growin, crows still crowin. Everythin turn out just fine. Just take time."

"Time's one thing I got a lot of," I says.

"I'm tellin ya. That's why they call me Furry. Furry Lewis is the name and I been bit by the dog, too. Your troubles is common, son. You think you got trouble like no one in the world ever caught before? No, you ain't. You got the plain old, mean old Beale Street blues and there's a cure for it, believe me or believe me not."

I could see he had his own problems. He pulled up his pants leg and showed me a wooden leg.

"Mislaid my leg, understand. Hoboin. Started goin 'long. Catchin freights how I lost it. The couplin, that's the thing you gotta watch out for. Furry goin down a grade, outside Du Quoin, Illinois, nineteen and seventeen. Furry caught his foot in a couplin. Took me to a hospital in Carbondale. Look right out my window and see the ice cream factory. Care to hear another song? Got plenty."

Learned "Casey Jones" from Furry. "Kassie Jones" as he called it. It was sorta connected to the story 'bout his leg in Furry's way of tellin it. 'Course in Furry's mind *everything* was connected. The couplin, the leg, the dog.

Furry's fingers was just *flashin* all 'round them strings. His action on bottleneck was a mournful cry. That slider was the guy who's in trouble but still don't know how bad.

Furry'd sing it like he knew Casey. Knew his *wife,* ya know? *Dreamt a dream, the night she bought her sewin machine.*

Furry played in Will Shade's Memphis Jug Band. Played parties with them, recorded with them, but he also like to play his own stuff. I soon began hangin with him, serenadin on the street. We'd meet at his house, walk down Brinkley to Poplar, go up Poplar to Dunlap, maybe all the way down to Main. People'd stop us along the way and say, "Do you know so and so?" and we'd play it.

One afternoon we was playin for a picnic in the park. Furry was a great storyteller—one of the best there ever was in the blues. But his real talent was for *not* tellin a story. Never could just tell the story straight from the beginnin to the end. He'd throw in anything that flew through his mind.

"Roll with it, leave it alone," Furry tell you slap in the middle of singin "Stackerlee." "Ain't 'bout a murder. No, it ain't. It's about you lose your money, don't let your mind slide down the street after it. Which is why I says *when you lose your money, learn to lose.*" With Furry a song could go on a hour or more. One song. I'm not kiddin.

Was in the middle of one of them endless songs I seen something make me turn white as a sheet. Might put it down to some bad cat whiskey or settin out in the sun too long but 'long 'bout four of the afternoon I seen Vida Lee clear as I'm talkin to you now, a-shakin her tail in a red shift under the shade of a tree not far from where we was playin. I told Furry, "Think I just seen someone I usta know in my other life."

"Don't go chasin ustabes," says Furry. "We lost more men to that than we done in the war."

I watched as she walked to the river and across by the railroad bridge and under the bluff. By the time I got there she was nowheres to be seen. Then I heard a cracklin of branches and run to the spot. All I come up on is a fat old mammy squattin in the bushes, cursin at me, "Goddamn, it's a pitiful thing a woman can't take a piss in the woods without you mens come a peekin."

This seein Vida Lee business gonna get me in trouble one of these days.

When Furry played in Will Shade's jug band I'd sometimes go along, play with them. Jug bands is a small street group. Guitar, harmonica, jug and a banjo plus a bunch of homemade instruments.

There was all kinds of tub, jug, washboard bands, or skiffle, jook and spasm bands in Memphis. The Memphis Jug Band and Gus Cannon's Jug Stompers were the two main ones. It's a tradition that goes back to slavery times when we wasn't allowed to own any instruments. Slaves'd do a thing called the juba pat—slappin your hands on your shoulders and over your body. W.C. Handy made rhythms as a child by scraping a nail across the jawbone of a dead horse. The jug in a jug band was a cheap alternative to a double bass. You put your lips up to the rim of the bottle, hold the jug close to your mouth and blow. Makes a low-pitched buzzin sound when you blow at different angles. Other instruments was kazoos and washtub bass.

Had some wicked harp players, too, and the king of the harp players was Noah Lewis. No relation to Furry. Could blow the hell out of that harp. He could play *two* harps at the same time. Through his mouth and through his nose. Same key, same melody. Noah, he was full of cocaine all the time, I reckon that's why he could play so loud, and aw, he was good. Had a real melancholy tone, driftin out and floatin back, blendin with the kazoo, or Gus Cannon's banjo.

In them days we had what you call moonlight picnics, you know, they'd last for three days straight, out in the woods. Lots of shade, and there ain't no one gonna bother you out there. Played sportin houses, hotels, white children's parties, college dances, even police parties. There were whole parties with nothin there but captains and sergeants.

That scene with Vida Lee had me worried ever since. I swear I'd seen her a-dancin there as clear as still whiskey in a glass fruit jar. My mind was goin sideways on me and I was gettin a queasy feelin 'bout all that. Figured I'd best get some professional advice on the subject, maybe consult with Mary the Wonder down at the Panama.

She was standin by the bar when I come in. Well-made, blue-lipped woman with big earrings and Spanish shawl. Had a room in the back of the club where she done her consultations. "You got thin-air trouble," she told me, "and that ain't good."

She read my palm, done the cards, told my fortune from a crystal ball.

"Honey," she says, "you under a enchantment. What you needs is a hex-withdrawin potion. Just happen to have a bottle over here. Come all the way from old Mexico. Made from the flesh of a cactus plant, ground-up scorpions, and other stuff I am not disposed to reveal."

"This stuff rid me of them visions?"

"Questions, questions. That's part of your problem," she say, and she laugh and laugh. "Drink up, baby. It won't bite you."

It was bitter and sour-tastin but I got it all down. I sat 'round her parlor while she read movie magazines, ate chocolates and drank sherry brought by clients come to consult. I was waitin to see if anything would happen or not. Tell me I best not go out on the street straight away. After awhile I got a dizzy feelin in my head. I was sweatin and pukin till I thought I must be dead. She said, "Coley, you feel kinda warm, why don'tcha go lie down?"

I laid on that pallet long time. Seem like a hour or more gone by when a beautiful woman come in the room, smellin of jasmine and honeysuckle. Thought nothin of it. Seem like the most natural thing what coulda happen. She was tall and skinny, long hair shakin as she walked, dressed in a long gown and there was bracelets all janglin on her wrists. Billie Holiday was singin on the radio. All at once I knew who she were.

"Vida Lee!" I shouted. Jump up and embrace her. There was tears streamin down my face. "Honey, honey, honey, I been seein you everywheres. Thought I was goin outta my mind. See, I *knew* you was here. Knew I hadn't imagined all that stuff."

"Hush, baby," she said. "Lie yourself down again, honey. It's gonna be all right. Mama always make it better, don't she?"

She caressed me and undressed me and then she positioned herself on top of me and it felt just like I was meltin and she was dissolvin and we was blendin.

I woked up and I got a big surprise. Was the blue-lipped woman starin into my eyes.

"Coley," she said, "know that woman you been seein 'round? You ain't gonna be seein her no more."

"What?"

"You wanted her gone, didn'tcha?"

"Yeah, but—"

"She gone now, baby. Long gone on that evenin train. Now what say we go over to Pee Wee's and get ourselves a drink?"

Monkey and the Baboon
Playin in the Grass

Big news was across the river in West Memphis. Everybody talkin 'bout "the Wolf" and the amplified blues. You know, soon as I heard of him I say to myself, gotta find my walkin cane, take a little trip across the river, and check this cat out.

Town had developed into a jumpin blues *jungle*. Finally get to the place where he's suppose to be playin but, man, I was not prepared for what I got. Howlin Wolf come out like he *was* the Big Bad Wolf —gonna eat us or something. Six foot three, two hundred seventy pounds. Wild and hairy-lookin like he lived down in a cave. Bones all spread about. Everybody scared of the Wolf, that's right.

He was a hair-raisin sight. His head—I can't explain it exactly —seem to stick way out in front of him like a big craggy rock. His face come out at ya. And he didn't sing, he *growled* the words. Like they was bones he's gnawin on. Electric guitar and drums and harp all pumpin away behind him like a turbine.

"Moanin at Midnight" begin with Willie Johnson playin a guitar riff he picked up from Tommy Johnson's "Cool Drink of Water Blues." Some songs he just moan and groan all the way through.

When Wolf go into them falsetto howls of his—that come outta Teejay's bag, too. But this *real* different. His eyes light up like a demon wolf, the veins on his neck stick out like a mule's milk vein. Took all the bad blues that had ever come outta the Delta, added a thunderstorm, two dozen rattlesnakes and several grizzly bears. The black dog Delta blues you hear howlin down your mind. Just two-chord songs, no changes in 'em at all, distilled down to 300 proof African white lightnin. Made the hair stand up on the back of your neck, made you look down at your feet see if the little snakes hadn't crawled outta that sound.

❖   ❖   ❖

Think I forgot 'bout B.B. King? You hear B.B. play, it's not something you're likely *to* forget. He was over in Memphis for what, three, four years? Twenty-three years old, baby face. Sweet guitar.

When he got out of the army in '45 he tried farmin but after runnin the tractor into the fence a few times he figured time to give it up and come to Memphis. That's where I met him. Playin on Beale Street, y'know, playin for nickels and dimes on the street. Sometimes he'd hook up with his cousin, Booker White. Booker was a shy kid, didn't want no fuss.

B.B. was a new breed of blues player. He come up rough like Wolf and them but he didn't end up like them. Didn't play like them neither. He didn't come to the blues by the usual route, see. The way everybody since the dawn of creation done it. In the old days—the way I come up and Robert Johnson and Wolf and so on—you learned the blues by hangin out with older cats, listenin to them playin the joints in your own little town. When you got good enough you worked the same joints you'd learned in, play to people who'd know you.

B.B. learned the blues from records and radio. Lonnie Johnson was his main man, him and jazz cats like Django Reinhardt. He started out playin to strangers.

Which mean you got to put out whatever it takes to grab 'em. B.B. would do anything to please an audience. He'd seen what happened to his idol Lonnie Johnson—ended up pushin a janitor's broom—and he didn't want it to happen to him. Worked one night stands, auditoriums, dance halls. All black audiences, three hundred fifty-two nights a year. Now I like the road but that's too much highway even for me.

"What keeps me out there?" he'll tell ya. "Thirteen kids, four wives. And women on the side? Don't even want to count 'em."

'Bout the time I come to Memphis, B.B. had just got hisself

a spot appearing on Sonny Boy Williamson's radio show on WDIA. Had this radio show called, uh…. Well anyway, it was sponsored by Hadacol—same patent medicine Colonel Tom Parker was involved with.

B.B. had a gig playin at Miss Ann's in West Memphis, Arkansas. He was wailin blues guitar nobody could touch. Could hit them swoopin, wingin notes. Develop this style of playin he call twingin. That's when you vibrate your finger on one note—give a similar feel as a slider but got more vibrato to it.

Was like he was fingerin with them women playin that guitar, toyin with their thingamajig, y'know. Women would faint dead away when B.B. play, and when he hit that wailin falsetto of his, forget it. One time I seen this lady, she just went limp, had to carry her outside. Like in church. That was his secret, see, he's a preacher, and that guitar is his congregation.

Usta say: "Everything that happen to us since we got took from Africa is in that sound. Hidden in there hollowed out like in a smuggler's bible. Slavery, plantations—it's all in there. Both a callin and a affliction, understand?" Told you he was a preacher.

How B.B. end up with his own show is this. Miss Ann's, they say to him, "Here's the deal—deal is we give you a permanent gig at the club if you can get yourself your own radio show." This is how things had progressed in the seven years or so since Sonny Boy got hisself on the radio. You gotta get a radio spot before they'll give you a gig. And before you can get a radio spot you gotta get a sponsor. Too much monkey business for me to be involved in.

So over at WDIA they got a blues show goin featurin B.B. King and his buddies Johnny Ace, Junior Parker and Bobby "Blue" Bland. Call theirselves the Beale Streeters. Furry and me, we old-time, and here this new generation of blues pickers comin on. We look at each other and say, "Fuck, man."

One day, B.B. come in this bar I'm at, ask me do I want to sit in as a guest on that show. Be on the radio, y'know. For 'bout five seconds I felt like I was gonna turn into Bing Crosby or something. I went 'round tellin everyone, "Man, tune me in. I'm gonna be on the radio at such and such a time."

Shoulda kept my damn mouth shut. Jesus!

Went along there at the radio station and B.B. ask me, "Whaddaya gonna sing us today, Coley?" And so I say, "I'd like to do this one about good Gulf gasoline, you know, that Robert Johnson sung."

So, he says, "Well, let's hear it then."

So I goes, *The monkey and the baboon playin in the grass,* but instead of singin, *Monkey stuck his finger in that old "Good Gulf Gas,"* I sung, *the monkey stuck his finger in the good girl's ass.* Deejay jump up all red in the face. See, they didn't have no five second delays in them days—it really *was* live. In three minutes I was out on my ass. You'd a thought I'd said, "Overthrow the government!" And that was my last appearance on the radio, folks. First *and* last.

B.B. had a big hit with "Three O'Clock Blues"—then he really took off. Played just about every night of the year except for Christmas and Thanksgiving. He was tourin so often sometimes they had to play old acetate disks of his program on the radio. When the sponsor found out, they fired him. Was supposed to be a live show, see? 'Course by that time he didn't need no radio show to get him a club gig. He was out there on the road, hummin, bringin the blues to the world.

41

It's Hard to Tell, It's Hard to Tell When All Your Love's in Vain

I only intended to stay in Memphis for awhile, but somehow that while stretched on and on and soon I'd been there six months. At least. Tell you what I was thinkin. I was thinkin maybe I get myself a solid gig, do another radio spot—get a little more prepared next time I go on the air kinda thing. My usual shit.

Told myself I'd be pullin down real money from makin music. Hey, we could all move to Memphis. Vida Lee and the kids and all. Anyway, that while streeeeeetched out into months. One day I woke up and realized I been gone over a year and, y'know, I was gettin one of my feelins. My feelins was twitchin. Tellin me, "Boy, you best get that girl on the phone and talk the sweetest talk you *ever* talked."

But I don't do it that day or the next or the next. It was a pain in the neck to organize in them days before everybody had a phone in their house like they do today. Could take weeks just to say "Hello!" So I kept puttin it off, knowin in the back of my mind I was just stokin the fire for my own doom.

One day I run into Furry Lewis—he was workin for the sanitation department sweepin the street. Lunchtime he'd sit on the curb, eat his sandwich and play his guitar.

Now with Furry you never know whether something was deliberate or just happen to come up. Don't honestly know if there's a difference there, actually.

He was singin this song—you know how you've heard a song a dozen times and as pretty as it is you don't really hear it? But when you hear it and you are in that place, it'll fang you just like a rattlesnake bite. That's the way I heard the song. It went,

> *I'd rather see my coffin come rollin from my door,*
> *I'd rather see my coffin come rollin from my door,*
> *Lord to hear my good girl tell, "I don't want you no mo."*
>
> *I'd rather hear the screws on my coffin sound,*
> *Than to hear my good girl says, "I'm jumpin down."*

That song bit me just as hard as the Beale Street beagle. Took a chunk right outta my mind.

I finally make the arrangements to speak to Vida Lee over the telephone. Figure I'll just call her up, explain a few things. Tell her I'm on my way, y'know. Be back in Lula any day. Well, I finally get her on the phone and instead of the voice of my own true love, it's *ice* on the line, baby. Thought I was gonna catch me pneumonia. Only on thirty seconds and she's ready to hang up.

"Vida Lee? Come on, don't be like that, girl. I know I shoulda been home sooner, but I done it for us…. Don't you go hangin up on me, chile, you know I don't love nobody but you. Vida Lee? Vida Lee?" Aw, shit.

Still, I'm thinkin it's easy enough to get mad over the phone. When I get back home she'll let me in, right?

I was sad to leave Memphis but I figured I won't be gone long. I'll tell Vida Lee 'bout all the places I seen there, all the fine stores and the big hotels and the fancy people.

Went to see the gypsy just to say goodbye. She kissed me and said, "You know I could put a spell on you, honey pie, make you stick right here in Tennessee."

"Know you could, baby, but you won't."

"Maybe not, sugar, but I'll see you again. Yes indeed."

Lyin under the train, ridin the blinds I'm singin to myself,

When I get back to Memphis
You can bet I'll stay,
And I ain't gonna leave
Until the Judgment Day.

Took me a while to get back home. I was hungry and ain't nobody offerin me a crust a bread. My mama say you leave the land, you be eatin outta a garbage can. My guitar was my only friend and it was all swole up, look like the rain got on it.

You know what they say, when you get unhappy your luck runs out. Every switchin yard I swung through there was bulls waitin to split my head. I was too tired and weak to take a beatin right then from them railroad dicks so I run into the bushes.

Come August in Mississippi you don't wanna get in the way of the law. They just layin to catch workers to bring in that cotton crop. Sheriff Jenkins pull me off the blinds. I say, "Boss, I ain't done nothin." He say, "Yeah, but you *gonna.* I'm just arrestin you in advance." After two weeks on the county farm they finally turn me loose.

Get back to Lula. See my home down the road. I'm a happy, happy man. I'm so elated I'm hummin some dopey pop song I heard somewheres that got stuck in my head.

Climb up on the porch. Turn the handle. Door's locked. Damn! Bolted on the *inside,* y'know, so I know she's home. Aw, she seen me comin and figured she gonna make me stew awhile. I committed the crime, now I gotta do my time. She's in there. Just needs to be wooed a spell.

"You got your outside man in there with you?" I'm kiddin around.

No reply. I go 'round the back, try a different tack. I can see her settin there in a rockin chair with her back to the window.

"Vida Lee, honey? What you want for your birthday—aside from me and the river? Vida Lee, can you hear me?"

Ah, I know. I'll sing her a little song, woo her with that. "Judge Harsh Blues." One of the things Furry Lewis usta sing:

> *Good mornin, Judge, what may be my fine?*
> *Good mornin, Judge, what may be my fine?*
> *Fifty dollars, eleven twenty-nine.*

> *Baby 'cause I'm arrested, please don't grieve and moan,*
> *'Cause I'm arrested baby, don't grieve and moan.*
> *Penitentiary seem just like my home.*

Before I even finish the next verse I hear the front door bolt bein pulled. Damn! It worked, I'm thinkin to myself. Made her laugh is what done it. She never could resist that. I run 'round to the front door, big smile on my face. Door opens and—it's my mama.

"What the—"

"Son, I heard you was on your way from Memphis and figured to be here when you got back. Haven't seen you in forever. Your dad's not well, you know."

"Vida Lee here?"

"'Fraid she ain't, Coley." Suddenly I'm not feelin too good.

"No one know where she gone, son. She stopped to say goodbye a couple of days ago. Said she'd write."

"Did she go back to her mother's?"

"Never did get along that well with her mother."

"Didn't even say what *town* she gone to?"

"Don't think she rightly knew herself."

I looked 'round the house. 'Cept for the rockin chair, everything was gone, even the victrola.

"What happened?"

"Bailiff come and take everything. That was the end for her, I think."

It was a empty house. Coupla windows broken. There was a toy sword and a rusty garbage can lid in the kitchen. Kids had been playin in the house. Just like them abandoned houses I used to play in with my brothers.

I'm feelin mighty sorry for myself, but Mama got no use for that.

"Coley," she say, "you was never home except on your way to someplace else. People in jail seen their wifes more often than you. Now, what kinda life is that for a woman? She was a pretty girl when you married her, real pretty. And she had to go and marry *you*. It's a cryin shame."

Sweet Home Chicago

Delta is a ghost country, strange things rise up right outta that ground—told you 'bout all that, didn't I? Well now it was full of haunted houses, too. Peoples was movin out from the Delta like there been a curse on the land. When they bring in the tractors and cotton-pickin machinery weren't no more use for the field hand. From Memphis down to Jackson there was empty shacks wherever you look, rottin and fallin in. Our house was gettin ready for the boneyard too. Windows was rattlin, boards bangin, shakes on the roof was shakin. Couldn't take my rest in that skeleton house no more.

I was studyin how to get outta the cotton patch but I couldn't summon the get-up-and-go. I got so tangled in my mind I catch myself talkin to that damn stone—one Marie the Prophetess gimme back there in New Orleans. Took out the stone and I said, "Thing, where we goin? Sure ain't stayin here."

Come the last of August, crops was blighted, well was dry, and Vida Lee was out there in the world somewheres. My mind was long gone on that evenin train, and I was plannin on joinin it real soon. *Black night is fallin, baby, oh, how I hate to be so alone.*

Told my brother, "Septimus, man, take the place. It's yours, don't wanna be here no more." Told him I was goin to the big city. See another mule or cotton row I'm gonna run like Jesse Owens. Goin up north to St. Louis, maybe. Or Chicago.

"Maybe I'll get a job in a packin plant," I'm tellin him. "Figure on makin some money on the side, y'know, playin my music." Know what he done? Laughed in my goddamn face.

"Dream on, little brother, dream on! How you plan on sellin that plinkety-plink funky-butt up North? Your stuff ain't nothin but down-home collard greens to them cats up in Chicago. Don't nobody listen to that shit no more. You a dreamer, Coley, and I don't think nothin ever gonna wake you up. Gonna read 'bout you some day in the paper. Crazy old man holdin up a liquor store, or shakin down some cat at a craps game. Maybe shot through the head. Poor old boy didn't have no sense to stay down on the farm. Bought every dream that blew through town. Goodbye Coley, 'cause I believe your time ain't long."

Man, that was cold. My own brother raggin on me, talkin like I was a bum. 'Course what he say was true. The Delta blues was gettin long in the tooth and so was I. You got your bebop, pop, country and western, sweet blues, combo blues, and rhythm and blues all comin out the radio at you. Louis Jordan and Billy Eckstine. You got to admit, one lone cat frailin and slidin on a guitar have a pretty hard time competin with that.

Nineteen fifty-one come along and if you was still playin down-home blues in the little towns 'round the Delta, it was like bein a clog dancer at the Apollo, baby. Gigs was scarcer than hens' teeth. You could hear whatever you want any old time you wanna hear it. Just slide your nickel right into the slot. What you want with some old black man pickin and slidin over in the corner for? Only people care to hear you saddlin up that old gray mare was folks who liked the old Delta blues, and that was gettin to be a small minority. Last ten years, you be hard pressed to find a country blues song on a jukebox 'round Clarksdale. I'm serious. In the forties it was all Fats Waller, Louis Jordan, Jazz Gillum and Peetie Wheatstraw. Only real country blues I seen on the box was Blind Boy Fuller's "Good Feelin Blues" and Tommy McClennan's "Whiskey Headed Man." Slim pickins.

'Course, the blues is like kudzu. Whack it down over here, gonna pop its scaly head up someplace else. Book of the blues weren't closed yet. Stick around.

You catch that? Yup, I hear that train a'comin. All aboard Illinois Central! Come on, I'll show you how the folks from the Delta headed north, takin the sacred and profaned blues with 'em, plug in to Chicago Gas & Electric and change the world, that's right.

Illinois Central ran from New Orleans up to Chicago in twenty-four hours. Cost you $10.11 from Memphis ridin the cushions. I was gettin a little old for catchin freights. Your auntie or your sweetheart pack some roast chicken and biscuits for the trip, you was in luck. All I had was a box of Ritz Crackers.

Man, you ain't gonna believe who all on this train. Musta been half of Clarksdale packed in carryin all their junk with them. There's Mrs. Budge clutchin her Victrola, and Mr. Cawthorne (to whom she ain't speakin, he run off with her second cousin), and there's Reverend Poole with his cage bird.

Some is singin hymns, some playin harp and old blues songs. When we cross the Ohio river everybody burst out at once into *I done come out of the Land of Egypt with the good news.* Them old sisters was testifyin and scripturizin the whole way.

"We done crossed over, crossed over the river a Jordan. Taken our souls into the promised land. Praise the Lord!"

"Amen, sister!" And pass the chicken.

They had the chicken and ham *and* biscuits so I wasn't gonna debate chapter and verse with them ladies. There was this one cat name of Willie settin on the train playin his harp. Big muthafucka. Gap-tooth, baby-faced cat, grinnin and laughin at all the holiness business.

"Sister, when you prayin," he ask the lady in the straw hat, "and you sayin 'Deliver us from evil,' who you mean was evil?"

"Why, from temptation of the Devil, 'course. We prayin so as God deliver us from his clutches."

"Amen!" say the one in the calico dress.

"Ain't *your* God, sister," he tells her. "You left your God back in Africa. Who taken away your everything there is? Rob you of your culture, your language? Who taken away your gods and give you a strange white god with chin whiskers and blue eyes?"

"Brother, have I got some good news for you!" the straw-hat lady tells him. "Jesus be black. Yes darlin, God be black. Chapter 1, verse fourteen Revelations. Right there in the Book of the Seventh Seal."

Willie just laughed and laughed. "If he black why ain' he takin care of his own?"

"You keep on like that, chile, you goin straight to Hell."

"That just fine with me, sister, I'll be in good company."

Comin into Chicago seventeen hours later through the South Side. Sure didn't look like no Promised Land. Mile after mile of dilapidated wooden-frame row houses tumblin down to the edge of the tracks. Some was keepin goats and chickens in their backyard, some growin tomatoes and corn and turnip greens and okra. Now you *know* them folks is from the Delta.

Willie see me gettin my box down off of the rack and he say, "What you got in there, a guitar or a hambone? If you can do anything any damn good on that thing, come see me and I'll fix you up."

Hand me his card. Says:

WILLIE DIXON
Bass, producer, & songwriter to the Stars.
"I am the blues."

CHESS RECORDS
4848 Cottage Grove
Chicago, Illinois

Had a phone number on there too. Felt like I just spent the last eighteen hours with Santy Claus. 'Cause this was the main cat to see in Chicago if you was in the blues line. Maybe my luck was changing.

By the time the train pull into the Union Station, I am starvin. Platform swarmin with relatives and sweethearts. Whistles blowin, taxis honkin, peoples hollerin. My head was dizzy. I was goin at $33^1/_3$ rpm, everybody else spinnin at 78.

Got on a streetcar, headed straight for Tampa Red's house. Red lived at 35th and State over a pawnshop. Madhouse filled with old-time musicians—did I tell you 'bout Red? Tampa Red, you know Hudson Whittaker was his real name. He was short and dapper. Light skinned, fine features. Always dress dignified—bow tie, three-piece tweed suits. You seen him on the street you'd never take him for a blues player. Coulda been a professor at a college from the way he dressed.

There's a bunch of other stuff I could tell you about Red, but later for that. Right now I'm so hungry I could eat mosquito pie. All I can think about is food. Red open the door, I head right for the refrigerator, which have a bottle of stale beer, a piece of moldy cheese and a coupla dinner rolls. He was goin through one of his altercations with his wife, Frances. She walked out a week before.

"Jesus, Red," I told him, "make up with the bitch. I'm starvin!"

Tampa's house was a sort of hotel for musicians come up from the South. There was a piano in the kitchen, another one in the livin room, a tin can bass, a kettle drum and a pile of guitars. Big Maceo, Red's piano player, hung there. Big Boy Crudup when he come to town. Bunch a guys. Drink wine, play, get high. I was havin a fine old time hangin 'round there, tellin lies and drinkin Kentucky Fly.

Lester Melrose from Bluebird records was there all the time, too. Drunk. He was a happy-go-lucky guy who liked to have a good time but he had one of them big pudgy potato faces that always looks glum. Lester dressed like a businessman but his suits was all baggy. He was as rumpled-lookin as a unmade bed. Tie all askew, shirt missin a few buttons. He was a white cat who loved the blues —sweet blues, combo blues, mainly—and he acted as the go-between for the black artists and the record companies. If you was a black artist in them days, you couldn't get a contract direct. So Lester was that man.

Lester gave Tampa Red money to pay the rent and buy food 'cause any musician come up from the South, that's where they'd go. To Red's. A lot safer than scoutin 'round the South as Lester discovered when he went to find Tommy McClennan.

McClennan worked on a big farm outside Yazoo City. They spy a white northerner snoopin 'round a plantation, they run Lester through the corn. Called out the dogs, had themselves a grand old time. Almost tarred and feathered him.

"Get hurt?" Lester would say when he tell the story. "Hell, they nearly *killed* me. They woulda done it, too, if they hadn't been too fat to catch me."

Bluebird, which was the label Lester ran, was the low-price label of RCA, the great mother of all record companies. RCA records sold for 75 cents, Bluebird was 35 cents. Cheap. For the colored, y'know.

Bluebird had this creamy, big-city blues style down, and Lester kept on turnin 'em out till they all sounded the same. Had a bunch of hits with this shit. He and Georgia Tom Dorsey—yeah, the one usta play behind Bessie—they had a monster hit with "Tight Like That." Big Bill Broonzy was always over at Red's. Practically live there. Big Bill very suave and agile for such a huge guy. Silk socks, wing-tip shoes, tiepin with his initials on it. Had the most beautiful guitar I ever seen, a Gibson cut-away scroll that been custom made for him.

Big Bill was the nicest guy I ever met. That was the trouble with these cats, they was *too* nice. And the blues ain't nice music. You nice it up, it gonna evaporate right before your eyes. Blame it on my old buddy Peetie Wheatstraw. That sweet, smooth piano style was so tasty when it come out that everybody was jumpin on them sugar bones.

When I arrive in Chicago there was only a coupla Delta blues bands goin: Muddy Waters and Elmore James when he was in town. In the clubs they was mostly into a swingin jazz-type thing and West Coast jump blues—type a thing that T-Bone was doin.

After awhile Red's wife come back. Frances was a big woman with big jewel-cat glasses and straight hair like an Indian. She was warm-hearted and jolly but you didn't want to cross her. She had a temper and in that house of old sinners she was set to go off as regularly as a egg timer. When she got mad she could pick Tampa right off the floor and shake him like he was a rag doll. Frances was always cookin up big pots of stew and grits night and day. Great steamin kettles on the stove of ham hocks, cabbage greens smothered down.

One day I go fishin with Big Bill and Tampa Red. Red tell Frances, "Baby, don't buy nothin for dinner 'cause we is gonna bring it on home." Red's wife rollin her eyes back in her head. "Help me, Lord! Man gone crazy," what she said. "Thinks he's Jesus Christ gonna feed the whole South Side with loaves and fishes."

So we go to this lake way out somewheres early in the mornin. Fishin and boozin, boozin and fishin with a little break for playin a few tunes and tellin lies. Evenin rolls 'round and we haven't caught diddly-squat. We might as well been playin pool for all we caught and that's what Frances woulda thought if we'd a come back empty-handed.

"Hell, Red, what you gonna do now?"

Red has an idea. On the way back he buys hisself a bunch of fish. Just any old fish they got layin there.

"She ain't never gone know the difference," says he.

"I don't know 'bout that," says Big Bill.

But Red, he's real pleased with hisself and when we get back he very grandly hands the day's catch to Frances, who inspects them like they was nasty wrapped in bad news.

"Where you get this mess?" she ask him right off.

"We caught 'em, what you think we done?"

"You catch any of these, Big Bill?"

"Uh well...."

"Thought so. How 'bout you, Coley?"

"Ma'am, I never did have no luck really with fishin."

"Red, now you mean to tell me you caught *all* them fish all by yourself?"

"That's what I said, woman, and if you don't believe me—"

"Well I damn well don't. These is old fishes. Them fishes' eyes is *dead*. They been caught days ago and kept on ice shavins. And half them damn fish is sea fish from the ocean. And y'all is damn liars and you can get the hell outta my kitchen and stay out." Woman chased us out the door and down the stairs with a fryin pan.

When we get down to the street, Big Bill says, "Told ya you can't slip nothin past that woman."

"Well whaddya call this?" Red say, and he's got a drumstick in each pocket.

Tampa introduce me all 'round. Elmore James, Memphis Slim, Eddie Boyd, Willie Mabon, Memphis Minnie. Minnie give these

Blue Mondays, at the Gate. A good-lookin woman but real tough. Great big earrings. Talkin in that gruff manner but big in her heart. She'd do them good old numbers of hers like "Bumble Bee," "In My Girlish Days."

Tommy McClennan was up next. He'd only been in Chicago awhile but he'd got slick. Like most blues cats, he dressed real sharp —snap-brim straw hat, big flashy tie, tailored jacket. Had big eyes like he was surprised by the world. Short but handsome. But as sharp as Tommy dress, he still look like a cropper who'd just got his yearly furnish money, gone to Clarksdale and bought hisself some brand-new threads.

Tommy done his hit, "Bottle Up and Go." He was a fierce player in the Delta style but he have this bad habit of throwin the word "nigger" 'bout. Down South blacks was usta callin each other nigger in a kiddin way, same as today—but back then in Chicago, uhn uhn. He say it once too often and they smash his guitar 'round his neck and heave him right through the window.

Most everyone got a gig, at least on the weekends. Big noise 'round then was Muddy Waters. He had a bunch of R&B hits already. Callin hisself the King of the Blues and ain't nobody gonna contradict him.

"You gotta go over to the club, listen at him," Red's tellin me. "Check out all what he puttin down, Coley. Get back! Delta blues electrified and layin track, baby. Swear I never thought I'd see the day."

We go over to the 708 Club—that was the address, 708 East 47. Was a nice little place. Booths and shit. You knew something big was happenin soon as you walk in that door. And I'm talkin here 'bout the *early* days of Muddy. When he and Little Walter would sit down and play just like the old guys usta do down South, settin on chairs. This was before he got his stage act together. Seen Otis Rush at the Alibi leapin about and took a page outta Otis's book. What Otis told me anyways.

But even sittin down, Muddy was a ball of fire. He could punch out them words like nailin rivets. Fists clenched like he was holdin on to a freight-train door, sweat pourin down his face, whole shirt soaked through. Was the king bee, baby. Gals lined up ten deep when he was singin. He was playin them freight-train blues like some wild thing that been hid in the blues done jumped right outta the box at ya, barkin feedback and distortion.

Was a cool little combo he got there, slap bass of Ernest "Big" Crawford, Jimmy Rogers on lead guitar, Little Walter playin harp, Baby Face Leroy on drums, Otis Spann on piano. Otis was like Muddy's adopted son. He usta hang out on Muddy's doorstep when he first come up from Belzoni, Mississippi, suckin on a bottle of cat whiskey till Muddy come out his door. Muddy was the doctor, see? He come to see the doctor.

Beautiful bottleneck sound he got on that guitar a his—like a summer afternoon in Coahoma County with lightnin streakin 'cross the sky. Muddy's slide tone stung hard. When he get excited he slide sharp—let it drift when he's feelin good. Dragonflies hummin over that note. When he want to throw some shadow on it, sour it up, he go flat, a frog-hair off. Muddy play like a cloud driftin over a field. Ain't 'bout no scales or frets. They say in the Chinese musics they got more notes than in any scale we know about. Ten thousand notes. That's what Charley Patton and Henry Sloan and Tommy Johnson knew. Knew all them invisible notes.

Delta roots music go down to the bottom of the world, the old blues wisdom what Muddy brung with him outta the cotton patch. He knows where them notes is buried. He's in Old Africa when he's slitherin on that bottleneck, man. The old Yoruba scale, that West African bird in the brain. The spirit *hovers*, baby, it moves. You ain't never gonna nail it down.

But when Muddy start hollerin he don't need to play no guitar. It was a loud shoutin band. He was chantin the blues like they was Mississippi hymns.

> *I gotta axe handle pistol*
> *On a graveyard frame*
> *That shoots tombstone bullets*
> *Wearin balls and chains.*
> *I'm drinkin TNT,*
> *I'm smokin dynamite,*
> *I hope some schoolboy*
> *Start a fight.*

Because I'm ready,
Ready as anybody can be.
I'm ready for you,
I hope you're ready for me.

Muddy could play distortion like some people play scales. Music come *at* you—hard, mean and raw. Drivin behind them blues with all six cylinders. Shift its gears and oil the whole joint to drinkin and dancin.

Man, I thought he was a god. A sad-faced, quiet-spoken, otherworldly, sweaty god. Had a serene disposition and the heavy-lidded eyes of a ancient soul. A face so solemn and mysterious that when he smile it was just like the sun comin out on a cloudy day. Muddy Waters had the most African face on him of any blues player I ever seen. Eyes like he was peekin outta a mask. Face just like Grandmaw Pie told me 'bout. Shaman's voice comin out through the mask.

Just 'bout every weekend there be head-cuttin contests. The prize was maybe five bucks and a bottle of whiskey. Just for the fun of it. Everybody showed up, black and white. They be crowded into the club, settin on the stairs, spillin out into the street. The hot three then was Muddy, Big Bill and Memphis Minnie. And Minnie almost always won them contests. She could connect with a audience better than anybody. She could make you laugh at the Killer Diller from the South that was so ugly he made mannequins walk outta store windows or she could sing hot like in "Me and My Chauffeur Blues." She was gonna buy that boy a brand-new V-8 Ford.

Frequently Red and Big Bill would get at that bottle before Minnie finished her set. She'd be chasin 'em down the street hollerin and cursin.

I Heard the Voice of a Porkchop

After awhile I had to split from the Tampa Red Hotel. Big Bill was quiet, never raise his voice, but Red would kick up a fuss over nothin and square it up all over the joint. He was testy when he got drunk, and he and Lester Melrose they was pretty much loaded all the time.

But however scrappy it got there, it was scarier leavin. I was on my own without a boot to piss in. I pawned my guitar and amp and when that money was gone I end up panhandlin on Maxwell Street, big open-air market in Chicago. Over 'round 14th and Halstead, what they call Jewtown. Mile-long wooden stalls all 'long the curbs. Mexicans and gypsies sellin spices, melons, taters—aromas of cooking could drive you wild. Cats hustlin appliances, windup toys. There was fortunetellers and doomsayers. You coulda filled a 'cyclopedia with the hustles goin down there. Some of them pitchmen was beautiful to see, they tricked it out so good. All *kinda* nonsense. Horses that could add and subtract, pigs that could read. And fights. Called it "Bloody Maxwell" for all the brawls they got there.

A whole mess of strange characters playin there. One-leg Sam Norwood, my old friend from Greenville, Daddy Stovepipe, Maxwell Street Jimmy, who been in the minstrel shows—and still dressed like he was in 'em, and a funny old cat in a jockey cap named Eddie "Porkchop" Hines who always toutin the odds—"Thirty-to-one on

McKinley's Bride, yessir!"—mighta been a jockey at some time in his life, I don't know. Man, there was singers and pickers hitchin all the way from Helena and Natchez 'cause they'd heard you could make a buck playin on Maxwell Street, and you could, too. You hear them electric guitars from half a mile away. Cuttin whine of bottlenecks wailin through the air like bandsaws. Electric guitars with pick-ups on 'em, y'know. They was playin Robert Johnson, Elmore James riffs like "Rollin and Tumblin" and "Dust My Broom," and they was rakin in the dough. I could see how it was. They was gettin so much coin throwed in their bucket they had to put newspaper in the bottom so as you wouldn't hear how much.

I was cursin myself for pawnin my guitar and amp. I was a gunslinger without no gun. And it was *cold*, boy. The hawk—you know that wind what come off Lake Michigan? Man, it'll cut right through your clothes and finger your bones. I was sleepin on gratings in cardboard boxes. Thought I'd wake up one mornin and find myself froze into a giant ice cube. Cops roustin you out in the middle of the night, too. "Better get on home, buster, if you have one."

Thought it might be a good oportunity to call Willie Dixon, my friend from the train. I dialed Chess Records and a loud, growly voice come over the line, sayin, "HELLO, MOTHER!" I hung up. Wasn't till later on that I heard this was Leonard Chess's way of answerin the phone.

Chicago, man. It's cold, it's mean, and ugly as a old whore. My mind was gettin clouded by the cold. And bein hungry. I begin casin some of the joints 'long Maxwell Street. On a corner there's Finkelstein's candy store. Easy pickins. You wasn't gonna get rich outta it but I wasn't goin for the big score anyways. What I didn't count on was there bein a cop shop right down the street. What did I know? I was new in town.

Got me a dumb plan. Whittle a chunk of wood to look something like a gun—that is if you didn't look too close, was shortsighted, and hadn't seen a gun in a while. Which the old guy hadn't. He was shakin like a leaf.

"I ain't too good at this," I told him, "so let's get it over fast."

It was all dimes and nickels and quarters and the old fella was tremblin so bad he spill it all over the floor. I'm helpin him pick it up when I hear a gruff voice sayin, "Can I give you a hand with that, sport?" I was lookin up at a big beefy cop in a checkered cap. I run down in the alley, jump a fence, up the back stairs, over the roof. I could hear Paddy huffin and puffin comin on. I'm runnin 'cross this roof lookin back, laughin at this big, beefy cop. Damn, if I don't run right into a pigeon coop, get myself all tangle up in the chicken wire. I was layin there giftwrapped when that police catch up with me.

Lockup was in the basement of the precinct. A real hellhole. They got troughs down there for you to piss and shit in. Rats as fat as rabbits was roostin on the water pipes. At least it was warm. It was *too* damn hot down there—was like a waitin room in Hell with cats throwin up all over you.

Two months later they pull me outta there. Figure I'm gonna get hauled in front of the judge. Sergeant takes my cuffs off, hands me my stuff in a brown paper bag.

"So long," I tell him.

"You'll be back," says he.

Can't even hold up a damn candy store and pull it off! I was just what my brother say I was—a old bum. No guitar, no wife, no friends, no home, no life.

I am scufflin down the street when a fat old broad come tearin outta a fortunetellin parlor. A gypsy woman runnin down the street after you means either you are about to catch on fire or she in worse trouble than you. At that point I didn't much care which.

"Come on in, cropper," she says. "I'll give you something make good come to you."

"Hell, I ain't no farmer, woman."

"Aw c'mon, I can still smell that hog shit on your shoes. Suck your dick, big boy. Uh-huh baby, make your eyeballs pop out your nappy head. Come back in here, I'll do you good. Say, damn if I ain't knowed you from somewheres."

"You don't know me, lady, and I don't *wanna* know you."

"Tough guy, huhn? Got news for you, mister cryin in his corn liquor. Oh yeah, I can see it in your eyes, big shot. Lost your baby, maybe?"

"Mind your own fuckin business."

"Wait a minute, it's *you*. You the fella what was seein things. Back in Memphis? Fuck me, my spell musta worked good on you, boy. You don't remember nothin, do ya?"

"Mary? Gypsy Mary from the Panama Club? Well, I'll be damn!" The woman had gained 'bout three hundred pound. Must be doin fairly well. She still hustlin them potions.

"Got strong Mexican mojos right here. *Suerte-podere-riquezas-alegrias*. I'll do you, dollar cheap."

"Mary, I ain't messin with no more stuff like that. Got me so turned around you wouldn't believe."

She gimme something anyways. On the house. Guaranteed Mama Sita love potion and damned if it didn't work—but not in the way I planned. Go messin in magic you never know what gonna happen.

Every day them policy wheels callin to me. Had names like Panama, White House, Snake, Hollywood. Sayin, "Coley, Coley, come over here lay your money down, lay your money, money down." Gonna do just that, soon as I could get me some numbers that vibrated right.

Then one night in my sleep Grandmaw Pie come to me, sing me a crazy song. She was whisperin a lullaby in a whale's ear. Went like this:

> *Eleven sailors ridin twenty-fi bees*
> *Was sailin, sailin over de seben seas.*
> *Dey was pickin pretty parrods outta palm trees*
> *And eatin by de dozen dem Panama's peas.*

The whale got the face of Thomas Jefferson on him and that Jefferson whale got a great big grin 'cross his kisser. Don't make no sense, but that exactly the things you gotta pay attention to. Soon as the credits roll on that dream I raise myself right up outta bed and head over to them policy wheels. Get there just before twelve—last spin be at midnight—and play the numbers Pie give to me. Bet my last dollar on the Panama wheel and won. Weren't much but it allow me to get my guitar outta Sy's Pawn, put a little De Armond pick-up on to it, get me a Silvertone amp. Boy, I was wailin. It buzz like a field of locusts but I loved it just the same.

Get to that Maxwell Street market on a Sunday mornin real early. Choose myself out a good spot, babe, on a corner. Got myself a long cord, pay a guy in a store a dollar to plug it in. You could make more money than God if you was good.

Them sassy women sashayin down the street, I wanted to show 'em just how I feel:

> *All you pretty little chicks widcha curly hair,*
> *I know you feel I ain't nowhere.*
> *But stop whadcha doin, come over here.*
> *I'll prove to you, baby, that I ain't no square.*

Yeah, Maxwell Street market a hubbub of black-ass barterin, banterin, bitchin, hawkin, whorin, and hustlin ingenuity like the world ain't never seen. People competin for every little piece of loose change. Them other blues sonsofbitches hangin on the bottom rung of the ladder hasslin me something fierce, but didn't bug me none till Little Walter Jacobs come along. Got the purple beret on, an El Pepe mustache, Hawaiian shirt, and a whatchagonnadoaboutit attitude. Walter was a hell of a harp player and a hell-*raiser*, too. Tough and rough, scrappy little guy. Never met a harp player didn't have a bad attitude. Junior Wells, Sonny Boy number two, all of 'em was menacin muthafuckas.

Walter, he was playin on the street with his friend Honeyboy Edwards. Tuft under his lip and the big gold tooth give him a fiendish appearance, but Honey have a pleasant nature underneath that. He was a slide player in the Delta style. Had a real nice action. "Man," he say to me, "play something on that box."

I do a coupla riffs and right off he say, "Helena? Yazoo City? Clarksdale?" Had me pegged real close.

Little Walter weren't that cordial.

"Get lost, amateur! This corner *mine*."

He been on a tour of the South with Muddy Waters, got into a fight, up and split. I heard he walked all the way from Hayti, Mississippi to the next bus station. He was a tough little punk been on his own since he was eight. Had a slug in him from when he got in a shootout and nailed hisself in the leg. He was too damn cussed to even take it out.

I moved off down the street. Hey, one corner good as another, right? Little Brother Montgomery come over, porkpie hat settin up on his head. He was an older cat—like me—with that worried aspect folks of my generation had, always lookin behind hisself, check if anything was gainin on him. Says, "Hell, come set yourself over here. I don't care who plays up next to me, I like the company."

Next Sunday, Walter come up on me. "Whatcha catchin, cousin?"

"Just small fries and cuttin bait."

"Stick with me, man, we might get a good something goin."

"What happen to Honey?"

"He went over to Chess records and cut a coupla tunes."

"Good for him."

"No, it ain't. That muthafuckin Muddy Waters was over there and he got hisself all puffed up over it. Didn't want nobody near that studio who got a style anything like he done, baby. So Mr. Chess give a hundred dollars to Honey and ease him on out the back door. Don't wanna upset his prize poodle. Honey got disgusted an took hisself off on the next train south."

We get a little combo goin. Me, Walter, that cat Porkchop on washtub bass—he could sing some, too. Ever heard a porkchop sing? And we got Evelyn Young on sax. Sax players was starvin on account of the harp players what was comin up from the Delta after Sonny Boy number one get to Chicago and have some hit records. That Sonny Boy was *John* Williamson, got killed in 1949 and after that Sonny Boy number two come 'long. Then come Little Walter, Big Walter Horton, Junior Wells and them. Harp players was scorin all the gigs.

Walter had one of the best sounds you could get from a harp, a down-in-the-cellar sound. Made that harp honk just like he was blowin sax. Evelyn had hair short as a man's and she weren't too pretty neither. None of the guys was even thinkin 'bout pickin up on her and she didn't want 'em to neither. Her taste run to her own sex.

Playin with Walter was a stone draw. Dead presidents was flyin 'round like leafs in a breeze. Walter had a bunch of girls 'round him.

Them bitches was drippin off of him. He coulda lived anywheres in any style he so desired. High society or lowlife. And he did. Lived fine. He was livin in a penthouse—what he said anyhow.

❖　　❖　　❖

We was makin good bread playin on the street but this was a Sunday deal, Maxwell Street, and I was gettin tired of my day gigs, jumpin from packin plant to slaughterhouse to some loadin-and-unloadin dock.

I ask Walter to help me get a gig in a club. There was so many in them days. The Pink Poodle, Theresa's, the Plantation Club, Cadillac Baby's, Club Alibi, the Congo Lounge, El Macombo Club, Ricky's Show Lounge, Club Zanzibar. Have I forgotten any? All this activity heated up the atmosphere something fine. Blues was runnin like a fever through Chicago. Nobody ever slept. We was up all night, worked all day. Buses ran twenty-four hours a day. So did the steel mills.

Chicago was a specialized kinda howlin hell dreamed up by some Delta demon—the worst kind you could think up, one that was disguised as the promised land.

Places like the Bucket O' Blood was real rough. Just as you passin along you see guys flyin outta the door—*through* the door. Shoes and hats and broke-up chairs comin down like a rainy night in Georgia. Blues and booze get 'em jacked up, man, and they go off like firecrackers. Somethin you played, something you *didn't* play —who knows what all? You had cats comin at you with hog legs, razors, meat cleavers, cue sticks.

Meanwhile just as I was countin on Walter doin me a solid, he got hotter than a pistol and split the scene. That song a his, "Juke," was doin real good. Chess put him on the road behind that. He didn't need to play the street no more though he was the kinda guy that come down and do it anyways. Get his vibes out on the street, y'know? Now Muddy was different like that. May have played down on Maxwell a coupla times when he first arrive but he just didn't agree with that. He was a proud cat. To him it was kin to beggin. He see Walter or Junior Wells doin it, he'd say, "You all gonna have to stop goin over there, playin on the street. You makin me look bad, man."

When I Came to Chicago in 1951 Muddy Waters Said, "Coley Boy, You Better Get a Gun"

I was scufflin and scabbin. If I got lucky some places let me do a few numbers, pick up a buck or two here and there and move on over to the next joint. Workin the small clubs, little hole-in-the-wall neighborhood joints. I'd get the gig if some cat didn't show, someone got a bookin outta town. That kinda trip. Club Alibi, five dollars a night. Little, low-ceilin joints. Sawdust on the floor. Steampipes runnin all 'round the top of the room with tinsel still wrapped 'round 'em. Some didn't even have tables. Just a little hole in the wall with the cats and kittens sittin at the bar and leanin up 'gainst the walls.

Club work can kill you. You're off twenty, play forty. Six and half hours in a joint like that, you wrecked. Get off 'round five in the mornin. Summertime it's day when you arrive and day when you leave. It ain't just the playin, it's all the drinkin and arguin. Gettin into fights. Hell, you got the musicians' union shakin you down. You don't pay 'em off, they pull you off the stage. My union card was a five dollar bill.

Over at Sylvio's on West Lake I met this cat who run crap games and manage some artists on the side. His name was Shakey Jake. He was smooth-looking, with a boyish face. Had that innocent expression of don't look at me, boss. But that cat was always up to his ears in mischief. Called him Shakey 'cause they usta say, "Shake 'em, Jake!" when they was layin bets. But see, I knew he didn't shake nothin. Them con men just click the dice together. As a result of fuckin 'round like this he been shot in the side and took up handlin musicians as a less dangerous occupation. Manage Magic Sam for awhile.

Tells me 'bout this place called the Congo Club where they was lookin for an act to bring people in from the street. Which is how I got my first steady gig.

Cats come into the Congo Friday night what worked at the meat packin plants and the slaughterhouses. Their coats was all splattered with blood from handlin carcasses but they got their do's *down*. Glossy slicked-up coifs standin up to attention like their hair was made of wax.

Shakey Jake at the Congo Village had hisself a girfriend with a pink poodle dog called Antoine. Dyed bright pink to match her lipstick color and Shakey had taught it to blow and suck on the harp. I swear. "Give Poochy Antoine his solo, now, give the poodle some!" they get to shoutin. I heard dogs sing "The Old Rugged Cross" better'n that, but the scroungy mutt always got a bigger round of applause than me.

Everybody was plugged in. You needed an electric guitar to cut through the noise in them taverns. At the start we was goin head to head with the jump-blues cats with the saxes and the axes. Once we got electrified you could just blow them suckers right off the bandstand.

Weirdest thing that happened to me 'round then was I run into myself. I'm tellin you the truth now. One night a short, feisty cat come in the club.

"Know who I am, muthafucka?"

Had on a zebra-striped jacket like J.B. Lenoir usta wear and he was carryin a big old Gibson guitar so I knew *he* thought he was somebody, but I myself had never laid eyes on him. Popped right outta the woodwork with some evil plan on his mind. You get these types. So I says, "Bet you're gone tell me, right?"

"Guess!" Now he's got his face right up on mine. I can see his nose hairs twitchin he's so close and I have bad feelin about this cat. Got a piece in his pocket or I ain't....

"You got the wrong guy," I say, tryin to back off.

"Do I? This name ring a bell, asshole? Freddy Fox. You heard what I said, Freddy Fuckin Fox."

Oh, Jesus! Knew this day gonna come. Now it have finally happened. I run up on the guy I was mistook for—y'know, when I cut "Ninety-Nine Years in Hell" or whatever that record was called.

Told the scout from the record company I *was* Freddy Fox.

"You sonofabitch," he says, "that dumb turpentine camp song pursued me like a ex-wife my whole life. I swore if I ever found the sucker who pulled that shit—"

I think he come in intendin to blow me away but something snapped in him and he just got over hisself. We ended laughin 'bout it. That's bars for you, man. Cats is either layin to kill you or bear-huggin you. Tellin you, "Fella, wanna know something for free? You my best friend. Don'tcha believe what I say, muthafucka? You callin me a liar?"

Maybe I shoulda asked Mary for a job potion, too, 'cause I got fired from my gig third week I'm there. Deal at the Congo was seven bucks a night and all the whiskey you could drink. Mighta took a bit too much advantage of the second part. That night I was layin right in the street. When the customers come in the bar they ask, "Where's the show?" the owner say, "You just stepped over him."

I pick myself up and I can only find some no-show gigs here and there. What really broke the cake was when this tall, skinny cat with a do-rag on his head come in the bar I was at and say, "You Coley Williams? Heard all 'bout you from my sister. Says you some player on that guitar, otherwise you a no-good sonofabitch."

"Uh, your sister, didja say?" I was thinkin on my feet, y'know. 'Fraid maybe I forgot somethin.

"Yeah," he says, "Vida Lee."

"Vida Lee, huhn. And what they call you, my man?"

"Jimmy. Jimmy Brown." Wait a damn minute. My mind was movin outta orbit and all the dogs in hell was barkin.

"The fuck you are," says I. "I *know* she got a brother named Jimmy, know that cat *real* well, and you ain't him."

"Hey, you sayin I don't know who I'm kin to? Go ask Vida Lee."

"Now how am I gonna do that?"

"She's livin over in Morgan Park. Go ask her, smartass, see what she say." And he split. Hell, what the fuck was goin down? This cat weren't no more like the other Jimmy than grits ain't groceries.

I was giggin that night. Just found me a slot at the Tempo Tap on

Indiana and the first night I'm there, in they come—Muddy Waters and company, newly vamped and callin themselves the Headhunters. They was out to cut heads, and, baby, they was hittin heavy. Breeze into a club and blow away whoever was playin there—like blues gangsters, y'know? If they'd get a chance they'd burn you, baby, and, man, did we get our short and curlies scorched.

We did our thing that night and it was cool as it goes, doin Tommy Johnson's "Big Road Blues," shit like that. Me and Tampa Red, a pick-up cat on bass and the bartender on drums. Now it was Muddy's boys' turn to play. They do that thing, their signature tune, "Your Cat Will Play." It was the same song as "Juke." You know, the one that became a hit for Little Walter? Muddy weren't settin in no chair no more. He was stampin, hollerin, jumpin up in the air, his whole body jerkin like Jimmy Rogers' guitar was givin him electric shocks. He'd double over like someone done shot him in the belly with a .44 and then flip back, sing the next verse. When he come to a heavy line— *goin down to Loosana, baby, behine the sun*—his eyes rolled back in his head like a ju-ju man.

We didn't stand a ice cube's chance in Hell. 'Cause Muddy's was the twenty-amp, shot-through-with-lightnin Frankenstein's blues. It stung you like the whole Chicago power company was runnin through them tiny amps.

Was like Muddy drove his Caddy right through the plate-glass window of the bar I was sittin in. I walked outta that club with all the guitars in all the bars in Hell ringin in my ears. But I was just as happy to be alive as catfish on a Sunday mornin. I had heard the kinda sound make the whole world go 'round. Lazarus got his old bones refried and rose up from the dead, that's right.

I could not get that Jimmy Brown business off of my mind so next mornin I set out to look up Vida Lee. Once I knew where to look she weren't that hard to locate. Over in Morgan Park all the sisters knew who she were.

She was lookin pretty good when she open up the door. Flower bandanna 'round her head, Camel danglin from her lips and a what-the-hell-you-want-now look on her face. "Jimmy" was gone to work but his stuff was all over the house. She was still playin that mess that Jimmy was her brother. So I play along. Keep askin them questions I already know the answer to.

"Aw, c'mon, you tryin to tell to me you and your brother sleeps in the same damn bed?"

"Where he suppose to lay? The kids' room? The couch? Ain't none of your business nohow." She was tryin to throw me off the track like a woman do.

"Honey, I just met your *other* brother Jimmy over at the Congo Club."

"We all brothers and sisters under the skin."

"Fuck that shit. Who this Jimmy dude? He ain't your brother, is he?"

"So fuckin what and how dare you?"

"All them years you tellin me 'bout your hardworkin brother you was carryin on with him behind my back?"

"Aw quit whinin, Coley. You got no right to talk to me like that. We through. We *been* through for years. I just felt sorry for you is all. A pathetic old man runnin 'round like he was some kid. Bettin Georgia Skin, sleepin in the alley, playin that old muddy river crap."

Slam the door in my face. I am halfway down the stairs when she come out on the landin and start throwin stuff at my head. Shoes and pots and cans.

Don't recall how I got home that night but I woke up with strange things bouncin 'round my brain and one shoe on. Like my mama usta say, if you lose your shoe—oh, to hell with that.

Next day I'm cuttin down the street when I see a bunch of people crowded 'round a store window. I thought it was an accident but turn out to be a television broadcast. The President speakin on the TV and everybody watchin it like God had come down and fitted hisself into that little box. They was sellin them TVs, havin a "flyin saucer sale." Old President Ike was sellin something, too, but I didn't catch what it was because outta the corner of my eye I seen a sight I didn't wanna see.

'Round the corner come big trouble with a .44 in the person of Sonny Boy Williamson. The second. If it'd been Sonny Boy number one, I'd a been even more scared seein he been dead three years now. But Sonny Boy number two was quite enough trouble. Man, them chickens was really comin home to roost. First Freddy Fox and now this.

Sonny Boy hadn't forgotten 'bout that gas station ripoff—you know the one where Jimmy told the cops he was Sonny Boy? It *was* Jimmy done that, right? That's what I was gonna tell Sonny Boy.

"You best say your prayers," he says.

"Sonny Boy, don't get all crazy, we was desperate."

"Not desperate as you gone be, fucker!" and *craaaack!* he fires off a round. I was lucky he been boozin 'cause he miss me by a mile. Stops and says, "Where's the other little creep. That's the cocksucker I want."

"Man, you got a minute?"

I musta lost my mind 'cause I start tellin him the "Jimmy" story, blow by fuckin blow. He was caught up in it, I could see that. Which gimme just enough time to slip off 'round the corner with Sonny Boy hot on my tail, snappin his pistol after me. Get back to my room, heart poundin, mind spinnin. Lord, how much more fun can one man have?

A Wolf Draggin His Tail

I was comin home late one Friday night—it was summer, everybody have their windows open to the street and seem like outta every window was comin Muddy's voice with that bass drum behind it,

> She moooooooves me mayun,
>   honey an I jus don see how it done.
> She godda pocketful a money,
>   li'l doll don't try ta help me none.

Everybody got the same song on their radio and it was beamin outta the barber shop, the candy store, the second-story window, from up on the roof, the beauty parlor, the bar on the corner. Everybody was tuned in to that muddy voice—slow, sure, sad—like the black god rose up from his riverbed and was wakin up the livin 'long with the dead. Gonna move mountains, gonna hide in the sea.

> She moved a crazy man who said, "Now I ain't so dumb."
> Ah took her to a fun'ral, boy, the dead jumped up an run.
> She looked at a dumb boy, said, "Now I can speak."
> She shove her finger in a blind man's eye.
>   "Once I was blind and now I can see."
> Shemooooooovesmemayun….

"She Moves Me" was a big seller amongst the black people. Muddy was sure 'nuff king of the blues, but you know how people is. You start sayin someone's king, they set out lookin for who gonna push him off his throne.

By and by 'long come Howlin Wolf. Man, he was a holy terror. The Delta been seepin into Chicago little by little but Wolf was like the whole seethin, heathen Delta in one bellowin package. Seem to me he have grown bigger and fiercer since I seen him last at West Memphis.

The band was vampin the openin number. All this crazy energy pourin through the joint. People gettin up outta their seats. A big commotion goin on. Women screamin, movin their chairs outta the way. Here come the Wolf, crawlin 'long the floor on his hands and knees like a moon-crazed coyote dog, hissin and snappin at people while he make his way to the front of the club. Wolf jump up on stage, grab all three mikes and begin pumpin his harp through 'em. Every time he jump in the air the whole damn room shake.

Sang like a man in a trance. Thrashin, writhin, and snappin his head back. Like some demon groanin and growlin under the floorboards, gonna pop up and eat your brains. He was talkin in the old *nasty* way. *I'm goin HOOOOWL fo ya put something to it now!* Crazy broke-up thoughts, little pieces of anger and fear flyin out at ya, send cold chills up and down my spine. Words would leap out and snatch you and run back into the dark piney woods.

It was like they put an electric cord into Wolf and plugged *him* in. Jump, chillen! He strutted and howled—was the hugest voice you ever heard—eyes wide and bulgin like he was havin a epileptic fit, roll 'round on his back, climb up the steampipes till the whole rack swayed and then slide down again and holler.

> *They take me to the doctor*
> *Shot full of holes.*
> *Nurse cried out*
> *Please save his soul.*
> *Accused a murder*
> *In the first degree.*
> *Judge wife cried*
> *Let the man go free.*

Said now cop's wife cried,
Don't take him down.
Rather be dead, six feet in the ground.
When you come home
You can eat pork and beans.
I eats more chicken
Any man seen.

Hubert Sumlin was followin his prowl, slicin the air with his over-amped solos. Got his amp turned up till his tone cracked, amp 'bout to burst in flame. And Wolf is eggin him on.

"Play that guitar till it *smoke*, baby! Blow your top, blow your *top*, blow your TOP!!! 'Cause lissen all you peoples, the Wolf is in town and you know he is. Lemme groooowl for y'all. *ARRRGHHHHHHH!* That's so sweet."

Earl Phillips back there beatin them drums to death. Sockin them skins like they done him some harm. And the Wolf—the Wolf was howlin his howl, goin "*Eeeeeful, Eeeeeful gone on* ..." and then there come a *crack-crack-crack*—staccato-type sound like Earl whacked his drumstick on the snare.

Big sweaty guy in a cowboy hat come staggerin up to the front of the stage. He was leanin over to Hubert Sumlin like he was gonna make him a request of a song. So he was pushin on Hubie—and Hubie, y'know, is this tall, very skinny kid. He's pushin Hubie backwards, this real heavy cat. Hubie was laughin till tears was runnin down his cheeks about this fool that was fallin over on him.

"Coley," he says, "whaddama gonna do, this crazy muthafucka done passed out on me."

But now I could see in the cat's eyes and they was not right. I said, "No baby, I think someone lighted him up."

Cat's face was right up against Hubert's now and Hubie looked in the guy's eyes and he went pale as a sheet 'cause that cat was *dead*. Hubie drop that guitar like it was a hot skillet and ran in the back until a police come. Meanwhile Wolf finish the set like nothin happen.

❖   ❖   ❖

Fella who own the Plantation Club called me on the phone in the hall where I was boardin. Could I spot for Sonny Boy? Now I had to think 'bout this one. Had to ask myself, Did I wanna die today? Sonny Boy still mad, maybe *real* mad by now. Hell, up on that stage I was gonna be like a duck in a shootin gallery. So I say, "Sure, long as Sonny Boy don't show." I needed the bread.

Well, I was over there at the club layin down a riff when in walks Sonny Boy lookin just like Beelzebub hisself. Little black cloud sendin out purple sparks. Sonny Boy could look at you meaner than anyone I ever seen. I froze. Then I start to run. He shouts, "Don't fuckin move. Play, muthafucka! You gone back me up."

So I seconded to Sonny Boy that night and I never played better in my whole damn life. Played like my life depended on it. When the set was over I ask him, "What happened? The other day you was layin to kill me."

"I done got over it," he says in that creepy voice a his. "Caught up with your muthafuckin pal, Jimmy. Sliced that sombitch. Left a trail of blood behind him all down Newberry. They gone be moppin that mess up for a week."

"Jesus, Sonny Boy, you—?"

"I scratched him real good…but he was still walkin last I seen him. *Hawh! hawh! hawh!*"

Played behind Sonny Boy a few nights along there but he was a hard cat to keep up with. He'd drink till seven in the mornin when the bar close down, go across the street, get two cups a coffee, eggs and grits, and be right back in that bar when the doors open. He'd be settin there when I come in with his switchblade and his harp. Didn't stagger none, didn't slur his words. Was like he been drinkin milkshakes all night.

Had a bunch of suits made up two-tone. One side would be pale blue, the other side green. Sonny Boy, he get his pictures taken in 'em sidewise. One side he was facin the camera it was blue, the other side was green. A whole bunch of cats was into this shit, Willie Dixon and them, but it was too clownish for me. Just get me a lime green shirt, purple boots and a nice plaid suit and I'm happy.

❖   ❖   ❖

So I go to this used clothin store over on the West Side that Sonny Boy tell me about. Outside was a bunch of girls skippin rope and rhymin and a old toothless dude sellin numbers and matchbooks. As I walk in I hear a woman yellin very loud, "Don't tolerate no wineheads in here, now out!"

Cat standin there, little unsteady, givin off ether fumes, sayin, "Whadidoo, lady?"

"Scram!"

I knew that voice. Kinda voice you never gonna misplace. That woman was Bertha Lee, Charley Patton's last squeeze. She was one tough broad with a sweet disposition behind that. Large woman. Big bones.

"One a God's chillen I suppose," she say, none too sure. And then she start to laugh, "So let *Him* take care of 'em."

Bertha Lee set there with all them wierd clothes piled up on tables, tellin me what happen in the end to Charley. Been almost thirty year since Charley pass.

"So he didn't die by the lightnin? Or bit by a bad fish?"

"Lord, no. Where peoples get them notions, I cannot understand. Reckon folks mix him up with his songs, y'know. Charley was a top liar and them stories just stuck to him. Charley died layin in my lap, son. Was light as a feather at the end. Wasn't no hoodoo spell or jealous bitch lightnin him up like they say. But folks won't rest lessen they spin up some crazy yarn."

She had a little plastic Zenith radio on her desk. Willie Mabon was wailin on that old Cripple Clarence Lofton number, "I Don't Know."

"Wasn't it 'round the time he gone to New York to do a recordin session?"

"He been back maybe three months or so and he go off, play this dance. We was stayin in a little old shack outside a Longswitch, near to Holly Grove. It was a dance what the whites give, and let me tell you they work you for that dollar."

"Don't I know it."

"Charley come home, couldn't speak. He was that hoarse from the singin, couldn't catch up with his breath. Was so choked he had to get up middle of the night throw open a window to get hisself a mouthful of air. Was 'bout three weeks after that his heart gave out."

She interrupt her story to tell a lady, "Honey, ain't no way you gonna fit into that. Try the other pile, over there by the bureau. Where you stayin at?"

"Over at Lawndale," I tell her.

"Well, good luck to you. Here, take a money-attractin candle, bring you some joy."

If Trouble Was Money

When I seen Howlin Wolf 'round town we frequently set and talk awhile after the show. Talk 'bout the old times, 'cause Wolf was old-time. Like me. Maybe ten, twelve years younger than me but we was among the same crowd pretty much. Charley Patton and Blind Lemon and people we known from the past was what Wolf like to talk 'bout.

"Hell, Muddy never even *seen* Robert Johnson," says Wolf. "He only knowed RL from records and from all them other people doin his songs. Me and RL we was born from the same she wolf."

"Bring me another drink," I told the waitress.

"Yeah," he say, talkin his poker-face voice. "They usta call me Bull Cow and Foot back home. Say I had big feet. But I just stuck to the Wolf. My grandfather usta tell me stories 'bout wolves and all what they could do. Told me if I misbehave they gone put a wolf on me. So everybody else went to callin me the Wolf."

We all knew he got his name from that Funny Paper Smith record but I weren't gonna cross Wolf over such nonsense. Everybody got the right to his own story, don't he?

"I started forty years too late," he said. "I was a farmer and I didn't know what was happenin. I was glad to get a sound out. All them years I diddled and daddled down on the farm. Got a GI loan in '45, got myself a tractor and forty acres. Blew the blues away again. In '48 I finally quit the land and headed for Chicago with my harp in my hand. Bought myself a brand-new DeSoto station wagon."

Wolf cut hisself a right of way with that harp, like Honeyboy say. Muddy was king on the South Side but now Wolf was givin him a run for his money. Muddy and Wolf, the Wolf and the Hoochie Coochie Man—they was always feudin 'bout who was gonna cut who. Muddy may been the king but nobody had the energy the Wolf had when he was draggin his tail.

Pretty soon, Delta-type plots start a-brewin twixt the two of them. Like the time Muddy stole away the Wolf's guitar player. Hubert Sumlin played lead in Wolf's band. Hubie was like a son to Wolf and Muddy knew that. But Hubie was just a kid then, and very easy to lead along. Muddy send his chauffeur over to a club where Hubie was playin. That chauffeur come inside and he's drippin in diamond rings and shit and flashin a big wad of money. I seen him come up to Hubie, offers him triple pay if he'll leave the Wolf and go with Muddy. Know what Hubie said to that? "Hell, yes."

His big problem now is how do he break it to the Wolf. He don't realize Wolf already know. Wolf just put his muzzle in the air and sniffed at the wind. Anyway, Hubie go into the washroom and he run right into Wolf. Just standin there, sayin nothin, lookin that ferocious look a his. And right there in front of him the Wolf start to change colors like a werewolf on a full moon. Got *blacker*. You might have thought Wolf was gonna rip Hubert's head off and eat it right there but he just shook his head and said, "You a damn fool, Hubie" and walked out. Three weeks later Hubert come back. He tell the Wolf, "I couldn't take that mess over there at Muddy's no more. So disorganized and sloppy. Drive me crazy, man."

See, that's a surprisin thing 'bout Wolf, bet you didn't know that, did you? He was a very particular individual, person what kept track of things, knew what was what. Wolf told everybody in his band how to do everything. How they should dress, when to come in for their break. Sent some to the Chicago Conservatory for music lessons, made his band join the musicians' union, pay their taxes. Muddy wouldn't have known what unemployment compensation was if it had bit him on the leg.

Biggest rivalry they got goin was the songs, and the cat what spun the tunes at that time was Willie Dixon. Let me tell you 'bout Willie.

Willie and his brother wrote up a version of the signifyin monkey and made a pamphlet they sold in the street. That was a story been 'round since Adam said to Eve—whatever he did say. Willie would recite a few lines, and the people would come up and want to buy a copy.

> *Deep down in the jungle so they say*
> *There's a signifyin muthafucka down the way.*
> *There hadn't been no disturbin in the jungle for quite a bit,*
> *For up jumped the monkey in the tree one day and laughed,*
>   *"I guess I'll start some shit."*
> *Now the lion come through the jungle one peaceful day,*
> *When the signifyin monkey stopped him and this what he*
>   *started to say.*
> *He said, "Mr Lion," he said, "a bad-assed muthafucka*
>   *down your way...."*

Wolf was always suspicious that Muddy and Willie had a conspiracy between theirselves. He was always on Willie, buggin him, "Why you give all a your best songs over to Muddy? Why don'tcha throw some my way, someone know what to do with them?"

But Willie—say he'd writ a song for the Wolf—well, if he come over and say, "Look Wolf, I got a song for you," Wolf might just say it didn't suit him. Might suspect that he been offered leftovers —song been given to Muddy already and Muddy turned it down. So Willie got this plan.

The Wolf ever see Willie with papers he come right over to where Willie is settin and slide right up beside him in that booth.

"Whatcha got cookin, Willie boy?" That voice. "Got somethin in your satchel for me?"

"Wolf, can't let you have this one this time. I done promised it to Muddy."

Wolf beg him to sing a verse. "Lemme have a taste a that." Willie start hummin it, mumblin to hisself, speakin the words. Big old Wolf eyes open wide. Now he's inspectin Willie like he's Little Red Ridin Hood. "Hell Willie, you know I can do this song like a muthafucka. I can run this song up a tree. You gotta give it me."

❖   ❖   ❖

The two big blues recordin companies in Chicago then was Chess and Veejay. Chess was run by Phil and Leonard Chess. Len was a little smoother and more into the music—he played the bass drum on Muddy Waters' "She Moves Me," y'know—but outside of that they was two peas in a pod. They was in that little office plottin and schemin twenty-four hours a day. Even if they was only nickel-and-dimin someone, they was happy.

Nobody got paid what they was due but that was pretty much par for the course back then. Even if it wasn't a square deal, Chess was run like a family. Len or Phil, one of them would always come to the session. Felt if they didn't show, the artists would think they didn't care. Sometimes they had such dumb suggestions that Willie Dixon would throw 'em out of the studio.

Every year Len Chess would buy Muddy a new Cadillac. When he had a record in the charts and come to the Chess brothers askin for his royalties, Len would throw a fit. "Royalties? How can you talk to me about royalties? Didn't I just give you a brand-new Caddy?"

Before they got their own recordin studio, Chess recorded their artists at an independent studio called Universal Recording. They'd have to stop every half hour 'cause that's when the furnace would kick in. If it was a rockin session they'd just roll right on over it.

Wolf was a rugged customer in the studio. Them old-time Delta blues players, they was set in their own ways. Wolf a natural singer but he couldn't read. Only way he could do a song was to learn it by heart, which he wasn't none too good at neither.

Mostly Willie would have to whisper the lyrics to him while he was singin the song. And right in the middle of a good take, Wolf would stop and say, "Oh man, what was that you said?" And they'd have to do it over.

Willie Dixon and him would have frequent disagreements. It was like monster to monster. Dixon was pushin three hundred pounds and Wolf was close to two hundred-fifty pounds hisself. Like two boxcars goin at each other. Wolf was ferocious-lookin but Willie weren't afraid of nobody. He won the Golden Gloves and been a sparrin partner for Joe Louis. That's right, started out bein a boxer. But he was versus fightin. Didn't like might is right and all that shit.

The Wolf never wanted to do the songs Willie Dixon made for

him. Like "Wang Dang Doodle"—he *hated* it. Now that record sold because of all that list of lowlife characters.

> *Tell Automatic Slim*
> *To tell Razor-Totin Jim*
> *To tell Butcher-Knife-Totin Annie*
> *To tell Fast-Talkin Fannie....*

"I ain't singin none of that trash," Wolf would say, "so you can forget 'bout it. Hell, sound like some old levee camp number." Actually, it was a old lesbian song called "The Bull Dikers' Ball."

Willie Dixon talk real slow and always use his x-ray eyes. You have to wear shades 'round Willie. Look like some jolly old fellow sellin produce off of a truck, but he was sharp. Could read you just like a book. What everybody don't know is that Willie was 'bout the toughest bass player I ever run into. He was two bass players, soundwise.

All the blues stuff was cut live. They'd run through the song a coupla times and then the red light come on that means it's money time. Sonny Boy would wing it if he had lost the words to a verse and often they was better than what been wrote. All that shit 'bout the "Unseen Eye." But then Sonny Boy was one mysterious individual. Paranoid and secretive—'cept when he was braggin. Like this one time Sonny is in an isolation booth singing his lead vocal and he's tryin to peer through the little window to see who else in the room. He was a very suspicious-type cat and while he's tryin to get a good look the isolation booth falls over—just when the drummer is makin a big break in the song—and Sonny Boy fall over with the booth and continues singin. And that, believe it or not, was the take they pressed.

This little kid he sold peanuts on my block—"Buy my nuts, five cents a bag"—told me he seen this cat from down South what knew me and did I know him. Old-time blues player. Tommy Somethin. Oh man, I'm thinkin, can it possibly be?

"Tommy Johnson?"

"Yeah, uh, I think so. Maybe. He's stayin out in this hobo jungle out by the dump."

Took the first streetcar out to the end of the line and walked through the junkyard—rusty washin machines, automobile skeletons, old baby carriages and bicycles, discarded toasters and chrome and plastic stuff sinkin back into the weeds.

Someone was out there howlin and smashin bottles but it weren't Teejay. Was the other Tommy, Tommy McClellan. Become a stone winehead hisself and was livin in a junked Oldsmobile.

"Oh man," he told me, "Teejay passed just this spring. Was playin at a frolic, don't ya know, and his heart attacked him. He was goin down slow, baby, last time I seen him. Heart didn't grab him, that liver disease would have. Planted him down in Crystal Springs."

Felt like I heard a stone dropped down a well that had no bottom.

"So I guess he never made it up to God."

"Hell no, man, not that cat. The Devil got him signed up and sealed years ago."

"You talkin 'bout that crossroads thing, right?" My mind was a crazy old man with no home runnin all over the places it been.

"Showed me where the Devil scratched him when he was tunin up that box a his."

"He did, huh?"

"Oh man, was three straight lines down his arm, just like a lizard claw. Gimme chills all over when I seen it."

"Well," I says, "God bless that sonofabitch."

"Fuck, yes," says he. "Anyway, I'm livin clean. Come out here to get the fresh air, can you dig it? Reminds me a little of Forest, Mississippi."

What can I say? He was the original whiskey-headed man. I give him a buck to go get a bottle and I walk back to the terminal.

One night I'm in the washroom at the Zanzibar. Gone in there to smoke a reefer when in come Muddy with Willie Dixon. They was all talkin away.

"Whatcha got for me, Dixon?"

"Man, this song's a natural for you. 'I'm the Hoochie Coochie Man.' That's you, babe."

Muddy goin, "Hmm-hmm, sounds good. Shoot! Coley, lemme have a hit on that reefer."

Willie start in tellin him, "This here's your riff, *Da-da-da-da-Da*."

"Oh, Dixon, ain't nothin to that."

Willie's feedin him the words and Muddy repeats 'em after, takin a drag while Willie tell to him the next line.

Willie layin the beat on him 'long with the line.

"I got a black cat bone—*Da-da-da-da-Da*."

Muddy singin 'em back back:

"*Ahgoddablaggatbo*."

Muddy had a way of jammin words all up together so it sound like some kinda hoodoo talk.

"I got a mojo, too," say Willie.

"*Ahgottamojotoo*."

"I got the John the Conquerer Root."

"*Goddejohndecongueroo*!"

"I'm gone mess with you."

"*Ahmgownamesswidjoo*!"

"Fuck, man," Willie says, "that's it, way you gotta sing it. Just like what you was doin."

"Whatcha say?"

"Like you was doin it, man, that stop-time thing. Got a real evil feel on to it."

Now Muddy try it:

> *Goddablaggatbo.*
> *Gottamojootoo.*
> *Goddejohndecongueroo.*
> *Ahmgownamesswidjoo.*

Willie and me went, "Wow, that scary now, cat!"

It was a humorous-type thing, tongue-in-cheek riff on what Muddy was already foolin with. *Go down in Nuohleeanz get me a mojo hand*. All that voodoo-hoodoo-mojo-hand was already on "Louisiana Blues." What Willie done when he wrote songs for these guys was to take the character of the singer and exaggerate it. Like "I Ain't Superstitious," which he wrote for Howlin Wolf. Or "My Babe" for Little Walter.

Muddy start half believin his hoodoo riff. Muddy like to gamble a bit, see, but he was one of them cats what *always* lost. Didn't know the dices was loaded with mercury. This one time he's losin real bad, musta dropped seventy or eighty bucks that night. Gets pissed off with this hand he been given by a doctor back in Clarksdale for good luck at gamblin. Finally, he tear it open. Inside weren't nothing but pieces of paper wrapped up in a bundle with some herbs. And all that was writ on the paper was: "You win, you win, you win." That was it. He was disgusted. But that don't mean he give up on mojos. Just that the two-headed men in the Delta don't know how to fix it. That was his opinion. You want strong mojo you got to go down to Louisiana— like he say in the song.

The Delta was the dreamworld of Chicago blues. That what they singin 'bout. What got lost, what they left behind. They may have a telephone, a TV, a new automobile, a brand-new washin machine and a clean shirt for every day of the week, but what they dream about is the Delta. In the memory that down-home life seem mighty good compared to the factory. You don't hear no Muddy Waters, Howlin Wolf songs 'bout workin in the meat packin plant on the South Side, do you? Or drivin a truck for the venetian blind factory. It's all mojo hands and cotton fields and born on the seventh hour of the seventh day and what the seventh doctor say.

> *Well, I'm goin away to leave, won't be back no more.*
> *Goin back down South, chile, don't you wanna go?*

For awhile I got myself a job drivin Muddy's car. Sweet gig, right? 'Cause Muddy, he didn't attract no trouble. He was a calm individual, face smooth as a pond.

One night I go by to Muddy's pad and, well, see, Muddy had this new harp player named Henry Strong. Muddy run through harp players after Walter went out on his own. First he got Junior Wells.

Junior was like bottled TNT. You was always waitin for him to blow up, he was so emotional in his music. He was a genius. Swoopin notes and short, stabbin phrases. But then Junior got drafted into the Korean war. Lasted about five minutes, then went AWOL. So nervous 'bout bein caught he'd miss half the gigs. Then Muddy got Big Walter Horton and then he got Henry Strong, good-lookin young kid who had all these girlfriends. We stop by Henry's house on the way to the gig. No answer. We was bangin on the door when a very weak voice come through the door so we push it in. There was Henry lyin on the floor in a pool of blood. His girlfriend was in the other room screamin, "What I done? What I done? That goddamn sonofabitch!"

Wasn't dead yet but he weren't long for this world neither. We got him in the Cadillac but he was dead before we reached the hospital. There was blood everywhere in that car. I leave Muddy off, he says, "You better clean this mess up 'fore it dry."

Man, I quit that job next day. Told Muddy, "Think I'll take my chances in the artillery, boss."

47

Got Them Eisenhower Blues

Okay, so DiMaggio married Marilyn Monroe, the Yankees won the World Series five times in a row, we got the H-bomb and TV—but what the world done for *me* lately? See what I'm sayin? Things was bad in '54. There was no work, and when the cats on the day shift ain't got jobs, they ain't goin to the clubs neither.

Whatever you done gonna end up a losin proposition, like J.B. Lenoir say in the "Eisenhower Blues," even the government out to get you.

I hadn't had a gig in three months. I lost my crib. I was back to sleepin on pool tables and eatin leftovers off of plates in the Automat. Been hustlin all my life, and I was sick in mind 'cause I kept hurtin the only somebody I cared 'bout.

I was beginnin to ponder if all this good luck got anything to do with Mary the Wonder. Maybe she put this something on me. Oh yeah, I was under a spell for sure. Just have to wake myself up and everything go back like it was. But when I woke up, seem like I stumbled into a worse nightmare than before. Maybe all Chicago was under some kinda spell, a sorta hell conjured outta the Delta.

I end up sleepin in the back of Mary's store. She had a big mouth and a kind heart and I had nowheres to go. I ask her can she help me with my wife.

"Coley baby, you ain't got no wife."

"Yeah I know it, and you was a lot of damn help with that one, too."

"Hell boy, you was *mine* first."

"What that suppose to mean?"

"Oh sugar, don't you remember? And I thought you recognize me that first time you come in Zeke's Cafe."

"Uh oh, here we go."

"No kiddin. Do you remember that night down the jook joint? Tommy Johnson was playin and you was just a pretty young boy and we went in the back and—"

"Omigod, the reincarnated spider."

"Uh-huhn."

"Jesus, that was the best first time anybody ever had."

"Come over here and prove it, baby."

Well, well. Suddenly my luck change. Begin gettin work pretty steady, got me a place. Even went down to Eli's and got my suit outta pawn. Awhile after that I run up on Little Walter. Should say he run up on me. I was standin outside the Congo Club and he come screechin up in his big black Cadillac, squealin his brakes. Everybody come out the club check out who this were. That the kinda cat he was. Like in that song he done, "My Babe." He like to brag what kinda chick he got, what kinda short he drivin. Behavin like a cowboy.

I get in his Caddy. Got his own funky little club in there. Couple of chicks, champagne and reefer. Wearin one fine suit, cloth layin on him just like a vine.

"Wha's shakin, Walter?"

"You!" Always the jive-ass.

"Okay, Walter, tell me what I come in here for? Whassup?"

"Not your dick, baby, that's for sure."

"Pull over," I says.

"Aw, don't be sore. I'm only shuckin with ya. But seriously, Coley, how you gone score with chicks lookin all raggedy like you do? You looks like my Uncle Silas shufflin in the rows. You is *soooo* down-home. I don't agree with that broken-down blues look. Not me, babe, I got my mohair workin. *Hawh! hawh! hawh!* Tell you what I'm gone do for you, Coley, gone get you fixed and flashed."

Took me over to Fox's the pimp tailor, got me a suit. Took me to Jerome's got me a do, my hair all pomaded up. Looked in the mirror at my new bad self, my threads, my process hair, and asks myself, "What in the *world have we here?*"

One day I'm walkin down Langley Avenue mindin my own business and I hear this sound pumpin down the street—*dunh-da-dunh-da-dunh*, *da-dunh-dunh*—a kinda bump-and-grind shuffle, y'know. African drums beatin out palm-wine time. Beamin their code, man, hummin that old Yoruba Western Union through the trees. Menace was comin off them maracas and a beat like to burst the heart of a grizzly bear. Moment I heard that sound I knew nothin ever gonna be the same again. Like the blues took its clothes off and was shakin its bare naked ass in the middle of the street.

"What you call that crazy thing anyhow?" I had to know what this was.

"Ain't got no name but we call it 'Dirty Muthafucka.'" They was jivin me.

"Man, that is some riff you got there. Where'd you catch that crazy thing?"

"Cajun, man, from Arcadia way down in N'Orleans, understand? Hot sauces, cotton rows and alligator shoes, baby. That's my blood beatin."

Tellin a funky little history—with beats. He was talkin *bop-didi-bo-didley-bop-bop-bop*. All janglin and chunga-ka-chunga-in off of him like a tin roof in a Louisiana rainstorm.

His name was Ellas McDaniel. Cowboy hat, glasses, leather jacket. He was playin on the corner with his friend Jerome Green. Jerome played maracas and washboard. He was like a big old possum. Talk real slow so when he come to the punch line it would creep up on you. Billy Boy Arnold was playin harp with him. Little kid, took after Little Walter's style pretty much. They was all teenagers.

"Been out here shakin for nickels and dimes since I was thirteen," says the cat in the cowboy hat. Had this little old band that go from corner to corner. They done a few things against that riff. Was like based on the dozens. One of 'em would say: "Your old lady so ugly she have to creep up on a glass to get a drink of water" and all that jive.

It been awhile before I seen him again. Fall of '54, maybe. I remember that 'cause it was 'round the time Willie Mabon's "Poison Ivy" come out. The down-on-the-corner band was playin the clubs —the Sawdust Trail, Castle Rock, 708 Club. They was callin theirselves the Langley Avenue Jive Cats, and Ellas McDaniel was callin hisself Bo Diddley.

They'd made a dub of "Dirty Muthafucka" and was tryin to shop it to the different labels. They took it over to Veejay, the other big blues label in Chicago. Had Jimmy Reed and John Lee Hooker. But Veejay turned 'em down.

"Me and Jerome and Billy Boy, we played it for Jimmy Bracken over at Veejay and he didn't go for it. Stole my harp player, though. Snatched Billy Boy right outta my hand."

"Hey man, could be the *name*, did you ever think of that? 'Dirty Muthafucka' ain't gonna play in Peoria."

"Oh, we ain't aimin to call it that. We call it 'Bo Diddley.'"

I told him I'd take him over to Chess Records if he wanted.

"Man, you work at Chess?"

"Sort of," I said. "I'm paintin Leonard's office."

Leonard liked it all right. Liked it *real* good. Recognized that smokin basic bottom beat. They cut it with Otis Spann on piano. Clifford James on drums was layin in that voodoo pulse.

Bo's songs was hipster Uncle Remus-type riffs, nursery rhyme street jive. Bo Diddley was a actor, see? Liked to paint pictures of hisself doin wild and crazy stuff. Bo the gunslinger, Bo the gladiator, Bo the bayou boy, Bo the roadrunner—or that nasty muthafucka in the cobra necktie who don't mean his woman no good in "Who Do You Love."

Bo traveled with some weird cats, some of 'em was in his head, some was real. There was Jerome (*You ain't no South American. Yeah I am, man. South Texas*) and then there was his half sister the Duchess, foxy chick in silver lamé toreador pants. There was other characters, too. Cookie, Sleepy King and them. Even his guitars have personalities. Had 'em customized. Like playin a big old customized dick. "This joker'll do everything but ball!"

"Bo Diddley" got in the r&b charts—had that revved-up

syncopated chopped-and-channeled Diddley boogie beat. Most imitated sound in all of rock 'n' roll. Bo went on to become a legend and Leonard gave him a new Cadillac every year, just like Muddy got. Last I heard of him, Diddley Daddy was runnin for Sheriff in New Mexico.

Bo was the first cat I knowed who was into aliens and all that extraterrestrial jive. He was fuckin convinced. "They been here already. Been up to all kinda shit the government ain't coppin to."

Nineteen fifty-two been the year of the saucers. Everybody was seein 'em and reportin on it. Takin a human specimen up in their spaceships, women gettin the clap from Venusian toilet seats. But Bo says this was all federal bullshit. He knew 'cause he knew a guy who knew a guy who worked out at the air base.

"Hell, man, they started sightin 'em back in '42. You don't believe me, check it out. It was durin the war, see, so they couldn't let it out to the public. They didn't tell nobody 'cause they figured people was gonna panic if they knew they got little green men in a lab in New Mexico. It was only when people started reportin 'em from all over that they had to cop to it. Said it was in '52, but I had a friend what said his daddy had seen all these weird lights in the sky over Seattle way back in '42."

"Yeah," says Jerome, "you know Ray Charles is from Seattle?"

"No man, Ray is from Florida."

"Well, he *moved* to Seattle. And do you know why?"

"What Ray Charles to do with all this?"

"He's got a woman, way over town, oh yeah. And he's got a hit record out 'bout that woman, and—wait, I'm comin up to it—Seattle is the farthest place from Florida on the map, you know that? *That's* why he went there."

"And?"

"So I ask him once, 'Ray, do you know of these flyin saucers they talkin 'bout?'

'Man,' he said, 'I see 'em every night.'"

❖   ❖   ❖

A few days later I'm comin downstairs and my landlady pokes her head 'round the bannisters. "Coley, that you, you sorry sonofabitch?"

It was the kinda sound you wouldn't easily mistake. She had a voice would strip the varnish off furniture. "A police was here today lookin for you. You ain't in any trouble, are you?"

"No, ma'am." Jesus, that's all I need. What the hell can that be?

Next mornin I get a letter. It said, "Son, you best come on home. Your dad done passed last night. We buryin him Friday. May the Good Lord forgive him. Mama."

I get down to 12th and Michigan, I'm standin in front of the big old Union Station. God damn, here we go again. I'm headin back to the land of cotton. What was it 'bout the Delta? Like they hid some huge magnet in the ground, buried down near Itta Bena somewheres.

The train was like watchin a movie in reverse. Seem like the same old sisters was on that train as been on the one I came up on. 'Cept now they was singin, *Praise the Lord, we goin home to Jesus.* When I heard that, I got afraid. Afraid everything that happen to me in my life gonna unravel, go back to the way it usta be. Which is pretty much the way it look when I got home. Got to Dockery's. See how it is. Like I was fourteen years old again.

Weren't no more Pea Vine. Most of the trains that run through the Delta was strictly freight, if they was runnin at all. So I took the Greyhound home. Kept lookin through the back window, see who was gainin on that bus. I was tired, fell into a troubled sleep. Up at the window I seen RL clingin on the back of that bus just like he promised. He had long talons like in a picture of the Devil, and leathery wings that flapped in the wind. When I woke up we was in Drew.

Got home to Mama. She was all in black and talkin 'bout how the angels was watchin over my daddy. He was laid out on a coupla chairs in the parlor, all dressed in his Sunday best. He'd a looked happier if I put a guitar in his arms. I composed a song for him, but Mama wouldn't allow no blues in her house.

"Ain't no profane deviltry of that kind gone be sung in my house. Don't wanna wreck your daddy's chance of takin the Lord's hand, do you, chile?"

I was beginnin to *feel* like a child, too. Felt I didn't know nothin. Like I was shrinkin down in size, gonna get smaller and smaller and disappear. After the funeral Septimus and me drove up to Lula, God knows why. Last thing I wanted to remember 'bout was my long-gone happy home. We're standin around and out of the blue Septimus slip somethin into my hand. It was cold and hard and round like a marble.

"Here," he says, "Daddy wanted you to have this." Open up my hand and there's Daddy's eyeball starin at me like when he was alive. I just about jumped ten feet in the air. "Old man musta figured you could use a little luck, I guess," he says. "Unseein eye seeth all, so you better watch your step, Coley. *Hawh, hawh, hawh*."

Then Septimus left me there and went into Lula to buy us some beer. I stood in front of the old place like I was hypnotized. I was back at that damn house lookin for what gone wrong with my life and it was like talkin to the wind. Could not even go inside. Maybe that weren't such a good idea anyway. House was listin sideways and the front porch dipped into a saddle in the middle. I felt just like that house. Whatever happen to it was gonna happen to me. Just hopin that old house weren't gonna fall down while I was standin there.

I was in a fine way of makin myself miserable when Septimus come up on me.

"Coley, you got a call down at the store. Fella says he gone call back at two o'clock. Probably callin to say you won the sweepstakes."

"More likely the long distance call remindin me another mule been kickin in my stall."

"Coley, you ever think you might be takin this blues thing too serious? It's just a damn phone call, fer chrissake, ain't the burnin bush, baby."

Call was from Tampa Red. Bein very mysterious and all about what it was he was callin for. Them old-time guys don't like to upset the spirits. Woods is full of eyes, and never say "Moses" after sundown. That jive. I finally got so aggravated with all his dancin 'round the point I tell him, "Red, I gotta go."

"Coley, I done had this dream the other night."

"Uh-oh."

"Wait."

"Red, you tellin me you called me 'bout a dream?"

"Listen to what it was. Had the sun comin up over the Mississippi in it, had the moon in it, had a lemon, a woodpecker, a large boy and his mama, a Victrola, a bottle of milk of magnesia, Beale Street and the state of Kentucky. And that ain't all it had."

"C'mon, Red, you're shuckin me."

"Tell you what else was in it. Had a crown in it, a fine crown of gold, a man in the electric chair, Union soldiers under General Grant, the planet Saturn—'cept instead of rings it had a phonograph record 'round it—and the numbers seven, zero, and six."

"You know, Red, you ain't been the same since Frances passed."

"Coley, I swear to you I seen it like God made green grass. Just like I'm talkin to you now."

"Well if it's a true dream, only a damn fool'd ignore a vision like that."

"Don't I know it. Went to Aunt Sally's Dream Book and look it up."

"And?"

"Weren't nothin in it 'bout that. So I went to see Mary—you know, your friend the gypsy woman."

"And?"

"Said it had something to do with Memphis, Big Boy, the Union soldiers, and a hillbilly guitar player."

"That ain't too revealin."

"Wait, I'm comin to it. What it all mean, she says, is something big gone happen there. A great unveilin what will change the world, make it spin backwards."

"She said all that, did she?"

"Coley, this ain't no joke. You best find Big Boy, go to Memphis. You don't wanna miss this one."

In my mind I could see Red's face all serious and worried so I ask him, "Red, you lit or something?"

"Well," he says, "here's the deal—"

"Red, forget it. I must be crazy but I'll go get Crudup."

Big Boy lived in Forest, Mississippi with his mom. He was extremely dubious 'bout our little expedition. And, worse for me, he had a mom even more sanctified than mine. A double-dipped woman. She was in the midst of persuadin Big Boy to give up blues entirely and come back to the church. She even got him a job sellin bibles door-to-door. She kept sayin, "Arthur," that was his name, "blues a infernal snare to catch your soul."

I practically had to haul Big Boy outta there, which weren't all that easy seein his size was large. He loved his mama's cookin and had increased on it considerably. Plus he got the holy shakes bad—he was just this side of snake-handlin. I am tryin to get him to see sense but he was further gone than I thought.

"Bible say you never know what form the Antichrist shall take," he tell me. "He might come as a postman or a judge or a insurance salesman or the President of the United States or some peckerwood singer or a—"

"Aw shut up!" He was startin to get on my nerves, but I shouldn't have shouted at the cat. A big tear come in his eye.

"Don't be ridiculous, Big Boy," I says. "Why, he's probably just some hillbilly kid who don't come from no hill."

Memphis City here we come. But first I went by my daddy's grave, poured a bottle of Wild Turkey down into the ground and sung him my song.

The King and I

It was the sixth day of July and we was sniffin for traces like a hound dog in the piney woods. If we interpret Tampa Red right, something real big was brewin in Memphis, something gonna make sparks fly outta the moon. Anything this big couldn't be that hard to find and we was gonna run it to ground. Outside of Tunica, a Hank Williams song come on the radio. The peddle steel was whaaa-whaaain like a train whistle in distress.

"That the redneck cat we lookin for?"

"I hope not."

"Why's that?"

"Dead."

"Hank Williams passed?"

"Last year."

"Soulful sound. For a hillbilly."

We come into Memphis on Highway 61, past K's Drive-in and on downtown—61 run into Third Street—then we hit Beale Street. I had to stop and take a look. It was a pitiful sight. Everything all plywooded up, shut down, burnt out. Nothin but pawnshops and five-ply far as you could see. In five years it was all gone. I seen Furry Lewis sweepin the curb, pushin his old metal garbage can on wheels. He was workin for Sanitation like he always done. Limpin along on that wooden leg a his—accident with that railroad couplin, remember that? Short-sleeve shirt, wash trousers and a gray beaver hat.

"How you doin, Furry?"

"Survivin. Beale Street ain't goin too good, though."

"I seen."

"All them years I kept thinkin things might go back to like it was, y'know, like when you was here."

"Playin much?"

"Nah, I hocked my guitar to get something to drink. Ain't nowhere to play no more, anyway. Man, nobody even knows I play. They think I'm a street sweeper."

"How's Versie?"

"Thank the Lord, we's back together."

"Glad to hear it, mighty glad. Listen, Furry, we'll see ya 'round, okay?"

"You know where to find me."

I told Big Boy, "Let's get outta here, man, this is scary."

"And go where? We don't have no address, we don't even have no street. Don't even know *what* in the fuck we lookin for."

"We'll just watch out for the signs."

"Can't read 'em too good with my eyes."

"Not street signs. Sign signs."

"Coley, you know this hoodoo shit don't sit too good with me. It's on the Devil's line."

"Look! The Peabody Hotel."

"Place with the damn ducks. Ducks in the lobby, now how stupid is that?"

"Okay, now turn here on Poplar."

"Coley, may I ask what navigation method you employin?"

"I'm usin the stone."

"A *stone*?"

"Yeah, a magic stone what is steeped with magic. Given me by my grandpaw."

"Your grandpaw a doctor?"

"No, man, it was all in this dream I had."

"You can inherit shit in dreams? Man, this is some good news!"

"I *seen* it in a dream. Later I got it from this two-headed woman down in New Orleans."

"You think I'm crazy? Pass that bottle over here."

Down Poplar, past Poplar Tunes and the Crown Electric Company. All *right*. When I seen that, I knew we was on the beam for sure.

"Baby, we is gettin hot now," I'm tellin Big Boy.

"Huhn?"

"Crown Electric. A crown was in the dream, dig. 'A fine crown of gold.' And so was the electric chair."

"Don't see no chair."

"Keep drivin. Hang another right. What's this?"

"Madison."

"Keep goin. What's the street comin up?"

"Union, it look like."

"That's it! The Union soldiers, remember?"

"You know, Coley, people been put away for less than this."

"What were them numbers, again?"

"We got a seven, a zero, and a sixer." Big Boy was callin out the numbers like he was readin off a policy wheel.

"Hit it."

And right there—at the numbers Tampa said—was Sun Records. 706 Union Avenue. My God, that's some fine hoodooin. But Sun Records was shut down. It was nighttime.

"I been with Howlin Wolf. Mr. Phillips record him, y'know, when he done 'Moanin in the Moonlight' and that."

"So what you figure this all is?"

"Dunno Big Boy, but we 'bout to find out. Let's go get something to eat."

"Okay, so where that conjure stone a yours say the best place to eat?"

It was Saturday night a little before nine o'clock. *High Noon* was playin at Loews State. Big Boy was flippin the stations, tune into Dewey Phillips' *Red, Hot and Blue* show.

"Daddy-O-Dewey playin the hits. We *way* uptown, all you cats and kittens out there, far uptown as we can get. Anybody out there wanna buy a fur-lined duck?"

"Sounds good," says Big Boy.

"Okaaaaay, now," says the deejay, "if this next number don't flat get you, I'll cloud up and rain all over you."

> *Well, that's all right, Mama, that's all right for you,*
> *That's all right, Mama, just any way you do.*
> *That's all right, that's all right now, Mama, any way you do.*

"Hey man, that's my song."

"What the—"

"Shhhh! Let's hear it."

> *Well, Mama she done told me, Papa done told me too,*
> *Son, that gal you foolin with ain't no good for you.*
> *But that's all right now, Mama, any way you do.*

We just settin there, lookin at each other like what was *that?*

"Well, ain't that some shit! Coley, I think that boy done the song better'n I done it myself."

"No kiddin."

Dewey Phillips come back on sayin, "Whew, that, that was— lemme catch up with my breath here—that was Elvis Aron Presley of our very own Humes High doin an old Big Boy Crudup number, 'That's All Right Mama' way back from nineteen and forty-seven. On the Bluebird label. Yes, sir! Let me tell you, that boy can sing, can't he? And, Mrs. Presley, if you're listenin—and I know you are —get that cottonpickin son a yours down to the station. Awright! Give us a call down here at WHBQ, baby, number at the station is…."

"Did he just say Humes High back there?"

"What about it?"

"It's *white*, that's what about it."

"You sayin this a white boy?"

"My, my, my! Could be the big deal down on Beale what we come 'bout."

"Where's the shepherds and the three wise men?"

"Stayin at the motor hotel, or maybe sleepin in their car. How the hell should I know?"

❖   ❖   ❖

Next day we come back to Sun Records. There was a '54 Bel Air Chevrolet and an old Lincoln settin outside.

"C'mon, Big Boy, let's see if Mr. Sam Phillips here."

"Sam Phillips, Dewey Phillips. Everybody in Memphis got the name Phillips?"

"Anybody that matters in Memphis, they give 'em that name at birth. Phillips or Booth. One of the two."

Sun Studios was just a storefront, like a paint store. You tell 'em what you want and they go in the storeroom in back and get it for you. In the front was a little office and in back the studio. There was a tiny recordin booth in the front, too, with some recordin equipment and a window cut in the wall.

Marion Keisker, Mr. Phillips' office manager, come out. Say hello and tell us to keep it down.

"Red light's on. They're recordin in there."

"Is that, uh—"

"Boy's name is Elvis, Elvis Presley."

"Heard his song on the radio last night. It was—"

"Wasn't that something, though? Dewey says they got so many phone calls the switchboard was jammed over at the station. Go on in the control room, I'm sure Sam will be glad to see you."

The studio at Sun was small compared to anything you see today, just one big room. You got this skinny shy cat, Scotty Moore, playin guitar, Bill Black on the stand-up bass—he was a real clown. These boys was regulars from a honky-tonk band—Doug Poindexter and the Starlight Wranglers. But the cat up to the microphone was something else. Tall, skinny kid—lean, strange and slinky. Jet black hair, long and greasy with sideburns that run down to Atlanta. Pink shirt, black jacket, pink pants with stripes down the legs and white shoes. High-tone fashion, hillbilly style. Bill Black took a close look at Elvis's greasy ducktail and said, "Gimme a fly-flapper and I'll help you kill it."

They done a coupla verses and Mr. Phillips said: "That last one sound pretty good through the door. Let me get a balance. All right boys, we just 'bout on it now. Do it one more time for Sam. Take two."

Bill Black was slappin that bass silly. He weren't no Willie Dixon playin that thing but he could do a good slap-beat thing with it, and Scotty Moore was dancin on them strings, sure could pick a beautiful, liltin country guitar. 'Bout halfway through Mr. Phllips interrupt him.

"Simplify, simplify! If we'd wanted Chet Atkins we'd've brought him up from Nashville and got *him* in the damn studio."

It was a old Bill Monroe tune, "Blue Moon of Kentucky." Bill Monroe done it as a waltz. But the way they was doin it weren't no waltz. Elvis was gettin into the rhythm and then he look over at Bill Black who was pretendin his bass was shakin from the vibrations and he blew the take.

Blue moon of Kentucky keep on shakin, shinin, shinin—

Over the intercom Elvis says, "I'm sorry, Mr. Phillips. Let me try it again."

"That's original," Mr. Phillips said.

"A big, original mistake."

"That's what Sun Records is, boys," Mr. Phillips said. "Okay, let's cut one this time."

Elvis was movin all nervous and loose like a crazy, spastic puppet on strings. All the vibrato movin back and forth like someone was shakin him from the inside. A tent-show trick with some old blues cat behind the curtains throwin his voice onto a boy, and the boy catchin that voice and singin with it.

When the take was done Mr. Phillips was jumpin outta his seat.

"That's fine, man," he says. "Hell, that's different. That's a pop song now, nearly 'bout!" And everybody laughed.

When Elvis come in the control room to hear the playback he was all jangly and tense.

"If I seem nervous," he said, "it's because I am."

Mrs. Keisker brought in some sodas and Mr. Phillips introduce everybody. Elvis couldn't get over Big Boy.

"Man, I can't believe it. I cut one of your songs day before yesterday."

"I know it, heard it over the radio last night. You done it better than me, man."

"Mr. Crudup, I'm honored to sing your songs, sir, I really am. Especially that one you done, uh, 'My Baby something....'"

"'My Baby Left Me.'"

"That's the one."

Big Boy asked him where he heard it.

"Well sir, it's like this. I listened to this music all my life on the radio. And I can remember when I first heard you—bangin on your box down in Tupelo, Mississippi. That's where I'm from."

Very polite and sincere, call everybody sir—even us. You don't call blacks sir in the South unless there's something funny with you.

Elvis was curious 'bout Muddy Waters and Little Walter. We got to talkin 'bout singin and he ask me 'bout Chess Records and Mr. Phillips brought up Howlin Wolf.

"I recorded him here, did you know that? Yup, he did his first records right here in this studio. Had the biggest feet I ever seen on a man. God, the fervor on that man's face when he sung! This is where the soul of man never dies. His eyes would light up, the veins on his neck come out. He sang with his whole damned soul."

"Howlin Wolf, that is the wildest stuff I *ever* heard!" cried Elvis.

"You want to hear that thing played back?"

We all said how great it sounded but Mr. Phillips wasn't sure what he could do with it.

"Tell ya, I'm up a gum stump. Everybody says I'm crazy. 'Sam, who in hell is gonna buy it?' Aren't that many black people buyin the r&b sound as it is."

"Yeah," says Bill Black, "they gonna run us outta town when they hear this."

"You know, Elvis," said Big Boy, "you are like *two* different people when you get goin."

"Only two? That's all?" Elvis said. Everybody laughed. "Well, what I do generally is, I think of a song. When I hear it I don't always know whichaway it's gone go but—it's kinda like this, once I'm singin, I know where I'm goin, man, I'm *gone*. I get into it and shift gears and—hey, fellas, I don't really know what happens."

And that is how we met "the King." He did another of Big Boy's songs a coupla years later but Big Boy never saw one red cent from neither of 'em.

❖   ❖   ❖

We heard Elvis was gonna be singin down at the openin of Katz's drugstore, which was on the corner of East Parkway and Lamar. They was performin on the back of a flatbed truck. The emcee introduce Elvis.

"And, now, we bring you the boppin hillbilly, his name is Elvis Presley. Please give him a big hand everybody, our own Elvis Presley from right here in Memphis."

"Thank you, thank you for comin. We'd like to do a song for you, we hope that you like it, it's called—I don't know what it's called but we're gone play it anyway."

And he went into "Good Rockin Tonight." It was a young crowd. There was a lotta kids, which was good, but he was something else. You had to adjust. He had these real spastic-lookin moves. Nobody had seen a white kid doin this stuff—or actin like he done. They didn't react right away, just kinda stood there. Bill Black started clownin, cuttin up, he was ridin his double bass like it was a mule, put a pair of bloomers on his head.

Halfway into the first song the crowd went wild. That wiggle, that shake thing, the thing with the hips? Chicks was screamin and hollerin like he was the second comin.

And I'll tell you what, by the end of that first song he had all of them people up on their feet. And I mean *everybody*. Old people, fat people, skinny people, kids, neighbors who had wandered over to see what all the fuss was 'bout. It was just one them things that occur in your life where you say to yourself, "Man, I'm not believin this!" Some old woman—she musta weighed two hundred pounds —took all her effort just to get up outta her seat, she was clappin along and hollerin, her big old freckle puddin face glowin with joy.

He sung and moved so hard he was winded by the time he got to the end of the show.

> *I'm leavin town, baby, I'm leavin town for sure.*
> *Then you won't be bothered with me hangin 'round your door.*

A little blonde in a blue print dress was shoutin, "Stick around, honey!"

But that's all right, that's all right,
That's all right, Mama, any way you do.
Ah, dah dah deedee, dee dee deedee, dee dee deedee
I need your lovin (I'm outta breath)

And the little blonde shouted, "That's all right, baby!"

After the show I saw him walkin to his car and the little blonde was sayin, "I didn't figure you for bein so tall. How tall are you?"

"Even six foot, ma'am—uh, honey."

"Aren't you the one," she said.

And he said, "I am the one, baby!"

Johnny B. Goode

Back in Chicago, I get a call from Leonard. Knew I been down to Sun Records and all, wanted to hear what the big deal in Memphis was and had I got the record by that boy—whatsisname?—and would I bring it along.

It was like a big old family meetin. The jukebox guys was there. Leonard was pacin up and down, smokin like a chimney, wringin his hands. Sales was down twenty-five percent he was sayin. "Twenty-five fuckin percent!" And the jukebox guys was tellin him, "Len, it's just a summer thing. We always get a dip in the summer."

Salesmen was blamin it on TV. The television was pullin people away from the radio and the radio was where you sold records. There was a recession goin on, nobody was buyin records. All kinda reasons.

"I'm tellin ya, dese kids would buy r&b if dey was exposed to it," Phil was sayin. That's the way he talked—he and his brother come over on a freighter from Poland. "Dose kids, dey don't hear it on de radio so how should dey know dey want it?"

"Nah," said Leonard. He weren't convinced.

"Dey bought de Moonglows, didn't dey?"

"Who bought it? Kids bought 'Sincerely,' but it's a ballad. I'm talkin dance music."

"Why don'tcha call Sam Evans or Al Benson over at de station?"

"Aw, dey ain't gone play r&b by a bunch of old black men. Dey're fightin for dere lives with dis TV thing as it is. De last thing dey need is r&b. No, what we need is—I want dat you should pay attention to dis."

Leonard was gonna read the lesson for today. *Cashbox* was their Bible.

"'Reports from key cities indicate it will be a big seller,' it says. 'Music Sales Company, Memphis, distributor for Sun, reportedly sold over four thousand copies de first week.' I tell you dis is something big, my friend. Very big. Hey Coley, you got dat single dat was makin steam down at Sun?"

I played both sides.

"It's fuckin—not fuckin bad," says Willie.

"Aw it's Ma and Pa Kettle with a beat," says Phil. He picks the record up and holds it in the air flipping it from one side to the other. "What is dis? R&b country, country r&b. It's a mishmash."

"Yeah well, dat's as may be," says Leonard, "but it's mishmash with a fuckin bullet, schmuck."

"You're sayin *we* should be doin dis shit?"

"Are we a hillbilly label? Have we ever been a hillbilly label? I said we gotta do *something*."

"Anyway," Willie says, "he's a caucasian."

"Caucasian? He's a hillbilly, ain't he? Have you been listenin to me, what I'm sayin? A white kid is what we need."

"Don't look at me," says Willie.

"You mean like that Orville Presley?" says a salesman.

"What did I say? Did I say a hillbilly? Where you gonna find hillbillies in Chicago, my friend?"

"Try Maxwell Street," says Willie.

'Round this time Mama decide she was gonna move to Chicago. Nothin to keep her in Mississippi now that Pop was gone. I went back home, help her pack up her stuff. Man, she wanted to take everything with her. She would of took the peach tree if she coulda got it out of the ground. I kept explainin, "Mama, you lucky you get yourself a little old room. There ain't gonna be place for all this mess." Finally I got tired of fightin over all this junk. I left Septimus to sort it out.

"Hell, let her take what she wants. If it don't fit she can take it down to Maxwell Street and sell it."

Muddy was playin at Huff's Garden and I figured I might be able to get a ride back to Chicago with him. After the gig he says, "Coley, c'mon, we're gone check out this piano player. Johnnie Johnson. You ever hear of him? Willie says he really something. You was in St. Louis awhile, wasn't you?"

"Muddy, I ain't been here in years. That was back in pre-historic times, man."

Johnnie Johnson was playin over at the Cosmopolitan Club. It was a big joint on the corner there in East St. Louis, which is in Illinois and a lot looser about the racial thing than Missouri. Across the Mississippi in St. Louis, if the cops saw a black and white couple in a car they'd arrest 'em. Take 'em down to the station to be tested for the clap. That's the truth. In East St. Louis blacks and whites was still segregated but they mingled together in the clubs. Naturally that made for a interestin mix. One of the reason music progressed in that town.

We come up to the cashier and Muddy announces hisself. He was usta gettin in free at clubs in Chicago. So he says, "Hi, I'm Muddy Waters." And the cashier just says, "A dollar fifty." No discounts, apparently, for visitin celebrities.

We go on in. There was three or four hundred people in there dancin to the music, a little combo called Sir John's Trio. Sir John was Johnnie Johnson. He was the big jolly, droopy-eyed cat sittin at the piano. There was a tall, skinny guitar player and a snaggly-tooth drummer who was cuttin up. Johnson had a eccentric style of playin which Muddy liked—he weren't lookin for hisself, mind. Otis Spann was his guy. He was scoutin for Willie Dixon, see, and Leonard Chess. They was always lookin for new talent. Especially now. The scene was movin away from r&b, and whatever the next wave gonna be they wanna catch it.

But the real leader of this band was the cat on electric guitar. Good-lookin fella, a real showman. Tellin stories and jokes between songs, winkin at people in the audience. Had that audience charmed like a snake.

In the fills he put that guitar way out front. Could play whole choruses without repeatin one lick. This was new, even among blues players. Guitar solos was considered jive. You'd just lay down a few licks in the break and get outta the way. Hell, Robert Johnson only recorded one solo in his whole life. Okay, so there was exceptions like T-Bone, but it weren't common.

Band was playin moody and slow, doin some smoky, jazz-tinged blues like T-Bone and Charlie Christian stuff. Mellow and dreamy. The clientele was dancin close, shufflin to the beat 'round the floor. Band played some Nat King Cole numbers, played some blues. Maybe he'd heard Muddy was in the house 'cause they done a version of Muddy's "Got My Mojo Workin." He was some actor, that guitar player. Done it in a real down-home voice, like some old rounder on the courthouse steps. He weren't a old sharecropper like Muddy and me but he was singin in that vein. Muddy laughed. "You think this cat ever seen the backside of a mule?"

"Muddy," I said, "he does you almost as good as you do yourself."

Midway into the set this guitar player sung some hillbilly numbers —stuff like "Jambalaya"—which he made up new words for. Would do all them honky-tonk gestures—openin his eyes wide, flappin his knees like a goofy cracker. St. Louis was a country music town so you heard a lot of it over the radio. 'Course, the country stuff was aimed at white folks and the clientele at the Cosmopolitan was mainly black. Still, they was attemptin to dance to this hillbilly beat. It was humorous, I'll grant you that.

This one song he done was to the tune of "Ida Red"—a country song—what we call western swing or hillbilly music—a old Bob Wills song. It went like:

> *Ida Red, Ida Red, I'm stuck on Ida Red.*
> *Can't get chicken outta my head*
> *Cause I'm stuck on Ida Red.*

He seemed to be makin up words right there on the bandstand. He was clownin, y'know. 'Bout a bunch of high school football players screwin chicks in the back of his Coupe de Ville and he was fantasizin 'bout how he wished he was back there with 'em.

The way he done it was like a little vaudeville show. A novelty song, you know. Just like a cartoon comes on before the movie. But it moved, man. He was doin this *da-da-da-da-da-da-da* guitar riff. I knew that riff. Carl Hogan usta lay down a riff just like that. He was the guitar player in Louis Jordan's Tympany Five. Back in the '40s they was the cat's pajamas. But the way this guy done it was more honky-tonk—he was playin double-string stuff, playin the two strings together, which makes for a real fat sound. Punches that sound out almost like a horn would.

After the set Johnnie and the guys come over. The drummer's name was Ebby Hardy. Guitar player was Chuck Berry. This musta been, oh, spring of nineteen and fifty-five.

Muddy told Chuck how he thought the hillbilly tune was "something real different, man."

"They're callin him the black hillbilly, did you know that?" Johnnie asked.

"The black hillbilly," Muddy said, and chuckled to hisself. "Ain't that something, though?"

Chuck was very much in awe of Muddy. Idolized him. You could see he was waitin to ask the King of the Blues something. What he wanted to say, he addressed it to Muddy very softly and politely, "Oh, Mr. Waters—"

"Muddy, call me Muddy. Ain't no such person as Mr. Waters."

"Well, uh, see, that hillbilly stuff's just our spacer, y'know, we run it just to break up the set. Lighten it up, y'know?"

Afraid Muddy might think this stuff was really him, that goofy hillbilly routine. Chuck wanted Muddy to know that what he really liked to play was them cool, sophisticated, creamy, T-Bone Walker guitar slurs—not this hillbilly jive. That was just a joke. Chuck aspired to be a jazz musician. "Wee, Wee Hours," that piano-bar number on the flip side of his first single, that's what he and Johnnie Johnson liked to play. But in his heart of hearts he knew he weren't no Charlie Christian nor Django Reinhardt neither. He was Johnny B. Goode, and he played that guitar just like a-ringin a bell.

"That's how we wake 'em up midway," Chuck was sayin, "so's everybody don't fall asleep durin the slow ones."

"You gots people dancin to it, that's more'n I can do," say Muddy.

"You call that dancin?" Chuck say and everybody laugh.

"Mr.—uh, Muddy, may I ask you a question?"

"Hell yes, you can ask me two."

"Me and the fellas have put down a few numbers on a tape—" Chuck said. "I bought this magnetic reel-to-reel recorder from a friend of mine I paint houses with. And see, we was thinkin if—"

"Leonard Chess. He's the guy to talk to. Go see Leonard at Chess Records in Chicago. Forty seventh and Cottage. He'll tell you what he thinks of it, don't worry 'bout that." You had to have met Leonard Chess to know how funny that was.

Now, that was Saturday night. The followin Friday Chuck Berry walk into Chess studios luggin his great big quarter-inch tape recorder just as Bo Diddley and me was leavin. I introduce the two of them and they talked 'bout guitars—pick-ups and action and shit.

When Leonard come out of his office Chuck introduce hisself. He kinda stood there and made a speech 'bout what he done and who all played on it and why he thought it might go. Leonard was standin there with his mouth open. He was usta us Mississippi boys amblin in and mumblin, y'know, and havin to draw 'em out. But Chuck could talk that talk.

So Leonard listened for a while. Chuck sang him "Wee Wee Hours." "Aw, dat's not for us. Too slow. Ya got anything else?" He liked the other one, the novelty song, the one Chuck was now callin "Ida Mae"—he'd put new words to it. It weren't no longer a sex in the back of the car song, it was a car song period.

Willie liked it all right. "But what concerns me, Chuck," he says to him, "is you usin someone else's melody here. If that gets into the charts, some hillbilly cat's gone come knockin at your door askin you for money. So you best lose that hillbilly tune. Needs a new title, too. That's too close, Ida Red, Ida Mae."

Chuck went over in the corner and talked to himself for a coupla minutes and he come back with, "How 'bout 'Maybellene?' Sounds out like Ida Mae—rhythmically."

"Dat ain't de real name of one of your girlfriends, is it?" Leonard was always cautious 'bout havin chicks comin after his artists for money. Chuck was laughin.

"No, sir, it was the name of a cow in my third grade reader."

"Well, dat's okay then. Work it up into a rhythm and blues number and we'll make a record out of it. Give you a contract. Fair enough?"

"Go home, let it set for a while," said Willie. "Do it more r&b, add some grits to it—then you'll really have something."

Chuck was not happy that he couldn't record it right then and there 'cause he was broke and had no way of gettin back to St. Louis. I believe he had to sell some blood to buy his ticket home. Me and Tampa Red was tellin him, "You don't need no ticket, man. We'll carry you over to the stockyards and you can just hop a freight. You be in St. Louis within a few hours."

"What you guys take me for? I ain't some old rounder ridin the rods. I got two jobs. I got a job at the automobile plant and I paint houses with my dad. I got a family, I got my own house, I got a degree from the Poro College of Cosmetology."

"What you want, a medal or something?" says Red. "You talkin to the wrong cats, baby. We ain't never had no jobs and we never want none."

"That's why you guys'll always be bums."

"Aw, go stuff yourself," says Red. He was gettin hotter than grits on Sunday. As we go off, Red is sayin, "Can you believe that shit, man? He'd rather sell his own blood than hop a freight. She-it! What's wrong with this new generation anyways?"

Willie got a call from Chuck the followin week. He played the reworked song to him over the phone and Willie told him to come on up. "How 'bout this Friday?" Chuck asks. Willie goes, "Friday wouldn't be good." Leonard didn't like to record on Fridays or any date that had a thirteen in it. "The seventh and eleventh of the month is always good days, though," Willie tells him. Chuck musta thought they was all nuts up at Chess but the place was happenin, right?

He'd not only fixed up "Maybellene," he'd written three new ones. Willie was impressed. Willie was a prolific songwriter, but this was like black magic.

"You wrote these since last week?"

"Poetry is my blood flow," said Chuck. Didn't mention nothin 'bout *sellin* the blood.

"That's true," said his piano player Johnnie Johnson. "Put him in a corner and he'll rhyme one up for you just like—"

"Little Jack Horner," said Chuck.

They cut "Maybellene," "Wee Wee Hours," "Too Much Monkey Business," and "Roll Over Beethoven." Took 'em thirty-six takes to get "Maybellene" down but they done "Wee Wee Hours" in three. It was perfect, but Willie wasn't happy. Willie was the producer and he was also playin bass on the session. Phil, Leonard's brother, was there that night. He was gettin impatient, walkin up and down the control room, runnin his hands through his hair.

"C'mon, guys, we been here three hours already and cut just two fuckin songs. Let's move on." Willie is settin there doin his Buddha act. "Willie," says Phil, "is dere something I'm missin here?"

"Yeah," says Willie. "It's too perfect."

"What? *What?*"

Willie was a perfectionist. He'd do as many as forty takes to get it right. But every record had to have a flaw in it. That's the way he was. Willie would not let a record go out unless it had at least one mistake in it, which wasn't all that hard. He figured only one to make something perfect was God, and even He messed up once in a while.

When "Maybellene" started tearin up the road, Willie put together a tourin band for Chuck. Lafayette Leake on piano (Johnnie Johnson couldn't leave his day job), Harold Ashby, tenor sax, Al Duncan, drums, Willie, bass. I would sub for Willie on the bass if he had to take care of business back at Chess. Mainly I got to move the equipment, drive the car. We was all squeezed into this old Cadillac with the double bass strapped on the top. Chuck liked to drive at night and he drove real fast, drove like he wanted to prove something.

Chuck had definite ideas about the sound he wanted to get. We'd rehearse all kinda ways, figure out the keys and chord changes, but when we come to play the show it all went out the window. He'd just wing it, play in any old key. We'd all be lookin at each other like "What was that?"

He was tourin so fast you couldn't catch him. Blowin like a cool breeze. String tie, white bucks, honkin guitar. He could really put on a show. And with them moves—the duck walk and that—the kids ate it up. He tapped right into the Teen Dream, baby—cars, guitars, girls and school days. Had it all figured out. "Everyone has gone to school, right? Everybody been in love or gonna be, and most people got a car."

Chuck had his eyes wide open—a natural born businessman. He thought stuff through. We'd barely heard 'bout copyrights then though nobody knew exactly what they was. But Chuck flew right through the ceilin when he saw his first royalty statement and saw what was goin down. Had this skinny little check in it and we all knew "Maybellene" gone over the moon.

"With Chess you're lucky to be seein royalties period," I told him.

If you were gettin royalties at all, half a cent was standard for a song. If you wrote songs on both sides of the record you'd be makin one cent a record. But that was the last time Chuck got took. Like he usta say, "Don't let the same dog bite you twice."

Bill Haley and Elvis gettin all the credit but we all know Chuck is the guy. There's not a lot of other ways of playin it than the way Chuck laid it down. Oh, and the other thing 'bout Chuck, you can't put out such a blast in the world like that without havin joy in your heart. I don't believe you can.

"That's one thing about rock 'n' roll, Coley."

"What's that?"

"There's freedom in that sound, baby. Deliver us from the days of old."

It the new thang, baby. Everybody doin it, everybody listenin to it on the juke boxes, dancin to it—ain't no place for a old broken-down blues player like me. Hey, even down at the Maxwell Street market they wanna hear rock 'n' roll. "Man, do you know that song Bo

Diddley do?" Like Mississippi Fred McDowell, "I don't play no rock 'n' roll." Not that I can't, just that I be too long in the tooth to do it right.

"Play 'Maybellene,'" they tellin me. "C'mon man, play me that car song." And I'm tellin 'em, "Get off of my case, man, I ain't got that long a breath. Chuck, he's a young guy, y'know, he's a *healthy* young cat, drinks buttermilk for breakfast. I can get that Cadillac motivatin over the hill but I ain't gonna make it to the top of that hill nohow."

Listen, I was happy for Leonard and Phil. They got themselves a brand-new bag. But we all knew what it meant for us old blues cats. Blues was a automobile, started out as a Model-T. As it was cruisin down Highway 61 the blues turned into a Terraplane. Now it was a coffee-colored Cadillac—got chrome and fins and dice danglin from the rearview mirror. I knew that car was goin places but I was just like a scraggly dog chasin its dust down the road.

50

White Boys Lost in the Blues

It was the stone. *That* stone. One that laid in the forest and soak up the light of stars for a million years, et cetera. My little greatgrandbaby, Nawassa, was playin on her hundred-piece jigsaw puzzle map of the world. Usin the stone as a car to drive cross the sea.

"Rrrrrmmmm! Rrrrrmmm! Rrrrmmmmm! My cars is layin eggs on the head of the Queen of Engulund."

"That so," I says. "Well, well, well. That's a magic stone, Nawassa, you know that? Can tell the future and see things 'bout to be."

"I knows that, Babu," she says. That's what she call me, y'know, Babu. "Found it in your shoe. See, it's glowin like a firefly."

"And where that stone landed, darlin?"

"Engulund, Babu, where the wind come from."

I looked down and it was settin right on a little old town in England, name of Dartford. That's right, baby. Look it up.

Aw sure, I had my beautiful greatgrandkids, my grandkids, my kids —where was my boy Willie, though?—but far as anything else in my life I was outdated and granulated.

After rock 'n' roll come in—the Little Richards, the Chuck Berrys, the Jerry Lee Lewises and what have you—I might as well have gone on the Social Security and hibernated 'cause it was over for me, baby. I had holes in my shoes and my blues was fadin down the railway lines. My life, my wife, my Saturday nights. All over, baby, and it ain't never comin back.

Even Muddy and them couldn't get by no more just singin the blues. So what was I suppose to do? They was the wizards of the South Side and they got them playin Little Richard tunes, Fats Domino songs. That's the rule, play what's cool.

Mother lode of the Delta blues was runnin thin. Junior Wells and Buddy Guy was the last of the Mohicans. Blacks wasn't interested in listenin to the blues. Down-home was a stone embarrassment. They don't find no encouragement in collard greens and hog lard. Ashamed to be associated with us.

When soul music come in—Ray Charles, James Brown, Motown, Stax and that—blues was really gone with the wind. Was a whole other country, plum outta my field. Got together for a different drift, understand, and I just weren't blowin that way. James Brown, man, was like a rhythm undertow.

Now soul music—you with me, baby?—it weren't nothin but gospel took into pop music. Like Big Bill said 'bout Ray Charles, "He's cryin sanctified!" Now listen here, ain't nobody from my year woulda ever dreamed in their most sterno-stewed brain of stealin the Holy Fire outta the church. Goddamn, you'd of feared for your life. Bolt a lightnin might strike you dead in the middle of the road. You wouldn't even make it to the highway.

But these cats was runnin into the chapel stealin the collection boxes right and left. And don't tell me there ain't consequences. Look what happen to Sam Cooke—shot dead. Otis Redding's plane crashed, Wilson Pickett doin hard time for murder, James Brown out there half crazy on hog tranquilizer pullin a gun on a state police. Ray Charles is blind.

But nothin goes away forever, see? Soon as it gets to the end of the line, it turns right 'round and comes back. That goes double for the blues. Blues is under everything. Blues is under your rap stoop, under your bebop bar stool, under your pile of CDs, in your sock drawer, in the linin of your hat. Pull them blues threads out and the whole damn world unravel.

First sign we had of it was the white boys. Jewish boys, y'know, and parochial school boys come from over on the North Side. Rich kids dressin poor. Denims, leather jacket, haven't took a shave in a coupla days. Come in the clubs on Friday, Saturday night. Sit over in the corner drinkin their beer, never sayin nothin to nobody. Figured they was cops, y'know? They was young for cops but I been sayin that for years, that the cops was gettin younger and younger every year.

Settin over in the corner there, tryin not to get noticed, dig? But one night Sonny Boy sees 'em slouched down in a booth just starin and he says, "I seen you cats hangin 'round here, just *lookin*. What you lookin at? Nobody gettin paid off what shouldn't be, so what's your fuckin problem?"

And these kids is talkin this spade jive, "Hey man, it's cool. We ain't here to cause no trouble."

"So whatcha come in here for, the decor?" Right in their faces.

"We're here for the music, man. We dig the blues, baby. We *play* the blues."

Sonny turn 'round real slow. He's lookin at Muddy—Muddy was playin that night—and real drawn out he says, "Muddy, what we got here is a confusion. Some honky muthafuckas as says they play the blues." Laugh so hard he fall off his barstool.

It was not long after that—or maybe it was long after, I dunno. The years start driftin together for me. Breakfast seem like every fifteen minutes. Was it '63? Thank you. Spring of '63, Willie Dixon was takin his crew to London— Muddy, Wolf, Sonny Boy and them. On this thing, the American Folk Blues Festival, and would I like to come 'long? Hell, I'd never seen Europe and I heard a lotta them blues guys done pretty good over there in Paris. Champion Jack Dupree and so forth. Treated like gods, you know. Way we should be. Maybe score myself one of them electric guitars and a little Pignose amp and come 'long after all.

The first night I was there, some Brit kids invited me down to the Crawdaddy Club, play a little blues, show 'em how it was done.

They was cranin their necks to see where my fingers was landin on the frets like I was B.B. King or something. Backin me up was a young fella named Charlie Watts on drums, Keith Richards playin bass, Mick something or other blowed a little harp. Not bad.

When I come off stage they was all over me askin questions and did I know this one and that one. Like I'd known King Solomon instead of Solomon Burke. I loved them boys, especially that Keith Richards. Real skinny kid with a bad case of acne but he was one soulful cat. We went out into the alley to smoke a joint and I ask him how did he get into the blues?

"In art school you got your packet of Weights cigarettes and go in the bog. One cat knew how to play 'Cocaine Blues.'"

"But where'd you get them records in the first place?"

"Guys would bring 'em in, stuff they'd bought off of merchant seamen and stuff. I got into Little Richard, then started to wonder where it had all come from. Big Bill Broonzy and Muddy Waters was the first names I heard anything about. Maybe you'd heard of Big Bill Broonzy and then someone would have a Elmore James LP and you'd go, 'Amazin. Another bloody master.'"

Ain't that some shit? All them years we was thinkin the blues is hemorrhagin. Felt like the rivers was runnin backwards, but all the little eggs was hatchin. The blues was pollinatin in places I'd never heard of—boys far from the Delta was teachin themselves Spanish tunin and learnin the sacred and funky Yoruba sound alphabet.

All those cats that was one day gonna be in them big bands. The Rollin Stones, the Yardbirds, Led Zeppelin, Cream, the Pretty Things, the Bluesbreakers—they was sittin in the front rows watchin every twitch and slouch. Brian Jones, Eric Clapton, Jimmy Page, Long John Baldry, Keith Richards, Mick Jagger—all sittin there just worshippin these blues guys. Never seen nothin the like of it. Damn cult is what it was. Clutch a Howlin Wolf single like it was a piece of the true cross. There weren't more than four r&b bands in England at the time but them four bands was spreadin the gospel.

This was a line, see, nobody in their wildest dreams thought the blues could cross. Record companies, radio ignored us until the British boys come along. Hell, in 1966 Howlin Wolf actually got hisself a hit in England with "Smokestack Lightnin." Musta thought he'd died and gone to heaven. All this idolizin went a bit to Sonny Boy's head. If he got Jimmy Page or Eric Clapton backin him, he'd tap 'em on the shoulders and make 'em kneel down on the stage while he blowed his solo.

After the shows we usta hang out at Alexis Korner's house. Alexis was short and wiry with a big bushy mustache and black curly hair. Looked like a gypsy. Everybody who was into the blues in London hung out at Alexis's house. Settin 'round his house at two in the mornin —this was some scene, man. Howlin Wolf, Muddy Waters, Sonny Boy Williamson, Willie Dixon. All settin on the sofa. *Huge* guys. And here was these skinny little English boys settin at their feet.

Willie Dixon start tappin on the back of a chair, Sonny Boy play harp, Wolf gettin down on his knees start hollerin "Wang Dang Doodle." It was a Delta storm in a fruit jar. Fireflies, hoodoo women, cotton rows, black cat bones. Like you'd showed fire to people what never seen it.

Any little scrap, they ate it up. This was the real history of the USA to them. Forget 'bout the Battle of Bull Run, tell us 'bout Robert Johnson. Muddy was a god, Wolf was a god, Sonny Boy was a god. We was all gods more or less accordin to them, but the god behind the god was Robert Johnson.

Eric Clapton was a real shy boy. Wouldn't even raise his eyes when he spoke. But curious. Couldn't hear enough 'bout Robert Johnson, and here was Muddy tellin him how he got hisself discovered on account of Robert. How Mr. Lomax come lookin for Robert but Robert had got killed so he made recordins of Muddy instead. Muddy say he regretted he'd never seen Robert play. "I listened to Robert's records till I wore 'em out but to my way of thinkin, best we had back then was Sonny House," Muddy said. "He'd touch them strings, Lord, he could make 'em sing like a bird."

Them conversations went on and on into the night. And it woulda gone on till mornin but Sonny Boy suddenly snap, "Fuck this shit, where's the broads?"

They took us all 'round to this sleazy club in Soho called the Kit-Kat. It was packed with all the lowlife and wildlife you'd ever want to see: sailors, drag queens, Jamaican dope dealers and hookers. Man, we felt right at home.

❖   ❖   ❖

Before we headed home them British boys got Muddy and Wolf and Sonny Boy to sign the singles and EPs and LPs they brought with 'em. I remember Jimmy Page got Muddy Waters to sign this EP had "You Need Love" on it. 'Cause that come up later on, y'know. Remember that? Willie had to sue Led Zeppelin over that. Said "Whole Lotta Love" was that song. And it was.

Now I'll tell ya, this is how the British Invasion come 'bout. When we was in England we was playin in Piccadilly Square. Memphis Slim and me was lettin them little English boys slip in backstage and Willie Dixon was back there, handin out tapes of his songs like hot cross buns.

Them blues kids was chasin up B-sides like gold coins and Willie come along with all them demos a his he'd put on tape. Was like Christmas in July. How'd you think they got some of them songs? Rollin Stones and Yardbirds had some songs before they been recorded. Like "You Shook Me" and "300 Pounds of Joy." Pretty funny seein them bony little Brit boys singin that one. And Muddy's thing, "I Just Wanna Make Love To You," that was a big hit on the first Rollin Stones album.

Muddy and Wolf was great heroes in England. Everybody's yellin, "Play 'Back Door Man!'" Go back home, next door neighbor don't know them from Adam and Noah. You know, when the Beatles come here, they was asked by a reporter what they wanted to see in America and they said: "Muddy Waters and Bo Diddley." And the reporters said to them, "Where's that?" Thought they was talkin 'bout some kinda resort area.

51

Baby, Let Me Follow You Down

In '58 we lost Tommy McClennan, Big Bill. The old-timers was goin down fast. I lost count. I didn't wanna know. *Beverly Hillbillies*, *Mr. Ed*, hula hoops and Ike and Tupperware. They was losin me real fast. Heard Elvis's Cadillac caught on fire—if that ain't a sign. Next thing you know they're puttin him in the army. Little Richard's become a minister, Chuck Berry's in jail. Hail, hail, rock 'n' roll.

When you're in your forties you know everything. You are at the height of your powers, baby. Just keep tellin yourself that. In your fifties you still think you ridin high, you got it all figured. It's a deception of yourself but you need it. You can still tell yourself you know what's goin down. You know the score. Just can't be bothered with all the shuckin and jivin goin down out there. But when your sixties roll 'round—and, mind, *the* sixties was *my* sixties—you wake up to some fucked-up thing every damn day. The world gone crazy and don't even know it. You don't understand it and you don't *wanna* understand it.

Like one day I run into Willie Dixon in the package store.

"You hear 'bout that shit in L.A.?" he says. Now, Willie at that time he was in his Aunt-Sally's-Dream-Book phase, see. So he still thinks he's connected. That everything *is* connected, and what's broke he can tell you how to fix it.

"Whassat?" says I.

"Y'know, shoot-out with the cops at the Black Muslim temple. Some shit, huh?"

"Wait a minute, Willie. What you talkin 'bout a temple?"

"Where you been? Elijah Mohammed, y'know, they callin him the Holy Apostle."

"Oh yeah? What line they layin down?"

"Raisin up the consciousness of the black people. Clean livin. No drinkin, no smokin, no adultery."

"Guess that excludes you and me."

"Well, I'm workin up to it, man."

"So far, I don't like it."

"Coley," he say, like a man who knows what's happenin, "if you don't wanna make yourself a fool, you best get some literature from the temple."

"From the *temple*? Willie, this place is gettin more and more like Babylon every day."

Been nearly ten years since Rosa Parks refused to move to the back of the bus. A hundred years since Emancipation and what? Bullshit with all deliberate speed.

If you'da been in the Shamrock Bar, spring of '63, you'da seen some nasty shit goin down on that TV set. Fire hoses turned on children, snarlin police dogs, people gettin clobbered, houses dynamited, churches burned, skulls cracked. You couldn't turn on the TV without seein some ugly tub of lard like commissioner "Bull" Connor down in Birmingham paradin his storm troopers. Now if God had went and gave rednecks brains we'd really be in trouble.

Look man, it could happen to anybody.

Things was that bad I had to break down, get me a job. Shuggy's Atomic Car Wash.

> *Scrub that grease and grime right offa your car.*
> *You need Shuggy's Atomic Car Wash whoever you are.*

You heard the jingle on WVON and you get a free wax. WVON was the radio station Leonard and Phil bought for one million dollars cash. And to show their appreciation for all them black folk who made 'em rich they named their radio station "Voice of the Negro." Tell it to Barrett Strong, baby. *They say the best things in life are free, but you can give 'em to the birds and bees....*

While I'm workin at Shuggy's my mama come by.

"What is this?" she asks me.

"What it look like, Mama? I'm workin my butt off. You oughta be proud. You need a wax job or something?"

"Don't get funny with me. What I don't need is to see a son of mine doin what's a summer job for a kid. Here, I got a postcard for you. Septimus sent it on from Lula."

"Read it to me," I says, "my hands is wet."

"It's addressed to Mr. Coley Williams, Old-time Blues Singer, Lula, Mississippi. Says here:

> If you are alive and well please call us here collect.
> P.S. Hope this reaches you. Got address from your song 'Last Time I Seen Lula' on the Vanguard *Delta Troubadors* series.
> P.P.S. Would you know whereabouts of Booker White or Son House?

Signed, Dick Waterman. Postmarked Cambridge, Massachusetts."

"So what does it mean?"

"Means someone know you're alive."

"Could be from a police."

"Do the police write people postcards with statues on 'em? I don't think so. Anyways I called the number. All they want is for you to show up at a Folk Festival they're holdin in Newport, Rhode Island and sing a few songs."

Now what in the name of Sam Hill was this? Bunch of botheration sound like, you know, that I don't need to get myself tangled up in. But when they say they ain't got but four hundred dollars for the weekend gig, what am I gonna say to that? Be right over. Ever since this rock 'n' roll business been goin on I been workin as a janitor, night watchman, delivery boy, caddy and pushcart vendor. Four hundred dollars? That more money than Robert Johnson make in his entire life.

The kid that writ to me, Dick Waterwhatsisname? Coupla weeks later he come through Chicago. Young fella with a mustache and big glasses. He was real serious like one of them cats who makes bombs in their basements. He was in this car with two other white boys. Want my help in findin old blues singers like myself.

Then Dick tells me this strange thing and I have to admit it did get my attention. Heard a rumor, he says, that Ma Rainey was alive and livin in St. Louis. Did I by any chance know her. *Know* her? Man!

"That would be a good trick," I says, "if Ma was still kickin!"

"Yeah," he says, "I've talked to her."

I knew the old girl was dead, dead as ragtime, but on the other hand I could not resist the idea she slipped through. Talk the Grim Reaper outta it. Sing him a song, give him a blow job. And weren't there the legend of the two Ma Raineys? Anyways, they're just talkin St. Louis and St. Louis ain't Mississippi, know what I mean?

So I get in the car with Dick and these other white college boys —what was their names? It'll come to me. Down in St. Louis we meet up with "Ma Rainey." A sweet old gal—and the size of two Ma Raineys—but she ain't no Mother of the Blues. "My friends is callin me that 'cause I sing so good." She ain't gonna sing "See See Rider" like Ma done but she was a veritable funky old bluesman switchboard. Told us where to look for Booker White and Skip James and a bunch of others I figured had passed long ago. "Son House? Yeah, he still kickin. Heard he was livin down by Lake Cormorant, somewhere over there."

I told this Dick fella, "Maybe he ain't dead but he ain't gonna play you no blues."

"Why's that?"

"He's caught the holy fire last time I heard a him."

"Well," says Dick, "what if we offered him a honorarium?"

"How's that?"

"You know, some money plus his expenses—same as we're givin you."

"Well now, that just might do the trick. Might fly outta that church faster than a bat outta Georgia."

❖   ❖   ❖

Once we hit Mississippi I knew this trip been a serious miscalculation. Hadn't I learned nothin? The rednecks figured we was there for voter registration, and that weren't much more popular than some white boys and a old black man ridin in the same automobile. Freedom Riders was gettin beat up right and left. I had no intention of rattlin no rednecks' cages. I knew the beast only too well and I knew what it could do if it got riled.

We was 'round Lake Cormorant area but no sign of Sonny House. Weren't nobody givin us no help neither. When Dick or the other white kids was askin directions these hillbillies would just say, "Thass nigrah music. What you want with that nigrah music for?" They wasn't gonna give no directions for the pursuit of nigrah music.

These kids was dumb as shit 'bout the South. They would wax on to these moron bigots 'bout how they come to preserve the traditional folk music, y'know? Well, that made 'em even more suspect than they already was. Library of Congress? Nigrah tunes? Shee-it!

The next bright idea they got is of me bein a preacher, the Reverend Williams. They gonna harass a man of the cloth? Well, this here's Mississippi, son, and they don't give a good goddamn if I been ordained by Elijah hisself.

Two fat peckerwoods was standin by the side of the road. Just puffed like a adder with venom when they seen our party come drivin by.

"Good afternoon, gentlemens," I says in the politest old darky voice I can muster. "Fine day, ain't it? May I introduce myself? I'm the Reverend Williams and I'm come to attend a funeral. Can you tell me how we might get to Son House's house, sir,"

"House's house?" They was snickerin. The dumb shits found this hilarious. Just stood there and wheezed. The younger one looked down the sights of his shotgun. White kids in the car was almost levitatin they was so terrified.

Long minute standin in the heat—I could hear my own heart beatin inside my head, I could hear the crickets sing a whole verse of "Ain't No Grave Can Hold My Body Down" while I stood there. Finally the older one spat on the ground. Outta the corner of his mouth he said, "Third farm down."

Son come out of his house, dignified and skinny in a string tie.

And drunk as a deacon. He was glad to see me but it took some persuadin to his wife that this was a bona fidy enterprise. She figured it were some excuse to pry Son loose and get him back into his bad old ways. She was not gonna lose him to liquor and gamblin and nasty heathenish practices. The kids showed her pictures and contracts and other pieces of paper and told her their parents was lawyers and dentists and such, and by-and-by she relented and let Son pack hisself a suitcase.

Now we got *two* old black men in the car. Try gettin outta Misssissippi without some busybody impedin your travels. Sure enough the sheriff of Tunica stop us. "Get outta the vehicle!" he suggest. Told him the whole story of what it was 'bout. The white boys was chimin in tryin to help, sayin, "Man, it's the truth we can show—"

"If you boys"—boys meant Son and me—"is who you says you is, do us a tune."

We played him a coupla songs and he says, "Well now, thass nice. Mighty fine, mighty fine. How would you boys like to play at a supper tonight over by Dundee?"

So we played that supper and eased ourselves on outta Mississippi with our fingers and toes crossed. We knew some shit was comin down, and we didn't wanna be 'round when it did.

We was drivin through Virginia when Son ask me are we gonna play for the Congress.

"No, man, this is a *folk* festival." I am a expert in these matters now. "These fine gentlemen here in this car is the genuine article," I says. "Real folkies!"

Son look at me like I am crazy.

"What the hell is a folkie?"

"Someone who drinks their tea with a cinnammon stick," says one of the kids in the car.

"A kid with a college education and a large record collection," says the other. "Or anyone who knows who Uncle Dave Macon is."

"You know, Son, it's Leadbelly-type things. 'Rock Island Line,'

'Midnight Special,' 'Goodnight Irene.' Down in the mine where the sun don't shine, and all that."

"Hey, I heard they made Leadbelly get in his prison stripes when he perform up North."

"Bet he loved that."

"So who is all gonna be there exactly?"

"Young cats playin jugs and kazoos and pretty girls playin dulcimers. You gone like it. I guarantee it."

"Plantation stuff?" says Son with some distaste. "Like from the minstrel shows?"

"Well, uh, not really."

"*Old*-time," Son says finally. "I get it. So where's the damn jug?"

Son didn't have a guitar of his own so they bought him one. But when it come time for him to perform—no guitar. What become of the guitar they wanted to know. I coulda told 'em. Pawned it for a bottle of hooch and, Son bein Son, he had a good explanation for what he done.

"Can't play no good lessen I'm drunk," he told 'em. Which was true. Had a tremor, see, which made it near impossible for him to play when he was sober. They fixed that by gettin him some medications.

But there was a more serious problem. Son had forgotten who he was. He hadn't picked up a guitar in many years and it'd been some twenty years since he'd played professionally. They'd found the great Son House, the apocalyptic blues slider hisself, but he played nothin like the old fiery Son they knew from records.

There was this owly-lookin young kid name Al Wilson and he could play them old blues real good. He'd tell Son, "In 1930, this is how you played 'My Black Mama.' Remember when Lomax recorded 'Levee Camp Moan' with you in 1941?" And Son would go, "Yeah! Yeah! There it is! My recollection's comin back to me now."

He spent a few hours every day with Son and in a couple of weeks Son House was playin like Son House again. Now he could play, but did he want to? At a performance he done at a little coffee house called the Unicorn he'd take up to five minutes to tune his guitar, then put it down. Interrupt hisself in the middle of a song or deliver one of his nonsensical ten-minute sermons. Still, by the time we got to Newport he was slidin and hammerin that guitar just like he usta.

Little by little they dug up a whole mess of old bluesmen. Turned over every rock and peeked in every hollow log. Some was pumpin gas, some was carpenters, some was workin as bellboys at hotels, some was settin on their porches waitin for the lights to go out. Brushed 'em off and put 'em on the bus north. Booker White, they found him. Big old farm boy. Booker had this huge head and terrible teeth— always looked like a farmer. Wherever he was playin, he was still settin on his Uncle Ben's porch strummin his guitar. Tom Hoskins found Mississippi John Hurt, brought him up from Mississippi. Found him from that record of his, "Avalon Blues." Avalon, Mississippi. He was still there. Mississippi John had a disposition that was sweet as honey. Sleepy alligator eyes and that big muddy-river smile.

We all got given badges with "Performer," "Staff," or "Kin" on 'em. Dependin. Mississippi Fred McDowell got one of each pinned on him, like he was some Civil War general.

All the old ghosts of the Delta and points south was there. Son House, Booker White, Lightnin Hopkins, Skip James, Mississippi John Hurt, John Lee Hooker, Mississippi Fred McDowell, Reverend Robert Wilkins, Sleepy John Estes, Hammie Nixon, Yank Rachell, Libba Cotton. I swear some of 'em they *did* dig up. Looked it too. Polyester don't rot, y'know. Buried in their plastic shirts. Only way some of 'em could've survived is they was so pickled from grain alcohol they was formaldehyded.

It was the zombie bash, baby, the ghost blues convention. All the haints from Beale to Bourbon Street was there. We was runnin into one another sayin, "Hell, thought you was dead." Some of them cats wasn't all that crazy 'bout bein found in the first place. "She-it! Fifteen hours on the fuckin bus, breakfast and a place to sleep, then they put you back on the damn bus."

But I don't care what they say, I had me a great old time at that festival. I never expected to see half of these cats again this side of the grave. It was like time had stopped and the past and the future was comin together. With the fog comin off the water at night, coulda been anytime anywhere. Cats from thirty years ago, forty years ago. These guys never been all in one place before 'cept in someone's record collection. You could walk 'round and see the whole length and breadth of the blues and all the different places it come from. Scraggly old mountain men, ancient blues singers. There was hillbilly players and mandolin pluckers and mountain yodelers there too. And bluegrass boys in big white hats. Ashley Boggs was there, Bill Monroe, Mother Maybelle. And there were the younger crowd folk musicians—Bob Dylan, Joan Baez, Eric von Schmidt.

And here was all these kids singin songs in little groups 'round campfires 'bout grizzly bears they never seen and workin on the railroad which ain't somethin they ever gonna do. There was Foggy Mountain breakdowns, piney woods yodellin, and deep in the mine where the sun never shine hootenannies. College kids eat that stuff up. Anything ancient, moss-covered. Hillbilly reels and moldy old bo weevil blues, bottleneck dobros, mountain men ballads.

It was a little toy world been lifted outta the misery and toil and poverty of the South and set up in Rhode Island. Fantasy world of boneyards, backwoods, canebrakes, mules, riverboat gamblers and jackleg preachers. Safe as figurines on a mantle.

Bluesville is what they was callin the blues workshop. A wooden pallet on the grass, and a chair on that pallet and on that chair was a old black man wearing a hat and heavy jacket—it's mid-summer, mind. White shirt, button up to the top button like the old blues guys wear 'em. And singin in such a thick Tunica County drawl you didn't know was it words or what. Kids was just stunned. Later they got to ask questions.

Furry's smilin. That sun-come-out-from-behind-a-thunderhead smile of his. Tellin 'em: "Son, you gotta paint that jug for it to sound right. It ain't gone have the right tone if it ain't got paint on it." These kids was learnin the tricks of the trade from Beale Street thirty years ago and eatin it up. Who woulda guessed jug bands would come back?

There was more jug bands playin 'round that festival than you'd a seen at one of Mayor Crump's picnics.

Skip James was settin there in his brand-new homburg, shirt button up to the neck. With his soul patch and fierce eyes he could make you shiver in the middle of July just by shootin you a look. He was singin in that high Delta ghost voice, brushin those strings as he sung:

> *When your knee-bones achin and your body cold,*
> *Said, when your knee-bones achin and your body cold,*
> *You just gettin ready, honey, for the cypress grove.*

John Lee Hooker could be found down in Bluesville. Look like a big old hoodoo doll hisself. Reelin out them single-chord drones. Make you believe to your bones. Them songs a his was little conjure-sack spells.

Lightnin was there, Sam Lightnin Hopkins, spinnin his old jive 'bout this and that, 'bout po Lightnin.

I ask him how he come to be there. Lightnin says, "Well, see now, Coley, I got this friend and his name is Long Gone Miles. And I had me another friend whose name was Not Long Gone Miles."

This the way he talk, you know. Like a sidewinder if a sidewinder could talk. He was a storyteller, a shaggy-dog type storyteller. He could keep you for a week if you set with him.

"This other friend a mine," Lightnin went on, "he gone into the hair processin as a hobby. And he'd done Long Gone's hair. I like the type a job he done so I ask him would he do my do? Would you do Lightin's hair?"

"Man," I says, "I'm lost already with this story a yours."

"That's 'cause you ain't listnin to me, Coley."

"Are we gettin to the point presently?"

"All in the Lord's good time, all in the Lord's good time. He drove me to the drugstore to get the stuff. Hair application for Lightin's hair, understand? And as we drove, he started tellin me about the club, and what kind of place it was. He said, 'Come out to the club one night and sing. And if you like it, they'll give you a paper and you can make some money.' It was a coffee house."

"This ain't like that story 'bout the snake by the railroad track you always tellin, is it?"

"Coley, I am tryin to supply you with information that might advance your betterment."

"Uh huh."

"Club 47 it's called. See Mr. Jim Rooney. And, uh, tell him Lightnin sent you."

"Uh-huhn."

This was good advice because I got me onto the coffee circuit—47 Club, Cafe Au Go Go in New York, colleges. Until then, I'd never been into the folk scene. Never been in a coffee house neither, but I cottoned onto it real quick. Been to a bunch of them festivals over the next few years. Little by little they begin lettin electric instruments in, but it wasn't till '67 they let Muddy bring his band. It was this kinda deal—you was a old-timer, made your guitar with your own bare hands—Wolf was makin fun of this routine when he come shufflin on in overalls sweepin the stage between acts at the Newport Folk Festival.

Muddy had knocked 'em out a few years earlier at the jazz festival but folkies was purists. Afeared of electricity as a old mammy.

The ones that broke the ice was the Paul Butterfield Blues Band. Butter—that's what we called him. Crazy eyes swirlin behind those shades of his. He had a cookin band. He'd stole Wolf's rhythm section, see. Jerome Arnold and Sam Lay. Somethin Wolf never forgave him for.

I remember the afternoon Butter's band played Bluesville. The place was packed. Maybe a thousand people there.

Alan Lomax and Eric von Schmidt was runnin Bluesville that day. With his big beard and wire glasses Eric looked like a old-time gold prospector. I weren't concerned that he would object to blues bein amplified but I knew Lomax weren't gonna care for it. But Alan outdid hisself that afternoon. He was the mayor of Bluesville and he was gonna lay down the law. Gets up on the stage, goes straight into this five-minute rant on used-to-be. Went something like this (though I may exaggerate it a little):

"Once upon a time a black sharecropper would take an axe handle, some bailin wire and a cigar box, make his own guitar. These tillers of the soil and hewers of wood sang their songs while they was plowin a mule. Today you've heard some of the greatest blues musicians in the world playing their simple music on simple instruments. I don't know why this Butterfield band needs all this equipment they've got piled up here. Let's just find out if these guys can play!"

Butter went on, and that ferocious undertow of sound blew everybody away. Albert Grossman was there—crewcut, glasses and white linen jacket. He was pudgy and belligerent. He managed Bob Dylan and people like that, and when Butter's band came off Grossman buttonholes Lomax.

"What kind of a fuckin introduction was that?" Lomax says, "Oh yeah, well, what're ya gonna do about it?" And before you know it these two big guys are rollin 'round in the dust punchin and kickin each other. Sammy Lay, Butter's drummer, cooled 'em out. Sammy was a big friendly guy but behind his shades he could look like one mean muthafucka and they backed off fast.

Bob Dylan and Mike Bloomfield come on stage—Dylan was just a scrawny, wiry-haired kid in cowboy boots and shades. All them boys wearin tea shades. They was just startin to smoke weed and didn't want people to see their eyes. Bloomfield was another of them kids who usta hang 'round Theresa's—tall, skinny, nervous kid, always shiftin from one foot to the other.

For some reason electricity really wigged some of them folkies out. When Dylan and Bloomfield plugged in their guitars Pete Seeger went nuts. He was runnin 'round backstage with a axe, shoutin, "If you don't get off the stage right now I'm gonna chop these cables." Seeger was a skinny, weedy-lookin guy, and Theodore Bikel, the beefy Israeli folk singer—looked like a plumber—was tryin to calm him down, sayin: "Leave 'em alone! You can't stop the future with an axe."

But that's what happens, baby, when you try to turn back the clock.

Mannish Boys

In the late '50s Chess had moved to bigger quarters at 2120 South Michigan Avenue. It was a two-story building, the offices was on the ground floor, the studio was upstairs. But in '64 it was still the same madhouse it always been when the Rollin Stones come to record there. People wanderin in off the street—some old lady who thought it was the Social Security office and wouldn't be convinced otherwise, a cat sellin knishes, a numbers runner, a salesman hustlin airtime, deejays and rackers, everybody talkin at once, and above it all Leonard's voice on the phone to someone, yellin, "Lissen, you shmuck—"

The Stones walk into their temple of the blues and it's more like Maxwell Street on a Sunday afternoon. Muddy's up on a ladder paintin the ceilin. King of the Blues—said so right on his card—and he's paintin the office. The Stones recognized Muddy, they was greetin him like a long-lost mate but Muddy didn't know who in hell these kids was 'cause they was grown and had a *lot* more hair.

In the studio you got Sonny Boy and Little Walter deep into a philosophical argument 'bout the flavor of some chick down in Mobile's pussy.

"Ooooow, man, her snatch taste sooooo nasty. Like a fish that had died and been marinated in a barrel."

"After you got done with her it was smellin more like Seacaucus in July."

The Stones was just standin there, eyes poppin out their head. There they was in the inner sanctum of the blues and the principle topic of conversation was pussy juice.

But the Stones idolized Muddy. Woulda done anything for him. When they ask him, "Is there something we can get you, man? Just name it, anyfing at all, it's done."

"Yeah," says Muddy. "How 'bout some tsivas regul?"

They was goin, "*Wot*? Wot did ee say?" They thought maybe it was some mojo hand—the mysterious, all-stupifyin tsivas regul, from way down in Louisiana, behind the sun. Muddy gonna perform some ceremony before they cut wax. And all Muddy was askin for was a bottle of whiskey. Only the best for Muddy.

We got on famously, me and the Stones. Next time you see 'em ask 'em 'bout Coley Williams. We was so tight they come right out and ask me to come on their U.S. tour. Keith is insistin on it. But open for them? You gotta be kiddin. They comin to see Mick Jagger wiggle his tight crushed-velvet ass and what do they get? A mummified old black man sittin on a chair singin "Saddle Up My Pony."

"It's awright, Coley," says Mick. "We'll get you a pair of bellbottoms, you'll fit right in, won't ee, Keef?"

"Yeah, get your penicillin shots and a packet of rubbers, mate, and you'll be all set."

Goin on the road with Chuck Berry did not in any way prepare me for what went down on that Stones tour. Police barricades, security guards bashin away, faintin kids gaspin for air, tits hangin out, chicks chokin, nurses runnin 'round with ambulances.

We was turnin up to gigs we couldn't get into, let alone play. Three bars and a terrifyin mob of crazed teenage girls sweep over the stage, tramplin everything in their path. Throwin candies, peanuts, stuffed animals, panties, bras. You know that weird sound that thousands of chicks make when they're really lettin it go? *Kyyyeeeeeeeeeeagh*!! Like a jet plane takin off.

The Stones had "Little Red Rooster" out then. Howlin Wolf's version sold maybe 20,000 copies, and that was pretty good for a r&b record. Sam Cooke came along and his version sold over a 100,000 records. But these cats was sellin records like catfish sandwiches on a Friday night. Half a million copies right outta the gate. Still, they did Wolf a real solid. Refused to go on *Shindig* unless they put him on first. You could see them producers lookin at each other. Who the hell is Howlin Wolf? They thought some Indian chief gonna come out on stage in a war bonnet.

In the '60s when the electric bass come in, Willie Dixon didn't play so much on sessions no more. The stand-up bass was his thing. And Willie not workin at Chess at the time the Stones come to record, but he'd stop by. Sit outside in his car. You always knew it was him, his Oldsmobile was weighted way down to the curb on the driver's side. He'd carry us over to his house on Calumet Street or to some club.

We'd be sittin in Theresa's Lounge. In them days it was fifty cents to get in. You might see Muddy, Sonny Boy, Little Walter all on one night. For fifty cents! And if it was Muddy's night you'd have all the blues stars in Chicago hangin out at the bar.

Muddy checkin out the vibe from behind them lazy-lookin hooded eyes, castin 'round the room like a old gator, eyes just above the surface of the water. Sizin up who he's talkin to, tunin in to the pitch of his voice. Got a built-in radar saved his life more than once.

Magic Sam, Otis Rush, all them cats would come by and sit in. Muddy weren't jealous of nobody, see. He'd say, "I don't contradict nobody's playin." Anybody who wanted to play the blues, that was okay with him.

53

The Jacks Are All
Back in Their Boxes

Where Bo Diddley get them crazy ideas on his guitar from? Sound effects and so forth? Some of his guitars *is* unidentified flyin objects. Bo, I'm convinced, musta had hisself a encounter. Bo was the gate. Through Bo-gate poured untold extraterrestrials, diddlies, diodes, infestin brains, guitars and rock stars.

Now I told you it was from Bo that I first heard of UFOs. It was him what told me the *actual date* the first UFO been sighted. 1942. *November 27*, 1942. Knew the exact date—that's how I knew he was tellin the truth. Now I been involved in every scene where the blues have gone just 'bout, but I musta missed one or two. Like where that alien blues spacecraft hover over Seattle. Aliens is most interested in the blues than anything else on earth. You didn't know that? That's what they come for. Take the so-call pentatonic scale, now that just *have* to come from outer space.

I thought 'bout that when I was playin the Cafe Au Go Go in New York City. People keep sayin to me, "Come on down the street, you gotta hear this cat play, man, you ain't heard nothin like it. Cat plays the Delta blues for sure—only his Delta is on Mars."

The Cafe Wha? was a little old funky, sweaty, jive tourist dive in Greenwich Village. "Ladies and gentlemen, a big hand for the a-mazing Jimmy James and the Flames!" Onstage come this skinny, awkward young cat, slams right into a speeded-up version of Wolf's

"Killin Floor." Went by faster than blue hair. And on into a spooky trance blues. Barebones guitar lopin outta the bayou. Had a sly, little whispery voice like a country blues singer. Outta nowhere comes these Bo Diddley spacey, sound-effects guitar lines *meep-meeep-meeepin* in the mind-fryin New York City night. Delta blues... Delta blues...look-'round-for-my-shoes, carryin-the-ol-African-curse blues. But these was blues that done caught the Chinese train. The Col-trane blues. Watch out, somebody done hoodoo the hoodoo man.

A UFO was beamin down dolphin-chant telegrams. Freaky sonic hieroglyphics from a alien tomb what turn into terrible chattering monkey talk of the wah-wah. And damn if them little electric men I asked to interpret wasn't meltin like wax dolls in the Venusian gravitational drizzle.

In the old days we could make trains whistle, birds sing, and dogs howl, but this cat could pull truly terrifyin stuff outta that Stratocaster. Police sirens and machine guns, the vicious, brain-devourin dogs of Hell. Damn! Helicopters flew outta that guitar and dropped flamin napalm on bamboo villages while snatches of "Strangers in the Night" come out of a transistor radio far away.

He was playin the guitar with his teeth, behind his back, between his legs, y'know, like Guitar Shorty done. Guitar Shorty was a trick player, usta twist his guitar 'round, throw it up in the air. Buddy Guy was into this jive, blowin them cats on Maxwell Street away with his trickifications. This was old, *old* shit that went all the ways back to griots and their talkin sticks most likely. Charley Patton ridin his guitar like a mule in a Robinsonville jook joint. And they was sayin back then that he was just a fool.

I went backstage. He was very shy, lookin down, pickin at his guitar, like a gypsy scrutinizin a crystal ball. But man, that boy could talk. He was a rapper like I never known.

"Hey man, I know you. Remember that day I come into Chess? Bet you don't remember. Just another skinny black kid thinks he's Robert Johnson. First cat I run into is this big fat black cat—"

"That would be Willie, Willie Dixon."

"He says 'Can you do anything with that or you lookin to pawn it?' I did, like, a few riffs and I thought I was goin pretty hot shit there for a while until Muddy come over. When I heard what he was layin down I slunk right outta there like a mangy mutt. I was crushed, see?"

"Hey now, Mr. uh, James...."

"Hendrix, Jimi Hendrix. James just our *nom-de-blues*, dig?"

"But you done come *long* ways since that day, man."

"Well, meantime I wheeled my shoppin cart 'round the blues to see what I could find. I frisked the Three Kings good—Albert, Freddie and B.B. See what cards fall outta their sleeves. From aisle number two I grab me some So'side jagged rusty razor blades off of brother Buddy Guy and snap-a-pistol-in-yo-face attack from Uncle Albert Collins. Then picked me up a few of B.B.'s tricks."

"You got a little Bo Diddley in there somewhere, too."

"Papa Bo Legba, man! Taught me how to make the guitar whine like a telephone line. Grindin the strings up against the frets, dig? More it grinds the more it whines. 'Cause you know your voice ain't never gonna be high enough to scream what you really wanna scream. Then the Fret Fairy come along and sprinkle that goofer dust on my axe, and she say, 'You got you your bag of tricks, Jimi, you know what you gotta do now? Boy, you gotta smash that glass.' So I pick up all those pieces of electricity. 'Cause, I usta live in a room full of mirrors—dig what I'm sayin?—and, uh, like, *that long-time curse hurts* and all that type of thing, y'know? I get up in the mornin and look 'round for my shoes and, uh, all I could see was me. But once I dived through the glass it was like, uh, y'know...like Charlie Parker in that chili house up on 139th, workin on the intervals on 'Cherokee,' dig? I heard the thing I'd been hearing in my head all my life. They usta call it Chinese music when you went out there on that lime-twig limb."

"You way past China now, baby."

Between '63 and '67 we was losin bluesmen fast. Sonny Boy, Little Walter, J.B. Lenoir, Elmore James. Wolf and Muddy was the end of a dyin breed at Chess. Little Walter, he messed hisself 'round by juicin and dopin too much. That's sad, y'know, 'cause he was a helluva talented guy, but he hung with a rough crowd and it done him in.

Didn't have no sense. He was the regular Saturday night skinballin, booze-guzzlin, pussy-sniffin, crap-shootin sonofabitch. And he got into the worst messes you could get into.

I walked into the bathroom at the place he's staying at one time, this white chick's pad, and there he was sittin on the john turnin blue with a needle stickin out his arm. His head had fallen over on the radiator and when we pick him up off it, his face look just like he'd laid it on a waffle iron. We put some coffee in him, walk him up and down awhile until he come to.

Sonny Boy was just as bad. Last time I seen him he was tryin to climb in the window at Chess. Now in the old days it was a family type deal. You could just stroll into Chess. But little by little it got more uptight. Soon it was interoffice memos, cash vouchers. Hell, if someone wanted to go to Detroit to see his sick sister—in the old way of doin things—and you needed a hundred dollars, Leonard would give it to you right outta his pocket. Now you needed a voucher just to go to the john. They got snotty-nose engineers in there trashin Muddy and Wolf. They was sayin shit like, "It was a miracle if those old blues singers could stay in the same key all through a song." Hell, we built this studio, asshole.

One day Sonny Boy comes by Chess and they won't let him in. "Do you have a appointment with Mr. Chess? Please take a seat and I'll buzz him on the intercom." Sonny Boy's a bit loaded and he starts shoutin, "Fuck this take a seat crap. You know who I am, bitch?" So they put him outside. There ain't no way they keepin Sonny Boy out. Now he's cursin a blue streak, "You fuckin sonsofbitches! I'm gone come in there and tear out your eyeballs!" And just at that moment a rabbi walks by. And the girl from the office is tellin Sonny Boy, "Watch your language in front of the rabbi." This just got Sonny Boy even more riled than he already were and he begin shoutin out in the street, "The fuck I will. Rabbi wants the same thing I do."

Well, I'll tell you, you can take the boy outta the Delta....

Hairy Green Buttons
And the Talking God

Things gettin worse, daily. Some cracker done killed Martin Luther King, a Arab shot Robert Kennedy. There was riots in Watts, Detroit, all over. War still grindin on over there in Vietnam. God look down on what was happenin in the world and say, "You tryin to break my heart?"

Had riots in Chicago, too. Day after Martin Luther King was shot in Memphis. Black smoke in the air and people lootin stores. Folks gone crazy. They was mad, see? Truth is, I felt the same way.

But my mama, well, you know how she was. Didn't abide no wrongdoin even if the cause was right. They was smashin in the front of an A&P, they got guns and baseball bats, and Mama is out on the street *lecturin* 'em. "What do you think you doin? You only destroyin your own neighborhood. Ain't no white folk gone miss them stores. You behavin just like a bunch a heathens."

When people told me what she was doin out there I wanted to scold her, y'know, the way you do when someone is gone. "Mama, what was you thinkin of, reprimandin folks with guns what's crazy with anger?" Poor Mama, got herself so aggravated yellin at the people lootin and burnin she give herself a heart attack. At least she died happy—fightin and carryin on and tellin people what to do.

Septimus come up for the funeral. He could see I blamed myself. He just said, "Mama died speakin her mind, she couldn't a done it no other way. Mama was Mama. Let her be."

When we laid her to rest I sung her that great old song of Blind Lemon's, "Motherless Children Have a Hard Time." It was all I could do to get through one verse.

> *When your mother is dead*
> *Father will do best he can.*
> *So many things father can't understand.*
> *No one else can take your mother's place*
> *When your mother is dead.*

Vida Lee come to the funeral. They was real close, them two. I'd been seein Vida Lee every little once in a while. Family shit. I was treadin on eggshells with her. Didn't know which way the wind blow. That's the thing with women, you can't always guess it out. I could see she had some plan but she weren't gonna reveal it right out and when I did hear it I thought she gone nuts. "Coley, now don't you interrupt me till I'm finished what I got to say."

"You got the floor, baby."

"Well, I been thinkin 'bout movin back down South...." That's how she began. And that was 'bout as much as I remember 'bout the conversation 'cause I had to stop her right there.

"When I start talkin 'bout goin back to Mississippi, you best lock me up," I says, "'cause then you know I am out of my mind crazy."

I was gettin a few gigs here and there, y'know, playin at colleges and spendin too much time in bus depots. This one time I drunk too much—I get bored hangin out in bus stations and I find the time pass more agreeably in them places when one is a little lit. 'Course, after a coupla pints of Night Train you can lose yourself real easy if you ain't payin attention.

Got on the wrong bus and it was mornin before I realized where I was. I shoulda taken it into the big city but I was so mad with myself I just got off the bus where we was. Which was in the middle of nowhere. Gas station, coffee shop, Indian tradin post, and that was 'bout it. The train tracks was the only encouragin sign of life in the place. The rest was just scrub brush, sagebrush, cactus, and sand. I already done my forty years in the wilderness, baby, I don't need this shit.

Way down the track was a bent over cat, kickin cans. How many times you come across this scene? A brother a little way down the railroad tracks tryin to kick out his blues.

Scufflin along, guitar slung across his back, dusty boots, throwin stones at a rusty Cadillac. Dressed raggedy, but raggedy velvets and satins with a big old feather stuck in his wide-brim padre hat. Was it that young Jimi Hendrix from the Cafe Wha?

"Man," he says, "did I just hallucinate you?"

"I don't think so. I ain't been showin up in too many people's dreams lately."

"I just got outta a nightmare myself—tourin with the fuckin Monkees. Pop fuckin slavery, man."

"You shoulda worked for Leonard Chess."

"Hey, it's you again. Now I *know* I'm trippin. Dig, you must be this little old man who comes outta the cactus where the Southern cross the Yellow Dog. Hear me, Señor Peyote, hear my prayer! I been walkin for a thousand miles to a destination that has escaped my memory, won't you show me the way to go home?"

"I'm lost as you are, baby."

"How'd you get all the way out here, anyway?"

"Just got on the wrong bus."

"Listen, man, there is no wrong bus." He handed me some green, hairy buttons.

"What have we here?"

"It's a little god that when you eat him he talks to you."

I took a bite. Real bitter tastin shit.

"Coley, Coley. Man, let us play us some blues, get ourselves some understandin. You know 'Catfish Blues,' right?"

"Baby, that catfish was me."

"Ha-ha-ha-ha-ha! I'm gonna call you Catfish Williams. Here we go,

> *Well, I wish I was a catfish,*
> *Swimmin in, Lord, the deep blue sea.*

I would have all, uh, you good-lookin women fishin after me.
Sho' 'nuff, after me, oh well, oh well.
Oh Lord! Oh Lord! Sho' 'nuff.
Well, I feel like, yes, I feel,
Baby, like a lowdown…my time ain't long.
I'm gonna catch this freight train smokin by
And back down the road I'm goin,
Back down the road I'm goin,
Back down the road I'm goin.
Sho' 'nuf ah—, sho' 'nuff.…

I started to feel funny but I didn't know why. The earth was spinnin like a 45, the King and Queen was playin cards, the Jack was out on bail and Jimi was floatin in the air just above my head.

"I think the cosmos is communin with itself," he said and then he said somethin 'bout Telstar and Nathan Hale. Listenin to him, it was like a radio switchin stations every ten seconds.

"Wait a minute, you say to yourself, the coffee I'm drinkin just turned to sand and the walls are made of glass but don't you pay no mind…turn to King Alpha's song in your intergalactic bibles and hear me when I say: *gwawawanggnggbwawawandzyyyyqwawawa* …the Vatican announced today that Little Richard and Elmore James would be made saints…don't mean to cause you no trouble but, baby, please pass me back my brain, 'cause, uh, Richard M. Nixon just turn orange and green on my TV screen…Aldrin packed the moon rock into the box and said he, uh, would leave it up to earth's scientists to decide what it was…baby, I been waiting here for a thousand years on Jupiter's purple hills…unilaterally endorsed the Christmas bombing of Laos…oh Mama, where will it all end, the alphabet has lost his suitcase and taken my goddamn name…get the cool refreshing taste of tomorrow today in new Rizla Menthols…all night long the power lines were wailing that synaptic jive in the cinema du mah mind…POP STAR TRASHES HOTEL ROOM, details at eleven …now what you're sayin, Mr. Operator, is that my name ain't in your book and when you call her number the phone just ringin offa the hook?…riots continued today in ten major U.S. cities…the interviewer flew down, and he said, 'Uh, Mr. Hendrix, is it true, is it true, we must know for the *Evening News?* Did you frame 'Voodoo Child' as a challenge to the hegemony of Western rationalism and an affirmation of Black American culture or is it, uh, just a lot of dazzling noise in which we discern—?' And I said to him, 'Man, why don't you take a drive with me in this song. Get in, Daddy, and I'll show you 'round the town. Red House is the house I came outta, dig? A blues shack back in the country, way down at the end of Lonely Street. You see that red house over yonder?' And the man from the paper said, 'Which house?' And I just said, 'Lord, Lord, won't someone help me find the door.'"

A lizard slithered down the railway tracks. Little clusters of blue notes scattered into the air—so that's what became of that night in Kentucky. Jimi's eyes was strayin down the railway lines.

"Did you catch that?" he asks me.

"Yeah, the tracks, man...."

"...they're, swayin."

"Must mean a train is just 'round that bend. 'Cept there ain't no bend and I don't hear no train."

"Well, dig it, Catfish, that's because this here is *my* train, and, uh, excuse me, but I hear my mind a howlin and I do believe it's time to go."

I didn't see no train so I didn't get on it. The wind was blowin up sand and dust in little gusts and the sage brush was rollin like dead souls along the ground, and when I turned 'round he was gone.

55

Gettin Ready for the Cypress Grove

I'm one hundred and two come March 15th give or take a few years and I'm just startin to realize what it is. Unfortunate luck, but that's nothin really to worry about. I'm just thankful that I'm livin, 'cause there was a good shot I coulda went out, you know, a few times there.

A blues singer—he'll never get rich. Seventy, eighty years old and he's still hustlin and scufflin. Look at me, I been blowin since I was twelve and I'm over one hundred years old. Imagine that! I been on the Johnny Carson's show, I been on *Top Hop* in Japan and *Dankeshön Fur Die Blues* over in Germany. I even sat on Bonnie Raitt's knee. Yes, I did.

Aw, these days my memory wanders like the Pea Vine—a rackety, branch-line milk train windin through the Delta, pickin passengers up outta the past, lettin 'em down. Lula, Alligator, Panther Burn, Nitta Yuma, Anguilla, Money, Rosedale, Itta Bena, Moon—all aboard! Names of them stations runnin through my mind like a Yeller Dog alphabet of creation.

When you're my age you remember stuff but it's all outta order. See, like when you just ask me what was the first blues I ever heard, what come up in my mind instead is a old lady dancin in the rain outside a Chess Records when "Juke" come out. They was playin a demo of it in the lobby—they usta do that sometimes, see if anybody bite. It was a hot day and they had the doors open onto the street and this old sister come by shakin her booty just like she was a young girl.

I remember them rafts loaded with provisions come inchin up the Yazoo and Sunflower rivers all the way from Vicksburg a hundred miles south. I remember the smile on my daddy's face the first time he heard me singin "East St. Louis Blues."

What was it you was askin me? Oh, yeah. How did I get back down here, that what you wanted to know? Well see, Chicago was startin to have too many memories for me—all my old friends was ghosts. Those that was left was plannin on becomin ministers, Shakey Jake and them. Just like down South. Oh man, I'm tellin you, this move over to the Lord produced some truly terrifyin jackleg preachers. I run up on Jake one day and he's talkin at me in his apocalyptic manner, "O foolish Galatians, who hath bewitched you?" and I says, "You can cool it, Shakey. It's me, Coley Williams."

Shakey Jake was gonna go door-to-door readin bits outta the Bible. He preached pretty good scriptures but it weren't nothin compared to the hustle he usta lay down. Anyways, he invite me to come along and feel my spirit rise. You know I ain't no washfoot Baptist and I can't do the Holy Roll but I come to see just what it was, understand?

Shakey Jake had a little storefront chapel called the Church of the Overwhelmin God. There was a picture of a airplane on the wall, pictures of the Holy Land and Martin Luther King and President Kennedy and a zinc tub down front for baptisin in. There was a ten-year-old kid playin drums, another kid playin a electric guitar that was as big as he was.

Shakey and his congregation was interpretin a verse outta *Corinthians.*

> God hath chosen the foolish things of the world to confound the wise; and God hath chosen the weak things of the world to confound the things which are mighty.

Amen! It was a inspirin sermon but they was takin it apart word by word, letter by letter while visions of grits and gravy was waftin through my head. Don't these cats ever eat lunch? The Reverend

Shakey y'know he don't want for victuals, he owns one of them fried chicken establishments. I got uncomfortable after a while listenin to all that burn-in-Hell business, know what I'm sayin? Maybe I was takin it all a bit too personal. I wished him good luck and went out into the sunlight.

Muddy was about the only one of the old gang left. Me and Junior Wells and Buddy Guy went out to see him at his house just before he passed. He was settin in his kitchen drinkin champagne—doctor's orders. I wouldn't mind goin down slow with a prescription like that. How many times a day, didya say, doc?

"Boys," say Muddy.

Junior goes, "Reverend Muddy?"

Muddy was real serious, and you never seen a face more serious than Muddy's when he was bein solemn. He had something to impart.

"I want you and Buddy and Junior to do me favor," he say. "Pour some of this stuff on my grave. And don't let the blues die."

"Muddy," I told him, "I don't think you got nothin to worry about. There's only one thing can kill the blues, and that's if we waked up one mornin and there was no more mean mistreaters, cheatin bitches, claim-jumpers or achin old heart diseases."

You know you gettin old when the music in a club is too loud for you. When Muddy passed in '83 I had no heart to stay in Chicago no longer. All the old-timers has left. All the big clubs closin up, foldin like a bad hand. I don't know why. Money was kinda plentiful 'round then I thought. Maybe they wasn't makin so much bread what with the rap musics comin in and all. If there's no club, where can you get your music together? It's rough.

I couldn't live up there no more. Hell, who could? People goin down the street shootin each other in the broad daylight. Lightin people up like they was rabbits. Rabbit huntin is something we usta do when we lived in the country. You shoot rabbits, but you shootin it for a cause. But these individuals was goin out in the street and poppin people from their cars. Shit man, nobody wants to lose their life over something like that. You have to lay in your house and call the grocery store, have them deliver your stuff. Then the delivery man gets shot and they close the store. I've never made sense with that stuff.

Had to leave town. But where in hell was I gonna go? Never in my wildest dream did I see myself catchin a southbound train. But the South become a relatively friendly place to live by this time.

Vida Lee had the right idea, see. She had the nicest little trailer outside Robinsonville, out there on the 61 highway. One day I show up there and she goes, "What took you so damn long?"

I was well ready to mosey home, sit in the shade, drink lemonade and smoke a big fat reefer. It really had all gone 'bout as far as it can go. I done just about all the migratin and syncopatin I intended.

So I been livin down here in Robinsonville, oh, seventeen years now. People come by me and they say the damndest things. A young fella with long greasy hair in a ponytail stop by the other day tell me, "Hey listen, mister, I built a boat and named it after you." Now what the hell is that?

Kids mostly. But Mr. Samuel Charters, Mr. Paul Oliver, Mr. Alan Lomax—they never come look me up. You got your Peter Guralnicks and your Stanley Booths rediscoverin just 'bout every damn blues singer has ever crawled out from under a rock. I'm still a-waitin, fellas. Me and old Ed Andrews stand ready for the great unveilin. Come to think of it, I don't know 'bout Ed—might be a little late for Ed.

But the TV and the radio and the newspapers, they located me all right. Every birthday of mine they come on out here. It's a damned circus. Most of these television reporters haven't a fuckin clue. They think the Blues Brothers is blues.

Last night I had that boxcar dream again. I was flyin over the Delta just like a crow flies. I seen the Yeller Dog crawlin between the cotton rows, laundry blowin on the line, kids swimmin in the Sunflower River and a country supper goin on in a field.

I was lookin down on the land, seein all the people and the wagons and I thought of Grandmaw Pie and how she wanted to fly over the earth. Over Dockery's I watched my mama collectin herbs before the first day of May, Grandpaw Scipio buryin the dead, seen my daddy creepin behind the water tower. Seen 'em just like God sees 'em. I looked down below me and I seen Lula lookin no bigger than a postage stamp. When I come to where the Southern cross the Dog I started thinkin how all that I seen in my life was like a book of the Bible—from the first time I heard the blues played to last Wednesday. Would be like if people still livin had known Cain and Abel.

The water rippled on Moon Lake and the islands there became the face of Mary the Wonder. She was lookin fine like the first time I seen her. Black dress with bright blue flowers on it, peony flower stuck in her nappy head.

"Honey, don't we even get a kiss first?" she said and laughed, and in that instant I knew she had passed.

She smiled and shook her head: "Well well, ain't this kinda inconvenient, baby, meetin this a-way?"

She vanished and I was standin alone at the crossroad of Three Forks. I began walkin down that dusty road, my shoes kickin stones. I heard a long, high moan, *uuhhh-uhh-uhh-ummmmm*, and a voice called out, "Coley, that you, baby?"

Standin before me in the road was Robert in his fedora hat and pinstripe suit, just the way I'd seen him that first night in the graveyard. Was so skinny he didn't even cast a shadow.

"How you, RL?"

"I'm so nasty they shouldn't allow me in the street," he said, talkin his usual jive. But I could see things wasn't right with him. He began to sing in a soft, high voice.

> *I got stones in my passway*
> *And my road seems dark as night,*
> *I have pains in my heart,*
> *They taken my appetite.*

His spiderlike fingers was crawlin all over the strings but they made no sound. He put the guitar down on the ground.

"Hell Coley, I can't play no more."

He cocked his head and put his finger to his lips.

"What's the matter, RL?"

"Aw, it's just the wind blowin in the cypress grove. Storm comin up, that's for sure." He laughed.

"Comin to get me. Outta Hell, brother, straight outta Hell. And oh, how that wind do howl."

But not a breath of wind stirred in the air. That howlin was all inside his head.

"Times is hard," he tell me, "and death have very sharp teeth. Oh baby, just to see Estelle walk out her door, sashay down the street one more time.… Hey, good seein ya, brother, but I gotta split. Dark don't catch me here." And with that he was gone, faded into the leaves.

I found myself on the edge of the Itta Bena wood. The way it was in the old days when it was full of panthers and bears. There was a crowd of faces stirrin behind the trees, shapes shiftin like you see them through the blinds from a movin train. A red lightbulb was swingin there in the dark.

I heard weepin and moanin. They was talkin about sandfoot women, the last true mojo left in the world and how you just can't get that stuff no more. I can scarcely remember what they said but they spoke speeches and hollered and hexed and broke dishes. They was on the telephone to God and cussed fire to the heart of the world. Out of the throng came Teejay. His heart sang a wild weird song under the needle of a phonograph. His lips was movin but he spoke no words—just the sense of it all tumblin out of his head.

"Mosquitoes is so bad in Hell," he say, "only thing to do is to take your head off and hide it somewhere." Spittin blood and barkin he sloped off into the woods behind the tracks of the Illinois Central.

And just as quick as it come it all fade away and I was sittin there on the ground holdin a guitar what was all swole up—the rain had got to it. I began to play a strange old tune, something I hadn't played since I was a boy. *Duhn-duhn duhn-duhn dah-dah-dah-dah-dah.*

> *I'm a poor boy long way from home,*
> *Oh, I'm a poor boy long way from home.*
> *I wish that midnight train would run,*
> *Carry me back where I come from.*

I was back in that boxcar. There was a bunch of rounders and drifters and hustlers congregated there. They was pourin in like rats to the granary. Blues singers, mostly. Fellas who have lived hard lives, have been rough in their lives. Some I seen in that dream was real rough, they was no more than bones theirselves. Then Junior Wells begin wailin on his harp, Muddy slid his bottleneck like greased lightnin and Willie Dixon was hummin on the stand-up bass. When they heard that noise, them bones came together just like in that verse of Ezekiel's. Skin covered them and the nine jive tailors dressed 'em in threads so fine they looked like jook-joint Nebuchadnezzars. All the fly dudes and all the fine mamas that I ever knowed was on that train. Heartbreakers, booty-shakers, party-makers—jokin and talkin trash, drinkin cat whiskey and smokin rope. You might accuse me of exaggeratin, but this was the greatest party ever had by all the bad company in all the world. Hoo-hoo! Well, well, *well!*

Some cat was shoutin, "Roll them bones!" and soon as I heard the rattle of the dice on the wood and the chantin of the players I wanted into that game bad. But just then I heard Vida Lee's voice sayin, "You gonna run yourself straight into the grave with this life, Coley Williams." I looked up and seen Vida Lee's eyes burnin into my soul.

"By the way," she say, "just so I know. When this party's over, you want to be buried or cremated?"

"Surprise me, baby," I told her. "Surprise me."

SOURCES
BIBLIOGRAPHY & LYRICS

BIBLIOGRAPHY

The rise of the blues is to me a miraculous event, a ray of blinding spiritual power cast over the soul-corrupting late twentieth century. The pervasive influence of the blues on rock, soul, rap, and country music seems a fitting fulfillment of the promises made in the Sermon on the Mount: the poorest, most abused people in America have created the most potent music on earth.

I have written about rock 'n' roll all my life and have always wanted to pay tribute to the source of this music. Once I had become smitten with the blues, I began to wonder what the lives of the mythic bluesmen were like. I wanted to enter the brooding landscape of the Delta, to see the world through the eyes of the great blues musicians.

Coley Williams is a fictional character, but in telling his story I have tried to write a collective autobiography of the blues, incorporating the voices, stories, and music of the actual bluesmen. To whatever extent I succeed, I owe this mainly to the writers on the blues who preceded me.

My models for this book have been the three great blues autobiographies: *Big Bill Blues,* the affable memoir (perhaps a bit too tidied up in places) of Big Bill Broonzy (with Yannick Bruynoghe); *The World Don't Owe Me Nothing,* the vivid, unsparing autobiography of Honeyboy Edwards (with Janis Martinson and Michael Robert Frank); and *I Say Me For a Parable,* the dialect-clotted memoir of

Mance Lipscomb with Glen Alyn (at first glance, the language here is so dense and impenetrable that it reads like Chaucerian English).

The classic collection of blues memoirs is, of course, Paul Oliver's *Conversations With the Blues* (republished in 1998 by Cambridge University Press with a CD). This is an inexhaustible resource of blues life and music, told with profound, rueful, and hilarious gusto by a fantastic cast of characters. The poetic diction of these reminiscences (with its biblical allusions and archaic language, its strange and soulful tales) comes to us as if from an age as remote as the Middle Ages—as if we were somehow hearing verbatim the utterances of saints and prophets, which in a sense we are.

From Paul Oliver's books, and from a number of other histories and personal accounts, I have learned much of what I know about the blues. I will mention a few others that have been indispensable.

For details of life in the Delta in the early part of the twentieth century, I have drawn on Robert Palmer's *Deep Blues,* William Ferris's *Blues from the Delta,* Zora Neale Hurston's *Mules and Men,* and Stephen Calt and Gayle Wardlow's *King of the Delta Blues: The Life and Music of Charlie Patton.* (Patton grew up, as did Coley Williams, on the Dockery Plantation.) For life in Chicago I drew principally on Mike Rowe's *Chicago Blues,* Peter Guralnick's *Feel Like Going Home,* and *I Am the Blues,* Willie Dixon's autobiography (with Don Snowden).

As much as possible I have tried to describe the great bluesmen Coley encounters in the words of their friends and fellow musicians. In so doing I have occasionally put their descriptions in Coley Williams's mouth. To coax the spectral Robert Johnson from the shadows, for instance, I have used accounts of him by Johnny Shines and Robert Junior Lockwood in Peter Guralnick's *Searching For Robert Johnson;* to capture the rambunctious, Rabelaisian Charley Patton I have drawn on the reminiscences of Son House, Booker Miller, Elizabeth Moore, Willie Moore, David Edwards, Frank Howard, Viola Cannon, and Sam Patton Chatmon in *King of the Delta Blues*; and to let Bessie Smith loose in all her outrageous glory I have made use of the recollections of her friends and acquaintances (principally Ruby Walker, Bessie's niece by marriage) in Chris Albertson's classic biography, *Bessie.* And, while I'm on the subject, I would like to acknowledge that numerous bluesmen in this book owe their likenesses to Samuel Charters' incisive portraits in *Blues Makers*.

For details of the lives and music of the other musicians Coley encounters I am in the debt of their biographers, the historians of the blues, and the autobiographies of the musicians listed below. If there were space enough and time I would gladly annotate each one, but for the moment you will have to read my gratitude between the lines. As for my sins of omission (and commission), *excusatio propter infirmitatem.*

David Dalton

Books

Abrahams, Roger D. *African Folktales: Traditional Stories of the Black World.* New York: Pantheon Books, 1983.

Albertson, Chris. *Bessie.* New York: Stein & Day, 1985.

Baraka, Amiri (see Leroi Jones)

Bennett, Lerone, Jr. *Before the Mayflower: A History of Black America.* New York: Penguin Books, 1993.

Berry, Chuck. *The Autobiography.* New York: Harmony Books, 1987.

Bogle, Donald. *Brown Sugar: Eighty Years of Black Female Superstars.* New York: Harmony Books, 1980.

Booth, Stanley. *Rhythm Oil.* New York: Pantheon Books, 1991.

Branch, Taylor. *Pillar of Fire: America in the King Years, 1963-65.* New York: Simon and Schuster,1998.

Broonzy, William, with Yannick Bruynoghe. *Big Bill Blues.* New York: Da Capo Press, 1992.

Brown, H. Rap. *Die Nigger Die!* New York: Dial Press, 1969.

Brown, Sterling A. *The Complete Poetry of Sterling A. Brown,* edited by Michael Harper. Chicago: TriQuarterly Books, 1983.

Calt, Stephen. *I'd Rather Be the Devil: Skip James and the Blues.* New York: Da Capo Press, 1994.

Calt, Stephen, and Gayle Wardlow. *King of the Delta Blues: The Life and Music of Charlie Patton.* Newton, NJ: Rock Chapel Press, 1988.

Charters, Samuel. *The Blues Masters.* New York: Da Capo Press, 1991.

———. *Poetry of the Blues.* New York: Oak Publishing, 1963.

———. *The Roots of the Blues.* New York: Perigee Books, 1982.

Cohn, Lawrence, ed. *Nothing But the Blues.* New York: Abbeville Press, 1993.

Collier, James Lincoln. *Louis Armstrong: An American Genius.* Oxford, England: Oxford University Press, 1983.

Cowdery, Charles K. *Blues Legends.* Salt Lake City: Gibbs Smith, 1995.

Dance, Daryl Cumber. *Shuckin' and Jivin': Folklore from Contemporary Black America.* Bloomington, IN: Indiana University Press, 1978.

Dance, Helen Oakley. *Stormy Monday: The T-Bone Walker Story.* New York: Da Capo Press, 1990.

Davis, Francis. *The History of the Blues: The Roots, the Music, the People: From Charley Patton to Robert Cray.* New York: Hyperion, 1995.

Dixon, Willie, with Don Snowden. *I Am the Blues.* New York: Da Capo Press, 1990.

Edwards, David Honeyboy, as told to Janis Martinson and Michael Robert Frank. *The World Don't Owe Me Nothing.* Chicago: Chicago Review Press, 1997.

Ellison, Ralph. *Invisible Man.* New York: Signet Books, 1964.

Evans, David. *Big Road Blues.* New York: Da Capo Press, 1987.

Faulkner, William. *The Mansion.* New York: Random House, 1987.

Field, Kim. *Harmonicas, Harps and Heavy Breathers.* New York: Fireside Books, 1993.

Feinstein, Elaine. *Bessie Smith: Empress of the Blues.* New York: Penguin Books, 1985.

Ferris, William. *Blues From the Delta.* New York: Da Capo Press, 1984.

Floyd, Samuel A., Jr. *The Power of Black Music.* New York: Oxford University Press, 1995.

Franklin, John Hope, and Alfred A. Moss, Jr. *From Slavery to Freedom: A History of African Americans.* New York: McGraw-Hill, 1994.

Garon, Paul. *Blues and the Poetic Spirit.* New York: Da Capo Press, 1979.

Garon, Paul, and Beth Garon. *Woman with Guitar: Memphis Minnie's Blues.* New York: Da Capo Press, 1992.

Gates, Henry Louis, Jr. *The Signifying Monkey: A Theory of African-American Literary Criticism.* New York and Oxford: Oxford University Press, 1988.

Governor, Alan. *Meeting the Blues.* Dallas, TX: Taylor, 1988.

Green, Martin I., and Bill Sienkiewicz. *Voodoo Child: The Illustrated Legend of Jimi Hendrix.* West Stockbridge, MA: Berkshire Studio, 1995.

Green, Stephen. *Going to Chicago: A Year on the Chicago Blues Scene.* San Francisco: Woodford Publishing, 1990.

Greenberg, Alan. *Love in Vain: A Vision of Robert Johnson.* New York: Da Capo Press, 1993.

Guralnick, Peter. *Feel Like Going Home.* New York: Back Bay Books, 1999.

————. *Last Train to Memphis: The Rise of Elvis Presley.* Boston: Little, Brown & Co., 1994.

————. *Lost Highway.* New York: Back Bay Books, 1999.

————. *Nighthawk Blues.* New York: Thunder's Mouth Press, 1988.

————. *Searching for Robert Johnson.* New York: E.P. Dutton, 1989.

Handy, W.C. *Father of the Blues: An Autobiography.* New York: Da Capo Press, 1991.

Harris, Sheldon. *Blues Who's Who.* New York: Da Capo Press, 1981.

Hurston, Zora Neale. *Mules and Men.* New York: Perennial Library, 1990.

Jones, Leroi. *Blues People.* New York: Morrow & Co, 1963.

Keil, Charles. *Urban Blues.* Chicago: University of Chicago Press, 1991.

King, B.B., with David Ritz. *Blues All Around Me: The Autobiography of B.B. King.* New York: Avon Books, 1996.

Lester, Julius. *The Tales of Uncle Remus: The Adventures of Brer Rabbit as Told by Julius Lester.* New York: Dial Books, 1987.

Lieb, Sandra. *Mother of the Blues: A Study of Ma Rainey.* Amherst, MA: The University of Massachusetts Press, 1981.

Lipscomb, Mance. *I Say Me for a Parable: The Oral Autobiography of Mance Lipscomb, Texas Bluesman,* As Told to and Compiled by Glen Alyn. New York: Da Capo Press, 1994.

Lomax, Alan. *The Land Where the Blues Began.* New York: Pantheon Books, 1993.

Major, Clarence. *Dirty Bird Blues.* New York: Berkley Books, 1997.

Marcus, Greil. *Mystery Train.* New York: E.P. Dutton, 1975.

Mellon, James. *Bullwhip Days.* New York: Weidenfield and Nicholson, 1988.

Murray, Albert. *The Hero and the Blues.* Columbia, MS: University of Missouri Press, 1973.

————. *Stomping the Blues.* New York: Vintage Books, 1982.

Murray, Charles Sharr. *Crosstown Traffic.* New York: St. Martin's Press, 1990.

Newman, Richard, and Marcus Sawyer. *Everybody Say Freedom.* New York: Plume, 1996.

Oakley, Giles. *The Devil's Music.* New York: Da Capo Press, 1997.

Oliver, Paul. *Blues Fell This Morning.* Cambridge, England: Cambridge University Press, 1990.

————. *Conversations with the Blues.* New York: Horizon Press, 1965.

————. *The Story of the Blues.* New York: Penguin Books, 1981.

Palmer, Robert. *Deep Blues.* New York: Penguin Books, 1981.

Pelton, Robert D. *The Trickster in West Africa: A Study of Mythic Irony and Sacred Delight.* Berkeley: University of California Press, 1980.

Robertson, Brian. *Little Blues Book.* Chapel Hill, NC: Algonquin Books, 1996.

Rooney, James. *Bossmen: Bill Monroe and Muddy Waters.* New York: Da Capo Press, 1991.

Rowe, Mike. *Chicago Blues [Chicago Breakdown].* New York: Da Capo Press, 1981.

Sackheim, Eric, ed. *The Blues Line: A Collection of Blues Lyrics.* Hopewell, NJ: The Ecco Press, 1993.

Schmidt, Eric von, and Jim Rooney. *Baby, Let Me Follow You Down: The Illustrated Story of the Cambridge Folk Years.* Garden City, NY: Anchor Books, 1979.

Shaw, Arnold. *Honkers and Shouters.* New York: Collier Books, 1978.

Smith, Willie The Lion, and George Hoefer. *Music on My Mind: The Memoirs of an American Pianist.* New York: Da Capo Press, 1978.

Stewart-Baxter, Derrick. *Ma Rainey and the Classic Blues Singers.* New York: Stein & Day, 1970.

Thompson, Robert Farris. *Flash of the Spirit: African & African-American Art & Philosophy.* New York: Vintage Books, 1984.

Turner, Victor. *Revelation and Divination in Ndembu Ritual.* Ithaca: Cornell University Press, 1975.

Welding, Pete, and Tony Bryan, eds. *Bluesland: Portraits of 12 American Blues Masters.* New York: E.P. Dutton, 1991.

Wilcock, Donald E., with Buddy Guy. *Damn Right I've Got the Blues.* San Francisco, Woodford Press, 1993.

Wolfe, Charles, and Kip Lornell. *The Life and Legend of Leadbelly.* New York: HarperCollins, 1992.

Magazines

"Afro Mud: A Personalized History of the Blues" by Pete Welding. *Down Beat,* February 27, 1975.

"Big Town Blues: A Chicago Breakdown" by Howard Mandel. Photos by D. Shipley. *Down Beat,* April 5, 1979.

"Blues in Black and White" by T.E. Mattox. *Blues Access,* Summer, 1993. No. 14.

"Buddy Guy" by Andrew M. Robble. *Living Blues,* December, 1993. No. 112.

"Child is Father to the Man: How Al Wilson Taught Son House How to Play Son House" by Rebecca Davis. *Blues Access,* Fall, 1998.

"Father and Son: An Interview with Muddy Waters and Mike Bloomfield" by Don DeMichael. *Down Beat,* August 7, 1969.

"Folk-Songs and Folk-Poetry as Found in the Secular Songs of the Southern Negroes" by Howard W. Odum. *Journal of American Folk-Lore,* Vol. 24, July-September 1911.

"Howlin' Wolf" by Paul Trynka and Tony Russel. *Mojo,* February 1996.

"Muddy Waters: Last King of the South Side?" by Pete Welding. *Down Beat,* October 8, 1964.

"Otis Rush: Ready for the Right Place" by Mike Floyd, edited by the Red Rooster. *Blues Access,* Summer 1993. No. 14.

"Pat Hare: A Blues Guitarist" by Kevin Hahn. *Juke Blues,* Summer 1991, No. 23.

"Willie Dixon: Poet Laureate of Modern Blues" Preface by Tom Townsley. Interview by Jas Obrecht. *Blues Review,* Winter/Holiday 1994.

"Willie Dixon: A Tribute" by Jim O'Neal. *Living Blues,* May/June 1992. No. 23.

LYRICS

We have gone to great lengths to ensure that every effort has been made to locate all possible copyright owners so that proper credit could be acknowledged wherever due.

If we have inadvertently given an incorrect credit or failed to acknowledge any existing copyrights, we sincerely apologize. In such an event, we request that the correct information be sent to us for inclusion in future printings.

It is our fondest hope that the readers of *Been Here and Gone* will explore the treasure trove of blues recordings and books available, and discover more about this remarkable music and the blues singers and musicians who lived it.

In addition to the Alan Lomax Collection from Rounder Records and the valuable anthologies from the Smithsonian, the Library of Congress and other sources, there are many wonderful reissues of classic blues, new recordings from those legends still alive, as well as contemporary music available from a wide array of fine blues labels. Happy hunting!

Page 28 *"A one room country shack…"*
Unidentified

32 *Cool Drink of Water*
By Tommy Johnson
Copyright © 1929 by Peer International Corporation
Copyright Renewed
International Copyright Secured. Used by Permission.

Catfish and the Whale
Unidentified

"black snake…"
Unidentified

Willie
By David Dalton
© 2000 Berkshire Studio Productions, Inc.

33 *"The reason I loves…"*
From "Folk-Songs and Folk-Poetry as Found in the Secular Songs of the Southern Negroes" by Howard W. Odum. *Journal of American Folk-Lore,* Vol. 24, July-September 1911.

41 *"When I gets worries…"*
Unidentified

"Polk an' Clay…"
From "Folk-Songs and Folk-Poetry as Found in the Secular Songs of the Southern Negroes" by Howard W. Odum. *Journal of American Folk-Lore,* Vol. 24, July-September 1911.

Emma
By David Dalton
© 2000 Berkshire Studio Productions, Inc.

Page 46 *"the time ain't long..."*
From "Folk-Songs and Folk-Poetry as Found in the Secular Songs of the Southern Negroes" by Howard W. Odum. *Journal of American Folk-Lore,* Vol. 24, July-September 1911.

54 *Pea Vine Blues*
By Charley Patton
No copyright information found

55 *"Well, you got your pistol..."*
By Blind Arvella Gray
From *Conversations With the Blues* by Paul Oliver
Reprinted with the permission of Cambridge University Press, New York and Cambridge, UK (1997)

56 *You Be Kind To Me*
Written by Mance Lipscomb
Published by TRADITION MUSIC (BMI) / Administered by BUG MUSIC
All Rights Reserved. Used By Permission.

58 *"Kusolola..."*
Traditional

64 *Vida Lee*
By David Dalton
© 2000 Berkshire Studio Productions, Inc.

65 *Big Road Blues*
By Tommy Johnson
Copyright © 1929 by Southern Music Publishing Co., Inc.
Copyright Renewed
International Copyright Secured. Used by Permission.

91/92 *Booze and Blues*
Words and Music by Guy Suddoth
© Copyright 1924 Universal-Northern Music Co.
A division of Universal Studios, Inc. (ASCAP)
Copyright renewed. International Copyright Secured.
All Rights Reserved. Used by Permission.

93 *Mississippi Bo Weavil Blues*
By Charley Patton
No copyright information found

Tom Rushin Blues
By Charley Patton
No copyright information found

94 *High Water Everywhere*
By Charley Patton
No copyright information found

99/100 *Shake It and Break It (Hang It on the Wall)*
By Charley Patton
No copyright information found

100 *Jelly Roll King*
By Charley Patton
No copyright information found

Up the Hickory
Traditional nursery rhyme

103 *Down the Dirt Road Blues*
By Charley Patton
No copyright information found

"Goin away to a world unknown..."
Unidentified

Page 103 *Joe Kirby*
By Charley Patton
No copyright information found

"I'm goin away, baby..."
Unidentified

105 *Moon Going Down*
By Charley Patton
No copyright information found

Jim Lee Blues: Part One
By Charley Patton
No copyright information found

107/108 *"...a lean, loose-limbed Negro..."*
From *Father of the Blues* by W.C. Handy
MacMillan, New York (1941)
Da Capo Press, New York (1991)
No current copyright found

108 *Green River Blues*
By Charley Patton
No copyright information found

113 *Nobody Knows the Trouble I've Seen*
Traditional folk song

118 *Don't Quit Now*
By Whistling Alex Moore
From *Conversations With the Blues* by Paul Oliver
Reprinted with the permission of Cambridge University
Press, New York and Cambridge, UK (1997)

Page 121 *The Midnight Special*
New Words and New Music Adaptation by
Huddie Ledbetter
Collected and adapted by John A. Lomax and Alan Lomax
TRO—© Copyright 1936 (Renewed) Folkways Music
Publishers, Inc., New York, NY
Used by permission

Penitentiary Blues
By Blind Lemon Jefferson
No copyright information found

122 *"Number one leader..."*
From "Folk-Songs and Folk-Poetry as Found in the Secular
Songs of the Southern Negroes" by Howard W. Odum.
Journal of American Folk-Lore, Vol. 24,
July-September 1911.

123 *"Lord, I been down yonder..."*
Unidentified

124 *Fannin' Street (Mr. Tom Hughes' Town)*
Words and Music by Huddie Ledbetter
Collected and adapted by John A. Lomax and Alan Lomax
TRO—© Copyright 1936 (Renewed) and 1959 (Renewed)
Folkways Music Publishers, Inc., New York, NY
Used by Permission

128/129 *Governor Pat Neff*
Words and Music by Huddie Ledbetter
Collected and adapted by John A. Lomax and Alan Lomax
TRO—© Copyright 1936 (Renewed) Folkways Music
Publishers, Inc., New York, NY
Used by Permission

Page 132 *Gambler's Blues*
Written by Melvin "Lil Son" Jackson
© 1970 TRADITION MUSIC (BMI) / Administered by
BUG MUSIC
All Rights Reserved. Used By Permission.

Meet Me in the Bottom
By Blind Arvella Gray
From *Conversations With the Blues* by Paul Oliver
Reprinted with the permission of Cambridge University
Press, New York and Cambridge, UK (1997)

132/133 *Jack A Diamonds Is A Hard Card To Play*
Written by Mance Lipscomb
© 1970 TRADITION MUSIC (BMI) / Administered by
BUG MUSIC
All Rights Reserved. Used By Permission.

133 *"raising good cotton crops..."*
By James Cotton
From *Conversations With the Blues* by Paul Oliver
Reprinted with the permission of Cambridge University
Press, New York and Cambridge, UK (1997)

135 *"Now place your deuces, Lord..."*
By Blind Arvella Gray
From *Conversations With the Blues* by Paul Oliver
Reprinted with the permission of Cambridge University
Press, New York and Cambridge, UK (1997)

136 *Chock House Blues*
By Blind Lemon Jefferson
No copyright information found

139 *Deceitful Brownskin Blues*
By Blind Lemon Jefferson
No copyright information found

Page 139 *Ghosts*
By David Dalton
© 2000 Berkshire Studio Productions, Inc.

143 *Dynamite Blues*
By Blind Lemon Jefferson
No copyright information found

Oil Well Blues
By Blind Lemon Jefferson
No copyright information found

145 *Long Distance Moan*
By Blind Lemon Jefferson
No copyright information found

Dry Southern Blues
By Blind Lemon Jefferson
No copyright information found

150 *Black Cat Hoot Owl Blues*
Words and Music by Thomas Dorsey
© Copyright 1929 Universal-Northern Music Co.
A division of Universal Studios, Inc. (ASCAP)
Copyright renewed. International Copyright Secured.
All Rights Reserved. Used by Permission.

See See Rider
Words and Music by J. Mayo Williams
© Copyright 1944 Universal-Northern Music Co.
A division of Universal Studios, Inc. (ASCAP)
Copyright renewed. International Copyright Secured.
All Rights Reserved. Used by Permission.

151 *Blues the World Forgot*
From *Mother of the Blues: A Study of Ma Rainey*
by Sandra Lieb
Reprinted with the permission of The University of
Massachusetts Press, Amherst, MA (1981)

Page 152 *Don't Fish in My Sea*
Words by Bessie Smith
Music by Ma Rainey
No copyright information found

163 *You've Been a Good Ole Wagon*
By Smith and Balcom
No copyright information found

Sobbin' Hearted Blues
By Bradford, Layer and Davis
No copyright information found

165 *Sobbin' Hearted Blues*
By Bradford, Layer and Davis
No copyright information found

168 *Shave 'Em Dry*
By Lucille Bogan
No copyright information found

176 *Backwater Blues*
By Bessie Smith
© 1927 (Renewed), 1974 FRANK MUSIC CORP.
All Rights Reserved. Used by Permission.

181 *Hell Hound On My Trail*
Words and Music by Robert Johnson
© (1978) 1990, 1991 King of Spades Music
All Rights Reserved. Used by Permission.

182 *Coley, Coley, Coley*
By David Dalton
© 2000 Berkshire Studio Productions, Inc.

183 Adapted from *Deep Shrimp Blues*
Words and Music by Robert Johnson
© (1978) 1990, 1991 King of Spades Music
All Rights Reserved. Used by Permission.

Page 206 *Stocking Feet Blues*
By Blind Lemon Jefferson
No copyright information found

"Tough luck has struck me..."
By Blind Lemon Jefferson
No copyright information found

208 *Terraplane Blues*
Words and Music by Robert Johnson
© (1978) 1990, 1991 King of Spades Music
All Rights Reserved. Used by Permission.

215 *High Sheriff Blues*
By Charley Patton
No copyright information found

218 *High Water Everywhere*
By Charley Patton
No copyright information found

You My All Time Dream
By Charley Patton
No copyright information found

219 Adapted from *Jesu, Lover of My Soul*
By John Wesley

222 *Some Summer Day*
By Charley Patton
No copyright information found

227 *Governor O.K. Allen*
Words and Music by Huddie Ledbetter
Collected and adapted by John A. Lomax and Alan Lomax
TRO—© Copyright 1936 (Renewed) Folkways Music
Publishers, Inc., New York, NY
Used by Permission

Page 233 Adapted from *Honeymoon Blues*
Words and Music by Robert Johnson
© (1978) 1990, 1991 King of Spades Music
All Rights Reserved. Used by Permission.

Cross Road Blues
Words and Music by Robert Johnson
© (1978) 1990, 1991 King of Spades Music
All Rights Reserved. Used by Permission.

234 *Cross Road Blues*
Words and Music by Robert Johnson
© (1978) 1990, 1991 King of Spades Music
All Rights Reserved. Used by Permission.

Me And The Devil Blues
Words and Music by Robert Johnson
© (1978) 1990, 1991 King of Spades Music
All Rights Reserved. Used by Permission.

237 *Peetie Wheatstraw Stomp No. 2*
by Peetie Wheatstraw
Copyright not renewed

238 *Night Time Is the Right TIme*
Words and Music by Leroy Carr
© Copyright 1938 Universal-Northern Music Co.
A division of Universal Studios, Inc. (ASCAP)
Copyright renewed. International Copyright Secured.
All Rights Reserved. Used by Permission.

248 *Me And The Devil Blues*
Words and Music by Robert Johnson
© (1978) 1990, 1991 King of Spades Music
All Rights Reserved. Used by Permission.

254 *"I want to pull up..."*
By Champion Jack Dupree
No copyright information found

Page 255 *Dirty Dozen*
> Words and Music by J. Mayo Williams and R. Perryman
> © Copyright 1929, 1957 Universal-MCA Music
> Publishing, Inc. A division of Universal Studios,
> Inc. (ASCAP)
> Copyright renewed. International Copyright Secured.
> All Rights Reserved. Used by Permission.

> *Long Gone*
> By W.C. Handy and Chris Smith
> By Permission of Handy Brothers Music Co., Inc.
> International Copyright Secured

271 *Stormy Monday*
> Written by Aaron T. Walker
> Used courtesy of Gregmark Music, Inc., and licensed by
> MizMo Enterprises.

279 *My Black Gal Blues*
> By Sleepy John Estes
> Copyright © 1933 by Peer International Corporation
> Copyright Renewed
> International Copyright Secured. Used by Permission.

> *Furry's Blues*
> By Furry Lewis
> Copyright © 1929 by Peer International Corporation
> Copyright Renewed
> International Copyright Secured. Used by Permission.

280 *"Dreamt a dream..."*
> By Furry Lewis
> No copyright information found

281 *"when you lose your money..."*
> By Furry Lewis
> No copyright information found

Page 287 *They're Red Hot*
Words and Music by Robert Johnson
© (1978) 1990, 1991 King of Spades Music
All Rights Reserved. Used by Permission.

289 *Everybody's Blues*
By Furry Lewis
Copyright © 1929 by Peer International Corporation
Copyright Renewed
International Copyright Secured. Used by Permission.

290 *Going Back to Memphis*
By Will Shade
Copyright © 1931 by Peer International Corporation
Copyright Renewed
International Copyright Secured. Used by Permission.

291 *Judge Harsh BLues*
By Furry Lewis
Copyright © 1929 by Peer International Corporation
Copyright Renewed
International Copyright Secured. Used by Permission.

293 *"Black night is fallin..."*
Unidentified

295 *"I done come out of the Land of Egypt..."*
Traditional hymn

301/302 *I'm Ready*
Written by Willie Dixon
© 1954, 1993 HOOCHIE COOCHIE MUSIC (BMI) /
Administered by BUG MUSIC
All Rights Reserved. Used By Permission.

306 *Eleven Sailors*
By David Dalton
© 2000 Berkshire Studio Productions, Inc.

Page 307 *I'm Ready*
Written by Willie Dixon
© 1954, 1993 HOOCHIE COOCHIE MUSIC (BMI) /
Administered by BUG MUSIC
All Rights Reserved. Used By Permission.

313 Adapted from *Louisiana Blues*
a/k/a *Going Down To Louisiana*
Written by Muddy Waters
© 1959, 1987 WATERTOONS MUSIC (BMI) /
Administered by BUG MUSIC
All Rights Reserved. Used By Permission.

316 *She Moves Me*
Written by Muddy Waters
© 1959, 1987 WATERTOONS MUSIC (BMI) /
Administered by BUG MUSIC
All Rights Reserved. Used By Permission.

317/318 *Back Door Man*
Written by Willie Dixon
© 1961, 1989 HOOCHIE COOCHIE MUSIC (BMI) /
Administered by BUG MUSIC
All Rights Reserved. Used By Permission.

324 *The Signifying Monkey and the Lion*
Adapted with modified spelling from *Deep Down in the Jungle* by Roger D. Abrahams
Copyright © 1963, 1970 by Roger D. Abrahams
Copyright renewed 1998
Used by permission of the publisher Aldine de Gruyter
A division of Walter de Gruyter, Inc., Berlin and New York

326 *Wang Dang Doodle*
Written by Willie Dixon
© 1962, 1968, 1996 HOOCHIE COOCHIE MUSIC
(BMI) / Administered by BUG MUSIC
All Rights Reserved. Used By Permission.

Page 328 *(I'm Your) Hoochie Coochie Man*
Written by Willie Dixon
© 1957, 1964, 1985 HOOCHIE COOCHIE MUSIC
(BMI) / Administered by BUG MUSIC
All Rights Reserved. Used By Permission.

Adapted from *Louisiana Blues*
a/k/a *Goin Down To Louisiana*
Written by Muddy Waters
© 1959, 1987 WATERTOONS MUSIC (BMI) /
Administered by BUG MUSIC
All Rights Reserved. Used By Permission.

329 *I Can't Be Satisfied*
Written by Muddy Waters
© 1959, 1987 WATERTOONS MUSIC (BMI) /
Administered by BUG MUSIC
All Rights Reserved. Used By Permission.

343 *That's All Right*
By Arthur Crudup
© 1947 (Renewed) Unichappell Music Inc. and
Crudup Music
All Rights Administered by Unichappell Music Inc.
All Rights Reserved. Used by Permission.
WARNER BROS. PUBLICATIONS U.S. INC.,
Miami, FL 33014

345 *Blue Moon of Kentucky*
By Bill Monroe
Copyright © 1947 by Peer International Corporation
Copyright Renewed
International Copyright Secured. Used by Permission.

Page 385 *Motherless Children Have a Hard TIme*
By Blind Lemon Jefferson
No copyright information found

386/387 *Rollin' Stone* a/k/a *Catfish Blues*
Written by Muddy Waters
© 1959, 1987 WATERTOONS MUSIC (BMI) /
Administered by BUG MUSIC
All Rights Reserved. Used By Permission.

393 *Stones in My Passway*
Words and Music by Robert Johnson
© (1978) 1990, 1991 King of Spades Music
All Rights Reserved. Used by Permission.

394 *"I'm a poor boy..."*
From "Folk-Songs and Folk-Poetry as Found in the Secular
Songs of the Southern Negroes" by Howard W. Odum.
Journal of American Folk-Lore, Vol. 24,
July-September 1911.